(OLLA...

I don't remember the e... ...
up, being deaf. My littl... ...nd
with singed holes on the back of his T-shirt. . . . Somebody lifted me up. . . . Mama. . . . She was screaming. . . .

Our corridor was destroyed. Across the street four
houses lay like broken teeth in a row of rubble, spilling
their pieces all the way to our patch of grass. I could see
past the houses and into the wall. It was black and fiery,
and lights flashed in red and yellow emergency colors.
The outer walls had closed. In school drills Mrs. Glantz
had told us that if the colony was ever breached, we
would not die from the outside moon environment. The
extra outer walls would shut tight to block up any holes.

There was a hole in Mishka's sleeve with nothing to
block it up. She just bled.

ACCLAIM FOR THE NOVELS OF
KARIN LOWACHEE

BURNDIVE

"Excellent . . . I recommend it without reservation."
—*Magazine of Fantasy and Science Fiction*

"Lowachee's characters have a way of getting inside
your head."
—**RevolutionSF.com**

more . . .

"Impresses with its ambition."
—*New York Times Book Review*

"*Warchild* unfolds with the slow beauty of growing springtime flowers."
—*Locus*

"Accomplished, vigorous, exciting . . . Lowachee's characters are rich and unclichéd."
—*SciFi.com*

"*Warchild*'s a small gem. Well, no, it's a bloody large gem, one that catches the whole of the attention and causes one to marvel at the hand that cut it so perfectly . . . Lowachee is not a talent to watch, she's a talent to enjoy *right now*, and I urge you to do just that."
—*Magazine of Fantasy and Science Fiction*

———————————

ALSO BY KARIN LOWACHEE

Warchild

Burndive

CAGEBIRD

KARIN LOWACHEE

ASPECT®

NEW YORK   BOSTON

Aspect is a registered trademark of Warner Books.

Cover design by Tony Russo
Book design by Giorgetta Bell McRee

Aspect Books

Time Warner Book Group
1271 Avenue of the Americas
New York, NY 10020
Visit our Web site at www.twbookmark.com

Printed in the United States of America

First Paperback Printing: April 2005

10 9 8 7 6 5 4 3 2 1

For Amber van Dyk and Nancy Proctor,
creative godmuses to Yuri and Finch,
even in the eleventh hours (and there were a few).

Thank Yous

2003 Blue Heaven Novel Workshoppers, incredible writers all, who critiqued and supported past the waters of the Isle: Christopher Barzak, Tobias Buckell, Roger Eichorn, Charles Coleman Finlay, Paul Melko, Cathy Morrison, Nancy Proctor, Mary Rickert, Benjamin Rosenbaum, James Stevens-Arce, and Amber van Dyk

Angela Boord
Hannah Bowen
Sue Glantz
Yukiko Kawakami
Jaime Levine
Shawna McCarthy
Derek "D'Ado" Molata
Monkeylint (Sock Monkeys, Sporks, and extra Lint)
Steve K. S. Perry
Devi Pillai
Matt Stawicki
The Team at Warner Aspect
Winifred Wong

My readers and street team (Sympathizer Network and Soljet Corps), from Mississauga to Malaysia.

And all my family and friends who support and love me even when it's difficult to understand what I'm doing, even when I'm a moody hermit soul, especially when I'm embedded in a book.

What did I feel that night? You are
  curious. How should I tell?
Does it matter so much what I felt?
  You rescued me—yet—was it well
That you came unwish'd for, uncall'd,
  between me and the deep and my dream.
Does it matter how many they saved?
  we are all of us wreck'd at last—
'Do you fear?' and there came thro' the
  roar of the breaker a whisper, a breath,
'Fear? am I not with you? I am frighted
  at life not death.'

—ALFRED, LORD TENNYSON
"Despair"
1881

CAGEBIRD

When I was fourteen I got the scarlet fever, at least that's what I called it and that's how I think of it still. It's not really the scarlet fever, not the one you read about in history files. Mine is just this feeling, and scarlet is its color. Red. You get so hot you have to release it, but it's the heat of a cold sweat. The fever eats you up inside and you shake like you're winter, like your blood is made of ice water and you need to see it run. You need to touch it and feel its warmth—because it has to be warm. Nobody is this dead inside.

When it comes out along your skin there isn't any pain. Just relief. Just the tiny red rivers of life. And you can breathe again, seeing that. You can look up. You can spread your arms and touch the edges of your emotions and maybe they touch back, like something new and curious. Or something old and almost forgotten.

And you think, This is who you are, Yurochka. This is what you're made of.

ME

* * ✦
✦ ☽ ✦
* ✦ *

2.25.2198 EHSD — Kalaallit Nunaat Military Prison

"Yuri Mikhailovich Terisov," the woman says to get my attention. Haven't heard that name, Terisov, in years—which is what she's counting on. *I'll remind you of who you were,* she might be thinking. I bet she thinks it. *Let me remind you of who you aren't anymore.* Yurochka. Terisov. But we all change whether we want to or not, our names are only a part of it, so her words don't cut. They fall between us like promises, hollow and encumbered.

I sit in a room the color of dirty ice, wrists cuffed to the table, arms spread and palms up like a martyred deity. She talks in deliberate paragraphs that're supposed to wrap around my head and smother me with authority. At the end of it, when I yawn, she says, "You're in here on consecutive life sentences with no opportunity for parole. You're only twenty-two years old. You should take this conversation more seriously."

I should, yeah. Except she's so serious she's funny. Her fixed attention on my face is downright entertaining. She thinks she can intimidate me just because she's a polly, but her stare isn't that different from all the stares I've ever gotten in my life.

The face of an angel and the eyes of a corpse, Falcone liked to say.

People look at me if I walk like I want to be noticed or smile like I want to be touched. Some people would just do anything for me—or anything *to* me—if I let them.

People are so easy. The galaxy's full of whores.

This polly woman thinks she can come in here, drag me to this shiny, sterile room, and pump me 'til I bleed emotion?

I can bang my head 'til I bleed a thought, but my real thoughts wouldn't interest her. Nobody's interested in hearing a whore speak. That's not what you buy them for.

But she waits for me to say something. I should respond to her Offer, like the prosecutor of my case had an Offer—which wasn't really an Offer, just a pat on the ass without the penetration. A reduced sentence for rolling on my contacts?

No. How many times, woman? *No.* You can't afford me.

Maybe once upon a time it was possible. Maybe in some fairy tale I thought about Offers, dreamed about the pass they could give me if I just rolled over and bit the pillow. But there's the morning after and all those furtive glances, and instead I chance juries, I chance lawyers, I let a lawyer talk hyperbole about how I was "torn from the loving arms of family and delivered into the clutches of a sadistic pirate" and that saves me from the death sentence. That saves me in a military prison where even pirates might have access. Because I know They can get me anywhere, and it's better They think I didn't help anyone, that I'm here against my will.

Because I am, really. Against my will.

Everyone knows my past, they put it in a File (there's always a File for my kind) and spread it out for me like it's a mirror above my head. I lie back and see it over me like Truth, and the one delivering it to me—the one delivering me—is also screwing me blind.

But she calls me mister as if she respects me. She claims she works for EarthHub, but maybe she hasn't gone farther outsystem than Pluto. Maybe she thinks "geisha" in my record refers to some female Japanese entertainer.

Protégé. I look at her and think it.

Falcone's.

The *Khan*.

Don't you know what I am?

Maybe she knows a little. She wants what's in my head.

"Mr. Terisov," she says, using my dead name again. She doesn't blink, and her eyes remind me of Finch's, my cellmate—black, Go game pieces. Her dark hair's pulled back in a tail to emphasize a wide mouth and a masculine jaw. Not pretty, but pleasing. Beneath the brown sweater her tits make shapes like two healthy, hydroponic oranges. She can look at my face and wait all day for my confession, but I'll look at those and we'll see who breaks first.

"Mr. Terisov." She sighs. "If you don't talk to me, I can't help you."

I yawn again and flex my fingers. Need a smoke, manita. These damn cuffs pinch my wrists, and the good pain's gone bad. I guess it's time to play now. "What agency did you say you work for?"

Her jaw tightens, just a small twitch, presaging a lie. She doesn't think I see it, so she lies anyway. "EarthHub Department of Justice."

So not a polly, technically.

Not a polly at all.

I nod my head like a slowpoke. "Uh-huh. Department of Justice. You a lawyer then?"

No lawyer has her eyes and her bearing. When she walked through that door her body language screamed polly. They announce themselves in small, telling ways, even the undercover ones. I never met a skin I couldn't finger, and she smelled just like one.

But now . . . not quite so badged.

Military?

"I do work for the Department of Justice," she says, without the twitch, convinced in her lie. Trying to convince me. "And I have the authority to table a deal with you, but you need to interact here, Mr. Terisov. You need to look at the facts of your situation."

I sniff like she's a drain of snot staining my good shirt. "What the *hell* d'you know about my 'situation'?"

She blinks, leans back, and folds her arms loosely, probably wishing for distance in this enclosed room. "I know they had to place you in solitary confinement for your own safety."

It's all on the slow, like she's wasting my time. "Sure they did. It was for *their* own safety. And for the safety of those two-bit criminals they shacked me with."

This doesn't impress her. "Deal with me, Mr. Terisov. Cut the games and deal. You can rot in here with your pretty words, or you can seize the opportunity in front of you."

"Seize the opportunity." It makes me laugh. "You write for vids or what?"

Her cheeks tighten. "Help us dismantle the pirate operations in space, and we'll lessen your sentence by a good portion."

"I heard this song before. It's tuneless."

She says, like a threat, "They're going to put you back in the general population once you walk out of this room."

Among the mundane murderers and pedophiles. Among ex–military men who were trained to hate people like me.

I don't blink, only smile. I speak to her slowly like I'm drugged or dumb. "You think that scares me?"

"It should. I know you have a big mouth and a misplaced sense of invulnerability, but it won't save you."

She keeps being funny.

"I was *in* genpop for three months, manita, *here*. Not in transfer. I don't like to brag, but it ain't all that hard."

She gestures to the shallow, precise scars on my forearms, tail ends curving to my wrists. Some are older than my time inside. "What are those then?"

"Boredom."

"You did that to yourself?" Sickened by it. Superior about it.

I shrug. I know it pisses her off. "The library here is shit."

"You *honestly* think you can survive a life sentence, much less more than one?" Abstract curiosity now.

And now I'm done playing.

"All my thoughts are honest, bitch."

The last straw, or maybe someone gives her an order on the silent bud in her ear. She rolls her chipsheet with my file in it, stands, and walks out.

Either way, I guess she's had enough of this pirate.

Poor, dishonest woman from the so-called EarthHub Department of Justice. Didn't anybody tell her? Doesn't she know the way it is?

You don't fuck with Falcone's protégés, ever, even though the bastard's dead.

＊ ＊ ＊

They leave me to stare at my blurry reflection in the polished gray tabletop. No guard to take me back to my cell, no God-voice through the intercom to pronounce my fate. No torture crew to come in and encourage my confession. Just the tabletop and me. Tiny white scratches mar the surface, somebody's defiant fever in a similar situation, who knows, but the marks are like everything. Imperfection is everywhere, in everybody. All the devils are in the details and you can exploit them—twist, stroke, or squeeze out what you want. Pollies and govies need optics to see those imperfections, but a good criminal knows them from the inside out.

Like optics. They surround where I sit, embedded black eyes in the grid lines of the walls, giving a three-sixty view of my immobility. If I fart they'll smell it somehow, that's the level of their attention in rooms like this. But what do optics really show them about me? They might gauge my body temperature and my voice stress, zoom on my dilated pupils, but nothing will tell them what the last thirteen years of my life were like.

I told one person, and he still put me in here.

Better to keep your mouth shut.

I learned long ago what it means to take favors from charitable people. No different from a cocktail who picks you up in a bar somewhere and screws you standing in the closest den. They all want to feel good. Even so-called service martyrs don't want to admit that they're whores for gratitude, but ultimately they're looking out for their own salvation. They believe their good works will get them to heaven.

Religiosos are pirates in denial. They'll broker your soul before the prayers are past your lips, but they don't call it that. They call it *charity*.

High moral ground always gives me a nosebleed.

Govies and their deals aren't much different from religiosos. They greet you with smiles and Offers in an attempt to hide flanking attacks. I still sit here because they aren't finished maneuvering. I know it for sure when the door opens and a beautiful man steps in. The woman didn't work, so they send a different thing. And beauty's a tool, like a knife or a drill or the little metal files you use to dig dirt from beneath your fingernails. This man knows it. His eyes fix on me as he shuts the heavy door behind him and walks up to the table, expensive shoes echoing on the floor. He holds a razor slate with both hands like a priest holds the word of God, standing in front of me to give a blessing or a curse. The tailored navy blue suit and white shirt make him look like some damn Universalist missionary, except there are no stars on his collar, no badge of peaceful intentions. The silk collar folds open at his neck like petals, revealing a column of swarthy skin. Above that, a smooth youngish face, deep-set dark eyes faintly rimmed by shadows more to do with race than fatigue. Thin lips smile with seeming honesty.

He knows I'm looking. Distantly interested, if not wholly affected—both of us are. Because he looks at me too, with a selective kind of scrutiny: my coin-round blue eyes and pale spacer skin; my naturally bruised lips and shoulder-length, beaten-gold hair, which I haven't combed except with fingers. You have to know your face to a narcissistic point, Falcone said. It's the only way to control it.

"My name's Andreas Lukacs," he says with an accent I don't recognize. Still smiling, but not the grin of a politician or a player, though I don't doubt he might be both. He sets his slate on the table with no particular emphasis. The display is dead transparency. He takes out a key from his pants pocket and points it at my cuffs, right and then the left, pressing the trigger.

The cuffs beep and fall away.

Now this is interesting.

He holds out his hand to me. I know this protocol, though it's not the culture of every ship or station. I take his hand and squeeze it, just so I can feel the temperature of his grip —warm against my cold fingers, dry and firm. I hold on and look up into his eyes, match his smile.

And then I kiss it, the back of his hand, and lick his skin in a long wet track.

Mmm, salty.

He jerks back with a disgusted frown.

Not so self-assured, are we?

"Yuri," he says, with more control than most would've mustered. He doesn't even blink. "Don't do that."

Like he's talking to a child.

"Andreas." I spread my arms on the table, palms up, free. "You can cuff me again if you want."

"No," he says. "You might like it."

I gift him with a grin and travel my gaze down his body. A long holiday. "Uh-huh. Then take a seat. Or not."

He decides to sit, but without haste or evident discomfort. Very neat in the way he pushes away both sides of his suit jacket so they don't bunch around his middle. The slate stays deactivated. He folds his hands on it and looks at me with the nice smile reasserted. Not a perfect set of teeth, one incisor's slightly crooked. So he isn't vain enough to spend cred on cosmetic work, despite the expensive suit.

"You gave my colleague quite a jar," Andreas Lukacs says. Soft like a sigh.

He came in armed, yeah. Not like that straightforward woman and her bullet-shaped vocabulary. He uses different weapons.

I fold my arms on the table, lean on them toward him, like a friend. "So you're from the Department of Justice too?"

His head tilts to the side a fraction. "No."

"Was she?"

A narrower stare, a flattening of the smile. "Yuri, I think you mistake why I'm here."

"I don't know why you're here, Andreas, so how could I mistake it?"

"I think you know."

He looks like a lawyer, but he's too comfortable with me. As if I don't pose a threat.

"You wanna offer me a deal like her? What, didn't she explain my point of view?"

He studies my face as if checking for flaws. "No," he says eventually. Maybe he found one. "I think she didn't explain mine."

So *he* was the eyes on the other side of those optics all the while she sat in here with me. He tested me on weaker prey.

Not a lawyer. Or a polly.

A crooked govie?

I don't open my mouth. Predators like him you have to watch in silence.

He wears a gold wedding band, caresses it with his thumb, and loses his smile. He leans back and presses the corner of his slate. The display lights up with a scroll of words. Black on white.

"Why did you never write to your family?" he asks, tilting the slate off the edge of the table, peering down at it as if the questions are all in there. But he doesn't need to look for them. He's got them behind his eyes.

My family.

"Yuri?" he says, eyes still on the slate. "Why did you never write to your family?"

"I'm not interested in answering any questions, Andreas. Didn't your colleague tell you?"

Now he looks up. "Oh, come on. Retreating already? I expected more from Falcone's second."

"I wasn't Falcone's second."

"Protégé, then."

He knows. He knows exactly what I am. But he pretends he doesn't, and, unlike the woman, he doesn't try to hide it. Showing your hand is a part of this play.

So I don't bother to smile. "You're baiting me. My silence is the only answer you're gonna get."

"No, your silence means that your family is still a raw subject."

Is it. "Did your wife take your last name when you married?"

One eyebrow lifts. "My wife?"

"Or husband. Whichever. That ring."

"What difference does it make if she did?"

Now I smile. I rest my chin on one hand, graze the table-top with a finger. "I want to know her name so I can arrange a hit."

He laughs. Surprised, but not nonplussed. "And you think you could, now that you've told me?"

He thinks he could stop me?

More than a crooked govie, then.

"Maybe you oughtta consult your slate." I point at it. "To see if I could."

I know my own file. I stroke the table again.

That should've scored something. Instead he keeps smiling. "How do you know I'm even married?"

I look at the ring.

"Appearances," he says, "can be deceiving. I thought you'd know that, geisha. Maybe I want you to think I'm married, so in your head you build a profile of a personal life that doesn't truly exist."

I feel my finger stop its movement.

"Now," he says, as if he doesn't notice, "tell me, why did you never write to your family?"

I'm on his field, and if I want to know what the game is I have to make him play. And I have to play along.

"I don't like to write," I tell him.

He gives me a big brotherly look. He pokes his slate again, then turns it around so I see the heading.

9.17.2185 EHSD.

This man visited the Camp, he says he's a captain.

Careful. Very careful. I look at him. "Where did you get that?"

"They're your journals, aren't they, Yuri? Quite extensive. All the way back to when you were nine years old. Took a long time to break into, but there they are. And yet you say you don't like to write."

This whore is Intel. Worse, as I stare at him, I recognize his sense of invulnerability.

Black Ops.

No other way he'd get that info unless he does this shit for a living. Unless this is his life.

My face is my instrument in this duet. I play it cold.

"I don't write to other people, Andreas."

"Not even family?"

"I don't know them."

"Surely a young man of your talents could get to know them."

"If he wanted to. I don't."

He tilts the slate away from me again. "Pity."

I shrug.

I need a cigret, but damned if I'll ask.

"Your father died five years ago in the Camp. On Colonial Grace. You know where the rest of your family is." Not a question.

"Tell me anyway if it'll get you off."

"What is important to you, Yuri, if not your family?"

"Eating, sleeping, screwing. I lead a simple life."

This amuses him. I amuse him. "Snappy. Still on the retreat?"

"You're the one sitting on the opposite side of this table, Andreas, when it's much more intimate on my side. What're you afraid of?"

He grins. "A young man of your talents."

Half-truth, maybe. That lick on his hand had put him off. But not enough to send him walking.

No, instead he dug in his heels.

"Let's talk about something else, then." He pokes his slate again, then slides it toward me. Not a skittering push, but a purposeful one, only releasing his hand once it sits dead center in front of me. "Your cellmate Stefano Finch."

My face is blank. I feel it. Geisha training.

The door opens behind Lukacs. He doesn't turn to look. A medium-height blond man walks in, a polar opposite image to dark and well-tailored Lukacs. This one wears gray manufiber pants, faintly reflective, and a rumpled black sweater. He drags a chair in with him, sets it at the short end of the table just at my periphery, sits, and loosely folds his arms.

I stare at him, he stares back with flint blue eyes. We get nowhere. So I smirk and look at Lukacs. "Your prom date? Or mine?"

He completely ignores the blond man and my question. "Finch. Twenty-five years old. EarthHub Naval, but a wrench monkey, nothing glamorous, nothing intelligent. Born and bred at Hephaestus Shipyard. Was a lifesystems mechanic." He gestures to the slate where Finch's dark-eyed image glows. "Killed his commanding officer."

"And yet they put him in prison." I can ignore the obvious too. "They shoulda given him a medal."

He rolls on like he doesn't hear, with Finch's file in front of me. He's got it memorized. "Father was also a lifesystems mechanic. Died ten years ago when a coolant pipe burst." Faint smile. "I suppose he wasn't very good, then, yeah? Mother had a slow decline after developing Kestral's disease. Too many hours spent around drive arrays in the early years."

His voice is about as warm as an Arctic handshake.

"He's led a rough life," Lukacs concludes. "But not as rough as yours, yeah?"

Your point being . . .

"Do you know why he killed his CO?" Lukacs says like this is normal conversation.

I shrug. In fact, no. You don't really ask those things in prison. And if you do, you don't expect a straight or truthful answer.

"I think you care," Lukacs says. "I think you care so much you screwed him."

There isn't any response to give this man but stillness. And even that might be saying too much.

"Suddenly quiet," Lukacs says.

"I'm waiting for you to quit self-gratifying. I don't like to interrupt intimate moments."

He smiles. It's as flat as this table and the other man's expression. Lukacs leans over and touches the face of the slate. The images start to cycle and I recognize the scenes. Me and Finch in our cell talking. Me, sleepwalking at lights-out like an insane person, around and around the cell. The both of us yelling at each other on different days. Snatches of sound before the image bleeds to yet another. To a shadowy frame and the sounds of sex.

I don't look at it. Instead I stare at Lukacs. Training makes my voice steady, when I want to reach across the table and beat him to death. "All your porn got a point, manito?"

"You tell me."

"I don't need to watch it, I can get it anytime."

"Yet you only did it once," he says, with a prurient tone.

"He wasn't all that good."

This makes Lukacs smile. He's heard all my arguments with Finch, my words now just get him off. "You really ought to ask the lad why he killed his CO. But of course that would require your release back to the general population. Would you like to see what went on when you weren't there?"

I don't answer. The blond man at the end of the table yawns, briefly covering his mouth.

"You've stopped talking?" Lukacs says.

He's bright.

"All right then." The slate still scrolls in front of him. In front of me. Cycling my business. Finch's business. Us.

Lukacs completely ignores it, even the volume. "I'll talk— about the fact I've been in your life since you landed on this planet; you just had no idea. I made sure the court closed your trial from the meedees; I watched you inside the system so you weren't prematurely killed; and now I've set you in solitary for two weeks so I can make my point."

"Then make it."

"Work with me to bring down the pirate organization. Or I might just get your lily Finch permanently transferred from your cell and in with someone else. And maybe he can add another murder to his sheet. Or maybe he won't last a night."

I have to push it. "Do what you want."

The blond man gets up without any signal that I can see from Lukacs, actually takes his chair and walks out.

The door shuts, heavy.

Now I hear my breath, a single intake. Likely Lukacs hears it too. "Where did he go?"

Lukacs shrugs.

"Where did he go?" Is he your boss, or are you his?

"Is that your answer?" Lukacs says. And waits. He's got nothing more to say until I drop the mask.

Here are all of my mistakes, encapsulated by dark eyes on a slate. I remember the night when I screwed him. When he asked. When I thought I was doing him a favor, but instead I caged myself. These feelings are iron bars.

I can't hide when they've mapped all the corners with optics. Not in that cell. And not in here, with this man and his game.

"Lay a hand on Finch, and you can forget any deal. I want him safe in our pod. Understand?" Even though there is no safety.

This is what Lukacs has wanted to hear from the moment he walked in. The bastard smiles.

"Perfectly," he says.

* * *

Lukacs doesn't smoke, but he came prepared to reward me with them now that I've accepted his hand in marriage. I blow white clouds into his face to blur the air between us. Once, twice, and by the third drag I'm jumping. Soaring. Damn near aroused, slouched back with my knees wide under the table. Smoke rolls over my tongue like spring rain or smooth booze. It's been a while, I ran out in the box, and Morry the Guard who took pity on me couldn't find my spacer brand. But Andreas Black Ops Lukacs knows it and knows how to get it, clever little puppy that he is.

The smoke in my lungs warms me a little in this cold, white-lit room. I wonder if that blond one watches through the optics, if he is the one who authorized this deal. He hasn't come back. I wonder if all the things Falcone said about Black Ops are true. Average people talk about them as if they only exist in vids, and sometimes you hear murmuring about it in the lower echelons of the government. Part myth, part dirty reality. Part dirty secret. Technically the Agency works for EarthHub Command, but you'll never find them listed on any govie budget reports. Falcone dealt with them when he was a carrier captain. He said never to trust them. He said he'd kill anyone in his crew or his network who waxed linen with Ops without his permission.

But Falcone's dead, and here I am.

"What happens after," I ask Lukacs.

"After?" He took his slate back, and now he scrolls it, reading something while I smoke.

"After I hand you the entire pirate organization in a big silver-beribboned gift box."

He still looks at his slate. Maybe reviewing the porn. "We'll grant you complete exoneration of your crimes. I'll even put it in writing."

Yeah, and it'll be stamped in my blood. "Say that again with a straight face, thanks."

Tiny, mocking smile, eyes down and reading. "Unlike other agencies or that rogue Captain Azarcon and his allies, we can actually make someone like you run clean in the eyes of the law. And we can protect you."

Someone like me. As if I'm all that different from an Intel whore like him. He screws people for a living too. "So does this free pass come before or after you eventually kill me?"

He laughs.

I don't. "If you're gonna wipe my slate, then you don't have to threaten Finch."

He says, "We like to cover the bases just in case you decide your own life isn't worth the trouble. Or his isn't." He pauses so I can figure it. "But I'll be generous. We'll protect him from the baser elements in here."

"Like you did when I was in the box." Did you?

"Oh, but we hadn't made a deal at that point." Now he looks up. "I asked you if you wanted to see what happened while you were in solitary. You were absolutely correct. Putting you there was for their safety. It certainly wasn't for your lily Finch's."

A beat.

I flick my burning cigret at him. He bats at it, instinctive, and I reach over in a dart and hit him in the face. He grabs at me, but I'm on the table with my hands locked around his throat. The chair makes a metallic clatter as it falls back on the floor.

Most people would seize my wrists and by then it would be too late. But he clamps a hand between my legs, the universal vulnerability of all men. No thanks. I let go of his neck and grip his hand, thumb in the pressure point to bend back his wrist. His free hand pushes against my face, and I grab that one too.

Then the door opens and the blond one's back, with a gun.

I let go immediately and move to get off the table, get behind it. But Lukacs's hand shoots out and knocks my head. His other fist grabs me between the legs, a vise. I flinch and lose breath. In a second he flips me onto my back and bangs my head to the table. I'm dazed. He's got me by the neck and crotch, and the blond agent stands over me with his gun against my temple.

Lukacs says, "Don't forget who has you by the balls, Terisov."

"Fuck you!" The room begins to dim. I want to throw up.

"Pirate," he says, leaning over me. "Remember who the bad guy is."

I can't get a grip on the table, and if I grip him I think that man will shoot. Maybe the gun isn't set on kill, but a paralysis pulse would not be pleasant.

Lukacs releases me with a shove. My eyes run. He moves away, then so does the other man.

"Get back in your seat," Lukacs says. Still standing and smoothing out his suit, his hair. Watching me.

I roll and slide off the table. I have to hold on to it for a second and I want to kill him. Both of them. In a messy manner. Instead I right the chair and sit in it, rubbing my mouth with my sleeve, trying not to wince. Swallowing my thoughts. I cup one hand between my legs, but nothing will help. I think he enjoyed it.

The blond one stands behind me. "Cuff him again."

"No," Lukacs says. "I think he's learned."

So Lukacs doesn't give the orders, or the blond one wouldn't have opened his mouth. But Lukacs doesn't listen to him, so maybe they're partners, not boss and stooge. After a moment the blond agent walks around me with a sidelong look down at my face, not a tilt of a smile. He keeps going out the door. Monitoring my reactions in this dealmaking, I know that now. He came in here quick enough.

Lukacs stays standing and rests his fingertips on the table, looking down at me. He carries on as if none of it happened.

"This is how it will work: you'll go back to your comrades with a cover and infiltrate."

So easy, sure. Wrapped up in nice unequivocal statements. I leave my sneer unchecked. "What cover could you possibly concoct that anyone's gonna believe?"

He says it like a smooth pickup. "Say some of your pirate comrades got you out. They're all factionalized now since Falcone died, the left hand ignorant of the right in most cases. Correct? Blaming your allies serves our purpose in three ways: one, when it breaks that you are actually alive and free, we can point the finger at the actual criminals. Two, since not all of your fellow pirates agree on your status, they'll spend more time watching one another and not our agenda. And three"—with that humorless smile—"the ones that do respect you will think you're still worthy enough to save and likely do business with. Which will open the doors for me." And this is the real point he wants me to get, the rest was telegraphing. "You'll say *eventually* that Black Ops helped you escape because a faction of the Agency wants a cut in with the pirates."

I can't help it. I stare. "That true?"

He doesn't blink. "That's what you can *tell* them. Eventually. After they trust you again."

"Is that true?"

"Of course not. EarthHub wants the pirates dismantled. Hence our deal for all the skills and info you have, Mr. Kirov."

Using my blood name, not the dead one. But I look at his wedding band.

"Believe me or not, it doesn't change the deal."

He keeps saying that word. It has the same sort of tone as Offer.

"You forget one thing, Lukacs—I was caught. By Azarcon." Evident by the fact I'm even here talking to you bastards. "There's no way in hell I can get back with my crew after being on his ship. They won't care that I didn't go willingly. Not to mention the fact I didn't manage to kill his kid. I got people kinda pissed at me for that."

He waves his hand in dismissal. "You'll explain to them that while you were inside you were approached by an agent who wishes to open communications between your contacts and his company."

I light another cigret from the pack he gave me and watch it burn for a second, an orange mouth eating its way up a stiff white stick. "That agent would be you."

"Yes. And when you've regained their trust and introduced me, we'll both have access to your friends."

And what a pretty picture that will make.

The cig deadens my nerves, smoothes me out like a soft thumb on metal foil. "Why would they even bother with you?" How much do you know?

He hasn't sat. He likes to look down at me when he sermonizes. "It seems *Kublai Khan*'s been struggling with your business contacts since you got caught. Your contacts"—he says it like it's a euphemism for sexual favors "much —prefer to deal with Caligtiera than with your ship, what with Caligtiera running Falcone's operation now. You knew that, yeah?" It's rhetorical, and he knows Cal's name might irk me. Falcone's lieutenant and a man who never much liked me or the protégé concept Falcone had pushed. "So an alliance with a—how should I say?—*ambivalent* faction of the Agency would be gold for your ship. We have access to a lot of information about the illegal activity in the Hub, I dare say more than even you could get. And let's also say this fictitious ambivalent faction of the Agency would really rather the aliens stay enemies. There's nothing good for Earth if we ally with those strits; they'll only weaken the Hub in the end. Fundamental Centralist views run rampant even in the Agency. Not so hard to believe, is it. And your hatred for Azarcon and his peace overtures do help in that, yeah?" Your. Pirates in general, yeah. Hate Azarcon. "Since you never testified against your former comrades, they won't, I believe, be hunting your head as ardently as you claim. And with you back on *Kublai Khan*, you might be able to wrest those contacts away from Caligtiera. Surely your captain would see all of this as an opportunity."

I'm the captain of *Kublai Khan*. Whoever's running her now is just keeping my seat warm. I suspect who would be running her now. Taja Roshan, who I dislike more than Cal. For some reason Lukacs doesn't bring up her name, so maybe he doesn't realize our rivalry. She was my lieutenant but not by choice, just because Falcone wanted one of his alpha crew to watch me on my own ship. But Lukacs doesn't need to know that either, at least I don't have to confirm it. Out loud I tell him, "You're counting on the fact they'll respect my link to you."

"Wouldn't it give you some cachet?" Just like Ops. An overblown sense of their own importance.

"If they believed me. If they didn't shoot me on sight."

"You're quite a convincing young man."

"I might not be that good. While we're being *honest*, Andreas."

He smiles again. "Oh, I think you're that good, Yuri."

I believe him on that. He's gone to a lot of trouble so far. "None of this will work if I can't even find the *Khan*. They probably don't use the same codes or sinkholes I used months ago, and the last I looked, space is kinda big."

"I trust you had a contingency plan, Yuri. Once it hits the Send that you 'died' in prison, you just follow your recovery protocol. I'm sure they'll find you."

He knows too much.

"And what if they don't trust it, and they meet me just to kill me?"

He shrugs. "Then I don't lose anything, do I."

"Except your precious plan of infiltration."

"Risk," he says. "We both accept it."

Especially if he wants something more. To bring down the pirates? How enterprising. How philanthropic of Black Ops. Like hell that's all he wants.

I look into his face, not that it makes a difference. "Without pirates or strits, you're out of business. That occur to you?"

Now he sits. He positions his slate in front of him once more and folds his hands on it. "Your kind don't die easy. Isn't that what you pirates always say? Don't fear for me or my job."

Just fear for your own life, he thinks. Fear for Finch's. He lets me read it in his eyes. Why destroy something if you can control it? Somewhere beneath his words is the full truth.

But Falcone trained me to be patient. So I'm obedient and listen to Andreas Lukacs lay it out, what he wants to lay out. What it'll take to get me off this dirt, if not a way to get the dirt off me.

* * *

Morry the Guard escorts me back to the general population, just like that woman had threatened and just like what Lukacs intended. To let me see Finch, no doubt. To remind me of this deal and the absolute mistake of it. But I make it anyway, like I've been making them for months, stitching them together in some desperate pattern that bleeds my fingers in the process.

Once Lukacs leaves the interview room it's a direct route for me, cuffed at both wrists and ankles, a shallow shuffle through the hallowed scrubbed-down halls of this high-security military prison. Straight back to the heart of hell.

Except this hell spews cold vapors, sitting in the polar region of planet Earth, on a still-preserved island called Greenland. And maybe there's color outside the tall gates and the reinforced steel chambers that keep our evil in, but we don't see it. Outside is death weather in the winter, anyway, and military spacer and dirtsider alike are sent here if the deed you did was bad enough.

They put me here because the majority of men inside these walls hate my kind. They wore uniforms in other lives, like Falcone had, and Falcone had bided time in this prison too, so maybe that was the thinking. I was never a part of EarthHub's elite, so there can't be any easy inside alliances for me, only hollow reminders of who I came from. Even the guards like to tell me. Pirate, they say, with a superior sneer. It becomes my name, like Whore or Geisha, but at least it's one that matters. Own it and use it. It goes ahead of me like a shadow, and once or twice a week when people test the edges of that darkness, it bites back. It leaves bloodstains on the floor that trail after my heels like starving children.

Even when they put me in solitary I can sit for hours with my eyes shut because darkness is nothing I haven't bedded already.

So even the guards became cautious.

This one, Morry, holds my arm like a dance partner. All of his kind learned early that I would cause no trouble if they caused none with me. One or two of them tried taunting me, but I broke their bones and they backed off. One or two of them fell victim to my smile, as sweet and meaningless as romance, and got me perks of cigs and soap. Eventually the mean ones got tired of singling me out and left that up to the other inmates. Morry, with his sloping shoulders and hooded eyes, he never raises his voice or his weapon and seems almost apologetic for our route.

"I'm taking you back to genpop," he says, like I haven't figured it already.

My pace is the jerk and slip of the reluctant. A zombie gait. In the narrowness of the hall, it doesn't even echo.

For such an old prison, Kalaallit Nunaat is well kept up like the discarded concubine of some ancient lord. Beneath the polished veneer is a scoured surface that might crack with a laugh. The walls are as gray as near-winter skies, with dull red accents on doors and signs, and glossy green floors the color of seaweed. Dozens of locked and guarded steel gates, like chastity belts for bored wives, stand between the private interview rooms in the sprawling administration complex and the stacked-unit wings where the maligned residents live. The noise of distant voices carries on the cool air that churns through the long corridors.

Not so different from pirate ships. Here you watch the shadows too, and take favors where you can.

"You were in that interview room a long time," Morry says conversationally, as he passes his nanobranded wrist through one gate scan and the next. The heavy bars clang and echo as they slide shut behind us, cutting off retreat. Black optic dots dog our asses, high and mighty on the walls.

I shrug. "They thought I was cute."

"Police?"

Spacers say pollies, dirtsiders say police. Morry is so much Earth-dirt that he bleeds grains of sand. Which doesn't make him stupid, necessarily. It can be natural curiosity on his part, but you never know the routes that information takes.

So I say, "Ask them."

And I wonder if Morry is one that Andreas Lukacs paid to plant optics in my cell or persecute Finch while I was in the box, if Morry knows everything already and just wants to play. His long face gives nothing but the stoic-guard glare. Some guards are notoriously easy to bribe. Or intimidate.

I could ask him, but that would reveal too much of my own concerns. So he just walks at a steady pace and I hobble along beside him like a marionette with one string cut.

Nothing changes in the landscape of clammy gray skin and arteries of red; we slip intravenous through one junkie's arm to the next and it just gets busier—blue-clad guards and dark-suited prison officials going about their business. And more security checks: narrow scanning arches and big armed men that paw you with dedicated sobriety. We stop longer at the second-to-last gate so they can run a scanwand from the tips of my hair to the bottoms of my shoes, seeing through my clothing and my skin.

Then we're at the gate to Santa's Workshop. That's what they call the genpop division, here at Earth's Northern Hemisphere. All the wicked little elves wait past that gate, eager to hammer you into someone's special toy.

My fingers grow stiff from the bone-chill air, so I curl them into fists behind me.

We pick up another guard. I don't recognize him, but it doesn't matter, they're all faceless at this point, like you make yourself faceless. He takes my arm from Morry, and Morry says, "See you later, Terisov." As if I've done something that amuses him. I don't have time to look closer at him; Mr. New Guard walks me through the final gate to the Workshop's wide processing room. Fresh prisoners cuffed and shoved already into nonidentity grays sit like dutiful schoolboys along the benches. They look up at me with shallow interest. I get moved to the head of the line. Seniority. Priority. Maybe Lukacs's doing.

"Back again, Terisov," Stafford says, the fat official behind his high desk. Santa Claus himself, if Santa was disgruntled and underpaid. He motions me forward and the guard shuffles me up. "Gimme your eyes."

I lean my chest to the desk and Stafford shines his scan into both retinas. He reads the pen display. It seems to take longer than it should, or maybe it's just my dread adding weight to the seconds.

"Welcome home," he says eventually, giving me a look as if he knows something I don't. "I think Finch missed you," he adds, not out of any concern. Maybe just to mock. Maybe to make me feel guilty.

Mr. Guard escorts me through the high arch of Santa's Workshop, past the corridor of optics and into the wide, half-occupied common area. We call it, not so creatively, the Hangout. It sits dead center of cell rings that rise three stories high, a coliseum of criminals controlled by a maneuverable, trijointed guard tower arm that can stretch from one side of the pit to the other in a matter of seconds. The tower bristles all around like a tank, protected by projectile-proof transparent plexpane.

Mounted on the west wall is a broad holoframe, currently deactivated. Scattered below this gaudy altar are a poor man's set of pews—plastic orange social seating nudged against long brown tables. The overall space gives a wide eyeline from the tiers of catwalks above. A few familiar enemies play games or cards at the tables. Nobody's allowed optical connection here, no surprise, for fear of burndives. They might not be able to access outside systems, but a good diver can still muck up the localized ones. Even games can be compromised, and that would just cause a hassle to fix or piss off some prisoners who need their battle drama.

In the center of the Hangout a dark man with a light beard laughs at me, looking up from his table's game display.

"See who come back to civilization." He says it loud, and everyone looks up.

I turn my ass and bound wrists to them and give a finger in greeting. "Hello, gentlemen."

The guard yanks me to the side.

"I'll be right back," I say over my shoulder. "Wave on the vid, will you?"

They laugh, but not from amusement. Anticipation. Like hyenas around a slab of day-old meat. My absence seems to have made them forget how many of them I bloodied in the past three months. Or maybe they remember all too well.

Mr. Guard propels me down one of the straight corridors on the ground level, past impact-resistant, plex-fronted cells, some of them occupied by idle murderers. Two and three doors gape open to help air circulation and invite allies and dealmaking. Nobody's locked down here until lights-out or inspection, or as a unitwide punishment. We can all walk around freely on most days, within gate parameters and under eyes and weapons. I doubt there are any corners unmonitored, especially if Ops has a hand in here, but what the guards and prison tyrants choose to notice is another thing.

My cell at the end of the corridor sits empty, or so it seems until I'm directly in front of it. Sticking out from under the blankets of the bottom bunk are the soles of dirty feet. I breathe out. The guard beeps off my cuffs, slides open the transparent door, and shoves me in. I bang a shoulder on the bunk and steady myself. The feet stir. One hand snakes out from the cover and pulls aside the crinkled pillow, revealing a dark eye, a slice of smooth forehead, and the shadowed angle of a sparsely stubbled cheek.

"You're back," Finch says, unimpressed. Not that I expected a laser light parade.

Maybe I should ask him how he is, but the sound of his voice reminds me of my own weakness. I rub my shoulder and step to the tiny sink in the corner of the cell. Aside from that and the toilet, there's nothing in here but the bunks. But it's all you need, really. A place to shit and sleep.

I turn on the tap and stick my mouth under the flow of bitter water. Not even that can get the taste of Lukacs off my tongue. I didn't need to blow him to swallow his offer, and now it's making me sick. My hands stay clammy even after I rub them on the front of my pants. Finch doesn't say a thing until I look up and around, squinting at the high far corner of our pod, across from the bunks. This is the angle that Ops footage was shot from.

"What're you doing?" He hasn't emerged from the blankets.

"Hoist me up." No chairs.

"What?"

I stand below the ceiling corner. Lukacs has to expect this. "Hoist me up, c'mon." I glance over my shoulder.

With a bit of a mumble he pushes down the blanket and shows me his full face, the discolored shapes on his skin and the severely short pattern of his hair, which used to be wavy long. Now it sticks up off the top of his head like a sloppy cut you keep sleeping on wrong. He has a striking face despite the abuse and fatigue, all cheekbones, jaw, and soul. You wear that around inside and people will want to screw with you. But he can't help it. He's not a real murderer like some of the others in here. Like me.

I don't say anything to his stare. There's no point in apologizing. None of it is my fault. Our silent alliance in this prison stops at self-survival.

"You got any cigs? I smell them on your clothes." He finally slides out from the bunk and stretches up to his full height. My height. He's tall and faintly muscled. A machete, not a butcher knife. He isn't wearing a shirt and his nipples are warm brown circles compared to the black stillness of his eyes.

Looks like they hit him on his body too.

He's being difficult on purpose, because I won't ask about it. "Forget the cigs, Finch. I need to get up into that corner."

"I'm not lifting your ass up there for no bloody reason." In that charming lilt. It makes even his insults sound like endearments.

I've been away too long. I move one stride and grab his

arm. Ignore it when he winces. And drag him to the wall. "Lift me up."

"Bloody hell, Yuri—" But he can't win and steadies himself. I step up onto his thigh, holding his shoulder, and reach my other hand to brace against the ceiling. He grabs the front of my shirt, swearing at me. The top of my head brushes the ceiling as I look all over the scuffed gray surface, into the shadowed lines that separate the walls.

There's a pinprick of black, like a mole, stuck between a smudge of dead insect and a piece of peeling paint. I dig it out with my fingernail. "Okay."

He lets go of me and I hop down.

"What is that?"

I drop the optic and crush it under my boot.

He knows but he still asks, "What was that?" What does it mean.

There's no telling if there might be more. It would take hours scouring the pod to find them just by raw sight. This is as safe as we'll get for talking without extra eyes and ears.

"We gave some Ops bastards a bit of a show that one time."

His face flattens white. And he says again, quieter, "What?"

I made him my lily because he asked for protection, and this is what the men in here understand. This is what they expect of me, or they would persecute Finch for his young looks. Claim and deference, even if it's only in front of others. He endured it without a sound or any kind of open resentment, and certainly without any show of pleasure. The screw wasn't anything artful or needy or even all that satisfying. But then it hasn't been any of those things in a long time.

"They were spying on us, Finch. From the moment the guard brought you in here two months ago." I'm beginning to think it wasn't just prison protocol that put him with me, young to young, pirate to pigeon. "Why'd you kill your CO? How'd you do it?" You seem too gentle.

He walks back to his bunk and sits on it. He badly wants that cigret, his knee bounces with nervous desire. "Ops. What the *hell* are you talking about?"

Not going to answer me? Lukacs harped on it, so I want to know. "Why'd you kill your CO. You're not a killer." Yet. A prison like this could make you a better one, or make you into one.

He sits there.

I stand in front of him. He watches the saggy knees of my pants, can bend and bite them if he wants. Not that he wants.

I fish out the pack of cigs Lukacs gave me, pull a stick and spark the end with my fingerband. Now Finch looks up as I blow a stream of blue smoke into his eyes. You want this.

"Why'd you kill your CO." Last time asking.

His jaw is tight. "I burned him through the gut with a pipecutter."

That sweet accent belies the violence of the words. And he still avoids. So I flick ashes onto his lap. "Hephaestus Shipyard?"

His teeth are clenched, but his breath shoots through them in a hiss. "The hell is this, Yuri?"

I made a deal with Ops because they want to get you killed. Now I'd like to know. Everything. "Shagging you was a big mistake. You're useless." I gesture to his bruised body. "Look at you. I was gone two weeks. Who did this?"

Now he's hurt, but in a way that makes him want to hit me. It's all in his eyes. He's not a killer because he can't hide it in his eyes. "If I'm useless then you don't need to know."

"Wex? Dulay?"

He doesn't answer.

I leave the pod.

"Yuri!"

I head to the Hangout, can hear the voices and the vid going. One sweep, and I zero on Wex playing Ghost at one of the game tables. Wex the rodenty bastard with upper-lip hair that never grows more than a sparse comb line. Dulay's nowhere in sight, nor is Jones, his crew. I approach on Wex's blind side, brief silence flanking me before someone gives a whoop of excitement. Fight. Wex turns in his seat just as I toss my cigret at him, then plant my fist into his eye.

He falls off the chair. I kick his ribs twice and a circle of men surround us as if they were called. Gladiatorial shouts and animal grunts erupt, and I've got maybe ten seconds before the guards pull me off him. He tries to grab my legs from his position on the floor, but I step aside, reach down to seize his shirtfront and pummel his face a few times. Wet thuds and cracks. Finch's voice behind me rises above the rest. "Yuri, stop it before they—"

But nobody's going to punish me. Not if Lukacs wants his plan to work. So I trust the agent just a little. I trust I'll get something out of this even while he gloats.

Wex on the floor, bleeding. I kick him again before official hands wrench me back and shove me facedown, yanking my arms behind me. Prison boot gray, then the shinier black of the guards swarming among them. The noise level declines all at once, and I'm laughing as they haul me up. Wex is still on the floor, cursing at me and dripping red. I spit on his lap.

"Go near him again, and I'll make you so pretty even Dulay will want up your ass."

"Shut up, Terisov!" Mr. Guard slaps my head and wheels me about, a brisk march back to my pod. Finch runs up beside me, glancing over his shoulder. Some of the prisoners laugh—at Wex. Wait until word gets to Dulay and Jones. I can count the seconds.

"You're locked down," Mr. Guard says, propelling both me and Finch inside. The door slams. A command into his commstud makes our pod beep. No leaving now. But also no getting in.

I go to the sink, turn it on, and stick my bruised knuckles under cold water. I hear Finch pace behind me.

"Quit prowling, it's annoying."

He stops. Doesn't reprimand me because beating the shite out of Wex is what I'm supposed to do, and it's sent a clear signal that I'm back with all previous rights and privileges.

Finch sits on the bunk, head in his hands. And I know exactly what happened in those two weeks I was gone.

As does Lukacs. Who put me in solitary so it could happen. So he could hang it over my head. So I could hate my decisions.

I almost reach out to put my hand in Finch's hair, but he turns away, still not looking up, and lies on the bunk with his back facing me, nose to the wall and arm tucked up under the pillow.

Go away, Yuri. You and your questions. He doesn't care about Ops now. But he's glad I'm back, in a way. I can tell by the way he refuses to look at me.

* * *

In darkness we can talk. Lights out, each of us in his own pocket of black and shifting restlessness, I stare up at the ceiling I know is there but can't see. His voice winds and twists up toward me like smoke from the bunk below.

"Why do you want to know?" he says. About Hephaestus.

Because Lukacs dropped the hint to make me feel dirty, dirty enough to get into bed with his kind. And why don't you hate me for what I did to you. Why don't I hate you for what you asked me to do.

"I'll tell you after you answer me." Some of it anyway. Enough so he doesn't mess up the deal.

He's quiet for a long few minutes. Then, "You know about Hephaestus Shipyard?"

"It's on the Rim and services mostly Guard stations. Right?" It was a target for pirates now and then, to get parts. I don't reckon it's a paradise.

"Yeah. No . . . I mean . . . you know about my parents or—"

"Yeah. But your CO?"

A long breath out. "It's a rough place. Sort of like here. In here. I used to get into scuffles with him. You know . . . fights. Bloody fights. I don't know, for whatever reason he liked to get at me for one thing or another. Either I did my work too well, or I was too quiet, or . . . whatever."

Because you look like you can't take care of yourself, Finch. But his defiance is the kind that brews.

"So one shift he got into me too much, and I jabbed him. With a live cutter. And that was it." He sniffs a little but not quite in remorse. Reliving the decision, maybe. Sorry to be in here because of it, but not sorry that he doesn't have to put up with the CO anymore. And probably his lack of shame made the sentence harsher.

"How'd he used to get into you?" There are a lot of ways to haze somebody.

"You know." Now he's irritated. "Taunts and shite."

"And from that you just assume that when you get into prison, you ask your cellmate to shag you for protection."

The dark can make you speak secrets.

I need to be clear, if for nothing else than my own guilt. "So your CO fucked with you."

He doesn't answer, at least not verbally.

He either let me do him, or it would be a dozen others, and life is all about the lesser of the two.

"So why did you?" he says eventually. "You didn't want to, so why did you?"

"Who says I didn't want to. You're sort of cute." We're having this conversation now when I never wanted to know before.

Before. Before a bastard in a nice suit showed me footage and said, This is where we control.

The minutes feel like heavy boots leaving imprints on my chest. A long march until tomorrow.

"You started walking," Finch says. "After."

"I've always walked." Not really.

"You walk in your sleep, and you talk to me. And it started after." His voice sounds hollow with the lack of light.

"Yeah, I told you about my dog, right?" The first time, he said. Then he never told me again what I said to him while I spun asleep.

"That's not all you talk about."

"Then what else?" Maybe my voice is a bit too sharp.

"Your life," he says, and it sinks like an anchor.

Sarcasm keeps me unmoved. "I was born, I grew up?"

He ignores it. "I told you about Hephaestus. So now what the hell was that optic?"

"Ops. They wanted to make a deal with me." If anyone's listening, they know this already.

"Black Ops."

"They're sending me back to space."

"Why?" Alarm. Thinking of his own skin, probably.

"Don't worry, the deal includes your safety. He said he'd protect you, and once I'm off-planet I'll have resources. I can follow up and make sure he does."

Why, is the silent question, but he doesn't ask it, and I don't offer. Why would you bother, Yuri.

"Won't people look for you?" he says instead. "How are they going to get you out? What does he want you to do once you're back in space?"

"You don't need to know all that."

"Well . . . when?"

Now the black feels oppressive. "Tomorrow."

"They're just going to waltz in here and free you?"

When are people like Lukacs ever that generous? "No. No, first they're gonna make me hurt."

* * *

The lockdown lifts for breakfast, and Finch and I go to the mess hall with looks and murmurs biting at our heels. The little humility lesson has become common gossip. Morry the Guard eyes me with something between fear and disdain—with a hint of something else that I read as smugness. Whatever he's smug about.

"There's Dulay," Finch murmurs, as we take our end of the table with our trays of prison gourmet.

I don't bother to look.

Start something, I think at them. Get it over with.

But they won't now. They've got better ideas, all electrified by EarthHub Black Ops.

* * *

It's an hour before lights-out and common lockdown, Finch is off in the shower, and I need his absence. There was a dread following behind us the entire day and maybe he saw it in me, felt it, because he hovered in the pod when I decided not to leave it. No games, no exercise, no idle benign deals with fellow inmates. And I didn't tell him to go; we were silent attendees to the same party, watching the festivities from the safety of the wall. But now he's off in his routine and I need a shank. Its weight could fool me into thinking I have defenses, but there are none when it comes to the fever and a deal. There's nothing but that itch and the heat, and the finality of a promise.

I crawl over to his bunk and edge my hand behind his pillow and down to the iron frame. There, right where I left it, a sharpened tip of a toothbrush. I yank it from its taped housing and lean back against the bunk, breathing hard even though it took no effort. My hands shake, my grip sliding damp against the plastic length. It's been a long time. I had nothing sharp in solitary.

But old friends or old sicknesses don't need introductions. They house in you like breath in your lungs.

I hold mine in until I let out the scarlet fever. A long line across my skin with that sharp point, and it doesn't really hurt. The path is familiar, the relief so strong I almost bone from it. My leg stops shaking and my eyes half shut. And my mind slips to that one time I had him and the way his hair smelled like cheap prison cigs, not like my spacer brand at all. Not like space. I ran those dark waves through my fingers and thought about the stars. How they winked with promises, but they always lied.

And he said, "Are you done?" with his cheek turned into the pillow so I could barely hear the words. But his neck was red from my marking him with my teeth, deep and damaged enough that anyone who saw it would know. You're mine. Are you done. No, this is just the start of it. The rest of my life in here, and some dark passing of yours.

But I climbed out from his bunk and went to the sink and

drank from the tap. I leaned a hand on the edge and expected to hear him turning to the wall, but instead I heard nothing and when I looked over he was staring at me, unmoved.

"What're you doing in here?" I asked him.

"I don't really have a choice."

He was answering the silent question, the thing I'd just done to him, but it wasn't what I asked. And maybe he just couldn't stomach the idea of men like his CO doing the same, and I was young at least. On the surface, I was young.

When I went back to the bunk I saw how still he got, how the shadows from the dim light cut his body into sharp edges. And I knew if I touched him again he would make me bleed.

Like I'm bleeding now, except with a cut along your arm you don't feel that stillness in anything but yourself. Nothing gazes back with that black judgment except that thing you see when you shut your own eyes. And my heart settles.

When I hear the door slide open I want to smile and say to Finch, C'mere. Because this is the last time before I go, and I promise it won't hurt. Not you, at least. Sex is no antidote to death, but it can give it a buzz.

"Pirate," they say, and it's not Finch's voice.

I open my eyes. Inside the cell are three men. Wex, Jones, and Dulay.

"Look," Dulay says, "he started without us."

The blood runs down my arm in a delicate rivulet. And everything it carried surges back to me in a rush.

* * *

In that interview room Andreas Lukacs sat across from me and said, "You're going to have to be killed. The only way to get you out of this prison without causing suspicion is through the morgue."

And I laughed, because at the time it was funny. And appropriate.

"It's the only way," Lukacs said, with this agreement between us, as raw and hard as a rape.

"You don't have to be so smug," I said. "They can kill me for real, and that won't get you anywhere."

"No," he said. "I gave specific instructions. And they have a stake in it. Cred, for one."

So Andreas Lukacs is my first Black Ops cocktail. But I doubt this drink will go down smooth. He says there are guards he can use. There are men I have to face. And there's pain I have to take, but it's all right, after that I'll be free. Like a soul on its way to heaven, if you believe that sort of shit.

I don't even believe in hell. But I think hell believes in me.

* ** *

I get to my feet as they edge in, two large men and one wiry sadist with a bare moustache. We all know why we're here and retaliation is only a small part of it, the official part of it. The part that will hit the Send and convince the govies until someone figures out the truth. Wex or his partners don't say a word. They look at me, waiting for some reason. For me to move, maybe. Or run. Because running game is much more of a challenge.

But there's nowhere to run, and that's not part of the deal.

* ** *

When someone beats you until you're unconscious, you stop feeling the blows long before the dark. These men are military. They're trained. They know exactly where to kick.

"Keep his face clean," one of them says. "Leave the head."

Brain damage is nearly impossible to repair. But everything else—

Dulay and Jones hold me by the arms and the hair, on my feet, and Wex works up a sweat with his boot and my body.

This pain fucks you from the inside out. Deeper than sex and more intimate than a kiss.

It feasts like an animal. I feel every bite.

Wex finally knees me in the groin, and they let me fall. On my knees and then on my face, and everything is a jumbled, pulsing netherworld. Sound pools around me and congeals to distant noise. Voices. Violent words. A kicking foot and a banging door. And I'm back in my memory to the first time I was ever on the floor like this. My cocktail slammed the toe of his boot into my side. My back, my thighs. Then he stroked my hair and called me pretty as sin.

"Yuri," he says. "I never should've left."

A strange, brutal thing to say.

"Yuri. Stay with me, stay awake. *One of you assholes get the doctor!*"

My body is a wet cocoon, upside down, hanging from my feet. All the blood rushes to my head. It must be there because I hear it flow through my ears. A loud roar, pulling at me, dashing me against a rocky shore. But someone's breath is in my face. Someone's breathing for me. Trying to anchor me, but I just want to float. To disappear in the dark where it's safe. But it's a kiss of rain on my tongue. I remember the taste from my childhood. Out by the lake, under gray skies. Cool droplets caressed my skin in misty touches. Gentle as tears.

And after that I die, but it's nothing I haven't felt before. It's nothing at all.

* * *

The first night I carried on a conversation with Finch in my sleep he said I'd slid down from the top bunk and went to the sink, drank water from the tap, then started to pace the width of the pod. He asked me what was wrong, and apparently I said, "I'm sorry, I didn't mean to." He asked me what I meant by that, and I answered, "I won't do it again." And I walked around and around the perimeter of our space, tracing my hand over surfaces, telling him about the dog I had on Colonial Grace. After an hour I climbed back up into bed and didn't speak for the rest of the night. I woke up the next morning, took a piss, looked over at him half-hidden under blankets and he was holding the sharpened toothbrush in his fist, his back to the wall. I threw my towel at his face to wake him up. I asked him if he'd had an urge to brush his teeth in the middle of the night or what.

And he stared at me with his dark eyes, and said, "What was all that shit about your dog?"

I didn't know. I was asleep. He must've been high.

He said, "You circled this pod like a whirling dervish and wouldn't shut up about your dog." And then his voice dropped. "About your ship."

Then I remembered sometimes on *Genghis Khan*, and later on my own ship, I used to sleepwalk through the corridors and talk to people — vacant-eyed, they said. I never remembered what I said. Sometimes it was gibberish, they told me. Sometimes it wasn't. Apparently one time I knifed somebody. It spooked them because I *knew* them and the ship, even without lights. And when I walked I made no sound.

Finch looked at me that morning as if I'd died and come back to life. Like he wasn't sure if something else had returned with me, or if I had returned at all.

* * *

Somebody's stroking my hair with icy fingers. I open my eyes to a dim white light glowing from the table beneath me, casting close shadows around my body. It isn't a gentle hand on my head. It's just the cycled air tinged with the breath of outside. Cold freedom.

I'm in the prison morgue, on a metal drainage table, covered with a sheet up to my chin. Above are round medical lamps and an examination arm leaning over me like a curious industrial dragon. I know it's the morgue from its chill air, its silence—the sarcophagi nothingness of a place where only the dead are kept. I'm naked. And the pain is a multitude of sharp fists pushing into my body, all over from the neck down. Beneath my skin and the transparent aidtape is the incessant itch of industrious bot-knitters, fiery nano-ants with healing purpose.

They gave me drugs. I feel them sailing through my system, hydroplaning, but they didn't last long enough to keep me asleep. I can't move though. I try to lift a hand, twitch it, and the sheet falls open. The frosty air against my skin makes the swollen areas around my bruises come alive. With teeth.

My breath sounds loud. After a moment I realize I'm crying.

The most useless thing.

But it's just pain and drugs, and it passes, like everything.

A door bangs open on my right, throwing light over me in shards. I squint. It shuts, and footsteps approach. A woman says, "You're awake? Good. That will make it easier." She grips my shoulder.

I flinch and jerk to the side, uncontrolled, one flop like a fish. The movement kicks me in the gut. All movement now is nothing more than extended abuse.

"We have to hurry," she says, and calls up a dim glow of yellow all around the room.

"Screw it." My throat is raw, my words like little icicles falling to the floor. Shattering in syllables.

She grabs my arm and tugs me to sit up. I flail a fist, hissing. It isn't much of a fight. I end up slumped against her shoulder, her hand gripping the back of my hair to get my face from her neck. And I recognize her clean female scent. Lovely Dr. Jorgasson, prison nightingale.

"So you shag Lukacs too," I slur at her.

"I'm *helping* you, Terisov." She pulls my legs off the table so they dangle. Blood runs down my limbs, from the inside this time, swirling circulation and pain through my nerve endings. She yanks me to my feet anyway, holds me up. Her grip around my chest finds the hard grooves of my ribs, sinking through the bandage. She can touch my guts and giblets, just dip her fingers into my sides and poke all the wet life around.

The shadows sway.

"Up," she says. "Up." Struggling with my near deadweight. "Turn around. Lean here." She plants my hands on the table and I feel the cold metal edge slide up against my pelvis. I shake but stay standing even though I can't much sense my legs. I look at the table and think of Finch and his big dark eyes and what he looked like facedown in his bunk. Right before I warmed myself against him. He was so warm.

"Finch . . ." Was he the one yelling for the doctor? It had to be, nobody else would.

She wraps one of my arms around her shoulders, helping me into a thick, nondescript coverall. One leg and the other. Loose, at least. My balls chafe against the fabric. It still hurts. I put my hand there.

Jorgasson says, "What?" Preoccupied with dressing me. With moving my hand as if I'm going to jerk off right in front of her.

"Finch . . ."

"He's not your worry now," she says.

He's my deal. My mistake. I'm going to space, and if I don't want him killed, like this, if I don't want to trust Lukacs that far . . .

The tendrils of my thoughts disintegrate.

But Finch's voice echoes in my head. A false memory or a brutal truth. The panicked sound of desperation, calling for help.

Just now or when he first arrived at the prison? It all muddles in my mind. I remember his face when the guard deposited him in my cell, announced him as my podmate, then slapped him on the ass. Finch stood there with all of his anger wrapped up inside his chest, but it pounded in the pulse beneath his jaw. And I knew he was going to get himself killed within the week.

Unless I did something. Unless I claimed him and cut anyone who came close. Wex got to him first in the mess hall. Flipped his tray. Tried to start something. Bloodied Finch's nose. Then I bloodied Wex. And at that point I was committed. Like a fool.

I can leave him and then. Then. Wex will kill him now just out of spite, before Lukacs gets Wex sprung for "murdering" me, and I don't see Lukacs caring or even telling me until I am done with his work.

"I can't leave him here." I knock Jorgasson's hands away, lean my ass against the table to zip myself up. These rough coveralls that burn my chilled skin.

She leaves me to it and digs into a lower cupboard for a pair of stashed, heat-adjusting boots. "The deal is you alone," she says. "We don't have time to worry about him, and neither do you. Morry'll be here in five minutes to take you out."

"I'm not going without him."

She stares at me, then shoves the boots into my arms. "Put these on."

I let them drop.

"Terisov, I have specific instructions. And so do you."

"Then put me back in my pod."

Middle management is easiest to confound. She gives a frustrated growl. Likely she sees her promised cred floating away with my stubborn words.

"It won't take much." If she doesn't cooperate, I'll have to hurt her. "Just comm Morry to pick Finch up on the way here."

"There's the tower guard to get past in the Hangout and one section gate. Not to mention he's in here for a reason. He deserves to be here."

I sit back on the table. It feels good to be off my feet even though my ass gets goose bumps on that metal. I press an arm to my gut. I think the pain is making me crazy or at least too determined about the wrong things. But her judgment gets under my skin. Where did you grow up? What pretty life did you lead? "You know they'll kill him tomorrow. Or worse."

"Why do you care?"

Why don't you.

I stare into her shadowed face. She's a small woman with calloused hands, but she keeps us patched up in here, stitched and stuffed no matter how many times our seams rip apart and our insides fall out. But compassion doesn't pay well, and she is scared of what Lukacs will do if she deviates from the deal. She must know him well. Maybe, probably, she's helped him in the past. Ops could have assets from the papacy to a prison.

"Just get him here," I tell her. "Get him here!" I kick at her thigh, even though it hurts. Breathing hurts. She doesn't expect it, nearly crumples where she stands, so I grip the table edge, stretch, and kick her again before she can recover. She falls down. And that makes my vision cloud. But I slide off, standing. Show her that if it comes down to it, you can get her. Corners dig into my palms, and she must've picked herself off the floor because her hands grip my arms. If her nails were claws I would be bleeding.

Don't want to be touched, especially by an Ops pigeon. Snarl and a shove, one-handed, then a supporting lean again, right hip to the edge. She backs off, lifting her hands.

I look over my shoulder at her, still holding to the table. I'll hurt you. You know I'll hurt you if I have to.

We stare at each other. I'm not so faded that I'm not determined. Probably she has orders not to exacerbate my injuries. So she goes to the comm. I sit again and breathe. She argues with Morry in a hushed voice. I hear him say, "Just cuff and gag the bastard, and I'll be there. Forget the other one."

Cred makes him care less too.

I lift my hand at her when she looks at me. I let her know from my face and the gesture that she'll have to tranq me to get me to obey, and with this much drugs already in my system that might annoy Lukacs when he wants me thinking.

She says, "Get Stefano Finch, Morry. Tell them I need to examine him because Terisov had an STD."

It's the last bit of absurd perfection to this plan, and it makes me laugh.

* **

Jorgasson paces while I sit on the table tucked in and dangling feet. Everywhere hurts but my face. Everywhere itches from those damn bot-knitters until I bully Jorgasson to injet me with more fade. Just a bit. Something to numb all the parts of me that can feel. Even for a little while. Soon I'm just an etherized spider on that table, thick with lack of sensation.

Eventually the door opens again. Two shadows fill the rectangle of white light that crawls in from the corridor. Then the door shuts, cutting it off, and Morry says, "Here's your baby doll."

Finch yanks from the guard's grip and trips up to me, stopping against the short edge of the drainage table. His hands are cuffed behind him but nothing restrains the expression on his face. The rage of shock.

You're alive, his eyes say. They don't move from mine.

"He needs to dress," Jorgasson says, "or he'll freeze."

He looks at her, then back at me. He wears nothing but a T-shirt and fleecy black pants, and now a confused and wary glaze in his eyes.

And something in my chest tightens and twists.

"What's happening?" Finch nearly shouts into my face.

"Shut up," Morry says, even though this room is as thick as a tomb.

"I told you." They're going to make me hurt. They made me hurt. I see him remembering our conversation. Patching it all together. My provocation of Wex, not entirely on his behalf.

The silence falls over his body language like a sudden muteness.

Jorgasson motions Morry to uncuff Finch, holding out the same winter coveralls. Except now that I'm more awake I see they aren't winter coveralls. They're designer body bags for those dead prisoners who don't have relatives to bury them proper.

"No bloody way," Finch says, looking at them, eyes wide. Looking all around at exactly where we are. "What in bloody hell is going on?"

"We're out," I tell him, pathetic optimism.

"This isn't out." Uncuffed, he points to the grid of metal drawers in the wall, sized to fit prone bodies.

Well, it's true. It's kind of morbid.

"Put these on." Jorgasson shakes the clothing at him. "Or we'll leave you in here with the rest of the dead."

I massage my arm. "Do it."

He stands motionless. Staring at me. As if I'm speaking, still asleep.

And maybe I am.

"Let's go." Morry yanks me off the table, and my knees buckle.

Finch comes to life, pushes himself toe-to-toe with the guard.

Jorgasson pulls him back and sets the clothes in his arms, even though he still looks at Morry. Suspicious. Unyielding.

This little bird that I thought needed protection. His jaw sets in stubborn menace.

"Get dressed," I tell him, as Morry propels me to the

door. And to Morry: "We're walking out of here? And I'm supposed to be dead?"

"Don't concern yourself with the details," Morry says. "Just move."

"We fixed the camfeed," Jorgasson says from behind us, shoving Finch along as he zips up the dead man's clothes.

"Ops is gonna be poor by the time we're done. I'm almost flattered." I'm the only one who seems to find it funny. Finch stares at me like I'm one spark short of a blast.

Still, all of these elaborate details for me. All the connections Mr. Black Ops called in. Just more information for me to pad a proper mental jacket on our boy Andreas.

He'll have his turn. I think of all the different ways and can't stop giggling. I can barely walk. The floor seems to undulate like it's made of water. I think the drugs have latent effects, and Finch's voice floats forward.

"Are you all right?"

"Just a little stiff, don't worry." I am the funniest piece of shit in the universe.

Nobody laughs.

The four of us creep through the corridor like revenants. Not a long walk, just around the corner to a couple of interlocked doors that lead out to a small retrieval bay. Where the bodies get picked up for shipment elsewhere. Jorgasson passes her nanobranded wrist over the verification pad and punches in the code to open the doors. They slide apart with a deep belch. Biting Arctic breath blasts us in the face. Wakes me up. A watery yellow light on the outer wall beams a piss puddle to the trodden snow on the ground. A black truck waits with the engine humming and a glow of blue from the chassis, floating it a foot off the packed snow. The back end of it aims toward us. So this is the way they transport the dead, Charon's vessel. A man in a white skinsuit lowers himself from the right side of the cab, leaving the door open. The furred hood and dark shades obscure his face. He comes toward us at a clip.

"What's that?" Cold smoke curls from his nostrils. A gloved finger points to Finch.

Lukacs's voice. Mad.

"My bonus." I tilt forward, grab the front of his skinsuit. My fingers slip on the sensitive fabric, but I dig in. His hands clamp around my wrists to shove me back. "Thanks for saving my face, mano, I knew you'd still want me pretty."

I can barely breathe in this cold. All my insides seem to crystallize.

"Get him in the back," Lukacs says, pushing me at Morry.

"What about him?" Morry jerks a chin at Finch, whose teeth chatter, eyes squinting against the wind. Fixed on Lukacs.

Lukacs looks back at him. A long time. Then at me, just a tilt of his chin. I can't see his eyes.

"Put him in," Lukacs says. "Both of them."

"We can't explain his absence," Jorgasson says, apologetic and not a little scared.

Lukacs says, "He was so traumatized by Terisov's death he committed suicide. Now do what I said."

I don't feel the cold. Not anymore. Just something deep and dark, like the water beneath a floe. Fine grains of snow whip against my skin like sand. Morry yanks open the back of the truck and tumbles me into its steel emptiness. At least it's empty. One cage to the next, this one barely tall enough to stand in. So I sit, and my legs burn with gratitude.

Lukacs peers in at me. He's eyeless behind the shades.

It's way past sundown and he still wears them. Maybe they're scopes. "You and I will talk."

I lean back on my hands, plant my feet, and spread my legs. "Anytime, sweetness."

Finch clambers in beside me and shoves my knees together. "The hell is this?" My attitude, this man, this deal. Why. It's in the curve of his back as he sits. The question mark. His breath clouds in my sight like smoke, but it smells like snow.

The truck doors slam in. Black now, and nothing else. The wind howls outside in muted complaint. In a second the vehicle jerks forward and the hum rises by a few pitches. We bob up and down, subjected to the repulse of the terrain. All my bones jar and quake, but I stifle any sound of pain until I taste blood on my lips.

I think of Lukacs.

✦ ✦ ✦

In the darkness our voices seem more intimate than we are, and he sounds closer than he is. But he isn't close at all, he's across the space where we can't accidentally touch in the tilt and rumble of the drive. The corrugated sides of the truck dig into my bruised back, but I don't care. I don't know how long we're going to be on this ride, so I tuck into the corner with my arms against my chest and my knees up, conserving warmth.

"Who is that wank?" Finch says, a ragged question that sounds more like an accusation.

"Our ticket out. Be grateful."

Silence and the sound of shifting. Then he says, "He's going to kill me."

"No he won't. If he wanted to he woulda done it already."

My throat burns with every breath. Pain shoves a heated stick into my chest and wiggles it around. "If anything he's going to use you."

"*Use* me?"

Or not. He'll decide. And when he sees Finch serves no purpose, my chivalry will be Finch's death sentence.

This is what you learn.

"I thought you were dead," Finch says finally, against my silence. His voice is raw from the cold. Close in the darkness.

It echoes in this hollow cage. I let it.

* * *

Impossible to know how much time passes, but it feels like hours. Most of it slips away in silence, nothing but our breaths and the grating thrum of movement over a barren scape. I doze despite myself and succumb to the invitation of the floor. Eventually the engine whines down to a low, steady hum, and movement stops. My aching body twitches in the dark, more when the sound of doors opening and shutting crack through the walls. I push myself to sit.

The injetted fade has long gone, and the pain is back with a vengeance. Soon the rear door opens and Andreas Lukacs stands there, hood lowered this time, hair dusted with specks of blowing snow. The sky bleeds lighter behind him. His shades are still on. Beside him is another man in a similar hooded skinny, aiming a rifle at us. The prom date. I can't see the lower half of his face from the high tight collar, but his eyes are that flint blue.

"Move," Lukacs says, one hand in his pocket.

Finch glances at me and eases out. I grit my teeth against the pain and hold the back of the truck for balance as my feet touch the ice-crusted ground. All around us is nothing but vast mountainous landscape, swept white with snow and illuminated like a comp console from the barely awake sun. At least the sun rises in this late February season, on this latitude. The cold air forces itself into my lungs, but it's clean. It reminds me of Colonial Grace in the winter. It all would be beautiful if not for the existence of Lukacs.

He grabs me by the right arm and pushes up my sleeve.

"Hey!" I yank back, but his grip is a vise, my skin already bruised.

Finch takes a step but the other man shoves him with the nose of his rifle. Finch slips and falls on the ground, ass first. It's just enough distraction for Lukacs to wrench my arm straight out and injet me just below the inside of my elbow, right on my *Genghis Khan* tattoo.

"What the fuck?"

"Just a nanotag," he says, letting me go. "So we can track you."

"That wasn't in the deal." I know it's useless to say as soon as I hear it. "If anybody scans my tat, they'll see it."

He smiles. "No. To standard scans this one reads like the ship ID code."

Ops technology.

I hear scientists do the same thing to endangered animals.

Which means he plans on being in fairly close proximity to me at all times. Or someone he knows will be in my orbit. That's not such a problem on a planet. Good tech can be tracked anywhere with a satellite pickup mate. But how that will work when I'm on a moving ship, I don't know.

Unless someone on *Kublai Khan* works for him. Someone who gave him my journal files.

The thought burns, but I still feel the slap of the cold.

"I don't need to tell you what will happen if you try to re-move it," he says.

No, you don't. And this is real, he will put me back in the stars. The prison was rotten, but among the pirates and their long memories there might be no appeal. To them I got caught, I couldn't kill Azarcon's son after Falcone's death, I couldn't finish the job or hold the network together. And you don't fill an empty seat by warming a prison cell. Six months EHSD since Azarcon put me on a ship and sent me insystem. I'm going back to a different landscape with an out-of-date map.

I could sit in the snow with my pain pooling at my feet and refuse to move. I could make Lukacs kill me, and maybe it's the right sort of fate for piled-upon months of mistakes. I should, I could, why didn't I a year go. Instead of nurtur-ing a conscience, I should've poured flames on my courage and burned it to the ground. The ashes pile up, and I can choke instead of facing Finch's dark eyes and the black above me in the sky.

Lukacs says, "I didn't plan for your lily."

And out of me doesn't come a denial. I'm protective still, when maybe I should be self-protective alone. "I didn't plan to be tagged."

He smiles. I know his thoughts. They would be mine if I was in his position. You let some things play out. You're nothing if not adaptable. You have to be adaptable.

"He's important to you," Lukacs says. Now we talk, with the wind blowing around us sharp enough to cut. This white world with its serrated edges giving back nothing but nature.

I just look at the bastard.

"You realize," he says, "that since he's here now, he can't leave."

"Leave this island?"

Lukacs smiles. "Leave your side. You're going to take him aboard *Kublai Khan* with you."

Among pirates? "No. I'm not."

"Doubtless you've told him who we are. Or at least what we are. He's come this far with you. I don't want him running around free. So either I kill him when he's out of your sight, or you take him with you. I'm being generous, Yuri. Clearly you feel something for the boy, so I'm giving him a chance."

He's leverage.

"Besides," the other man speaks for the first time. Blue-eyed and chilled in his tone. With the rifle comfortably strapped off his shoulder, aimed. "He's a criminal."

His words are nearly drowned out by the approach of an insect-bellied small transport. The wind kicks up worse under its descent and I have to shield my eyes. Through the scissor gap of my fingers I see Lukacs approach it first. The starboard ramp yawns with an unfurled tongue that tastes the snow with a soft lick. Inside is red-lit steel.

The other agent gives Finch a shove forward, after Lukacs. As I start to hobble after them, the man grabs my arm. Swift words, whipped free by the wind like a tattered banner.

"Watch him."

Finch or Lukacs? Meaning what exactly?

But he shoves me. I glance at his eyes, and there's nothing there but ice-hard impassivity.

I step up into the red interior. Finch is seated already in one of the forward-facing chairs, strapped in. He looks at me through the tint, but all of his questions, maybe his fear if he feels fear, he should be feeling fear . . . all of it is swallowed by the metallic scent and cold scrape of the air. And I have no answers now. We both face the same shadow. I hold on to the overhead grips and turn as the ramp begins to shut. The other agent climbs back inside the truck. Not coming with us to space, at least not now. Only Lukacs, who grabs my arm to shove me into a seat across from Finch.

Outside the truck tilts and half circles before tearing off in a straight line away from our transport. Soon it disappears over a rise of jagged land. The blue glow of the repulsors melds with the awakening sky.

Then the door completely shuts and I am inside the red.

CURIOUS

2.25.2180 EHSD—Plymouth Moon

I fell in love for the first time when I was four years old, if it can be called love at that age. Maybe it was just proximity and appearance, but either way she had most of my attention. She was a blond pixie named Mishka and her *mat* worked in the Transplanetary loading office with my papa. Sometimes Papa invited them over for dinner unexpectedly and Mama always frowned and complained under her breath to Babushka while Babushka chopped the vegetables with mild, silent violence. "He never comms ahead to tell me that woman's coming," Mama said, and Babushka made a soft noise while the knife went chop and chop. "Yurochka," Babushka said. "Stop lurking and take this salad out to the table."

So I held the bowl with both hands and backed out of the kitchen to the round table that nearly overlapped into the family room. There, three-year-old Jascha sat waving his arms in front of the vid so it changed colors. My year-old sister Isobel lay tummy down on a blanket by his feet, grasping at his toes. If Mishka and her *mat* weren't visiting I'd go over there and bug them, but instead I reached up to try and put the bowl on the table without it toppling onto my head. My papa sat there smoking a cigret that always seemed to be near its filter, even when he just put it to his mouth, and Mishka's *mat* propped beside him with her cat green eyes and shadowed stares, blinking a lot. "Mishka," she said. "Help Yurochka with the food."

Mishka slid off the chair beside her *mat* and came round to take one side of the salad bowl and together we both managed to slide it onto the table. She had her *mat*'s eyes but with a shy gaze that never looked at me for long. She was only a couple of months older than me, born February 3. At her recent birthday party Mama made me kiss her cheek so they could vid it to Mishka's papa, who was on station above our Plymouth Moon. I smiled at her now because I remembered how she'd smelled like chocolate cake.

"Hi, Yura," Mishka said, smiling back in her serious way.

"Hi. Wanna play outside?"

She nodded. Her silky ponytail, tied up with a blue bauble, swung up and down.

"Papa, can we play outside until supper?"

Papa didn't hear me right away. He was talking in a low voice to Mishka's *mat*. I saw the smoke curling to the ceiling as he held his cigret, letting it burn as if he'd forgotten it.

"Papa!"

"What, Yurochka?" He peered down at me with a weary blink. He had tiny black points in the centers of his blue eyes. Sometimes Mama said that I had his eyes, and for some reason I never liked to hear it.

Mishka's *mat* leaned over and plucked a baby radish from the salad bowl and popped it into her mouth. She let her teeth hold it for a second, and the white round end looked out at me like a blind eye before she pulled it into her mouth and crunched down.

Ew.

"Papa, can we play outside? Please?"

"Only if your mother doesn't need you in the kitchen. Go on, ask her."

I thought he just wanted me out of sight, which I didn't understand, but I pushed open the tall narrow door and poked my head into the kitchen.

"Mama, can I play outside with Mishka?"

She was talking at the hot-table to tell it what to do and ignored me. Babushka still sat on the high stool by the counter, chopping green onions and tossing them into the big silver pot beside her. She smiled at me, and I smiled back. Babushka had scars on her face from a flight accident way before I was born, one on her chin, another on the left corner of her mouth, and one on her cheek. It made her look like she was frowning all the time, even when she wasn't. At night sometimes when she tucked me into bed I'd ask her to tell me about the day she'd gotten them.

She was a pilot for our Moon's hauling company, Quad-star Transplanetary Shipping. Papa's suit had the pin emblem on his lapel, the red streak across four gray circles. Babushka's uniform had the same emblem patch on her arm, with wings. One time just before I was born she was on a normal run up to Plymouth Station with a load of ore that was going to be picked up by a merchant at the end of the week. She'd smile at the beginning of the story; she said she always looked forward to these runs because Grandpa (she said "Dedushka") lived on station and she'd get a couple of days with him before flying back to the Moon. If I wanted, she would tell me stories about how she met Dedushka, how he'd "wooed" her with a picnic facing the stars, somewhere on a dusty part of the station that happened to have a viewport, and how she'd sneezed and "drank wine until the stars outside looked like tiny pearls in an ocean of night." Babushka loved these stories. She'd smile, then she'd pause, and her eyes would go far away and soon the smile would die.

And then she always held my hand as she told me how she got those scars, years after the picnic. How when the strits attacked the station they blew out an entire section. She ran to her shuttle and knew the section was the off-loading bay where Dedushka worked. And she never got to her shuttle. The strits kept attacking, and as she ran the corridor caved in. Pieces of metal and parts of people hit her face and her body, and she fell unconscious. The Rim Guard drove back the strits, and when she woke up she was in the station hospital and the doctor told her Dedushka was dead.

She said she didn't want to fix the scars. She said the scars on her body were a journal of her life, and even when she cried she remembered how she'd fallen in love with Dedushka at that dusty picnic years ago. She liked to tell me stories of her life. She said it was the way we remembered, and she never wanted to forget Dedushka. She'd kiss my head after telling the stories and say I reminded her of Dedushka, with my bright eyes and dark blond hair and the way I smiled right before I did something sneaky. She never said I looked like Papa. I was my mother's son.

Now she smiled at me while the silver pot whistled and shook and Mama talked to the hot-table. Babushka said, "Go play with Mishka, Yurochka, and we'll call you when supper's ready. But kisses first."

So I ran up and threw my arms around her legs because that was all I could reach as she sat on the high stool. But she picked me up by the waist and noisily kissed my cheek. Then she set me down, plop.

"Go on." She slapped my bottom, and I ran out.

"C'mon!" I grabbed Mishka's sleeve as I passed, and she followed, munching on a carrot stick that she'd stolen from the salad bowl.

"Me too!" Jascha said, pushing himself up from the family room floor, butt first.

"No, you can't come," I said.

"Yurochka," Papa said, in a Tone. "Take your brother with you."

Isobel burbled and smiled toothlessly at me. Surely they wouldn't make me take her out too? I'd never get to play with Mishka if I had to babysit them.

Jascha came up to me and took my hand, so I sighed and looked at Papa, but he didn't say I had to take Isobel. I pulled my brother out the front door before Papa changed his mind. Mishka followed, holding Jascha's other hand.

We had a small porch made of smooth cement. Farther out was a square patch of grass, edged up against a wide road that separated our homes from those across the street. You couldn't go outside on the Moon without a suit on, so all of our play areas, everywhere we went, were closed in. But it was still big. The ceiling arched above us, sprayed blue and broken by ovals of windowed black space. Trees dotted every corner, carefully monitored and attended by environmental engineers like Mama. Our section of grass had low lamps with thriving flowers beneath, their petals spread like painted lips to the light.

Mama had made us a multicolored sandbox just right of the porch. I let go of Jascha and jumped in, digging for toys.

Mishka sat on the rim with her feet together and traced a finger in the rainbow grains. Jascha helped me dig even though he didn't know what we were looking for. Eventually I uncovered my plastic hunter-killer and all of my *Battlemech Bear* figures, five of them. Mishka liked Bear the best, so I gave her the one that had the movable armor, and she smiled and knelt down beside me in the sand. I carved a trench and put Kit the Cat Commando in it, to guard the Bear.

Jascha tottered right through it. "Yura," he said, "I can't find Panda. Can you find me Panda?"

"You just messed up my trench!" I pushed him out of the way, but Kit was facedown already and half-buried from Jascha's fat feet.

He sat hard in the sand and hit my arm. His eyes squinted up like he was going to cry, but Jascha wasn't much of a crybaby. He said, "Don't do that!"

"Find Panda yourself."

Panda Paratrooper was his favorite because Panda had a big round head, and Jascha liked to chew on the ears.

"Here," Mishka said, leaning to the corner of the box where Panda's black paw stuck out from beneath a ripped parachute. She dusted off the toy and held it out to Jascha, and it made me feel bad for pushing him.

Jascha took it and growled Panda at my Kit.

"Say thank you," I told him, like Mama always told me.

"Thank you, *Mishka*," he said.

"We can all play," Mishka said. "Panda can help dig another trench."

She always had ideas like that. So we dug another trench, and when the hunter-killer came in to shoot we all powpowed it back until it crashed nose-first into the sand and blew up. Jascha liked making blown-up noises. He jumped up and down on the hunter-killer until it was super destroyed.

And then I thought it would be fun to bury Jascha, so I tickled him into the sand and sprinkled it all over his bright yellow hair. Mishka laughed, but she didn't help. So I sprinkled some on her too, and Jascha jumped on my back and wrapped his arms around my neck. I went down in surrender.

The front door opened, and Mama called, "Yurochka! Supper!" Then she got a good look at us. "Boys! I told you not to mess up before we eat!"

It was a standing order. Her forehead wrinkled when she was displeased. I tried to shake Jascha off, but he giggled and pulled my hair and I yelped.

"Yurochka!" Mama snapped. "Get in here now and clean yourself up!"

It was always Yurochka, Yurochka, even when I wasn't the only bad one.

"Jascha!" I elbowed him. "Stop it!"

Mishka was giggling. I couldn't really be mad at Jascha when Mishka smiled at me like that.

When she smiled at me.

Before the world erupted and it was branded into my memory with heat and flame.

*　*　*

I don't remember the explosion, but I remember waking up, being deaf. My little brother lay facedown in the sand with singed holes on the back of his T-shirt. I reached to touch him, but somebody lifted me up. Mama. I grabbed on to her blouse, feet flailing until her arm went under me, and she crushed me against her breast. She was screaming, or it was something else in my head going off like an alarm.

I looked down over Mama's shoulder. Mishka stood in a circle of red sand. The sand was red because she was bleeding. She wasn't crying. She had only one arm, and her eyes were wide and unblinking, and the sand kept getting redder at her feet, making a dark puddle. The ragged sleeve on her left side was empty and soaked black.

The drops of blood seemed to fall in a slow warp, making a crash as they hit the sand.

My mouth opened. The air tasted burned. I coughed and looked away, pressed my cheek to Mama's.

Mama turned, and I saw Jascha with colorful grit all over his face. He was crying, kneeling in the box, holding Panda Paratrooper in a little fist. Mama bent to gather him up, trying to pick him up and hold me at the same time. She set me on my feet, and I twisted my fingers in her pant leg. Mishka's *mat* stumbled out of our cracked front door with her mouth open. She looked as if someone had sucked all the color and the life from beneath her skin, leaving only white bone. She held Mishka to her side with one hand and picked up Mishka's arm with the other. Mishka's arm.

She said, "We'll fix it, darling, we'll fix it," as if the words were separated from her voice.

Half-buried in the sandbox was an arrow of sheetmetal with red on its edges.

"Wrap it, Katarina!" my mother said. "You must wrap it tight! Quickly! Do it, woman!" And she pushed Jascha against me so she could help Mishka's *mat*.

I held on to Jascha. He wailed. He never really cried, but now he opened his mouth and lost his voice among the sirens.

Our corridor was destroyed. Across the street four houses

lay like broken teeth in a row of rubble, spilling their pieces all the way to our patch of grass. I could see past the houses and into the wall. It was black and fiery, and lights flashed in red and yellow emergency colors. The outer walls had closed. In school drills Mrs. Glantz had told us that if the colony was ever breached, we would not die from the outside moon environment. The extra outer walls would shut tight to block up any holes.

There was a hole in Mishka's sleeve with nothing to block it up. She just bled.

Papa was there now, cuts on his face, holding Isobel's tiny head against his shoulder. She was covered in her animal-print blanket. The dust and burned smell swirled around me and my hand was frozen to Mama's pant leg. Jascha's grip on my waist hurt like claws. Papa said, "The shelters—"

People ran, spilled from their houses like they'd been tipped over the side of a table. A deep voice talked from overhead but it was too noisy to hear any words. Papa said again, "The shelters!" but he didn't grab Mama. He took Mishka's *mat* by the shoulder. And for a second Mama seemed to stop and grow dark, like someone had shut off the lights around her face. Papa started pulling Mishka's *mat* down the street.

"Hold on!" Mama said, sweeping Jascha up into her arms. Jascha's arms went around her neck like a knot, and we all ran. Mishka's *mat* was ahead of us with Mishka, but Mishka couldn't wrap her arms. Mishka stared down at me with her wide eyes. Red rivers swept down her *mat*'s arm. Miskha's *mat* still held Mishka's arm with its bits of white and black and red on one end, like wet, mashed-up popcorn.

"Babushka!" I cried. "Mama, where's Babushka!"

But she didn't answer, she held Jascha with one arm tight

around him and clutched my hand with her other, and we ran after Papa.

It was so loud by then I couldn't hear our footsteps, couldn't hear the voice from the ceiling, could barely see Papa ahead of us cutting through the dust, lit by fires that licked the smooth walls.

"Slow down!" Mama said, coughing. I couldn't feel my hand, she held it so tight. But it was okay. Just as long as she held it.

Papa didn't slow down. People gathered around us running too until I couldn't see the walls and barely saw the ceiling. Only bodies stampeding in a herd, shouting, screaming, and streaks of faces blurred by tears. The press of flesh and clothing nearly squeezed out all my breath.

Then Mama let go of me.

People sliced between us. I couldn't see her anymore. They pushed from behind, moving me along, but they were so tall, and Mama disappeared in the shadows of the crowd.

"Mama!" I screamed.

The sirens swallowed my voice.

"Maaamaaa!"

The sounds were like a raging beast, like all the enemies of Battlemech Bear were falling to our Moon. The world was crashing down. And I couldn't see anything. I cried so hard that everything melted and bled away, and Mama didn't find me, Papa didn't find me. Babushka was lost, and Mishka was bleeding, I saw her standing there with one arm gone. It was just in my mind, but it was all I saw.

* * *

Huddled in the corner under the shelter's aqua light, I peed myself. The stream of heat cascaded down my legs, and I shifted. I tugged on my pants and the bottom of my shirt, wringing it. A teenager standing nearby looked down at me, then all around at the talking groups of people, the families in their pockets of self-protection. People went deep through the narrow corridors and rooms of this solid building. The shelter was one of three and I didn't know if my parents were in this one. I'd stopped calling when nobody answered, when nobody could help, and ran away to the corner. If they looked, they would find me, I wasn't going to move. I clawed at my arms with blunt fingernails, looking up at the tall, milling grown-ups. I couldn't speak anymore. My throat was swollen by too many tears.

The walls blocked all but the most distant racket from overhead. Booms and echoes. Every once in a while the lights flickered.

The teenager leaned down near me and put his hand on my hair. "What's your name?"

I couldn't answer. He rubbed my head for a second, then straightened and spoke to a man at his elbow, maybe his father, who gave him a slim packet from a shelf overhead. Now they both looked down at me as the teenager handed me the packet, squeezing out the straw for me. I grabbed it and drank, and he asked when I was done, "What's your name?"

"Yuri Mikhailovich Terisov," I said. "Have you seen my mama or my papa? Have you seen Babushka?"

"Mikhail Terisov," the man said to the teen. "Did you see him down here earlier?"

The teenager shook his head. "I can go walk around again."

The man said, "No, stay here with the boy. I'll go look." And he disappeared among the elbows and legs.

"I peed," I said, twisting my clothing.

"Yeah," the teenager said. "It's okay. Yuri, right? I'll get you something new. Take off the wet things." He started to move away.

"No, don't go!" I grabbed at his leg.

He stopped and put his hand on my shoulder. "It's all right. I'll come back, I promise. Just stay here, okay?"

I didn't believe him, so I just stared at him. He had blue hair under the lights and very dark eyes. His skin looked like chocolate and I thought of Mishka and the tears all came down again.

"It's all right." He hugged my head for a bit and patted my back, then set me against the wall. "Stay here and I'll be back in, like, thirty seconds. Promise."

I put my thumb in my mouth and he went off. The other man didn't come back. I waited, biting my finger, pulling at the skin on the inside of my elbow with my other hand. When the teenager showed up again he kind of frowned, then smiled. "I told you to take off your wet clothes."

"I didn't want to."

"Embarrassed, huh?" He set some folded clothes on a shelf next to my head and reached to tug at my sleeves. I let him.

"You were gone a long time," I told him.

"It's crowded. And I came back anyway. See?"

He smiled again but I didn't smile back. I didn't feel like it. And I didn't think he felt like it either.

He helped me remove all the pee-smelling clothes, then ripped open a little package and shook out a square of scrubby. He handed it to me and I rubbed myself all over like Mama would tell me to do in the shower with the soap. The scrubby smelled like—fresh. Like Mama's garden. I sucked up the tears so I wouldn't cry in front of him and just ground the scrubby into my skin. It came away black and brown and yellow. From the sand and the destruction. And the pee. Then he helped me dress. The soft sweater and pants were just a little too large, but I didn't care. I reached up to him and for a second he paused. Then he lifted me up by the waist and let me hug him around the neck.

He said, "It'll be all right, Yuri. The strits'll go away and we'll get to go back home. My dad said so. He was here when they attacked the last time, and the time before that."

I didn't want to hear about any attacks. I just wanted to see Mama and Babushka again. And Jascha and Isobel. And Papa.

I was scared to see Mishka. Or her *mat*. And the way her *mat* had picked up her arm like it was a toy.

I fell asleep on his shoulder, and my dreams were nothing but noise and red.

* * *

Papa woke me up. It was Papa leaning over me with a hand on my shoulder, shaking it. I shot toward his chest and hung on. He held me for a long second with one hand, then disengaged my grip and stood, pulling me to my feet. I blinked in the dim light, saw him supporting Isobel in the basket of his other arm. Behind him stood Mishka's *mat*, holding Mishka in her arms. Mishka was asleep on her *mat*'s shoulder and there was a plug of bandages on the nub where her arm had been. A monitoring chip attached to it blinked colorful little dots.

We weren't where the teenager had sat with me. All around were grown-ups and kids on thin stretchers, hooked up to doctor pods. All the pods were full, so some of the injured people leaned against walls, cradling themselves. Blood stained the floor in places. It was quiet like a church, and the murmuring around me could have been prayers. Except the smell was ugly, like burned or dying things.

The boy with the chocolate-colored skin was nowhere in sight. But it was okay. Papa was here.

He said, "Yurochka, we have to go. You aren't hurt, you can walk, yeah?"

"Yes, Papa. Where're we going? Are we going home?"

"No." He glanced at Mishka's *mat*.

"Where's Mama?" I wished he would pick me up, even though he held Isobel. "Why can't we go home?"

"Mama is waiting for us in our new home, Yurochka. Come now. Come." He held out his hand, gripping my sister with the other.

Up above went *boom*.

"I don't want to go to a new home . . ." I looked up at the blue ceiling. "Why can't we go back home? Where's Babushka?"

"Yuri!" he snapped, shaking his hand at me. "No more questions! We're leaving now, and I don't want another word out of you!"

Isobel bawled. Papa grabbed my hand and tugged me to the exit. Mishka's *mat* followed, silent.

"Where's Mama?" I looked all around at the people, all of them walking like zombies in little groups under the watery light. Going somewhere. Going up to where it boomed. "I want Mama!"

"Yurochka! I won't tell you again."

He didn't look at me; he watched above the heads of everyone, where I couldn't see. His grip on my hand hurt. Isobel still cried, her voice joining others, babies and babies. Scared. I wished I could cry like that, but I wasn't a baby anymore.

I pressed up against Papa's side as we shuffled around the

shelter. We didn't seem to be going anywhere. The bits of floor I saw through the feet lay dirty and shadowed.

Then the booming stopped, and we all shifted. Somebody's bag jabbed into my back. I tried to twist away, but Papa tugged me to the right, and soon we were going up concrete stairs. One step at a time. Up and stop. Up and stop. A flickering yellow light beat above us like something was flying in front of it. It got brighter as we got higher. Voices buzzed. When we broke from the shelter it was like God had come to guide us to the next life. A man shouted into something that made his words fall around us like little bombs.

I didn't know where we were. It didn't look a thing like the Moon and our home. All the houses stood gap-toothed and burst open. The long corridor was puckered and bumpy with debris, unrolling into a black mouth that swirled and blinked with lights. Red-uniformed Rim Guardians walked around holding big, long guns. A dozen of them choked one section by the wall, checking people as they went through the tall, bent doors leading out from the residential area. People went through those doors when they had to work in the mines or the port or the school and the offices. But Papa wasn't going to work now. People bled. People hardly spoke. A lot of them wept.

The man with the God voice told us to stay in line and board this shuttle, and if we were missing family it would be sorted out on the transit station, and if not there, then at Grace. There were two shuttles going. We would all be reunited on Grace.

I looked up at Papa. Where was Grace? Would Mama meet us on Grace? Would Babushka?

But he didn't answer me. He didn't look down. And through the legs of all the grown-ups, there among the patrolling Guardians in their bloodred uniforms, lay bodies of other mamas. Other parents. And children. I didn't see Mama or Jascha among them, even though I looked. I stared until the broken, mashed-up people seemed to stare back.

Except I knew they didn't.

* * *

In the shuttle I looked out the oval window beside my seat. Down below was our colony. It was far away and small, round and gray like blind eyes. The long grooves in the ground, where the adults used to mine and dig and carve, could have been the trenches me and Jascha made in our sandbox.

My home lay cracked and jagged, shoved into the Moon like a giant had stepped on it.

2.27.2180 EHSD — Basquenal Rimstation 19, Transit Center

We waited in line, on the floor, while field officers from the EHRRO asked questions and issued IDs. I asked Papa what "aero" meant. He said it stood for EarthHub Refugee Relief Organization. I asked him what "refugee" meant. He said, People who are forced to leave their homes because of war or persecution. Then he told me not to ask any more questions, even though I wanted to know what "persecution" meant.

There was a big crowd ahead of us, in this long blue room with its bright lights high up on the ceiling. They'd led us off the shuttle and walked us through narrow corridors to this room, then made us sit and wait while people talked to us one by one, or family by family. It felt like nowhere, like we were in a room that nobody knew about and nobody could leave. Rim Guards stood at the exits. We'd been waiting for a full shift already. They'd fed us rounded little meals of wet vegetables and meat patties, but it seemed like too long ago, and I was hungry again. Isobel fell asleep on Papa's lap. Mishka sat against the wall with her legs stretched out, ankles slack, staring across the aisle at another little girl who rolled marbles on the floor between her feet. I tried not to look at Mishka's nub, all bandaged and thick and wanting. Mishka's *mat* had her arm around Mishka. I wondered where Mishka's missing arm was and if they would ever put it back on. I asked Papa.

"Don't ask such things," Papa said, then he looked over my head at Mishka's *mat*.

Mishka suddenly screamed and hit me. "Don't talk about it!" she yelled. "Don't you talk about it!"

Isobel woke up and started to cry.

I moved away from Mishka's fist, against the wall.

Everyone in the center looked at us. A Rim Guardian came over, her rifle pointed down.

"What's the problem here?"

"My daughter, she is just upset," Mishka's *mat* said, patting Mishka and hugging her, even though Mishka just sat there now, quiet like before. I stared at the floor. A pair of high heels approached. Not a Guardian.

"What about some food? Are you hungry?"

They were passing out drinks and packets of biscuits. They still hadn't gotten to us. But maybe now they thought it would shut us up. The lady in the high heels took some wrapped squares and envelopes of drinks from her plastic box and gave a set to each of us. The silver box had a symbol stamped on it in white—a ring of stars with an open palm in the center.

"Thank you," Papa said to the woman.

She smiled at us. Her eyes were sad, as if we were never going to eat another meal again.

* * *

Papa took me and Isobel up to the desk when our number was called. There was a man there, younger than Papa, and he looked at us with watery red eyes. I wondered why he would be crying. He hadn't been on the Moon.

"Name?" he said.

So Papa gave him all of our names. Then Papa said, "My wife. My wife and other son. Have they arrived? Ilyana is her name. And Jascha. Jakob. They were on the other shuttle."

The man didn't even look down at his slate. "The other shuttle's been redirected to Rimstation Twenty-three. Once they've been processed, you will all be sent to Colonial Grace in the Spokes. I'm sure you'll see your family there."

"When?" Papa asked, jiggling Isobel, who was fretting. "When will we be going?"

"A Guardian ship will take you to the relocation colony as soon as everyone here is registered."

"I need more food for the baby."

"One of our health service officers will bring that by. I've noted it here." He tapped his pen on the slate. It beeped. The other people in their silver EHRRO shirts all had similar slates. Passing information about us back and forth.

I tried to look at what he input, but he slid his hand over it as if by accident. I looked up into his face. He said, kind of soft, "It won't be long."

He gave Papa a holocube and explained that it was supposed to tell people who we were and where we came from and where we needed to go now that our home was destroyed. It told people we were Hub citizens, we weren't criminals, and that we had a right to be helped.

I wanted to know why we couldn't stay on this station. But Papa said that Rimstations didn't have the facilities to take on refugees forever. So we were going to a planet. Where it was safe. And Mama would meet us there with Jascha, and we would be together.

With Mishka and Mishka's *mat* too. But I didn't want that. I didn't say anything though. I didn't say that if I had to look at Mishka and her no-arm all the time, I was going to be sick.

4.30.2180 EHSD — Colonial Grace

The planet was called Colonial Grace because it had started to be a colony for EarthHub, one they had planned to make into a green paradise. But now it was just a half-terraformed rock that the Hub had abandoned when the war started decades ago. But they didn't want to just leave it empty, so now it was a refugee planet buried somewhere in the Spokes, far enough away from the main theater of war that its transplanted citizens didn't have to fear more alien attacks.

I heard the grown-ups call it the Camp. Not Grace.

It was barren until you looked a little closer at the knuckled land; lifeless until you felt the striking hand of wind on your cheek and knew it came from across the lake that edged up against this eyelid of homes. Houses? They were boxes that hugged one another against the cold. Gusts swept in from the wide expanse of unpopulated country, given free rein from the lack of development.

That's where we were—in the dregs of an idea.

It wasn't much of a home, nothing like they had on most stations or even on planet Earth, the oldest of homes. The Camp was quickly built, barely maintained, and not made to accommodate the hundreds of refugees they crammed in there. Most were children like me. Most were orphans because their parents were soldiers who'd died or were too injured to care for them, and the nearest stations were too overcrowded.

But the Camp was overcrowded. There was one toilet for every twenty people and not much to do but run around with a stray dog or toss pebbles into the water. I avoided the EarthHub Army guards because they were usually bored, peeved, and weary at this dead-end assignment, frustrated at our questions, and sometimes mean. The relief workers were generally harried, understaffed, underfunded, and traumatized by being around us in these conditions. The medical center was filled by sick kids and adults with nightmares too real to be swept away with drugs. People roamed the dirt paths between buildings, remembering the things they'd seen, muttering about them, while the guards sat on porches or walked the edges of the Camp, smoking and silent.

Mama wasn't there when we arrived. I went to the landing pad every day, as far as the guards let me, and peeked through the wire. But the shuttle didn't come. For weeks.

In other hours sometimes I went to school and listened to some worn-out adult drone on about subjects that had nothing to do with the fact I was always hungry, dirty, and cold. School had no link to the Send or other colonies or stations because the sat hookup in the Camp had been busted for months, and the govies hadn't sent anyone out to fix it. The military or the other adults never could keep it running for long. Not when the proper parts took years to get, or so the adults said.

Instead, govies dropped bins of nonperishable food into the Camp, and everyone had to line up on distribution day to get our ration. Once a week there was enough food and energy to have a hot meal of rice and beans and some sort of meat. And every once in a while some charity group from some No-Name Station sent secondhand clothing or handmade blankets and we were supposed to be grateful for how generous people were, how lucky we were that we were away from the strits and the rest of the Hub hadn't forgotten about us.

The guards should've been out there killing aliens, not standing around looking at us to make sure we didn't cause trouble with the relief workers. Why weren't they looking for Mama? Every day Papa went to Administration to ask about Mama and Jascha, but they told him they didn't have that information yet, that the shuttle was always Coming, and he would just have to be patient.

Isobel cried a lot. Sometimes Papa handed her off to Mishka's *mat*, or to me, and went outside to smoke. For the fresh air, he'd say. But I saw how sometimes his face got red when Isobel refused to stop crying, and I'd usually take her from Mishka's *mat* because she was my sister, and she'd go quiet when I held her. I liked to hold her.

Two months after we landed in the Camp, Papa found me under a pile of blankets on the cot they'd given us in the big, peeling cafeteria. There were about fifty of us jammed up nearest to the wall with the huge silver EHRRO seal painted on it. We weren't yet assigned a home. The Camp administrators had hustled most people into prefabs until things could be better sorted, but some of us were still left in public until the EHRRO dropped more prefabs. I'd gone to sleep while Papa and Mishka's *mat* sat up talking on the floor. Papa had held Isobel against his shoulder, and Mishka slept with her head on her *mat*'s lap and her one nub of an arm stretched out, as if it searched for the rest of itself.

When Papa woke me he was smoking, even though there were signs that said you weren't allowed to smoke indoors. But nobody really cared. He leaned down and touched my shoulder, and said, "Mama and Jascha won't be coming."

The track lighting right above us had blown out two days earlier. Yellow glow backlit his body, so I couldn't see his eyes. His fingers squeezed. I didn't say anything and maybe he thought I hadn't heard, because he repeated it.

I thought of the bodies back home, on our Moon, and the way they'd lain there as if somebody had forgotten about them. I twisted the blanket in my hands. "Why? Papa, why?"

"Their shuttle went to another camp."

"Why?"

"Damn bureaucrats," Papa said. "Their transit station thought they were from a different colony and redirected them to another planet. And now they have to sort them from some other colonists and the whole damn thing is taking too damn long . . ." He rubbed his cheek, blinking and unshaven.

I didn't know what he meant. "Can't someone go get them? Why can't the Rim Guard go get Mama? You said Mama would be meeting us here!"

My voice echoed. Someone five rows down started to cry. Papa held both my shoulders now.

"Yurochka!" He gave me a little shake. "That's enough. They've put your mother and Jascha somewhere else, and it's going to take a while for them to sort it. In the meantime we are here, you and your sister and me. We will have to make do." He released me and smoked and looked around. "We will make do."

I asked about Babushka, and he didn't answer for a long time. He just sat on the edge of my cot, looking across the cafeteria as if he expected someone to wave at him. I put my cheek against his arm, and after a few moments he gathered me to his side. Then he said, "Babushka's dead, Yurochka. She died in the house. Part of it fell on top of her."

And maybe it was the calm way he said it, or maybe it was because I was too tired and numb, but the words went through me like a ghost and left behind nothing but an absence.

* * *

Sometimes Babushka told me stories about my parents, like how they grew up together on Plymouth Station. Dedushka was friends with Papa's *otyets*, his father, they both worked in the loading bays, and Jerzy Terisov used to complain about Papa, his son, to Dedushka. "Head in the stars, that one. What am I to do? You're so lucky that Ilyana has her eye on a good solid career. I don't want Mikhail to end up like me. I want him to go to Austro or even Pax Terra, you know?" Babushka told me this and I never believed Papa could have had his head in the stars. He was always looking at the ground, or his cigrets, and only sometimes seemed to really look at Mama. But Babushka said when he was young he used to write stories and poems to Mama that made Dedushka roll his eyes until Babushka reminded him about their dusty picnic. All the poems worked because Papa proposed to Mama when they were nineteen. When Mama was in university, Papa took an office job to help her through it because it was expensive. And then Mama got a job on Plymouth Moon to work with the environment team, and Papa went with her to work in another office; and then I was born, and Jascha, and soon after that, Isobel. And I grew up in that house on the Moon with the sandbox on the front lawn that Mama had made for us. Grew up for four years.

And I remembered a lot of it, sitting there with Papa in the big cafeteria, with strangers handing us food as if we were poor, and it was cold in there even with Papa's arm around my shoulders. Everywhere was so big it echoed, and I could even see my breath.

Now Babushka was dead, and Mama was lost. The strits might have broken us up, but everyone else kept us apart.

2.11.2181 EHSD—The Camp

I have a lot of memories of sitting at lake's edge with my dog Seamus. I ditched boring school a half hour after Papa dropped me off, bundled in secondhand coat and scarf and hat, and picked my way through the brightly colored rocks along the shore. Seamus wasn't really my dog, it wasn't like I owned him in any sort of records, or that he was even given to me. He just found me one afternoon down at the shore and followed me around when he wanted. When he got tired of me he loped through the slant-roofed buildings of the Camp, nosing under porches and around the cafeteria doors for scraps and affection. Once he'd had a collar because the short brown fur around his neck was permanently flat, though the rest of him was haphazardly fluffy. But nobody in the Camp claimed him. Maybe his owner had died, like people did every month — frozen or sick or just in despair. Or maybe his owner just didn't want him anymore.

I don't know where I got the name from. A story or a song, but he came to me when I called him. Most of the time I followed Seamus around as he gnawed at mermaid-hair seaweed that had washed up on the rocks, bloodred curls streaming from his jaws. The water stank around the Camp from pollution or a lack of whatever was needed during the broken terraform process. We were told strictly not to drink it, but Seamus seemed unaffected by the things that slithered up from its depths. He bit them and shook them about with his jaws like one of his wild ancestors from Earth, and I trailed along after him, sometimes using his damp furry back to steady my footing along the churned-up rocks. They lay tumbled and jagged in places, remnants left behind from melted, receding ice.

One day Seamus led me to Mishka. She sat on a black, overturned dropbin that was cracked from time and weather like a tombstone. Its insides had long been gutted of nonperishables. She faced the gray water and curled her one hand in her lap. The brisk wind whipped her hair across pale skin blotched red by the weather's abuse. Her *mat* let her run wild in the Camp, too sorry or too tired to restrict her. *Poor Mishka*, our neighbors said. Even Papa and her *mat* said it. All the time. Even when she threw tantrums during meals and damaged our cabin.

We had our own home now, with our own stove, since a couple of months ago some company somewhere donated a bunch with independent energy cells. Papa always sat at the tilted table and smoked the sweet leaf our neighbors grew under the noses of the Camp administrators. Mishka's *mat* steamed eggs and onions for breakfast, and sometimes had to clean it all up when Mishka decided to pitch it on the floor. Papa never said anything to Mishka's tantrums, but once when I told her to stop it, and Mishka's *mat* had yelled at me, Papa told her never to speak to me like that or he would ask Administration to find her and Mishka another cabin.

The silence between our families sometimes fell thick like the snow, or ran as cold as the lake water.

Mishka didn't look up when Seamus pushed his nose into her hand. She didn't pet him or push him away. I tottered up behind him and scratched my nose with a mittened hand. She didn't wear a mitten and her coat was open. She looked made of ice, so white and hardened on the edges. But I thought if I pressed her skin she'd flake apart, and beneath would be the pale redness of an unhealed wound.

Our clothes were old, not the latest lightweight skin-clingers. Her wrist jutting out from the padded sleeve looked like one of those sticks you cracked and shook to get light, except she wasn't see-through or glowing. She was pale and opaque.

"Hi," I said, stopping just in front of her with a hand on Seamus's back. He nosed at something near her booted feet.

She looked up at me, but she didn't say anything. Her gaze slid to the rolling water. Her lips were stripped white from the wind and hurt to look at.

"Mishka," I said. "How come you don't go to school?"

She breathed out, ran her tongue over her bottom lip. "You don't go to school either, Yura."

I leaned against the bin and toed a black pebble lodged in the ground between us. "Sometimes I go. But you never do."

She didn't speak for a long time. I thought she might've forgotten I was even there. I tossed rocks into the lake and watched Seamus bound after them. Then she said, "I bet your mama's dead. And Jascha."

I looked at her and forgot about the rocks. "Don't say that."

"I bet the aliens killed them."

"Papa said they're on another colony. So shut up." I wanted to hit her, but I saw her flat sleeve where her arm should've been and just curled my fingers inside my mittens. "Why do you say things like that? Why're you so mean?"

She got up and walked to the shoreline, squatted and tucked her elbow against her stomach. Just stared at the horizon of water rippling under the wind.

"They say we'll never go home," she said, and I had to step closer to hear the creak of her words bending in the air. "I heard them. They say the strits won't let us go home because the Moon used to belong to them. They say the war started because of the Moon, and the strits are still mad about it. That's why they attacked. And they'll never stop attacking."

Her one hand fingered the loose, empty sleeve of the other.

"Your babushka's dead too," she said. "Isn't she?"

I hit her.

She didn't make a sound, so I hit her again across the shoulder. And I started to cry even though it didn't hurt me at all. She was the one with the missing arm and the hollow eyes. She was only five like me, and I'd loved the way she used to be so nice to my brother, the way she used to smile at me. But now she never smiled, and she screamed sometimes, or threw things, or she hid herself away, and now she told me my brother was dead and she didn't even seem to care.

I couldn't touch her, even when I hit her. She didn't make a sound.

9.10.2184 EHSD— Cigrets and Cookies

I got in the habit of avoiding Mishka and her *mat*. Every
other day I skipped school, hung out by the lake with Seamus or skulked around the Pediatric Ward looking pitiful so
the nurses gave me extra food and sweets. Most of the time
I took it all back to Isobel, who was nearly five years old
now, a pale-skinned girl with hair the color of brown sugar
and eyes that seemed too large for her face; they stretched
the skin around her sockets and made her look older than she
was. She didn't go to school, I think because she screamed
the entire day when Papa had tried to drop her off, so instead
he sat with her at home and read books with her from the
primary slate he got from the school. Sometimes she read on
her own, or traced the animation with her finger, tucked into
the corner of the bed we shared. Sometimes she talked to her
doll. She invited me to play but mostly she occupied herself,
which gave me some freedom to explore the Camp.

Not that I didn't know every square meter of it already,
like where the guards went when they wanted to do something illegal like smoke a leaf or screw someone while on
duty. One time around the EHRRO Staff Dormitory I caught
this guard with his face up some orphan girl's skirt, and I
just laughed and pointed. She must've been barely sixteen
and ran off when she saw me. The guard chased me all the
way back to the family cabins and kicked me to the gravel.
But I never saw him around the dorm again.

Bo-Sheng found me when I sat covered in pebble dust,
scraped bloody. I was picking at a flap of skin on the palm
of my hand and blowing on the red underbelly when this boy
crouched down beside me, black-haired, black-eyed, and

sharply angled like an adult even though he didn't seem much older than me. Maybe nine.

"You all right?" he asked, blowing smoke in my face. Then I saw the rolled leaf between his fingers. The smell was like Papa's, except with something tangy underneath, as if he'd just eaten an orange.

"Yeah . . . stupid guard." I spat on the path where the guard had gone. It was an impressive gob, and I grinned at the boy.

He made a face. "What's your name?"

"Yuri." I stood.

He looked surprised and got up too, and I was glad that I was taller than him. "I thought you were a girl," he said.

"You're stupid."

"Well your hair's so long," he said, squinting at me. Then he said, "My name's Bo-Sheng. Want one?" He offered the cigret leaf.

I shrugged and took it. Papa never let me smoke, but he wasn't around. I put it to my lips and it tasted like orange and burned leaves and that honey sweetness. Maybe the orange was from Bo-Sheng. I sucked on it and immediately started to cough. Bo-Sheng laughed and tried to take it back but I shoved him one-handed and tried again. After about five times it started to get easier. He let me have it and took out another roll from his dirty pants pocket and lit it with a blackened fingerband. I liked how his cheeks hollowed when he sucked on it. It made him look tough. His skin was brown from being outside a lot, and his hair fell into his eyes in jagged black spikes.

"I got cookies," I told him. I dug out the packet the nurse had given me and ripped it open.

He took one and ate it in two seconds, then held out his hand for another. The packet had four.

"One's for my sister," I said.

"There's three left," he said.

I guessed I could get more. So I gave him a second. He ate it just as quickly, then started to walk away. "C'mon," he said over his shoulder.

So I followed him.

6.17.2185 EHSD — Bo-Sheng

Bo-Sheng was an orphan. He had grown up in the Camp since he was two. He didn't remember anywhere else. His homeship had been destroyed in some battle long ago, and he didn't know details. The woman who'd survived with him died when he was five, and he was too young to look at his own records. They wouldn't let him. He knew the Camp and all the guards and aid workers, even when they'd just rotated on planet, and he grew his own sweet leaf in a long box on the windowsill above his bunk. He went where he wanted because he was fast and smart and didn't have to answer to anybody. There were older kids in his cabin and adults who kind of tried to get him to go to school, but like me, he preferred to wander.

I liked how his hands were always sprinkled with gray dust in the summer. He liked to pick up rocks and toss them against the sides of buildings. He could throw them hard. We started to toss rocks into the water a lot, and he always pitched them farther than me.

But I could get food from the nurses. They liked to comb my hair and fuss about how I needed a shower. A nurse lady named Nancy called me "child" a lot, and took my ripped clothes and sewed patches along the collars and on the knees of my jeans. Sometimes she tied my hair back for me with black elastic. Bo-Sheng said they must've thought I was a girl. We fought sometimes about it, when he said that, but I didn't mind too much. I could wrestle better than him. He was nice to Isobel though. Sometimes I took her with me out to the lake, and Bo-Sheng would always give her his ratty jacket if he thought she was cold. And he'd sit there shivering on the shore until I leaned against him to share the warmth.

And it was nice like that. It was better than the cigs.

9.9.2185 EHSD — School

Papa asked me once at breakfast, before school, "Who is that boy I always see lurking outside the classroom? Doesn't he go in? Is he a friend of yours?"

I said, "Yes," and left it up to Papa to figure out which question I meant to answer.

Papa sighed. "Yurochka, the teachers have been telling me that you sneak out of class in the mornings and don't go back. Is this true?"

I chewed the inside of my cheek and pushed the cereal around in my bowl, letting the milk glop-glop from the spoon and typhoon against the wheat flakes. "School's boring. And everyone's noisy and never pays attention. And the teachers always yell at us."

"That's because you don't listen. They have to yell."

"Why do I have to go anyway? I'm never going to do anything with it."

He leaned over and put his hand on my arm to stop me from playing with the food. "What do you mean?"

"We're never getting out of the Camp."

"That's not true," he said.

But the tightness of his fingers on my arm said another thing. He "worked" with some EHRRO crew in inventory, but he wasn't getting paid, and it made his back hurt, lifting boxes. Sometimes when I came home in the evenings, after playing in the cool hours with Bo-Sheng, I caught him hunched over the table with a scratched and dented slate in front of him, writing. I'd go and hug him, and he'd kiss my hair and pat me a few times, but then he'd tell me to go to bed. Up close, I caught glimpses of the words he input.

Every day gets longer on this planet until I think it will outlast my own life. And my children's.

But I didn't tell him I saw that. Instead, I said, "Look how long it's been and they haven't even brought Mama back."

He squeezed my arm tighter. "They will. And if you don't go to school, then why don't you stay home with me in the mornings, and we can read together. You, me, and Isobel. Yeah?"

I shrugged.

"I'd like it if we could," he said. "We can play games too." Then he leaned over and kissed my hair, smoothing the back of it with his hand.

I looked at him, tiny smile. He hugged me more since we left the Moon. Maybe he missed Mama and Jascha as much as I did.

* * *

Since I didn't go to school in the mornings, but stayed with Papa and Isobel, after a week Bo-Sheng got in the habit of rapping on my bedroom window after lunch to draw me out. We walked along the lakeshore and he gave me a pack of cigs and a fingerband that he said he stole from one of the older boys in his cabin, who'd got them from a guard.

I wiped my nose with the back of my hand, then lit one of the sticks. It took a few tries because the fingerband was too large and kept slipping down before I could get a decent spark.

The water rolled in gray at our feet, and I felt the cold tickle even through my boots. Seamus sniffed my ankles for a bit, then loped off to dig among the rocks. Bo-Sheng led me to an abandoned dropbin and we climbed on and lay back on its dented surface, looking up at the sky. I could see a round patch of pale blue, the only break in the clouds, like an eye. The wind always sounded hollow when you were lying down.

"I wonder if the war's over," I said.

Bo-Sheng laughed. "The war's not over. We'd hear about it." He blew a stream of smoke up toward the clouds, to join them. "I wish I was up there killing some strits."

I chewed the edge of my thumb where the skin cracked and frayed. "Like you could kill a strit? Maybe with your ugly looks."

He nudged me with his elbow. "I could. All you need is a gun."

Killing strits would be good. Especially the strits that had attacked the Moon. I barely remembered, now, but I still felt it.

And I missed Mama. Especially when Mishka's *mat* would get on my back to go to school just because she didn't want me underfoot, as if she had a right, as if she shouldn't have just tried to make her own daughter less of a zombie. Sometimes missing Mama came on so strong I couldn't control it. But I shook my head and wiped my face with my sleeve, and in a second it was gone. Like her face. I couldn't remember her face. Papa didn't have any images.

I sat up and slipped down from the bin, picked up a rock, and threw it into the lake. Bo-Sheng eased up and dangled his feet for a second, then jumped down and joined me. He cast his rock farther than mine. I elbowed him out of the way, held the cig between my lips, and threw another rock. It made a hollow splash, way out.

"I think you just knocked out some strit's brains," he said.

We grinned at each other. Tossed more rocks. Then I chased him down the shore.

* * *

That night the wind was so loud, rattling my bedroom window, that it woke me. I lay in the dark, feeling Isobel nestled against my back in a warm lump, and stared across the tiny space at the shadows moving behind the curtain.

Someone was outside.

I pulled the blanket up to my chin just as a tapping sounded, sharp against the glass.

"Yuri!"

I slid out from the bed and padded to the window, knocking my ankle against one of Isobel's spinning toys that she'd left on the floor. Biting my lip, I swept the curtain aside and came nose to nose with Bo-Sheng, the grimy barrier of the window between us.

"Open it," he said, his voice slightly muffled but still night-clear.

I undid the latch and slid aside the glass. Cool air rushed in, raising goose bumps along my arms.

"What're you doing?" I glanced over my shoulder at my bedroom door. The sliver of space beneath the door was dark; Papa and Mishka's *mat* had gone to bed already.

"Get dressed and come on," Bo-Sheng whispered. "There's a shuttle landing!"

For a second I didn't know what he meant. But the cold and his words woke me up with a slap. It wasn't distribution day for another two weeks, and the Army had just dropped a rotation of guards last month. So any shuttle coming to the Camp wouldn't be for food or protection. It had to be for something else.

Like Mama. Finally sent back to us?

"Hurry!" Bo-Sheng said.

I grabbed my coat and boots from the floor, had to pause to pull on the boots but ran after Bo-Sheng in a stumble, coat flapping open. He finally lost patience and grabbed my arm, hauled me along to the fence around the landing pad, where we saw the shuttle squatting in a pool of white from the control tower. Red-and-blue lights from the little ship strobed the tarmac all around its shark body.

I didn't see the Guard seal on its flank, the distinctive round shield with a flaring sun in the center, ringed by stars. It wasn't a Rim Guardian.

Unless some merchant brought Mama home?

My fingers curled through the wire as the rear door whined down.

A couple of men emerged under the lights, met by an Army guard from the tower. They stood around talking on the tarmac, and nobody else showed up.

Bo-Sheng looked at me. "Ah, I'm sorry, Yuri."

I just shook my head. I didn't know why. It wasn't like I expected good things to happen.

Hope was a rabid animal, and it ate you alive.

* * *

Bo-Sheng left because I wasn't in the mood to do anything, not even smoke. I just sat against the fence and looked

at my shadow cast black on the gravel in front of me from
the landing lights. Going home seemed the worst thing to
do, even though I'd at least be warm in bed. But sometimes
the weight of Isobel's silence and her sad eyes pressed hard
against me, and the memory of my father's words in his
journal seemed to tattoo black into my skin.

It was easier outside in the cold. I wrapped my arms
around my knees and put my chin on top and tried not to
think of Mama. Or Jascha. And what it might've been like if
I'd been able to stay with them. Were they on a warm planet,
or slowly freezing, becoming numb?

The fence rattled behind me. "Kid."

I jumped and turned around, saw a pair of green-clad
legs, and squinted up against the lights. It was a man, but I
couldn't see his face, just the outline of short pale hair that
looked like fire in the white glare.

I'd been chased by guards before for hanging around this
site.

So I got up and ran.

9.18.2185 EHSD — The Captain

I went to school, I didn't know why. But something out of
routine seemed like a good idea so I wouldn't think so much
about Mama. I took the slate that Papa had gotten for me,
with my journal in it, and wrote in that. The teacher was glad
to see me, after she'd reprimanded me for skipping all the
time in the first place. I didn't bother telling her that Papa
was teaching me fine at home. I just ignored her and all the
other things she talked about, and just poked at my slate. I
liked that I could save my entries encoded so nobody could

see. I drew some shapes beside the words, long ships with fins like fishes.

"Yuri."

I looked up toward the door of the classroom. Bo-Sheng stood in the foyer, motioning me to come out.

I glanced at the teacher. She was leaning over a girl's desk, explaining something. All the other kids were working. There were about three grade levels in here, fifty kids, most of them so obedient they bored me.

"Yuri," Bo-Sheng hissed.

I slid from my seat, gathered my slate and my coat, and went out to him. He tugged me out the door, making me trip over someone's discarded shoes. Outside was gray and cold, a typical day, and we paused at the top of the steps so I could put on my coat and bum a cig from him.

He smiled. "I want you to meet somebody."

"Who?" I followed him down the metallic steps and across the front quad, which wasn't much more than a square of gravel, sparse brown grass, and strewn toys. The skeletal swing had been broken for at least a year, torn up by a bad storm.

"He's from the shuttle," Bo-Sheng said, and I realized he was leading me to the landing pad.

"You met one of the men from the shuttle?" I hadn't told him about my scare that night. I wasn't sure if it had been a guard or one of the visitors.

"He came by the orphans' quarters."

"Why?" The cig tasted rotten for some reason. It must've been a bad batch, or maybe it was my own spit. I wiped the corners of my mouth.

Bo-Sheng said, "You'll see. I told him all about you. He wanted to meet you."

I wrinkled my nose. "Why would you talk about me? Why would he bother with kids?"

"He wanted to know if I had any friends. And adults bother all the time."

I knew what he meant. The guards bothered with us when we explored where we weren't supposed to. A few of them bothered with the older kids in a way that got the kids perks like cigs and extra food and clothes.

But this man from the shuttle couldn't be like that, or Bo-Sheng wouldn't deal with him. Bo-Sheng didn't play those games.

By the time we reached the gate leading to the tower and landing pad, my cig was almost done. I dug into Bo-Sheng's coat pocket as we walked to try and get another one and not drop my slate at the same time. He stopped to let me, and I fumbled for a while until he took the run-down cig from between my fingers and finished it off for me, freeing my other hand. I tucked my hair behind my ear so I could see what I was doing. The wind was strong.

I lit the second cig and looked up, and there was a man watching us, standing near the base of the landing tower, using it as a windbreak.

Bo-Sheng elbowed me as if I wasn't already paying attention.

The man had short silver hair, even though his face was younger than that, and wide blue eyes, like the bottom of a flame. He wore green fatigues and a gray jacket with some sort of merchant patch on the arm. When he got close enough that I saw the stubble on his face, I wanted to run again.

Because he was staring at me. And I knew he was the one I'd run from last night.

"So this is your friend," he said. He had an accent that

sounded somehow rich, like chocolate when it melted on your tongue.

"Yuri," I said, before Bo-Sheng could speak. I stared straight up at him. Couldn't run now and show I was scared. But there was nothing to be scared of, Bo-Sheng was here. "Who're you?"

He didn't blink. He hadn't blinked. He watched me smoke.

"I'm the captain of a ship that's in orbit right now. And I'm recruiting."

I glanced at Bo-Sheng, who was smiling at me as if he'd just stumbled on a table of desserts.

"Recruiting?" I said.

"To work on my ship."

I scratched the back of my hair. Tried not to glare at Bo-Sheng, who was clearly in love with the idea.

"I don't wanna work on your ship."

Bo-Sheng said, "Yuri . . ."

The man looked around like he was bored, not irritated or disappointed. He fished inside his jacket pocket and pulled out a silver case. He flipped it open and slid free a long white cig, then lit it with his fingerband. A clean rooty scent floated over our heads, strong enough to cut through the cold air. A slight whiff of it seemed immediately to warm my insides. It was an expensive smoke.

"You'd rather stay in this pit?" he asked, breathing dragon funnels at me.

Bo-Sheng caught my sleeve. "We can work for real up in space, Yuri. Quit here for good."

"I got my family here. Isobel and Papa."

The man wasn't paying any attention to Bo-Sheng. He just kept staring at me. And I didn't like it.

"You can take care of them from space, if you have cred,"

Bo-Sheng said. "When you get enough you can bring them with you too."

I looked up at the blue-eyed man. He brought the cig to his lips, and the smoke swirled from his mouth like water, flooding up to the white sky.

"Why don't we talk first," he said, like I was an adult. "And then if you want, you can take me to meet your papa."

*　＊　*

He told me his name was Marcus and his ship was called *The Abyssinian,* which I couldn't even pronounce. He said it came from a poem about a "pleasure dome," whatever that meant. He asked if we'd like to see the shuttle, and Bo-Sheng immediately said yes. I didn't mind seeing it either; I couldn't much remember the one we'd rode in to Colonial Grace, and besides, this one was a merchant outrider. So I dropped my cig and crushed it out and followed them through the gate and onto the landing pad. While Marcus strode ahead I snagged Bo-Sheng's sleeve and slowed him down.

"I don't know about him," I said.

"Ah, Yuri . . ." Bo-Sheng looked at the clouds. "I been talking to him all morning. Captains recruit all the time for their ships, especially orphans."

"But I'm not—"

He stared into my face. "Don't you want to get off this planet? Fight strits, after what they did to your Moon?"

"Merchants don't fight strits."

"Merchants with guns do. A lot of them have 'em. Marcus says he does. Sometimes they even run missions for the military. You never know."

I shifted the slate in my arms. "Are you going? With him?"

Bo-Sheng looked down at the ground and kicked the concrete with the toe of his shoe. He buried his hands in his coat pockets. "I want to, Yuri. And I want you to come with me." He chewed his lip and looked to the side.

His cheeks were windburned, and if I touched them, they would be cold. Like this world. Maybe soon we'd turn gray like the skies, or poisonous like the lakes.

"Hey," Marcus called, standing at the bottom of the shuttle ramp. "You kids coming?"

Bo-Sheng blinked at me, flicked his hair from his eyes. It couldn't hurt; I could practically hear his thoughts. So I went with him to the shadow of the shuttle. Marcus led us up the steep ramp, our smaller footsteps echoing lightly on the ridged steel. I stayed behind Bo-Sheng's shoulder, peered over it as warmth engulfed us. Inside was well lit in a soft blue glow, with clean beige walls and cushioned seats in the passenger cab, running on both sides with an aisle in the middle. Cabinets tracked the same path on the ceiling toward a single door leading to the cockpit. Everywhere smelled like fresh caff and those high-end cigrets. My stomach gurgled, and Bo-Sheng elbowed me.

Marcus pressed a hand to a panel on the wall, and the ramp whined up behind us, cutting off the cold. He said, "Are you boys hungry?"

"Yes," Bo-Sheng said. I didn't bother answering.

Marcus reached into one of the overheads and pulled out a few sealed bags. He folded up a couple of the seats, tapped at something on the bulkhead, and a table came down from the wall. He dropped the bags on top. "Here you go, dig in."

We swiveled a couple of chairs around, climbed on, and tore open the bags. There were chips and crackers and strips of fruit. I lost where Marcus went, my fingers buried in the bags and Bo-Sheng grinning across at me, but he soon came back, this time with two boxes of hot food and frothy juice drinks. The scent of tangy meat sauce and steamed, candied vegetables made my stomach grumble more, even though half of the chips were gone already.

For a while nobody spoke. Marcus just sat across the cabin, smoked, and watched us gobble down the food. Then he said, "So what do you like to do, Yuri?"

"Do?" Eat. I was alternating between the meal and the flavored chips.

"Well, even though there must not be much to do here, I assume you boys occupy yourselves in some way."

"He gets the nurses to give him cookies because they think he's pretty." Bo-Sheng laughed.

I kicked him below the table.

"Oh?" Marcus said, amused.

"No." I glared at Bo-Sheng. "They give to a lot of kids. But not him because he's stupid." I looked at Marcus and shrugged. "I like to do lots of stuff. I draw and write in my slate, and sometimes we hang around the lake. There's this dog . . . or we throw stuff in the lake."

"We like to smoke," Bo-Sheng added.

"I like to beat him up. And I have a sister and sometimes Papa reads to us or we play games and stuff, like puzzle games. I like puzzle games, and I like playing with my sister sometimes . . ."

He was watching so fixedly I got nervous and ate more food.

"Do you go to school or do you skip it like Bo-Sheng?"

I sipped my fruit juice and wrinkled my nose, but not at the drink. "I don't like school. It's boring and there's too many kids and the teachers are always busy and mad."

He nodded as if this wasn't a surprise. "Yeah, these camps aren't all that good for learning. Kids should be given more individual attention."

Yeah, maybe. I scraped my plate to get the last bit of gravy. All the food was so yummy by the time I was done I didn't mind so much how Marcus stared. He was probably just curious. Or pitying. Which was all right if it got us food like this. The nurses pitied me too, and it kept me and Isobel fed with sweets.

The shuttle seemed more warm, now that I had a full meal in my stomach. In a few minutes I started to get sleepy. I was so stuffed I thought I'd roll right off my chair. The burned-wood scent of that expensive cig wafted around my head, and I blinked when Bo-Sheng nudged my arm. I blinked again and saw Marcus standing over me holding out a stick. Offering.

I looked at Bo-Sheng. He was smiling. So I took the cig and held it as Marcus sparked the end. His fingerband winked at me, reflecting the shuttle's cabin light. I took a deep drag, and it was like breathing silk. It warmed me to the inside, steamed my blood until it quickened, and the scent of it made me think of clean things.

I looked up at the captain and grinned.

* **

Marcus said that on his ship he took care of his crew. Nobody went hungry, everybody contributed to the work, everybody could learn new skills and be rewarded for them, and everybody got leave on lots of stations where you could play games and meet new people. He said he'd take anybody who was willing to work and willing to give back to the ship and his crew. He said *The Abyssinian* was respected throughout EarthHub. For kids our age, underage, he would sign an agreement to make him our guardian.

He said his ship was like a family, and he was the papa.

* * *

Marcus wanted to leave the next morning. Too soon. Bo-Sheng and I waited outside the shuttle while Marcus talked to his comrade, a young man he'd introduced as Estienne. We were going to go home so Marcus could talk to Papa. But maybe my nervousness was written on my face; Bo-Sheng said, "The captain says he'll help you look for your mama and Jascha."

"When did he say that?"

"When I talked to him this morning. I made sure and asked."

Marcus was a merchant who went to a lot of ports. He was an adult, and people would listen to him, maybe even Rim Guardians. He could find Mama easy.

I held my slate to my chest and squinted at Bo-Sheng through the whipping breeze.

"Okay," I said. My gut clenched.

He smiled at me and held my sleeve. "Okay?" Excitement made his eyes shine like the winter lakes.

I smiled back, and he hugged me.

"It'll be us," he said, squeezing me almost out of my coat. He let go and pointed at the sky. "Up there!"

But I was too busy looking down the road toward my cabin.

* * *

Papa listened to everything Marcus had to say, there at
our kitchen table with Mishka's *mat* while Mishka was sent
to Isobel's room to mind her. Papa didn't nod or interrupt,
and Marcus laid it all out as clearly as he had for me and Bo-
Sheng: if Papa and him both signed a contract, all the earnings I made on *The Abyssinian* would be put in a fund
accessible by Papa. And Marcus said he'd do everything in
his power to locate Mama and Jascha.

"Why can't you hire Mikhail?" Mishka's *mat* asked.

"And who would take care of Isobel?" Papa said. "No . . .
she is still too young to work on a merchant. She needs her
father."

I clasped my hands on the table and didn't speak. Papa
gazed at me a long moment while Marcus lit another cigret.
He'd given Papa a pack.

Papa said, "Yurochka, what do you want to do?"

Bo-Sheng sat to my right, slurping at noodles Mishka's
mat had made for us. He looked at me with his face bent
over the bowl.

"It would be good to go," I said, even though I felt sick
at the idea of leaving. Even if it was to go with Bo-Sheng.
But I had to stop thinking of just myself. I was getting older,
and so was my father. "Papa, if I made enough cred, we
could all leave the Camp. Maybe even before Isobel's my
age."

I knew it hurt him to look at Isobel, who was so quiet and
so tiny, smaller than she should've been. When I held her at
night it was like hugging one of her dolls, slack and barely
stitched together.

I looked down at the table because when I thought of my
sister, sometimes I wanted to cry. Sometimes I talked to her
about Mama, but she had no real idea. She thought Mishka's
mat was our mama.

Papa took a deep breath, stubbed out the end of his cig in the ashtray, and looked across at Marcus.

"Can I see the contract, sir?"

* * *

I had no real possessions, so all that I wanted to take with me—like my slate—fit into one shoulder bag. Marcus said he'd supply us with what we needed anyway, until we had enough earnings to buy our own gear. Papa bundled me up in my coat and scarf and hat, and I hugged Isobel. I told her I was going to come back, but she cried. She hit my arm and my chest.

Mishka's *mat* had to tear her away and take her to her room, but I still heard the crying even through the shut door.

Mishka stared at me for a second as if I'd hit her or shouted at her, then ran after her *mat*. Without a word.

"It's okay," Papa said, putting an arm around my shoulders.

I didn't cry. We walked to the landing pad and my stomach just got tighter. But I gripped the strap pressing against my chest and listened to the scrape and clump of my steps along the road. Once at the gate, Papa stopped and stared at the shuttle. Specks of early snow blew around its struts. Shadows ran from the tall tower and huddled around the body of the little ship. Dots of red and blue surrounded the pad like bits of glowing candy.

Bo-Sheng was already there by the shuttle's nose. He waved at me.

I didn't wave back. I looked up at Papa.

"Well," he said. Then he paused. His mouth worked as if words were trying to get out, but he wasn't letting them. Then he hugged me hard, patted my back, and let me go.

"Papa," I said.

But his hand pressed my shoulder, he was looking over my head, and in the next moment he made his way back down the road, toward home.

* *,*

My feet didn't touch the floor of the shuttle. Me and Bo-Sheng were the youngest ones there. Six other kids from the Camp, all older, sat scattered around the cabin talking or just staring out the windows. Beside me, Bo-Sheng shifted restlessly, anxious and excited as we roared into the air. Beneath us growled and rumbled with the force of the firing jets. I peered out the cabin window as the Camp drifted away like a small pebble dropped in a large, dense lake. Soon the clouds mottled the gray haphazard expanse of occupied land. The homes and buildings and carved, scratched pathways were nothing but toy models on the surface, a playground made of plastic and paint, with tiny robotic figurines going about their day.

I'd forgotten to say good-bye to Seamus.

I thought of his dark amber eyes, cold nose, and dirty fur. He used to lick my hand if I held it out, like he expected treats.

But dogs didn't belong in space, among steel and cold and narrow corridors, and I was never going to see him again.

And I cried then. Because of that animal.

9.20.2185 EHSD—Estienne

Estienne was warm gold to Marcus's cool silver. He was a
lot younger than the captain and his hair shone the color of
reflected sunlight, thrown forward on his face as if he
looked at everything with his head bowed. He had to look
down at me a lot, and something about the way he smiled
put me at ease. There was nothing nervous or twitchy about
him, just a calm acceptance of everything and everyone. He
watched Bo-Sheng's energetic stride down the corridors of
The Abyssinian, hanging back from it as if he was afraid the
enthusiasm would infect him. The older kids were ahead of
Bo-Sheng, their own little group. I was slower going, clutching the bag strap across my chest, keeping myself in among
the shadows and tall walls, and Estienne walked beside me,
slowing down to match my smaller steps. He spoke in a low
voice with words that took their time to fall through the air.

"It doesn't look like a lot, but you'll get used to it."

If I were Jonah, like in the stories I'd read about, then this
was really the belly of the whale. The ship seemed to have
ribs, arching dark and smooth over my head, with small
round lights running along the spine, bumpy gray. The deck
was triple-paneled and opened below through the tiny holes
into black. Our steps echoed, and my face started to itch
from the cold.

"Bo-Sheng," I said, to call him back to my side. He
waited until we caught up, somewhere between Marcus,
who walked ahead with the older kids, and the silence coming up from behind.

"It's creepy," Bo-Sheng said, and giggled. "Like
Halloween!"

Estienne said again, "You'll get used to it. And it's just the passageways that're like this. The rooms are different."

Marcus paused at a lev, holding the doors open with his hand on the call pad, and looked back at us. At Estienne. "Take the kids to Dorm Two. Then come to my office."

Estienne nodded and Marcus half smiled at us before disappearing into the lev with the older group. So far he hadn't shown much interest once he got us aboard his shuttle. It had been mostly Estienne sitting with me and Bo-Sheng in the passenger cabin, talking to us about the ports he'd seen and the strits he'd killed (because, he said, *The Abyssinian* did in fact run information for the military sometimes, and sometimes they ran into a strit ship; Marcus, he said, wasn't the type to back away from a fight). Now it was Estienne looming over us in the dim corridor, looking perfectly at ease in the shadows, wearing a thin jacket for the cold. I was bundled in my Camp coat and sweater and scarf, and I still wanted to crawl under some blankets to warm up.

"Where's everyone else?" I said, peering up at him.

"Working," he said. "People work on this ship." The smile slid across his face again, but his gaze drifted over our heads.

"Where're the other kids going?" How come they got to go with the captain?

"You ask a lot of questions." He looked down at us again. "They have a different schedule because they're older. C'mon, let's get you both settled."

His hand rested on my shoulder as we went, but not to hold me back or even for comfort in this strange place. He leaned a little as if he needed me in order to walk. Bo-Sheng was quiet and slower now, looking all around from behind his bangs, staying close to my elbow. There was just enough room for the three of us to walk side by side.

"I think it's kind of cool," Bo-Sheng whispered to me.

He didn't seem scared, but I think he knew I was. I couldn't think of anything except how much I wanted to be back in the Camp, even with its grit and grayness, instead of here without Papa or Isobel. But maybe that was baby talk. Maybe I needed to just grow up.

Estienne paused in front of a hatch and tapped the control pad above our heads. We'd have to stretch to reach it. Then he turned the latch and shoved with his shoulder, and the hatch swung in. Light came up automatically, stark white, and we squinted into it, poking our heads under his arm to look in. It was a small cabin even for a kid's size, with a fold-down bunk, web storage, one locker wedged into the corner, and a narrow door leading to something else. Maybe a bathroom. The blanket had a red stripe on it, but everything else was steel gray. Even the walls.

"Sorry, but this is the best we've got right now until you guys earn it," Estienne said, sounding like he really was sorry. "Bo-Sheng, this is for you."

"We're not staying together?" I said, before Bo-Sheng could speak. My voice sounded too thin in the cold, heavy air.

"Does this look like it can fit two people?" Estienne asked, squeezing my shoulder. "Don't worry, you'll be right next door."

I didn't like it. I started to follow Bo-Sheng into the quarters. But Estienne caught my hood.

"Yuri. Let him get settled."

"It's okay," Bo-Sheng said, smiling, standing in the middle of that small space like it was some rich palace. "We each get our own. I mean, it's better this way. We're old enough to be by ourselves."

Maybe he was. But I'd liked sharing a room with my sister, even though I was nine.

"You'll see him again," Estienne said, laughing beneath the words.

So I didn't say anything when he shut the hatch and guided me to my own, right next to Bo-Sheng's like he had said. He opened it up and it looked exactly the same, except the blankets were pale yellow. I went in and turned all around, then looked up at him. He stood in the hatchway.

"Unpack your things, and I'll come back. If you're tired you can take a nap. Explore in here if you want." He ruffled my hair, gently. I didn't hit him, even though I thought about it.

He stepped out and shut the hatch, and I heard something beep. I went to it and tried to open it, but it wouldn't open. So I banged on it and yelled, but nothing came back but an echo.

* * *

I sat unmoving on the bunk with my bag still solid across my back, holding on to the straps on my chest, and watched the hatch. I didn't need to explore this narrow space. I wanted to know if I'd ever get out.

Eventually Estienne came back, dressed in different clothes, all black and shiny, with black dots around his eyes that faded into smudged darkness on his lids. It made his gaze fierce, too shiny, but then he smiled, and it was that same soft expression, as if all his thoughts were gentle.

"You didn't even take off your coat?"

I stared at him, then shot toward the corridor.

"Hey!" He caught me around the waist and lifted me off

my feet. My legs flailed but his arms held me tight. "Settle down, Yuri! Hey!"

"I wanna go! Take me back!"

He carried me into that horrible little space and kicked the hatch shut. I clawed at his arms, but he set me on the bunk. I wasn't that small, but he didn't even flinch or seem bothered by my activity. He grabbed my wrists but not hard enough to bruise. Just to hold me still.

"Yuri." The pale color of his eyes pierced through the feather cut of his bangs and those painted dark smudges. "I'm sorry, it took me longer than I expected. Please just relax."

"You locked the door!"

"For your own safety. If you wandered around this ship, you might get into trouble. Marcus wants to orient you first before he lets you loose. There's a certain way of doing things here. Just like any other place. Okay?"

It sounded reasonable. But I stared at him, quiet.

"You're awfully cute." He grinned. It was a Bo-Sheng thing to say. Just to bug me.

"Shut up."

"You are," he said, and poked my stomach.

"Stop it!"

Of course he didn't. He picked me up under my knees and shoulders and dumped me on the bunk, then started to tickle me. I hit him and shoved, but he rolled me back on the blankets. And I couldn't help it, I laughed until I couldn't breathe and then he sat back, satisfied.

I kicked him. Just so he wouldn't think he could do that *any*time. He winced.

"Come on, let's get you settled, then I'll take you to Marcus. He wants to talk to you."

"What about Bo-Sheng?"

Estienne rolled his eyes. "He already talked to Bo-Sheng. You're the lazy one that hasn't even unpacked your bag."

So I let him help me unload my few items of clothing, my slate, my socks and extra pair of mittens and the little robot Isobel had made for me a long time ago, out of spare plastic parts we'd fished from the lakeshore and glued together in school.

"What's that?" Estienne said.

"A robot."

His eyebrows went up. He tilted his head and gazed at it. "It looks like it encountered a strit."

I kicked him, but not too hard. He grabbed me by the collar and hauled me to the hatch.

"You need maintenance," he said. But nicely.

"Why're you dressed like that anyway?" I walked beside him down the corridor, and he kept his arm around me. I could've easily twitched it off, but his sleeve brushed the back of my neck beneath my hair, and the material was velvet soft.

"I'm going to meet somebody," he said.

"At a party?"

"Kind of," he said.

"When's the ship going to move?" That was scary, but in a fun way. We'd leaped once to get from that Rimstation to Colonial Grace. Mostly I blacked out, but I wanted to know if it'd be different for the second time.

"Don't worry," Estienne said, "you'll know it when we do. There'll be an announcement, and you'll be in quarters."

It had taken long hours in the shuttle to get to *The Abyssinian*. Maybe we weren't even near Colonial Grace anymore. I didn't like to think about how far away I was from Papa and Isobel, but it was natural to worry. Wasn't it?

And maybe it was going to feel better. Estienne liked to play, at least. And Bo-Sheng was just next door.

"What will we be doing first? For work?"

Estienne smiled and pulled me to a stop in front of a hatch. "Marcus will explain." He hit the call pad up on the wall, and when it flashed green he shoved open the hatch with his shoulder and a hand on the latch. It sounded like a deep sigh. I peered under his arm and saw Marcus on the bunk, holding a black boot.

"C'mon in," he said. And, "Thanks, Estienne."

"Welcome, sir," Estienne said, and gave me a small push inside. "See you later, Yuri."

"Uh-huh." I waved a little then tucked my hands up my sleeves, looking at Marcus. At his quarters. He had a small desk jammed up against the wall, across from a single bunk. It was all larger than my quarters but still small for a man. I gazed up at the bright panels of lights, the smooth scars on the walls as if people had dented the surface with furniture. But aside from the desk and the bunk, there wasn't anything else in the room but a couple of narrow tower lockers, webbing, and another door. So I looked back at Marcus. "What're you doing?"

He patted beside him on the bunk. "Have a seat and I'll show you."

I walked over and sat on the edge of the mattress, resting my hands beside me. After a second I slid farther back until my boots didn't touch the deck. The blanket was scratchy warm beneath my hands, and I picked at it idly, making fuzz. He didn't seem to mind even though I knew he noticed. I saw mostly the back of his shoulders, how they made two sharp lines beneath his thin gray jacket. He leaned on his elbows, holding the boot in his left hand and wiping at it with a blackened cloth in his right. The boot shone so much I saw the overhead lights reflected on its tip.

"Why don't you use a spray stain?"

He sighed, but not at the question. "Doing it this way allows me to think."

"About what?"

"This war. My ship in this war. Things like that." He slid a look back at me. His eyes were bluer than Papa's. Bluer than mine.

"Bo-Sheng says we can kill strits here."

"Does he?" Marcus smiled. His profile showed a sharp nose, more obvious because his hair was so short. Like a military cut. I wondered about that. "Bo-Sheng's right," he said. "My ship runs across the aliens sometimes."

"And you fight?"

"Of course we fight. Why, do you want to fight them too?"

I picked at the blanket some more. "Yeah, I wouldn't mind."

"They attacked your colony, didn't they?"

I shrugged.

"Bo-Sheng told me," he said. "You have a right to be angry at the strits and the government. Too many attacks like that happen, and the Hub doesn't do anything."

I wasn't thinking of the government, just the strits. "The Rim Guard tried to help."

"But did they?" He stopped polishing. I didn't say anything, just bounced my feet over the side of the bed until he put his hand on my ankle and stopped me. "Come up here, you want to try?"

I dragged myself forward, and he reached down to the plastic box at his feet and took out another smaller blackened cloth and handed it to me.

"Here. Your boots are scuffy."

It didn't sound mean like how the teachers in the Camp sounded sometimes, or the guards. So I watched him rub the heel of his boot and slid mine off, sticking my hand inside to hold it while I swirled the cloth in circles on the toe. Soon it was shiny black just like his, and I worked my way around it toward the heel.

"How come I can't stay with Bo-Sheng?" I didn't wait for him to answer or roll his eyes like Estienne. "I don't like it by myself."

"You're special," he said, polishing his boots.

"No I'm not."

Now he looked at me. For a long second before he answered, ignoring it when I fidgeted. "You know you're smarter than he is."

"No I'm not."

"Oh, don't play around, Yuri." His lips curled, and I wasn't sure if he meant it, or if it was the kind of smile you gave when you thought the kid couldn't understand.

"I'm not playing, *Marcus*," I said. In case he got all Papatone on me. "I don't get what you mean."

"I think you do. That planet was holding you back. You love your family but it was killing you to be there. What did you used to do with Bo-Sheng aside from run around the lake? Nothing good, I bet. But you brought your slate aboard. You read or write a lot, don't you? Even though you didn't like school?"

He must've talked to Bo-Sheng more than I knew.

"Bo-Sheng isn't nearly as concerned about you as you are for him. He's well-adjusted and ready to begin his training."

I didn't want that to hurt, but it did. A lot. "He hasn't asked about me?"

Marcus looked at me for a moment, then leaned on his hand, closer to me. His voice lowered, as if someone could be listening. "Yuri, this ship can be a great opportunity for you. I've decided to train you myself."

I blinked. Watched him, but he stared so completely that I couldn't hold it. He wasn't dismissing me like the teachers did. And he didn't look tired like Papa. His eyes were wide like cam-orbs.

"Training in what?" I asked, rubbing my boot again.

"Well, to begin with, weapons."

I doubted that. "Really?"

He set aside his cloth on the deck and pulled on his boot. "Everyone learns weapons on my ship. Kids included." Then the other boot, which he'd finished with earlier. "Come on, you must be hungry. I'll show you the ship, then we can go eat."

Without Bo-Sheng. Because Bo-Sheng had already eaten probably, and didn't seem to care where I was. So why should I care where he was?

I pulled on my boots and climbed off the bunk. "Got a cigret?"

That made Marcus smirk. But he dug out a pack from his breast pocket and tossed it to me. The expensive brand. "Keep it. But I don't want you to overdo it."

I slid out a stick and sparked the end with the old finger-band I always wore, and grinned up at him. "Why not?"

He laughed. "Yuri, the first thing you better get straight is when I tell you to do something, you don't question me. Not yet, anyway, when you don't know a thing about anything."

That stopped my smile. Above the laugh, his eyes didn't move. So I nodded. And blew the smoke out toward the deck.

He put his arm around my shoulders and walked me out of the quarters. "Good. You know, I'm fair. And my ship is good. But that's because my people do what I tell them. I'm not exactly your father, and this isn't quite like school, but I am going to take care of you. You'll do well here, I know it. I think you'll do extremely well."

"Really?" Nobody had ever said such a thing to me. "Why?"

"I told you why. But you won't believe me until you start looking at yourself apart from that boy."

Bo-Sheng.

"He's my best friend."

"Only?" Marcus said, and I had no idea what he meant. Then he dropped it. "We do need to get you new clothes, those are practically in rags. But don't worry, I won't make you cut your hair. I think I like it long."

"Bo-Sheng says it makes me look like a girl, but I don't care." Even though I did.

"Bo-Sheng's jealous," Marcus said, which sounded stupid until I thought about it. And then it didn't seem so unlikely. "And looking like a girl can have its advantages."

I made a face.

"You don't think so? Those nurses gave you sweets, didn't they? Because they thought you were pretty?"

"Yeah. I guess."

He laughed. I didn't see what was so funny, but as we walked he ruffled my hair, then settled his arm back around my shoulders. I didn't dare hit him like I would have Estienne.

Here and there people passed us in the corridors. His crew seemed to respect him a lot. Men and women, shadowed beneath the dim lights, appeared angry and mean with their tattooed skin and graffitied clothes, but then the shadows passed and I saw how their eyes acknowledged Marcus with quiet acceptance. Some even talked to him, briefly, with "sir" and "Captain," and when they saw me they nodded as well, as if I were a grown-up. One man stopped with us at a lev. He was stocky and hawk-nosed, and Marcus introduced him as Caligtiera. Cal, he said.

"Sir," I said, because everyone else used the word.

Cal squinted down at me, sniffed. "Yuri, eh?" His gaze slid to Marcus, and the corner of his mouth quirked. That was all. He didn't end up getting in the lev with us. Marcus led me in and when I turned around Cal remained outside, staring in at me. I folded my arms against my body and the doors slid shut.

"He's just curious," Marcus said. "And he doesn't talk much."

"Why's he curious about me?"

Marcus looked down at me as the lev grated and roared on its ascent. "Because one day you might take his job." He grinned.

I laughed. "Yeah, right!"

"You never know," Marcus said. "I told you that you're smart."

Even though he was joking, it still made me smile to think about.

* * *

He called it a "mess hall," not a cafeteria, and I wasn't sure why since there was nothing messy about it. Shadowed like the rest of the ship, noisy and full of the drifting scents of different hot foods, it was otherwise bare of any overall grit. Maybe because people ate here. It would have to be clean. The spine-wrought walls, a continued design from the

corridors, formed odd reflections of light on their twisted
dark steel.

Marcus sat with me while I scarfed down the free ham-
burger and fries and fizzy caff. All around us some of the
crew milled, eating and talking. The noise climbed high,
harsh voices and laughter and the occasional angry word,
but it was so alive and generally everyone seemed to like
being together. The people pulsed with energy. They didn't
drag around like the bodies in the Camp, wistful for better
things. Some of them looked over at us, curious, silent,
maybe even in a strange kind of recognition as if they knew
who I was already, but nobody approached. Marcus brought
me dessert too — chocolate ice cream.

He said, "Estienne will take you to get your new clothes,
you have a good shift of sleep, and tomorrow we begin."

Maybe he saw how nervous I felt despite the ice cream
treat.

"It'll be fine, Yuri," he said. "And I haven't forgotten.
We'll find your mother and brother."

I didn't want to hope, but maybe I could. I wasn't in the
Camp anymore. Things were different in space. And when
his hand stroked my arm it felt like he really cared.

* * *

Estienne took me to Supply for the clothes and toiletries.
Warm sweaters in dark blue, black, red. Light blue that Estienne said matched my eyes. T-shirts. Underclothes. Pants of
strong, faded manufiber and denim in just as many colors.
The man distributing them peered down at me with a secret
smile. He was bald, and his head was tattooed and studded
with dots of silver. I stared until Estienne put his hand on my
shoulder and turned me away.

"He's like that with all the new recruits," Estienne explained, though I wasn't quite sure what he meant.

Back in quarters he helped me fold and stack the clothes in my locker and sling the little bag of toiletries in the webbing beside my bunk. Isobel's robot sat up beside my pillow. If I had been allowed to paste up pictures, it might've started to look like my room on the Camp.

"Go brush your teeth," he said, squeezing my shoulder.

I was glad he stayed, and heard him singing something to himself as I fumbled around in the narrow, stainless-steel bathroom. It was built for an adult, and even though I wasn't short for my age, I had to stretch to adjust the mirror above the sink so it tilted down.

When I came out he'd laid out my sleepwear and was sitting on the end of the bunk, his back to the bulkhead and his knees bent so his arms rested against them. He was looking at a black-handled switchblade, turning it around in his fingers.

"What's that?" What do you use it for? Since he wasn't looking at me it was easier to just change into my pajamas right then. When I was done he glanced over.

"My little friend," he said. "Wanna see?"

I smiled and nodded, held out my hand, and he closed the blade and placed it in my palm. It was worn, but when I flipped it open again, the long sheen of metal shone like brand-new. I sat on the bunk and closed my fist around the hilt. It was small enough I could easily fold my fingers. Estienne scooted closer and arranged my grip, then held my arm and moved it slowly like I was going to slice somebody. I giggled when he put his other arm around me and moved my left hand, as if it had a knife in it too. I watched the movements I made, even though I wasn't controlling them. It was like a language.

"Does it work? Could I kill something this way?"

"Oh yeah," Estienne said. "But only if you were faster." He slipped his hand down my forearm and took the blade back, then his wrist flicked so fast I didn't see it.

The knife embedded in the slats of the tower locker.

I looked at him, eyes wide, and he grinned. "Go get it. And you can keep it."

"Really?" I scrambled off the bunk and went to the blade, tugged it out of the locker and turned to him.

"Really," he said, and slid off the blankets. "Now go to bed, we've got a long shift tomorrow."

I closed the blade and crawled into the bed, beneath the covers. After a second I slid it under my pillow.

"I'm going to lock the hatch again," Estienne said, crouching down beside me. "Okay? For your own safety."

I nodded. If that was the way this ship ran, then I had to learn it.

"Do you want to keep the lights up a little?"

I made a face. "I'm not afraid of the dark."

He laughed. "All right then." His hand went into my hair, but I leaned away. That made him laugh more. "Funny kid."

I watched as he stood and went to the hatch. Somehow I knew he was going to turn around, and he did, for a last look. His hair covered most of his eyes, almost white under the lights, framing his face like a glow.

Then he left, and the hatch beeped, and I called off the lights.

Pure darkness.

* * *

I expected to feel Isobel's warmth along my back, but there was nothing but the bulkhead. I tried not to think of her though; otherwise, I'd feel the loneliness just as cold as the cycled air. Eventually I slept, and the dreams stretched out ahead of me until I couldn't see them anymore.

* * *

I didn't hear Estienne come in, I just felt a hand on my forehead. I blinked open my eyes, confronted soft light and the halo of his hair hanging down, a crown of brightness that cast his face in shadow. He said quietly, "Time to get up. We've leaped."

"We leaped?" I croaked out, pushing myself to sit.

He nodded. "You slept right through it. That's a good sign for you living here. And you say you didn't grow up on a ship?"

I shook my head. He helped me disentangle from the blankets, and I went to the bathroom to pee and wash up. When I came out he had some of my clothes in his hands. Black like what he wore.

"Put these on." He smiled.

So I did that while he made up my bed. He held out the switchblade to me as I ran my hands over my hair to smooth it down. Once I had it in my pocket, looking up at him, none of this early shift felt so strange after all. I'd seen him the most since lifting off from the Camp, and he wasn't demanding at all. Maybe Marcus had asked him to take care of me especially, like Marcus himself was going to train me especially?

Me and not Bo-Sheng. I bit my tongue before I asked how Bo-Sheng was doing. I would probably see him today at some point.

"I start with the guns now?" I asked Estienne as he took me out to the corridor, toward the mess hall for breakfast.

"You might. The captain will tell you." He slid his arm around my shoulders again like he did yesterday, steering me around the corners and out of the way of passing crew. They all looked like they had somewhere to go and barely glanced at us. I asked him about that, if something was going on, and he said, "We've mated with one of our sister ships, and some of the crew are going over there."

"Another ship?"

He grinned. "*Shiva*. It's a merchant. We have lots of friends there."

"How long are we going to be — mated?"

He shrugged. "As long as the captain wants. Apparently they have some strits aboard."

I nearly stopped walking. I didn't think he'd say it so casually. "How do they have *strits*?"

"The way any Hub ship gets strits. They saw a ship where it wasn't supposed to be and attacked it. And *Shiva* won." He smiled. "*Shiva*'s as heavily armed as we are. You have to be now, every ship."

"What are they going to do with them?"

"Hmmm, maybe take them to the nearest military port."

He didn't sound too concerned. I said, "Maybe?"

"Well, after we have a bit of fun. You know how many of our comrades died because of strit attacks?"

Maybe he read my face.

He said, softly, "I'm sorry, Yuri. I forgot. Marcus told me . . . your family, huh? The strits attacked your colony?"

I nodded, then shrugged. "Long ago. When I was little."

Mishka's bloody stump where her arm had been.

I hadn't thought of that in a long time. Now it was there in front of my face like a blinding light. But Estienne's arm was around my shoulders, and I kept walking.

By then we were at the mess hall. It was a lot quieter than

the last shift. Only a quarter of it was occupied. Maybe the others were over on *Shiva*.

I wondered what a strit looked like up close. I wondered if it would understand me if I yelled at it.

Halfway through my breakfast of peanut butter toast and warm cereal, Marcus came in. He didn't acknowledge anybody, just approached our table directly and put his hand on the back of my seat in greeting.

"So how was your sleep, Yuri?"

I swallowed my bite and looked up at him. "Good. Sir."

The corner of his mouth twitched. "The leap didn't bother you?"

"He slept right through," Estienne said, with a glance of approval at me.

Marcus seemed surprised. "Well then . . . are you just about finished with your meal? I thought maybe you'd like to come over to *Shiva* with me. Estienne told you we were mated?"

"Yeah! He said they have strits there." Maybe I'd see one. With Marcus there with me they couldn't do anything. They must've been locked up somewhere. "Can Bo-Sheng come too? The strits killed his homeship, you know."

"Someone will take Bo-Sheng later, if we have time. But I'm going over there now, and Estienne has duties to see to. If you're going to go, let's get on."

I stood so suddenly Marcus had to step back or I would've plowed my seat into him. I tried a smile. "Sorry."

He only raised his eyebrows at me and helped me clamp my chair back to the deck. I turned and waved a little at Estienne. "See you later."

Estienne nodded. "Absolutely."

"Excited," Marcus commented as he took me out.

"It's an alien." People heard about them, and I remem-

bered vaguely seeing pictures on the Send, but to see one
live would be so much different. I'd smell them. They
must've had a scent. They must've had a reason for attacking ships and colonies. What I really wanted to do was kick
them hard for making me lose my mama and Jascha. Why
was their war so important that it killed people and lost
others?

"Are you interested in seeing them just because they're
alien?" Marcus said.

"I hate them," I said. "I want to see them because . . ." I
imagined them scared of me. Begging not to be hurt, or
blamed, or yelled at.

"Because?" Marcus said.

"Have you killed any? Like, by yourself?"

"Oh, sure," he said. "It's what we do, humans. Kill
aliens."

For a second I thought he might be joking, but when I
looked up his face was serious.

"It's quite satisfying," he continued.

I chewed my lip. "Why do they keep attacking us? Why
can't the Hub do something to stop them?"

Marcus was silent, walking along. He didn't touch me
like Estienne did but kept his pace short so I didn't have to
trot to keep up with him. After a moment, he said, "The Hub
made a deal with them a long time ago. The Hub expects
them to keep to this deal, to stay in their place. But obviously they don't. And everybody in between strit space and
the Spokes suffers for it. Like your family."

That was the end result. Camps full of people like Papa.
"But *why*?"

"Some people in the government are more concerned
about keeping things as they are instead of trying to make
them better. I know it doesn't make any sense to you . . . it

hardly does to me . . . but that's the way it is. Frustrating. Which is why most of the time we don't bother handing over the strits we capture. The Hub might just end up letting them go, and how does that help? It's just easier and more fair to vent them."

His voice was soft. He didn't brag about it.

I would've. To Bo-Sheng. And I'd write comms to Papa and tell him.

"Do you truly want to meet them?" Marcus asked, looking down at me as we paused outside the airlock.

"You'll be there, right?"

He nodded once. He wasn't going to make up my mind for me, and that made me stand a little taller.

I said, "Then yeah."

* * *

Shiva was white. It didn't look a thing like *The Abyssinian*. Its walls were white, its lights covered by smooth panels. Dots ran along the deck, iridescent paint. Red, green, blue, and yellow that Marcus said led to different places on the ship. So you wouldn't get lost even if all the lights went out. The crew seemed neater, somehow, not as ragged on the edges of their clothing. Not studded or so tattooed. And there were far more kids weaving past us, holding slates or following behind adults. We glanced at each other, but they didn't speak.

Everyone walked wide of Marcus. And me, because I trailed alongside him. Even the adults. But they didn't have any reason to respect me. They didn't quite look Marcus in the face. He didn't say a thing to any of them, but we didn't get far down the corridor before a dark-haired woman approached, a little hurried, smiling.

"Captain," she said. "Sorry I didn't meet you at the lock."

Behind her stood a sullen boy with a shaved head. No more than light brown stubble crowned his skull, and his gaze was flat. He might've been my age. He had his hands behind him and didn't look at me, even though I tried to catch his eyes to say hi. They were rimmed red, his skin was ashen as if he had a fever. I wondered why he was out of bed.

Marcus was saying to the woman, "I'd like to take Yuri to the strits."

She nodded. "Of course."

"Is this your protégé?" Marcus asked.

The woman stepped aside with a nod and put her arm around the boy. "Evan, say hello to Captain Falcone."

The boy's eyes came up and he smiled. "Hello, sir."

Even I could see he didn't mean it.

Marcus stared at him. "Does he give you trouble?"

"No," the woman said. I thought she must be the captain. "He might."

The woman didn't seem able to answer that. Her mouth looked wilted. Then she said, "He's still in training." Her eyes slid to me. "He does well."

Marcus said, "Come with me and leave the boy." Then he touched my shoulder and guided me around the woman and Evan. I glanced back, and the woman stroked Evan's neck and said something in a low voice. He nodded, turned, and headed away down the corridor. Maybe Evan was her son? Although Marcus called him a "protégé"—whatever that meant. Maybe he got special training like me.

The woman walked fast to join us at the lev. She and Marcus didn't speak as we got in and shot down the decks. I watched the blinking lights, my back to the wall.

Marcus led us both out as if the ship were his own. It

could've been the same deck except the lights were dimmer here. It was colder, emptier, but the walls were still white. Two men with rifles stood outside a double hatch, but Marcus ignored them, just gave the woman a glance, and she moved up and palmed the call pad. The doors slid aside and Marcus put his hands on both my shoulders and walked me in. To *Shiva*'s brig.

I didn't notice anything except the blurry white figures inside one of the steel cages. Marcus led me up to it so I could see inside.

The aliens. Trussed to the bulkhead in chains, their arms apart. Transparent wings fell from their wrists to both sides of their waists, attached. Wings, like the flies I used to find collected on the windowsill of my bedroom in the summer. These wings were shredded or torn. Five strits in this cell. I glanced to the other cells, ten in all, but could only make out shadows. None of the lights were lit except in this one.

They were white-faced, black-eyed, and one of them bared sharp little teeth at me. I stepped back against Marcus, but he squeezed my shoulders.

"They can't hurt you," he said. "Open the gate," he ordered the woman.

"No, wait," I said.

"You'll have to face them sometime," he said. "For what they did. You're not hiding away on that planet anymore."

I hadn't been hiding. I twitched away from his touch and glanced up.

He held my shoulder. Held on. "What're you going to do about it *now*? What're you going to do for your *father*?"

Papa wasn't here. Only me.

And I was already forgetting Mama. And Babushka. I didn't remember Jascha's face.

But I remembered Papa and Isobel, and how Isobel had

no memory of Mama at all, and how Papa sat at the kitchen table late at night and wrote words about pain.

And it was all the fault of these things. When the gate slid aside they stirred in their chains. Even their ankles were bound. Their clothing peeled off their skin in shreds, in long strips, so I saw the white skin beneath. White like the walls of this ship.

They could be human, with their basic faces. Their limbs. Their hair, though the colors were all wrong.

But they weren't human.

My heart galloped. I stood in front of the one in the center of the wall. It was tied and bruised, with dark yellow stains on its body as if it had wet itself. I pointed at it and smiled. Couldn't stop the smile.

"It peed."

"No," Marcus said. "That's their blood. It's yellow. See?" He walked up to that one and grabbed its silver-white hair, lifted its head so I saw the gold drops on its skin. Their blood looked like honey. And its face was marked around the bottomless eyes and down the cheeks with dark blue tattoos. "Aliens," Marcus said, and let it go.

Now that I saw that none of them could move, even when Marcus touched one, I went closer, looked up at the black eyes. It seemed to stare down at me with hatred, without lines or expression except that dark emptiness.

It yelled at me.

The sound was a raw call, no word I understood, just something from deep in its throat that shot through my nerves and shredded them.

I kicked it, heart thudding in my ears but not loud enough to drown out the thing as it wailed and cried in that inhuman voice. I pounded on its chest to stop it. I thought Marcus might pull me back, but he didn't. "It hurt your family," he said. "Take your revenge."

I kicked it again. For some reason that seemed to make them all erupt. All of those strit voices calling to me, each with an echo as if some smaller version of themselves sat deep within their chests, clawing to get out. The cawing rose high through the steel cages, hurting my ears. I remembered the switchblade in my pocket, pulled it out, and flicked it open.

The chains rattled. Marcus didn't stop me. And I jabbed the blade into the strit's chest.

It didn't make a sound. The noise cut off all around me as if someone had finally gagged them. And the silence was worse. It stung.

So I stabbed it again, around the same area high on its chest, to get it to cry out. Anything. Now they all looked at me, all of those strits with their demon black eyes and sharp little teeth, and they were just *things*. They were things that killed humans, attacked homes, and took away half my family. Who would miss them? Who would care?

I stabbed the thing in front of me until its chest was the color of frozen amber, jeweled and flecked black. Until my arm throbbed and my fingers felt swollen and slick; then I stepped back, nearly falling over if Marcus hadn't held my shoulder. His fingers squeezed. The other things didn't yell or even move now, as if they didn't care. Cold and heartless. For all I knew strits didn't feel. Not like humans felt. Not like I felt.

That was for Babushka.

The blade was sticky all up the handle. I tried to wipe it on my splattered clothes, but Marcus plucked it from my grip.

"Let me," he said, and rubbed my hair with affection. He

cleaned the blade on his own pants, then folded it and handed it back to me. "Estienne gave this to you, didn't he?"

I nodded. I wanted to sit down but I blinked, breathed in until it wasn't so much of an effort.

"It'll be all right," Marcus said. "Something crosses you, you teach it a lesson, then you move on. And aliens are always the enemy. Kill it or use it, but keep it at the end of your blade. Understand?"

I nodded, though his words seemed to gush too suddenly in my ears, as if I'd tilted my head wrong in the shower. Heavy sound.

"You'll be just fine," he said. And when I looked up, he was smiling.

* * *

The woman walked us to the airlock. She'd stood in her own brig and hadn't said a word. Now as we left she still didn't say anything until Marcus turned to her. "I'll be in touch."

"Yes, Captain," she said.

He still had his arm around me, and my hands were clenched up in their sleeve cuffs. They still shook for some reason and felt cold. Had I just killed a strit? Their voices still echoed in my head. Except they weren't voices, really, not any more than some animal had a voice. Even Seamus had looked at me different from those strits. Seamus knew me, even though I wasn't his owner. These strits were just— strange other things. My skin crawled from the thought of their black eyes and big insect wings.

Marcus's hand gripped my shoulder. Maybe he felt me shiver. I went with him through the mating tube to our own

airlock. Our own. *The Abyssinian*. I glanced once over my
shoulder at the other captain, in parting. She met my stare.

And for some reason she looked afraid.

10.5.2185 EHSD—Captain Falcone

Every goldshift now, as they called it on ships (not day and
night, a habit I wasn't going to break soon), Estienne took
me to Marcus's quarters for breakfast. Captain Marcus Falcone. I'd put it together and started calling him "Captain"
like his crew did, or Captain Falcone, and the first time I did
he'd asked if I'd picked that up from Estienne. "No," I said.
"The lady from *Shiva*."

"Observant," he said, with a smile.

He had meals brought to his quarters instead of the captain's galley in the morning before he went on bridge and we
sat across from each other and ate. He showed me maps of
the Hub on his slate and pointed out features like leap points
and the Demilitarized Zone where the strits were never supposed to cross but always did, to attack us. He didn't mind
it if I put my feet up on his bunk, or tried on his jackets, or
crawled all over his desk chair when he was in the bathroom
shaving or taking a shower. Sometimes he came out of the
bathroom dressed only in his pants and I saw the tattoos on
his body. Glimpses, until the third time when I worked up
enough courage to ask him if I could see them up close.

So he stood in front of me, patient with my curiosity. He
had two tats: a blood-covered four-armed woman on the left
side of his chest that danced with knives and dangling hands
about her waist; and on his right wrist was the detail of her
dark face. They were ugly but they were pretty in how de-

tailed and how colorful. I reached up to touch the lines of the ink, its rich reds and staining blacks, but stopped, peering up at him.

He put a hand on my hair. "Go ahead. One day you'll get one too."

"Really?" I pressed the pad of my forefinger against his skin and traced the lines. "What does it mean? It's kind of gross."

He laughed. "This symbol"—he touched the dancing woman—"is Kali. The Hindu goddess of destruction. Fitting for a warship, in its way. She was my ship before this one. My carrier, *Kali*." His voice lowered to barely a whisper. "Saving lives and taking down enemies."

"You were a carrier captain?" Maybe that was why his crew sometimes looked scared of him when he walked down the corridors. I thought of the Rim Guards and their long black guns.

He nodded. "A long time ago. Now this is my ship. How do you like it?" He sat on the bunk beside me.

I fell back on the tucked blankets and leaned against the bulkhead. "I like when we go to the shooting gallery." Guns. He'd taken me after I'd killed the strit. I grinned at him. "I like the chocolate. I like Estienne . . ."

"But?"

"But can I send messages to Papa? It's been two weeks and . . . I haven't seen Bo-Sheng either."

"You've been keeping track, have you?" He tousled my hair. I made a face, but I didn't mind so much. He didn't do it to make fun of me. "You know your father doesn't have private communications in the Camp. So . . . if you write to him, I'll send it to their general comm, and they can pass it along to him." He paused. "I gave him my private comm, but he's never sent anything."

I sat straighter. "He hasn't?" It cored me out to hear that. "Maybe it got lost. Papa would send something!"

Marcus shook his head slowly. "I'm sorry, Yuri."

I stared across the quarters at nothing.

Marcus slipped his arm around my shoulders. "It's difficult for them on that planet. I didn't want to tell you, I knew you'd be upset. But Yuri . . . you're in a different place now. And your father wanted you to come. And I'm glad you're here, you're doing very well."

"I am." It was a question, but my voice was flat. What would be the point of all this if Papa didn't even care? What if Isobel had forgotten about me too?

"You are." Marcus turned my head to face him. "Doing *very* well."

I wasn't going to cry, even though the span of space seemed to yawn inside my gut. I was alone on this ship. "What about Bo-Sheng? Can I see him please?"

"How about I give you this first." Marcus reached into his pants pocket and pulled out a pair of tags on a silver chain. He draped them around my neck.

I looked down. One of them was a tagcomm with tiny contact pads and a sliver for the input display.

"I've already programmed my and Estienne's comm numbers in there. This is for if you get lost on the ship or something happens, you just hit the right button and you'll get us. Ask it questions, and it'll tell you how to work it. Okay?"

"Does that mean I get to walk around? By myself?" I must've passed something, even though I hadn't actually been tested. Now I could go talk to Bo-Sheng. I could explore.

"You can walk around by yourself. You can come and go

in your quarters." He smiled. "All of that." His hand played softly in my hair.

He liked to touch me the way Papa sometimes did. As if I were his son.

Papa.

I picked up one of the tags and looked down at it. "Why wouldn't he ask about me?"

Marcus didn't answer. And the silence was enough.

Nobody cared anymore except on this ship.

Things weren't so strange here. I got used to the whump and whine of the ship's drives, the way the shadows squatted in the corners of the corridors, and even the way the crew looked. Their studs and tattoos, harsh words and occasional fights. Marcus had told me long ago that I didn't have to be scared, though, because nobody on the ship would ever touch me.

He said they knew he was my guardian, and I was his protégé.

* * *

I went to Bo-Sheng's quarters first. Even with Estienne or Marcus escorting me back and forth all over the ship for two weeks, and living right beside him, I had never crossed paths with Bo-Sheng. I wanted to tell him about killing the strit, and the gun and knife training I was getting, plus all the slate work about how the Hub ran and the important stations and leap points . . . it was so much and was Bo-Sheng doing it all too? Was he beating me at it? But there'd never been time. If Marcus wasn't talking and teaching me, it was Estienne, and I'd learned to stop asking about Bo-Sheng. Clearly he didn't ask about me.

Nobody did.

I fingered my new tags and buzzed Bo-Sheng's hatch. Maybe he wasn't even inside. It was just after breakfast. Maybe he was still in the mess hall? Or off to his own training?

But the hatch opened and a teenaged girl stood there. Behind her I saw Bo-Sheng and I didn't think, I just shoved past her and careened into him, hugged him.

"Yuri!"

I held on. I was more glad to see him now that he was standing right in front of me. He still smelled like those cheap cigrets. I only smoked the kind Marcus gave me. I touched the ends of his hair, and they were ragged. He hadn't changed.

He returned the hug for a long second and behind me the hatch shut. "She left," he said, sounding surprised. Then, "Where've you been?"

"Training! Like you." I dragged my eyes from his face— maybe he was a little thinner, but not surprising with the exercise they made us do — and looked around the quarters. A sweater was strewn here and there, the locker stood open, spilling toiletries. The bunk was unmade. I jumped on it and bounced. "I got so much to tell you!"

He didn't join me. He just stood there, looking surprised still. He rubbed his hair from his eyes. "Yuri . . . what's been going on? Are you all right?"

"Of course I'm all right. Look." I stopped bouncing and pulled out my switchblade. "Estienne gave this to me. I killed a *strit* with it. D'you know they have, like, yellow blood? It's so gross."

"You killed a strit? Where?" He still had that just-woke-up look. Like he was shocked the galaxy was still here.

I scratched my head. "Over on *Shiva*. Our sister ship. They had a bunch of strits in the brig, and Marcus let me kill one. They're like . . ." I twitched, plucking at my sleeve and holding out the blade to him. I wasn't ecstatic anymore. "Like animals. Don't you want to look at it?"

"No," he said, and looked around as if someone else were in here with us.

I shrugged and sat on the bed, flipping the switchblade in my hand. "Well, I've been learning to use it, and to shoot, and basically they gave me a free pass around the ship, Marcus just gave me these tags . . ." He didn't seem excited for me. "What's wrong?"

He said, "Yuri . . ." Now he approached and sat beside me on the bunk. And whispered, "Yuri, this was a mistake."

"What're you talking about? And why are you whispering?"

"Because!" His eyes darted. "I don't think this ship is a merchant."

I kind of laughed.

"Look," he said. "The crew . . . I *came* from a merchant. This ship isn't a merchant."

"Not every ship is your ship, Bo-Sheng. Besides, what do you remember about your ship? You were too little when the strits killed it. When I went across to *Shiva*, it had a totally different look and—" I didn't understand why he wanted to ruin this for us.

"Yuri, you gotta listen." His fingers dug through my sleeve. "I don't *like* it here."

I pulled away. "Well I do. And since you never even cared where I was all this time—"

"What?"

I got up. "I have to meet Estienne. You go and do what you want."

"Wait!" He snagged my wrist. "Yuri, this is a *pirate* ship. We have to get out of here!"

I yanked away. "You're being stupid."

"They haven't been all that nice to me!" His voice cracked. He stood and came close, holding both my arms.

"What do you mean?" I tried not to flinch from his grip.

"They just . . ." His face bled a deep pink beneath his skin. "Yuri, I just want to go. Please, can we go?"

Was he chickening out? He was always the one who got me into trouble in the Camp. "I don't want to go, Bo-Sheng. Besides, where would we go? Back to the Camp? I don't even know how to get off this ship or what to do if we were on station. And I like it here! They're nice to *me*." I looked in his eyes. "Maybe you're just not doing what they want. Maybe you're just no good at it."

He dropped his hands from my arms and moved away, his nose wrinkling as if I smelled bad. His voice was harsh. "What's wrong with you?"

"Well what's so bad about being here, even if it *is* a pirate ship? So what?"

"Pirates are criminals!"

"So what? Did the Hub ever do anything for us? They just stuck us on that planet to rot. At least here I'm doing stuff."

"Bad stuff, Yuri. They—"

"Like killing strits? They deserve it!"

He flinched from my shout, but said, "Has he found your mama yet?"

I didn't know why, but I wanted to hit him for mentioning Mama. "No. He says Hub bureaucracy is slow as shit, but he's trying."

"He says."

"What's *wrong* with you?"

"I don't like to be forced to do things!" Bo-Sheng shouted in my face. "And you shouldn't either!"

"Nobody's forcing me to do anything. What are they making you do?"

He saw my doubt. It seemed to piss him off. "I have to go."

"Where are you going?" First he yelled at me, then he was going to walk away? "How come you get to go around by yourself?" *Before me?*

He stared at me. Then he opened the hatch, and the girl was outside waiting. She looked at us, blank-faced. "I don't," he said. Then he just went with her, not even looking back at me.

As if I'd let him down in some way. As if he hadn't brought me here himself.

And before it made me sad, it made me angry.

⋆ ⋆ ⋆

Estienne noticed my foul mood but didn't comment on it until the end of the shift, after gym and shooting and fighting class (I sparred mostly with Estienne, and sometimes Marcus if he didn't need to be on the bridge or somewhere else, and it wasn't really fighting, just punching and kicking pads and "learning balance," Estienne said). We also had lunch, and more book work about the stations in the Dragons, and finally on our way back to my quarters he said, "What's wrong?"

I didn't want to go to my quarters in case Bo-Sheng was around, so I glanced up at Estienne. "Can I see your q?"

One eyebrow quirked. "Sure. Why now?"

"I just never seen it."

He shrugged. "Okay. This way." He put his hand on my shoulder and guided me ahead of himself, up a flight of stairs. It wound around twice before we ended up on another deck, quieter, its shadows receded from cones of pale blue light that washed down from the ceiling. There was a landing and a wall with two doors, no other exits but the stairs and a little to the right of us, a lev. He had to tap a code into a side panel before the doors parted, then he took me through. Every hatch on this deck had a lockpad beside it, and numbers. No names. He took me down to the end of the corridor, to the last hatch, and palmed another panel. Then he pushed it open with his shoulder and called up the lights.

Inside the room was black. And red. The walls and floor were gloss dark, reflective as a mirror, the pipes and lights overhead coated black like they'd been carved and frozen out of space. Red transparent material hung from the ceiling in airy waves and dripped down the walls. As if the pipes bled. I ran my hand along the curtain covering the bathroom door. It was so soft it seemed to slip through my fingers, no more solid than water.

Estienne set his slate on the desk, even the furniture was black, and collapsed on his bunk. "Now what happened?"

I walked all around the quarters. It looked as small as mine, but I knew just from the five strides this way and the other that it was in fact twice the size. Finally, I sat beside him on the bed, rubbed the puffy soft red comforter, and looked up at him. He slouched against the wall with one foot on the mattress, biting the edge of his thumb with concentration.

"I went to see Bo-Sheng," I said.

"Yeah?" His eyes flashed at me from behind blond shards of hair.

"He complained. He doesn't like it here. He thinks we're a pirate ship."

Estienne dropped his hand with a sigh and leaned forward, slinging his arm around my neck like he usually did.

"We *are* a pirate ship, Yuri. Technically."

"What? What do you mean 'technically'?" It wasn't a great shock, and in the end it didn't much matter now, but the secrecy?

"Technically we don't like to answer to the Hub. So technically we are a pirate." He shrugged. "Does that bother you?"

"No, not really."

"But it bothers Bo-Sheng."

Now I shrugged. "I don't know what his problem is. He says people make him do things."

"What things?"

"I don't know, he didn't say." I looked at Estienne instead of at the black floor. "Do you?"

"Do I what?"

"Make him do things."

He squinted in disapproval. "Yuri, he came on this ship voluntarily just like you. He's being trained just the same as any crewmember. *You* get extra-special treatment because Marcus—Captain Falcone—thinks you have that potential. Maybe Bo-Sheng is jealous."

"I don't know." Suddenly I didn't want to talk about it. Or remember the way he'd looked at me. "Why does the captain think I'm special?" Because I didn't believe it, really.

It made Estienne laugh, but not at me. And it was a quiet sound. "You're smart."

Was I? "But how'd he know?"

Estienne rubbed my hair. "He's smart. He said when he talked to you he could see it in your eyes. And how much you wanted something different. And even though Bo-Sheng acted like the big tough one, you were the one who would survive."

"Survive what?"

"You know. Just survive. In life." He tugged my hair. "Plus you're cuter."

I made a face.

"See?" He grinned.

Now I didn't want to talk about that either. "I don't want Bo-Sheng to be sad, being here."

"Do you think he's been treated badly? Have we ever mistreated you?"

I looked at my hands. "No."

He squeezed my neck a little with his arm, then ruffled my hair. "You know, it's good of you to be concerned about your friend. But you really don't have to be. Maybe he just hasn't, you know, gotten along as well as you. Do you want me to check up on him?"

"No. I'll . . . I'll see him again, won't I? I'll go tomorrow—next shift."

Estienne glanced at the ceiling as if pulling a reminder message from the pipes. "I don't know . . . actually I think his training schedule's changed. He'll be awake when you're asleep. Sometimes shifts work out that way. I think they're training him in technical stuff, you know, like how to fix things on the ship."

"Why am I not learning that?"

"You will eventually. Marcus is just doing things differently with you."

Because I was special. But that meant I wouldn't see Bo-Sheng for a while.

But I had Estienne.

He hugged me, both arms, until my chin scrunched to my

shoulder. "I'm glad you came to me. Never keep your worries bottled up, deal?"

Estienne was my best friend now. I liked how he never hesitated to hug me. I felt swallowed up by him, and sometimes in my quarters, in the dark, I wished . . . I wished. I missed the comfort of Isobel beside me just so I knew even asleep that I wasn't alone.

Maybe Estienne felt something of it. He kept holding me, so I wrapped my arms around his waist. I looked up at the cascades of red all around the quarters, and it was warm, like his arms were warm.

"I like your room," I said.

I felt him smile against my hair. "You want to stay a while?"

I nodded.

"How about a nap before dinner then? You worked hard today."

I nodded again, glanced up at him. He let me go and slid back on the bed, tucked against the wall on one elbow. I curled up beside him and sank into one of the pillows. He had two, and they were both thick and smelled like his hair—clean and touched by the sun, even though there wasn't a sun on this ship. He draped his arm over me and rested his chin near the top of my head.

"Estienne," I said.

"Yeah?"

"Do you like it here? Even though it's a pirate? I mean . . . would you ever leave?"

"No," he said immediately. "I would never leave. This is my home." He paused. "I want it to be your home too, Yuri."

I said, "It is. It is now."

I'd never go back to the Camp. Not now. Not if Papa

didn't even comm and especially not just because Bo-Sheng couldn't handle it in space.

I shut my eyes. Estienne's arm tightened around me and his face pressed into the back of my hair. Behind my lids the black lay divided by the red, an imprint.

RESCUED

2.27.2198 EHSD — Pax Terra Station

Andreas Lukacs takes us up to the station in his transport but
he doesn't disembark with us. "I'll be in touch," he says.
"With both of you." Meaning, Finch better not start thinking
he can go on vacation to Austro Station just because he's
free.

"What's he going to do," Finch mutters to me as we pass
through the security arch between this dock and the check-
point Customs booths, ten in all even though only five are
manned. Typical. We wait in line in harsh lighting and forest green walls to hand over our false IDs. Lukacs had mine
made already, coded on a finger-sized chipsheet, along with
a couple hundred cred because he's generous like that apparently. On the twelve-hour ride to the station he'd gotten
the same transmitted and encoded for Finch. Black Ops are
nothing if not expedient.

"Hang out and smoke a sweet leaf, I dunno." I want to smoke, but we can't in the open deck without pollies ready to haul you away.

"I mean," Finch says. "What's he going to do with me."

Because Lukacs gave no indication on the ride what he was planning or thinking, didn't much communicate with us at all. He knows what I have to do, and he'll deal with Finch when he's ready.

I'm still stiff and distractingly sore from the beat down, and while talking to Finch serves to keep me awake, it also takes more effort than I have right now. And I need to store up my energy to deal with Petra, my contingency plan, who has to get me in touch with my ship.

"Yuri?" Finch asks, when I zone out.

"Best that he hasn't done anything yet. Look, whatever you do, just don't get in my way." It comes out bitchier than it sounds in my head, but I don't qualify it. It shuts him up.

We pass through Customs without incident, thanks to the IDs and the change of clothes Lukacs had for us—navy blue flight crew uniforms, ubiquitous on any station—and enter the busy traffic of Pax Terra's main concourse. I look first for a public washroom. Easy to find once you find the food, it's hidden between two eateries. A long corridor into a blue-tiled room and Finch waits outside, he says, while I do what I have to do.

I look in the mirror at my unmarred face, feeling the bruises beneath my clothing from the neck down. I smooth my hair, splash my face with cold water to get myself alert. Petra won't want me to walk into her club looking like drug addict dross. She has an image, and I have an obligation. Even here and now. Even for a room to stay in and a secure link to borrow. She knows me as geisha and Falcone's protégé, so this is what she'll get. I rub beneath my eyes, get some color there other than dark circles, bite my lips into a more natural state. The cold on that planet bleached most color away in the last few months. Now, back in space, I tear at them with my teeth, not to break skin but just to get the red.

When I come out Finch asks, "What took you so long?" But I don't answer. I try to pick up my feet as we walk so my stride isn't so crippled. He follows at my right shoulder like a wraith. Two ghosts, it seems, haunting this old station. Pax Terra was the first commercial station in the Hub and became, pretty quickly, just as diverse as the planet "below" it. You can see Earth from most view windows around any of the twelve connected modules. You can put out your hand and touch another world. Inside, among transsteel corridors and the latest fashions, we're just two of 120,000 people flowing from one module to the next like blood cells converging on disparate diseases. This dock, that office. This apartment and that shop.

Austro Station, half its size, was modeled after Pax Terra, it's just considered the Rim version of this first jewel of Hubcentral. But Austro is far newer by fifty-some years, and Pax shows its age most of all in the pleasure district, where I take Finch. Where Petra is, mistress of one of ten flash houses in the section. The one we go to is called Red Square, her headquarters.

Low ceiling, flickering light, and there's a definite hiccup of moderated temperature, moisture, and airflow control through the corridors in this district. Scents released here tend to stick, and we're not five minutes wandering the burrow holes between flash houses, pushing by the press of bodies, before Finch presses his sleeve to his nose and mouth. How many people—cigret smoke, alcohol, and drug scent clinging to their clothes—have passed through here?

"Why don't they do something about the ventilation?" He coughs behind me. As if I can do something about it.

"Who's gonna pay for it? You?"

"They should shut this place down. At the very least a health inspector . . ."

"Govies come by here every year. But the amount of money it would cost to clear people out . . ." They don't think it's worth it. It serves one good purpose though. People in places like this don't look at you too closely or ask too many questions.

I just wish Finch didn't have to tail me. Wish that if I got him out, he could at least be on his way, and me on mine, though my track back to deep space feels like looking into the long barrel of a gun. Any minute now someone's going to pull the trigger and you won't see anything but a flash, and maybe you won't even feel the shot impact. Sometimes it's so sudden you don't have time to feel anything.

And that can be lucky.

But with Finch I feel him by my side with all of his questions and his nervousness, and when the shot comes I think I'll get the pain. Or maybe thinking you feel anything is just the sort of lie you tell yourself to make your universe make sense. To make you think you still have that capacity, and you're not just filled with dread.

He's looking off the wrong way, so I grab his sleeve and tug him toward the opaque front of the club—black sheen with a red star on the door. It's 1340 hours and the place is closed, but we can at least get in the foyer. Once the door shuts, casting us in russet half-light, Finch lowers his sleeve and takes a breath of the latent smoke-and-alcohol scent. But it's fresher air cycling down from the house's internal system.

He's quiet, I'm quiet. I think of past business I've done with this woman and hit the intercom.

"*Da?*" the man says on the other end.

I answer back in the same Russian. "*Kublai Khan*. Turn on your scan."

In a second a square of red light appears on the wall at elbow height, camouflaged until activated. I pull my sleeve up and press my *Khan* tattoo to the surface. Now we'll see if Andreas Lukacs's fancy Ops technology can pass muster in the underworld. The scan will pick up my ship ID since I helped them calibrate it to my nanocode long ago, but for all I know they could've upgraded, dropped my code once I was incarcerated, or received kill orders from Taja "just in case." I wouldn't be surprised.

But the scan shuts off after a moment, and the inner doors buzz briefly. Finch says, "Maybe I should—"

"You're coming with me, or they might decide to sweep you off their entrance while I'm inside." I yank the door open and step through to the club's bottleneck front space. The walls morph on a cycle of snowy sunset, antique soldiers in a goose-stepping march, and large graven images of dead politicians. The door shuts behind Finch and he has the good sense to be quiet when a small Asian man approaches from behind the heavy-laden bar that runs along the right side of the wall.

"You're out," he says, in accented majority language. His eyes are flat.

"Where's Petra?"

"Who's he?" Mr. Asian points behind my shoulder.

"Crew."

He doesn't believe me. Obviously. One look at Finch. "No *crew* allowed in here."

I remember my command voice. "Look, you can sass me

for an hour, or you can tell Petra I came, got fed up, and left in two minutes. And then I'll come back when you're no longer in service."

The man doesn't argue. He just walks off, straight into the shadowed back area of the club.

In five minutes she comes out, a stout woman with a round face and long black hair, straight down to her ass. She's all smiles, and I return it, leaning down to kiss both of her offered cheeks. This is where the work begins.

"Yuri, I had no idea you'd got out. When? How?"

"Maybe we can sit? It's been a long flight." And I want to curl up somewhere and just let my body heal. The bot-knitters still work, but it's a maddening itch easiest ignored when asleep.

But not yet.

"Of course, of course . . ." She takes my arm and leads me to one of the empty cushioned booths, glancing over her shoulder. "And who's your friend?"

"Prison mate. Busted him out too."

Finch hangs back, but Petra motions him forward. So he goes. I sit with a sigh, because I ache, and watch her take Finch by both arms and look him up and down. He does well not to flinch or look too discomfitted. He has no idea that she's broken boys in half with those same hands, and would do it to him if I pay her. "You trust him?" she asks.

If I say no, she'll kick him out. If I say yes, she might use him against me in some way once she gets tired of the pleasant routine.

"I trust him as long as he's in my sight," I tell her.

She laughs. "Then by all means. Sit." To Finch.

He does, right beside me, without a word. Mr. Asian brings across drinks as if he was silently called—which he probably was from a subvocalizer or commstud—and sets them down in front of me and Finch. White Russian for me, she remembers. Some amber-colored booze for him. I don't touch mine, and won't, until I'm relatively positive Petra isn't out to poison me. Finch takes his cues from me and doesn't even look at the glass.

"So tell me a good story," Petra says, leaning back in her seat across from us and lighting a long black cigret.

I open my mouth.

"No," she says. "Not you. Him." She points the cigret to Finch. "I want him to tell me how you got out."

I don't say anything. Protest would make it worse. But we have to do this, or I won't get the help I need. I don't even look at Finch, because Petra is looking at Finch, and at me though not directly. Mr. Asian behind the long bar, facing our seats dead on, can see me too, and I don't doubt that he might have ocular zoom implants. So I pull my own cigrets out of my pocket, cheap ones Lukacs gave me on the transport because I bitched for an hour straight. I light one and smoke, mingling the scent of our two different drugs.

Finch holds his hands in his lap and says in his sweet accent, "We had help. The military might be stupid, but we still couldn't just walk out of one of their prisons."

"True," Petra says with a nod. "What help?"

Finch shrugs and jerks his chin at me. "Not anyone I know. That's his area."

I don't look at him even though Petra still does. Maybe he did learn a thing or two inside. He at least learned how to keep a straight face.

"Pirates," I tell her. "Who else?"

"How?" she says.

"Killed me," I answer. I roll up my sleeve so she can see the bruises on my arm. "Beat me to death, you know. I guess I deserved it." Geisha can smile even in the face of that. If we don't kill because of it first. So I smile at her, to keep it pleasant.

She looks almost impressed. "You do deserve it. Which captain ordered it?"

"They told me Cal, as they were tossing me into the morgue." Because her and Cal never did get along, and the chances of her comming him are slim.

"Cal and not Taja?" Her smile is mocking. She knows I despise Taja more than Cal. "You trust that?" One painted eyebrow goes up.

"No." I laugh. "But so far I'll go along with it. I'm sitting here having a drink with you, after all."

Lies. Just all lies.

"And I don't mean to be rude, but I really need to comm my ship." That's true.

"Of course," she says smoothly. "But you won't at least relax in one of our dens?" Her eyes shift to Finch.

"Sure we will. But you know my ship comes first."

"Ah, business with you, Yuri. Even when some business is a pleasure."

"It's my upbringing." Training sounds far too cold. And some people don't want to be reminded that it's a job for me.

She grins now, and hauls herself off her seat. "I'll tell Koto to link you. And give you some privacy. Afterward, you come see me."

"Of course." This isn't something we haven't done before.

She moves off toward the broader back rooms, hidden behind a long velvet curtain, and I don't look at Finch. He doesn't say anything. Koto from behind the bar comes over and plops down a commmpad. "It's secure," he says, and walks off.

"Go stand by the bar," I tell Finch.

"Why?"

Now I look at him and tap my ashes in the silver tray on the table. Fatigue keeps kicking in my brain for attention. "Go stand by the bloody bar and make sure nobody's loitering around the corner or by the doors."

"This place is probably bugged anyway."

"It's not. Not that detailed, or do you think anyone would do business with her in these seats?" Drugs. Small weapons. Bodies. She trades in them all. "Just get over there."

He slides out and goes, but not without a tired glare. The hours since the prison weigh on him too.

Deal with him later. I poke the pad to activate it and run my finger along the options. Won't be a real-time talk, but text will do. Probably better. Less explanation.

There's a distress commcode that my ship will immediately recognize, and unless Taja somehow got into my primary command keys these won't have changed, even if she implemented new ones. Mine just lie dormant until I send a signal, a kind of fail-safe in case the ship gets usurped. Which isn't unheard of among pirates.

So I send the activation set to the system and wait. Comm officer Chris will see the alert and answer back.

And he does, in about ten minutes. The ship must not be in the Dragons for the signal to hop back so quickly, considering verification time. The message pops up on the pad.

Identify.

I tap in my old captain's ID.

Nothing.

Then, *Identify.*

I sink my burned-out cigret into the ashtray then input: *It's your captain. I need a pickup on Pax Terra, Red Square. Make it quick. And Chris? If Taja removed Dexter from my quarters, I'm going to kill her.*

Nobody but shipmates know about my pet bird. And nobody but intimate crew knows that I threatened Taja more than once about how she treated Dexter when I had to be off ship for one reason or another.

I wait for the reply.

Yuri? Holy shit.

Come get me. I palm off and motion Finch over. "We're set. Stay here while I go see Petra. Don't drink anything."

"What're you going to tell her?"

"Nothing. We're not gonna speak."

"Meaning what?" His voice is sharp.

I don't look at him. He doesn't know anything about me, certainly not enough to judge.

"Figure it out."

I leave him there to sit.

* * *

Petra asks for perks, so I give her a half hour of body barter and she makes sympathetic faces at the bruises and bandages. I let her do most of the work but still I ache afterward and I want to sleep and just not have to move. But to show that would insult her, so I keep it all to myself. While I'm pulling up my pants she lights a cigret, lying there on the couch in her office with her naked legs crossed and her long hair draped over her breasts like a mermaid.

"They coming?" she says.

"Yeah. Got a room for me and my mate for a few shifts?"

"Sure. Just don't wear yourself out on him, I want more of this." I hear the smirk in her words. "It's nice to see prison didn't ruin you, *Captain.*"

I let my hair hide my expression as I look down to seam

up the pants, because now I'd like to kill her. "You never have to worry about that."

She motions to the door with her chin, licking her bottom lip briefly. "Take the Argenta room."

I nod and leave. I meet Finch, who hasn't moved from his seat or touched the glass as ordered, and ignore his stare.

Koto unlocks the room for us from the master controls behind the bar, then leads us down a narrow hall. The den area of the club is a ten-room curtained-off section just past the VIP lounge. The room she lends us is midnight purple and silver, draped with a canopy. At least it's not red, but it's gaudy, really, with its main feature being the single middle-sized bed with an ostentatious peacock headboard.

Finch says, "I think we need two rooms."

I unload my pockets on the side table. "Get over it. She's not going to waste an extra room when she already thinks we're shagging."

"We're *not* shagging."

"Don't flatter yourself." I collapse onto the plush covers, on my back, and shut my eyes. I hear him walk around the room and poke into corners, opening the bathroom door, investigating things like some curious animal. Eventually he must have gotten tired because the end of the bed sinks down under his weight, then hesitation, and finally I feel him stretch out beside me. He doesn't move at all.

I roll my back to him, and I feel him do the same.

*　*　*

I wake up halfway through the shift with my back to the peacock headboard and the lights up at a low glow. And Finch is sitting at the foot of the bed with one of the pillows in his lap, staring at me.

I pull my knees up, rest my elbows against them, and rub my eyes. Again. What did I say? I don't want to ask.

"Yuri," he says.

"Don't." Don't tell me, don't look at me, I don't want to know.

This started when you screwed me, his eyes say. With guilt? But he's wrong. My active body and deadened consciousness didn't need him to trigger it.

"Go back to sleep," I tell him. So you won't hear me.

But he doesn't move. "Who's Estienne?"

I can't tell if he knows already and just wants me to say it awake. I look at the bathroom door and miss the switchblade in my pocket.

"Bo-Sheng?" he says.

So I slide up and go inside the bathroom and lock the door. I sit on the tiles with my eyes open.

* *

For the next week the routine is simple. We lie low in Petra's flash house, drinking and eating there, and I have sex with her every other night to pay the rent and feed us without having to spend all our cred. That's what I've come to and me and Finch don't talk about it, even though every time he sees Petra his face goes solid blank. He doesn't quite look at me that way. Mostly I think he's disgusted. I would be too since doing this for rent seems to degrade the years of geisha training in the Hanamachi on Falcone's ship, whatever that means now, except I can't have that much pride and work for Ops at the same time. There's no pride involved here, any more than there is emotion.

While Finch goes out on forays for first aid, food, clothes, and smokes—easier for him to show his face on the decks than me—I scroll the Send for info on the comp in our room. In the heart of Hubcentral, there isn't much on the popular links but Centralist propaganda. President Judy Damiani seems to be basking in the glory of diminishing strit attacks on ships and military bases in the Dragons. Her politics makes no mention of Captain Cairo Azarcon or his adoptive father EarthHub Joint Chief Admiral Ashrafi and their attempts to make peace with the strits and their human sympathizers, nor is there much mention, of course, of her subtle Fundamental Centralist opinions and ties to antialien terrorist groups like the Family of Humanity—which I know for a fact.

She and her followers play it up as if the strits are quiet because of better work by the deep-space carriers, but anybody who's skated deep space—wasn't that long ago I was in Azarcon's brig—knows that pulling back has more to do with Azarcon's voluntary exile to the strit side and his communication with the sympathizer Warboy. But Damiani hates Azarcon, and the thing she wants to do least of all is keep his name in the collective consciousness of the Hub, where he can do damage.

Like his son Ryan seems to be doing damage. A bit of a burndiver, that one, intelligent and inherently rebellious—like his father, whose ship he's on right now thanks to Family action that resulted in his mother's death on Austro Station. Not my family, not pirates. Family of Humanity. The boy can be vengeful, encouraged by his father, I don't know. Bit of a meedee darling thanks to good looks and a sharp tongue. I scroll a few marginalized reports apparently transmitted from across the Demilitarized Zone, origins no doubt heavily coded with deep-space military technology. And maybe some strit protocols too, I wouldn't be surprised. That'd make them pretty much impossible to trace. Ryan

Azarcon, drumming up suspicion about Damiani's real motives in the EarthHub presidency. He's immune just like his father, who Damiani already branded a traitor when he refused to be recalled. Her mistake, forcing his hand. To prosecute the son for slander or conspiracy or treason they'd have to find him, and there isn't a carrier in the Hub that would go up against Cairo Azarcon and the Warboy, at least not without plenty of persuasion.

From the moment Falcone died, the persecution of pirates by those same carriers stepped up, and it's not a far stretch to believe they're too busy chasing pirates to be that engaged with a fallen brother like Azarcon. Deep spacers tend to stick together, and they all hated us.

Not a lot of mention about pirates on the Send, but then we never seem to make the main news cycles this far insystem. Deep-space links make passing mention, but it's not advantageous to harp on pirate attacks when you want merchant ships to take quicker routes to deliver goods instead of the long way around in order to avoid interception.

We prefer it that way. Lack of meedee attention means people are more ignorant of our existence, or at least in a healthy denial, and criminals do work better in the dark.

Reading all of this, hearing the reports, there is nothing more sure in the Hub right now than constant jockeying for political power. No matter the faction. Within the Hub government, out in deep space, and especially among the pirates. I don't need to find reports to remember how I left it. Why I left it. Why I regretted leaving it, stuck in Azarcon's brig with a man too angry over a wife's death and a son's blindness.

Push and pull of attention, desire, and agenda. Now I'm here with this warlord woman so she doesn't give me up to badder elements, and that's all politics is, really—this give-and-take on your back in someone else's bed.

I suppose I must please Petra a lot because she gives me a gun, nothing fancy, but it works and it's small. Finch and I sequester ourselves in the room in late blueshifts when the music and voices of the club penetrate into the dens, loud and teeming. The less people see me here the better. He bought a deck of cards, cheapest entertainment, and we play that on the bed, sitting amid little avalanches of sheets, blankets, and pillows. He doesn't talk much. Once or twice I catch him smiling when he beats me at a game, but then he seems to remember the situation, and it all fades.

On the seventh full shift, at 1200 hours, when the club is in full swing and we're holed up in here, he finally asks: "When are your people going to get here?"

"They have to send someone in from the Rim. They weren't in the Dragons I don't think, but it's still not a short haul. Anyway, don't be so eager. They might just decide to kill us." I lay down a card. We've resorted to playing Go Fish. We've played every other game ever invented for a deck.

After a minute of concentration that doesn't seem needed for a child's game, he says, "How're your injuries?"

"Better." And I know I'm baiting. "Concerned?"

He blinks, his only reaction. His voice is wry. "Since my well-being is directly tied to yours, thanks to—him—then yeah."

The devil must've heard that tangential invocation because the very next shift, when I'm in the bathroom taking a piss, Finch bangs on the door.

"Yuri, come out."

I sent him to buy cigs. After washing my hands I open the door, and he says, "Lukacs. Out there. Told me he wants to see you."

"Where're my cigs?"

"Did you hear what I said?"

I hold out my hand. "Of course I did, you're yelling it in my face. Petra probably even heard, and now she's going to ask questions, thanks, now gimme my cigs."

He pulls them from his pocket and takes out a stick before handing me the pack. "I wasn't yelling," he whispers.

No, he wasn't. "If talking to that man makes you so freaky, then maybe you should just let me kill you and be done."

This is what passes for humor between us. He doesn't answer it, just lights his cig. My expensive spacer brand. I inhale his smoke before lighting my own, then I head to the door. "Put on your game face."

* * *

Finch leads me to the shadowed back booth of an off-ramp Irish pub, a little away from the main strip of higher-end clubs and dens on the primary concourse. It's still part of the regularly patronized shops and restaurants that fuel the resident population, tourists, and stopover travelers heading outsystem, so there's enough of a crowd to obscure us in a rear booth. Andreas Lukacs sits with his back to the wall and a beer in his hand, sips it casually as we slide into our seats—one on each side of him. Finch takes the cue from my eyes.

But our benign outflanking maneuver is counteracted by the other agent who disengages himself from the bar and pulls up a chair to sit across from Lukacs, back facing out but with clear lines of sight to both of us. He leans back with his fingers laced across his belly, watching us. Less of a bodyguard pose and more of a partner. They must be partners, and yet that odd warning before liftoff from Earth. *Watch him.* I try to see behind the shadows cutting his face from the dim lights, but there's no getting through that. His expression is the same hard evaluation and despite the relaxed pose I can feel he's hair-triggered.

Lukacs is casual and undisturbed at being fenced in. He eyes my new dark sweater and cargo jacket and pants. "You're looking better."

"You mean better-looking," I reply.

"Your boy here let me know that you're waiting for someone from your ship to pick you up."

I don't say anything, just poke the table menu with my order. White Russian. And I plan on leaving him with the tab.

"Once you're aboard, I expect you to get in their good graces in a reasonable amount of time and get to work setting up my cover." He slides over a small chipsheet and a reader. "My contact information. Memorize it now."

I stick the sheet on the interface and peruse the codes. Trained memory, and he gives me the silence. Five minutes, then he holds his hand out and I pass it all back.

And what will you be doing in the meantime while I arrange all of this? My eyes drift to the blond man. And you? But I don't bother to ask because they won't give any answers.

We don't speak as the waitress comes by to set down a small square napkin and my White Russian. She leaves, and I sip, and then I say, "You're paying."

"Then why don't you order?" Lukacs glances at Finch. The question somehow sounds like a challenge.

I don't want Lukacs to focus on Finch but Finch says, evenly enough, "No thanks."

"Trained him well," the blond man says.

I look at him, razor-cut direct. And that means what?

"Not to take favors from strangers," the man continues, with a thin smile, as if he heard my thoughts.

"But you're not strangers now. We're all practically kissing cousins." I can smile too if just for the entertainment of it.

"I'd advise you not to get too attached," Lukacs says, talking to me but looking at Finch. "But I think my words come a bit too late."

Enough. "Because you plan to—what? Use him against me somehow?"

Now Lukacs is the only one smiling. "Of course. The moment I knew you'd do this thing in order to save his life, the better the odds for success if he's in the picture. Isn't that so? And how do you feel about that, Mr. Finch?"

Finch says, "I think you can guess," in the sort of tone you take right before you kill someone. Maybe he's this brave because I'm sitting right here, or maybe he really is so angry it provides a kind of focus.

Lukacs finishes his beer. "Yes, I probably could." He looks at me, expectant, as the blond agent rises from his seat.

So I have to slide out so Lukacs can get to his feet. I only edge away far enough to give him wiggle room, and our bodies brush as he passes.

"Thank you," he says, with studied politeness. "Thank you for making this so easy." Just to me, while his eyes cut to Finch like an edge of paper on soft flesh.

This is what happens, I can almost hear him think, when

you allow yourself to be compromised. Or maybe it's just my own voice, louder than memory.

I sit back down after they leave the pub.

Finch says, "What now?" Showing discomfort in the way both his hands lie flat on the table, fingers digging slightly.

I pick up my glass and look down into its white depths before taking a sip. "You can do what you want, but I'm finishing this drink."

* * *

Oh-three-fifty in my blueshift and someone knocks on our door. I'm up and off the bed before Finch even rolls over and calls up the lights to a comfortable 30 percent.

Rika, finally, geisha sister once upon a time and the Elder Sister of *Kublai Khan*'s Hanamachi. Of course Taja wouldn't come herself, but I'm surprised she sent someone that I actually trust. Or had trusted. Or maybe she knew I wouldn't go quietly at gunpoint.

For a second I wonder if Rika will shoot me.

But she just says, "Hey, brother," in her naturally hoarse voice. As if it hasn't been months. "What idiot let you out?"

I'm not ashamed, suddenly, to grab her into a tight hug while I hear Finch climb out of the bed behind me.

"Oh, what's this?" she says.

I feel her hand leave my shoulder and drop to her waist, where her gun's hidden. I hold her wrist.

"He's mine, don't shoot him. Let's get the hell out of here."

* * *

I sit in the copilot seat with Finch behind me at the artillery controls while Rika pilots the outrider, part of her training. It's a little shuttle registered to my ship whose skin ID is *Orlando*. But seeing Rika again, I think of nothing but the *Khan*. Both of them. The one that's dead, Falcone's, and the one I'm going back to—mine. I haven't been back to mine in . . .

"Been like a year," Rika says. "Bastard."

That long.

"What the *hell* were you doing?" An old anger pushes to the surface of her eyes. "How the *hell* did you get cuffed by Azarcon?"

Do I go into my catalogue of mistakes, missteps, and misconceptions? No. I'm her captain, and better she thinks for as long as she can that I was maybe outwitted instead of simply out of joint. She can't know my dislocation from the moment Falcone died. From before that, in corners that the geisha weren't supposed to reveal.

"Azarcon caught up to me." I stare at her. The hard veneer of bitterness. No I don't want to talk about the fact he's a better captain than me. "What'd Taja say?"

Her response is delayed because she's trying to chip at my shell. See if I'm soft inside. But her tools aren't sharp enough, and eventually she shrugs a bit, leaves it alone, whatever she thinks of me and my absence. "Taja said to come get you." Rika pokes at the system display, swirling her finger around to elicit some information for the ride. She said we've got two leaps to go through before we can get to the sinkhole where *Kublai Khan* waits. "The bitch hasn't told me if she wants to kill you or not, but there's folks on board who'd kill her if she left you adrift."

"Good to know. I'll need your help with that."

Her glance pins me, but I don't elaborate. Not yet. So she jerks her chin back at Finch. "Who the hell is he?"

"Cellmate."

Her eyebrow lifts.

"Not like that. I'll tell you later." I have no intention of explaining Finch in detail to anyone, but Rika, my Elder Sister, she at least deserves to know something. But not while Finch is behind us listening.

"He's cute," she says. "Maybe he'll dance for us? With a fan?"

"You'd have better luck trying to blow up *Macedon* buck naked. He's feisty."

Finch mutters something incoherent, but I don't ask what.

"You know this exclusively, do you?" Her grin is familiar.

"Speaking of *Macedon* . . ."

She leans back, on autopilot, and props her foot up on the seat, rocking it back a little and gazing out the cockpit at motionless space. "Behind the DMZ still. Sleeping with the strits. Every once in a while that Azarcon kid stirs up the meedees with some political criticism, but nothin' from Azarcon Sr. at all. I bet the govies're worried."

Falcone used to go under the radar sometimes too and come out a dragon. Govies got to think that the captain's plotting. President Damiani and her terrorist connections at the very least must be getting very little sleep.

"The sanctioned carriers still on our asses?" I don't want to talk about Azarcon too deeply with Rika since she has no idea I tried to get on his ship. Twice. Both mistakes, but she wouldn't split hairs that finely.

"*Archangel*'s the worst." *Macedon*'s sister ship, whose jets' reputations are only upstaged by Azarcon's. They run joint exercises sometimes and I saw the cross-pollination from the vantage of both brigs, less than a year ago. Their crews are close, know each other by name, and sometimes jump from one or the other ship if deep relationships form. Rare but not unheard of, and when *Macedon* handed me over, the abuse was much the same.

Falcone knew carriers.

Rika lights a cigret that she pulls from her pant leg pocket and blows smoke in disdain. "*Archangel*'s basically taken up the slack in the Dragons."

No surprise there. "And how's my ship."

She's silent for a second. It makes the hair on my arms crawl. A new captain and she obviously feels some loyalty— or fear—toward Taja.

But it's only a second, and she says, "Taja isn't as con- vincing as you were with the clients. And whatever charm she had with Marcus doesn't work on Cal."

So everything Lukacs said was true. My ship's hurting because Taja doesn't know her shit. Or the shit she offers nobody wants. It's a backward sort of compliment to me, I guess, although it points more to the fact of the backstabbing nature of this business if the benefits are right.

I lean over and take the cig from her fingers, just for a drag, that's all I want right now, then hand it back. "What's Cal been up to."

Rika smiles without humor. "Stealing your contacts and reorganizing the trade."

Not surprising in the least. He's had his eye on it for decades. Which only means he won't be that happy to know I'm out.

"And I'm curious," she says. "How *did* you get free?"

"The same way Marcus did, in his time. Some of those cats remember who scratched their backs." I say it because it's simplest, and even though we shared a Hanamachi I was always a protégé first.

3.10.2198 EHSD—The Blood

A week and a half later *Kublai Khan* guides us into bay two with winking red lights. I'm groggy from the last leap, which was deep, Finch is nearly still unconscious in his seat, but Rika's stimmed on rapid infeed and floats us easily to the grappling marks. As soon as we hear the clamps secure on either side of the shuttle she powers down and turns to us. "Home."

The ramp grates open behind us, and she edges by me. I stand and follow, feeling for the gun in my backwaist, snagging Finch's arm on the way. He's not steady on his feet.

But it doesn't matter. Taja's sent an escort—five men with rifles. They meet us there as we hit deck, and Rika glances at me in apology. No apologies, really. It's expected.

Taja's there herself, her hair pulled back from her face, emphasizing her cheeks and the dark cant of her eyes. Her features pinch and seem to fix like that, the mark of stress.

"You look like shit," I tell her, fully aware that it's mutual. But I'm not going to pretend that I'm glad to see her.

She says, "You should've stayed gone, Yuri." Her eyes cut across my shoulder. "At least you brought a friend."

He's leverage for her too, unless she thinks he's here just as extra muscle. I don't look at him.

She motions one of the men forward. Tall, with a blond half-hawk haircut. I don't recognize him, which means it's someone she recruited in my absence. Someone who doesn't know me or care. He pats me down roughly and confiscates the gun and my fake ID and even my cigrets, which I glare at him for, but he's paid and dispassionate and doesn't crack an expression. Then he does the same to Finch.

And Taja says, "You know where you're going, don't you?"

* * *

The walk through my own ship, under guard, is both tense and humiliating. Some of the crew stare in disdain, others turn their eyes away because the gun pointed at my back is embarrassing for them too. I'm someone they supported, and maybe if Taja sees them react any other way, their names will go on the list all pirate captains keep about their crews. A few look with anger, but not at me. Those I take note of in particular. Loyalty can be used.

My *Khan* looks the same, though it's been a year removed. It's a Komodo-class merchant like its bloodmother, outfitted with the same grade of weaponry as Falcone had. The familiar glow of the lights along the spine of the corridor make the shadows in the corners come alive, little black dancers at the edges of my sight. Our footsteps echo on the deck grille.

All the way to the brig. Imprisonment is a lifestyle.

* * *

She makes us stew in silence and blinding overhead lights. One cell for the both of us, frigid and bare with nothing but a crooked bunk, a dirty toilet, and a sink that spills only ice water. Looks familiar, I tell Finch.

"Shite," he says, with his hands tucked into his armpits.

"This place's got optics," I mutter, before he starts cursing Lukacs aloud.

"It's your ship? I figured." He sits on the bunk with his arms against his stomach. He's holding up well, but a long stay in a pirate brig will kick that down soon enough.

"Well." I sit beside him with my back to the cold wall and my legs over the edge of the bunk. "At least we won't die of suspense. Likely she'll just starve us with neglect."

"Didn't you know this was going to happen?"

"Pretty much. But what am I going to do about it? Nothing I can do if she doesn't come down here. She's just being a bitch." I hope the optics pick that up.

He doesn't say anything.

"But. She might also see the benefit of keeping me alive." That for the optics too. Then I poke his back with one foot. "There's only one bunk here. Are you going to be freaky about it?"

Why in my own distress do I persecute him, even mildly. Maybe because I like it when he retaliates.

His eyes slice to me, black blades. "No, I won't be freaky. You're gonna sleep on the floor."

* * *

I don't sleep, as it turns out, so I give him the bunk and just sit against it with my arms around my knees, listening to him breathe behind me. Now that he's in it maybe it would've been kinder to leave him back in the prison to deal with things alone. Saddled with me here and on the radar of someone like Andreas Lukacs, he has less of a choice. It's a prolonged death here.

I know this. I count my own years backward to the beginning and all the times I slept like him, with interrupted breaths.

The thoughts spin around, and I can't turn and look at him, or shake him awake and demand he tell me everything, all of it, what's in his head and why he never tried to kill me for what I did to him in the prison.

Instead, just his silence. Protection with a price is just mutual prostitution, so maybe that's why he can't hate me enough to kill me.

He sleeps, and I'm almost dozing when the brig hatch clangs open. I haul myself up and go to the bars, glancing back over my shoulder. Finch faces the wall in a tight curl, so far asleep after the stress of those leaps that he doesn't hear a thing. So I lean against the bars and watch Taja approach on the other side.

"Why are you still alive?" she says, meaning in the general sense.

But I answer her in specifics. "Because you haven't killed me yet."

"Right," she says slowly, folding her arms and looking at me up and down. "And remind me why you're not dead now. In my brig."

Her brig. What reason does she have to keep me alive?

"Because you've fucked up my operation, and you need my help."

She snorts.

"What're our resources like, Taja. Our caches. When's the last time you've met with a client and shook a deal?"

"You lost the right to take that tone when you got your ass captured by Azarcon."

"Yeah, but look at me now, a boomerang. And you need me."

She doesn't dance around that. She just looks at me.

"I can help," I tell her, flat out.

"And take my ship?"

"You know you've just been babysitting. By the way, where's my bird?"

She ignores that and gestures behind me. "Who is he? One of your playmates? A client? What?"

"Lint."

"Handsome lint. Right up your—alley."

I grin at her the way animals do. "You know the crew will kill you before they allow you to run this ship aground."

She turns and walks out, slamming the hatch.

Finch wakes up and rolls over. "Yuri?"

Maybe he thinks I've been sleepwalking again.

"Your watch now. I want the bed." I turn to look at him. The light's high bright, so it's harder to get a true restful sleep. He squints at me. "Unless." I move closer and look down at him. With the glow behind my head I know my face is shadowed. I touch his shoulder. "You want to cuddle with me."

That makes him move, and I laugh. It's cruel, but my thoughts are on Taja and my ship when I lie down. The bunk is warm from his body and holds his scent. It helps me to fall asleep.

* * *

When I wake up, minutes or hours later, he's gone. My mind's fuzzy from something more than sleep, and when I glance down the transparent shininess of a drug tape winks at me from my arm. They snuck in here and put me down so I didn't hear them kidnap Finch.

I rip it off and look up to the corners where I know the optics are embedded.

"You bitch!"

But of course nobody answers.

* *

She doesn't waste food on me. Or soap. Or time. I don't see or hear from anybody for maybe three days. Three full shifts. Impossible to tell. I think about gnawing at my own arm. I'm nauseous from the lack of eating, and I piss too much from just drinking water. The tap makes the water metallic and icy, and it sits in my gut like the cold ocean depths. My nails aren't even sharp enough as I scratch at the healed cuts on my arms. Nothing from Finch, or Rika, or anyone else. Maybe there are guards outside the brig. I know somebody watches. I lie on the bunk, or stretch and pace, but mostly I just sit and concoct elaborate scenarios of murder. Andreas Lukacs. Taja Roshan. That nameless blond agent.

All of them.

* *

The hatch opens, and it's Finch. I'm too tired to roll off the bunk, and he approaches the door of the cage. He's dressed in black. Not geisha black, but they aren't the clothes he arrived in. He carries a tray of food and the aroma sinks its teeth into my gut and makes it open wide.

"Where've you been?"

He says, "On the ship." Hesitant. Maybe because of the optics or maybe he just doesn't want to tell me.

"Get me out," I tell him. Because I won't be bought even with toast and eggs.

"She will," he says, in a quiet voice, and sets the tray edge in the delivery slot. "Here, take this."

"What's in it?"

He looks down. "Bread, tomatoes . . ."

"What's she been doing with you? Is there poison in there, drugs maybe? What the hell is going on?" I don't care about the optics now. He looks far too well fed.

"Yuri, take the food. I wrangled that out of her at least, and you need it."

So I get up and I take it and go back to the bunk. "What's she been asking?" Because she would have asked something. Interrogation didn't always come with beatings and intimidation.

"About the prison, mostly."

I gaze at him as I eat, try not to gobble it all down and make myself sick. If it's poisoned, at least I'll die quicker than starving to death. "And?"

"Not really anything else."

"That's bullshit."

"She didn't ask anything else, Yuri."

"That's still bullshit, and if you're playing me I swear I'll kill you bare-handed if I ever get out of here."

His head tilts, and his eyes narrow. "I'm not playing you, dammit."

Paranoia comes easy when you're alone. I set aside the food, full after a couple of bites, and approach the bars again, sliding my hands around the cold columns. "Finch." What can I say that they won't hear? It's impossible. But I risk it anyway. "If you mean it, then at least try to check on my bird."

Now he looks at me as if I'm speaking gibberish. "Bird?"

"Yeah, my bird. Dexter. Haven't seen him in months, and he better be still alive. If you can find Rika, she'll take you to him." I stare at his eyes. "Rika sometimes took care of him when I was off ship."

I need to get to Rika somehow. I need to know who I can count on.

His face is guarded. Or maybe just scared. "I'll see what I can do."

I reach through the bars and grab hold of him to make him listen. "Finch, don't believe a thing she says. Understand? Don't trust it, any of it." This isn't your world.

He locks his hands around my wrists as if to shove me off, but instead he just holds there.

I stare into his face. "Has she touched you?"

Now he wrenches away and steps back. "No. You think I'd let her?"

"I think you can't stop her." She's no bullying Army officer, for all of her faults. When it came to men she got what she wanted. And he's marked because of me. "What happened."

He doesn't answer.

I push against the bars but don't reach through them. "She wants to work you against me. She'll give you things and let you go so far, then she'll ask for a favor."

He wants to know how I know in such specifics, but I read it in his eyes—he answers that himself.

"She won't get anything from me," he says, a low voice. "The optics, Yuri."

I feel my jaw tighten. That sinks into the cold like a bare hook.

Hunger and fatigue, or maybe compassion, have made me stupid. If she wasn't sure why he was with me, she'll be positive now. But I had to warn him. I have to make him hide himself before she lulls him into a bit of safety. Even a bit. This ship isn't safe in any way.

"I'll be all right," he says, out loud maybe for his own benefit, not for mine.

Because I know better.

* * *

There's a fork with the food. It isn't as sharp as a knife, and they don't care that I have it because whenever they come back to get the tray they can just make me toss it out before even stepping close to the bars. Guards with guns who'd begrudge me a fork.

I use it. I think of all the things Taja might be doing to Finch, and like everything else he keeps most of it silent. Things that I did, because she's one of us, and although she wasn't a protégé, she still knows the common language. Exploitation for your own ends. Innocence, or ignorance, is a tool you can use.

I sit on the bunk with my back to the wall and dig the tines of that fork into my arm. This is all the tool I've got in this brig.

Blood.

And then I breathe.

* * *

She makes me sit another shift. It seems like a full additional shift by how hungry I get after that one meal, but I'm hungry all the time now, so maybe it's shorter than that.

Two guards I don't recognize come to get me, cuff my wrists behind my back, and yank me out. They take me up the lev to the command deck, and I'm so blind with hunger and the borderline state of permanent nausea that I don't notice anything except there are no crew here, maybe they've been told to stay inside quarters.

The guards dump me inside the captain's mess, which is laden on both sides of the main table with fruits and vegetables. They uncuff me and push me into the seat. Then they both leave though I'm sure at least one stays outside the hatch.

On the far side of the table Taja sits. No Finch. But I don't ask. I just stare at her, and we could be a married couple if she isn't wearing a gun somewhere below my line of sight, like I know she is.

"Feel free," she says, gesturing to the food.

"I'd rather talk."

She picks up a celery stick and bites the end. "So talk."

"If all you're doing is pampering my cellmate and asking him about prison, then I think you know more than you give off."

"Isn't that what you claim, Kirov?" Using my pirate name, of course. It's been so long since I've heard it said aloud, when dirtsiders, officials, all insisted I was that other person. The one who owned Terisov. But this name falls from her lips and settles on me like a familiar arm. "You claim," she says, "to know so much more to make my ship run better."

"And you would seem to agree since I'm still alive." Unless. "Have you talked to Caligtiera?"

I see in her face before she even answers. "Why? Do you want to? Maybe make a little alliance to get me out of the equation?"

"Well, Cal would never put up with your lack of take, would he. He likes his people productive." And you are below him, make no mistake, just like you were below Falcone.

She sees that in my face because I let her. "Obnoxious even in cuffs." She means figuratively, as she's got the guns.

"You mean I'm right. Let's cut this off, okay. I know—" I stare at her, the way she leans back in her seat, rocking slightly, eating vegetables with a certain smugness in her eyes. Of course she should be smug, she thinks she's holding all the cards—me under her whim. But it's not only that. The fact I'm even free doesn't surprise her in the least. The fact I was able to bring someone else out with me. Finch didn't tell her about Lukacs, or she'd be spitting fury at me for hooking up with Black Ops. Like all pirates would, or at the very least she'd call me an idiot.

So she doesn't know about Ops.

Or maybe she does. My encoded journals, last left in my private system, booby-trapped to delete on any detection of invasion—in the hands of Black Ops. And their fancy tech.

And how would they get it?

And how would they track this nanotag under my skin?

I was thinking of a traitor, standing in the snow and cold of Earth. I'm looking at her now. I recognize it. Of course I do.

And agents for Black Ops can double-deal in their sleep. Bring down the pirates? Maybe build a bridge instead. Maybe my cover isn't a cover at all.

"What do you know?" she says, with a mocking bite.

I don't move. "You're in bed with that Ops agent."

She sniffs. Doesn't even try to deny it. Why should she? I'm the one under her gun. "You know, Yuri, for someone whose job was to be in bed with any number of our clients . . ."

"Black Ops, Taja! Falcone—"

"Is dead." Her eyes flare.

"Just because he's dead doesn't mean he was stupid. He

warned us about them for a reason, and here you go giving them my fucking files!"

"Well you didn't need them in jail."

"What deal did you make?"

She smiles, false sweetness. "What deal did *you* make?"

"Like you don't know? What did he promise you if you let me back on the ship? To keep me in line or get rid of me once I served my purpose, so you can keep my captaincy?"

"The captaincy's mine to begin with."

"We can stop pissing in arcs, Taja. Lukacs wants me here because you're messing up the operation, none of the other captains like you very much, and I'm your way back inside. Admit it, I'm the only one who's got a chance with Cal, and Ops can give you a few perks if you cooperate. Because *my* ship's been failing under *your* command. Hasn't it."

"It didn't start with me," she says, leaning forward and pushing her forefinger onto the table veneer. "When you decided to take a vacation on Austro instead of taking out Azarcon's son, we were well on our way. I came in to clean up *your* mess, Kirov! And while we're at it, let's take note of the fact that you couldn't even do your job for Estienne."

I grab up the plate of food and throw it at her like a weapon, then rush around the table. But she's fast, knocks the plate away with a crash. She's on her feet and back toward the corner, her gun out and aimed.

"Back!" she yells.

The hatch opens. Her men are there.

"Sit your ass down!" she says.

I feel the snarl on my lips. I know she's not above shooting me in the leg or arm, so I ignore her goons and walk back to my side of the table. Not an immediate move as I slowly retake my seat and look at her. "You've been eyeing this ship since *Genghis Khan*."

She walks back slowly but doesn't sit, just leans her gun on the table and stares at me. And waits until the men leave. "If Ops offers a deal," she says, ignoring that, "and the only dark spot is getting your ass back here, then I'll take it, yeah. But don't think just because you're out of those cuffs that you got any freedom here. You breathe wrong, and I'll take it out on your little friend before I move on to you."

Of course this all works so well for Lukacs. I'm guessing his motivations, she's convinced she knows, and we're fighting among ourselves.

I don't say anything.

Her eyes hunt. "This is the way it's going to work. You make *nice* with Cal, you regain the trust of your contacts— any way you can. If they ask you to shoot Azarcon himself, you'll walk all the way to stritside and put a gun to his head. Once that's cemented you set Lukacs up with Cal, and whatever deal Black Ops makes with *our* network, *Kublai Khan* will get the lion's share." She picks up her glass and sips the concoction. Confident in her plan now that she's got me at gunpoint. "You know you don't want Cal running Falcone's operation and directing our allies. That'll leave no room for us except as his lapdogs. As far as I'm concerned, trading spit with Ops will give us an actual foothold in the government, and it'll be a lot less tenuous than shadow puppetry with the Family of Humanity or second-tier Centralist fanatics."

"You're a fool to trust Lukacs," I tell her, because that's what it comes down to, past the pretty ambitions.

"I don't trust him. Any more than I trust you. But Ops is none too pleased about the treaty, and if they want to encourage us to harass Azarcon and his allies, it's pretty much what we want to do anyway."

"What treaty? Azarcon's *exiled*, for all intents and purposes. There is no treaty that the Hub will recognize."

She smirks. And I could hit her for that face. "You've been too far insystem for far too long, Kirov. There's no *official* treaty. But we all know who's been supplying *Macedon* these past few months, and they aren't human. Now why don't you stop worrying and eat from the plate you haven't broken. You'll need it."

That's all I'm going to get out of her for now. For all I know she's bedded Lukacs already, in the literal sense, and thinks that makes her immune to his betrayal.

She's not geisha, and she never did get that part right.

* * *

At least she doesn't put me back in the brig. I get my own quarters. Not the captain's quarters, since she's in them, but quarters on the command crew deck with a guard outside my hatch who I don't recognize. How much of my crew did she put off, kill, or otherwise alienate in order to bring her own allies on board?

Something I can ask Rika if I ever see her again.

Taja is all smiles as she locks me up. "Get some rest. You'll want it next shift when you talk to Caligtiera."

"You're setting it up?"

She says, "He thinks I want to grovel, and he will probably think we're playing him, but he doesn't know my deal with Ops. And you're not going to tell him if you want your boy alive. So you'd best get your geisha skills together."

She shuts me in.

I go over those bare quarters millimeter by millimeter, looking for optics. I have nothing else to do. Surprisingly, I see none. It's possible she's adhered to that unspoken rule—

you'll never get loyalty from your crew if you spy on them unduly. Not even Falcone pushed that far with his people, at least not with optics. He tended to use the kind of optics that traveled on two legs, as they always saw and heard much more through interaction than pure observation.

So I'm not surprised when Finch shows up, carrying Dexter in his black cage. She lets us talk, then she'll talk to him, I can't stop it. Finch doesn't say anything as I take the cage from him. The little bird is losing feathers from the excitement of seeing me. The guard locks us in, and Finch stands out of the way as Dexter flutters, frantic. I immediately put the cage on the floor and crouch down to open the door.

"You're not going to let him out." Finch comes alive, unfolding his crossed arms.

"Of course I'm going to let him out, he's been in here for months I bet." I coo at the bird. His small eyes roll at me, and his screech echoes in the space. No curtains or soft cushions in here to dampen the sound. Lovebirds are loud.

"Shit," Finch says, putting a hand to his right ear.

"He doesn't like strangers." I cast him a look, then I open the cage. Dexter darts out and flies straight at Finch.

"Gah!" His hands go up.

"Don't hit him!"

Finch covers his head with his arms. I call at Dexter and after a bit of bullying he flies back and lands on top of the cage, fluffing his wings, then sticking his beak into them.

"That animal's mad!" Finch says, brushing bits of green feather from his shoulders.

"He's a bird." I turn my shoulder and stroke Dexter's soft, feathered head. He bites me gently on the fingertip. He remembers me. That small contact makes my eyes suddenly water. I keep my back to Finch. "Where've you been?"

"Is it safe to talk in here?"

"Maybe not."

I hear him walk over to the bunk and sit on it. "She's put me next door. And she invites me to meals and tries to get me to talk about you. About what it was like in the prison."

For smug, prurient reasons, maybe. Or maybe just as lead-up. She thinks she has all the time in the universe to slowly pull Finch in. I can't hear much from his voice, so I turn and look at him finally. Clear-eyed now. "And you tell her . . . what?"

He eyes Dexter on the cage then meets my stare. "That it was prison. Not a resort."

In this small quarters, it's almost the same. Behind me Dexter squawks for no apparent reason. Fatigue presses behind my eyes, and I move to the bunk and drop down. Finch gets up like I have some sort of disease, but it gives me more room to stretch out.

"You're going to sleep," he says.

"Unlike you, I haven't been given the five-star treatment." I can't look at him now, all the threat that he is for me without even trying. I've made him stand in that position like a mad general in a losing battle, and now both Lukacs and Taja don't need to point a gun at me. They just point it at him. And I can't think about it, or think about being here, or what I'll have to do tomorrow to make Caligtiera not shoot me. How well I'll have to lie. This ship is too familiar and my thoughts too muddled. I roll to my side, facing out, and stretch a hand to Dexter, who tilts his head at me. "Did you talk to Rika at all?"

He watches the bird, and me. "No, I haven't actually been able to move around without escort."

"If you can, try to get to her. She'll help us."

"With what?"

Now I look up at him as Dexter darts with his clipped

wings across the short distance from his cage to my finger. I bring him close, roll over to my back, and let him perch on my chest. He hops forward and pecks my lips with his little beak. Bird kisses. "To retake the ship, of course. You wouldn't happen to have any cigs on you?"

* * *

The next goldshift Taja and three guards escort me from my quarters, past Finch's silent one, and we take a shuttle across to Caligtiera's ship, *Iron Cross*. His is an Orca-class modified merchant—heavily modified, larger than *Kublai Khan* and outfitted like a battleship. No scan could mistake his silhouette for some war-era Rim hauler, and that probably suits him fine since he prefers to deal in the shadows. His ports aren't EarthHub-sanctioned, but pirate-maintained, deep-space sinkhole stopovers that are the nodes of the illegal network—where we refuel sometimes, store merchandise and maintain caches, execute repairs and just simply relax outside the purview of military interests.

The empire Falcone built.

Everyone wants control of it, so far nobody's been able to dethrone Cal, who worked as Falcone's second for most of Falcone's illegal career. All of our contacts respect Cal, know Cal, and would definitely go to Cal first over any other captain with something to prove—like Taja. I was an exception, handpicked by Falcone, proven to follow in his footsteps, and our allies knew that. But Cal knew the operation just as much as I did as the protégé, and he never wanted me to forget it.

His ship, his rules. His superiority, as I walk off the shuttle under Taja's guard. Of course the man himself isn't there to meet me, but there are a couple of brawnies with guns and a woman in a tight gray suit who says, "Sorry, Taja, just Yuri alone."

Taja says, "What?"

And now I smile.

The gray-skirted woman says, "You set this up, but the captain wants to speak to Yuri alone. Meaning, without you butting in."

I continue to grin.

Taja turns to me, takes my arm in a hard grip, and leans close to my ear. Whispers, "Don't fuck with me, Kirov, or I'll space your toy dog before you're even back on my ship. Got it?" Her fingers dig.

I let her threaten, wordless, ignoring. Which I know aggravates her even more. When she releases me I walk over to the unfamiliar woman. One of Cal's men frisks me thoroughly, comes up with nothing of course. The woman says to Taja, "Wait here with your shuttle."

And I don't need to see Taja's face to feel her expression. There is nothing more humbling in this business than the knowledge that you are not the one in control.

* * *

The woman doesn't tell me her name, just leads me through the ship, one of the men trailing us with a gun aimed at my back. *Iron Cross* is a dark ship, not just in lighting but in steel surfaces and ambient noise. Kept full of shadows, its crew has no time or inclination to slack or dull their senses. If you aren't always on the lookout here, chances are you won't survive. *Genghis Khan*'s crew deck had the same feeling; but here it's all over the ship as she takes me into a lev and up, then back out again on another deck that differs in no way I can discern from where we've been on flight. The

schematics of this ship are different from mine, but I think
we must be headed toward one of the conference rooms.
Trust Caligtiera not to wine and dine a guest.

And I'm right, as the hatch opens, and the woman steps
in after me. And there Cal sits at a long discussion table,
holding court in a room of one.

"Captain Kirov," the woman says, then leaves us.

The man hasn't aged. He doesn't seem to age, in all the
years I've known him. Maybe he's got a bit of voodoo hidden in his quarters, or maybe he's just that wily. Time itself
can't corner him.

"Yuri," he says, still sitting. I feel his eyes. "You look surprisingly—"

"Alive? Yeah, it shocks me too." I walk over to the seat
directly across from him, unclamp it, and drop down.
There's a glass of water on the table, so I pick it up and
drink. It soothes the rawness in my throat. "How've you
been?"

He doesn't answer that idle question. He just picks up as
if the length of time we've been apart in our separate deals
is only as long as this table. "So Taja actually managed to
spring you. I didn't think she had it in her."

"Me neither."

"Why would she do that? I thought she wanted you dead,
or at least out of the picture. Which you were on that for-
saken planet."

I smirk. "Clearly she wants me to get my ship back in the
game, since she's effectively dealt us out. Right?"

His smile stays longer than mine. "Right. But Taja's
known to have more pride than sense. And it must be a big
insult, not to mention a threat, to have you on board."

He won't let it go. "I don't think you really understand
how badly she's doing."

"Tell me." His face is as flat as his voice, but it doesn't fool me. Of course he's got his eye on my ship.

"Well, for one, the crew's divided."

"You've talked to your crew already?"

"I talked to Rika." So far I haven't had to lie much. Truth is always easier to deliver. "And you know the geisha . . ."

They often have sway on a ship, ambassadors and assassins for their captain, and generally respected by the crew. It's the only reason Rika's still on board. If Taja got rid of her and the rest of the Hanamachi, it would cause more problems than it would solve.

Cal's never had a Hanamachi. His smile is wry now. "So Roshan hasn't got the balls to vent your whores, eh?"

I know better than to take that bait. "Which is why she's losing my ship and a good deal of cred that could, possibly, go partly to you." If she had sense to swallow her pride and make a solid alliance.

"I don't need a captain like her." A statement that provides an opening.

"But you could use one like me."

He shrugs. "And here you are with an offer, hm? She was rather eager to set this up."

"I'm here for me, not for her."

"I'll believe that when you can board my ship without a guard of your own crew."

It's a mild insult, but accurate. I lean back and tap the table twice with a finger. "That's just a matter of time. In the meanwhile I don't want to waste yours. I do have a proposal."

"I thought you might."

"Just because Azarcon's gone stritside doesn't mean we're in the clear, does it? If anything the carriers're more pervasive because the strits've stopped attacking altogether.

As long as the Hub doesn't cross the DMZ. That's what the Send says."

He just looks at me because he knows this.

"So right now we've got a whole lot of product and not a lot of opportunity to move it."

He doesn't say anything.

"What about our contacts in the Family of Humanity?"

"They're lying low," he says finally, swinging his seat gently from side to side, hands laced on his stomach. "That Azarcon kid and his big mouth with the meedees"—his eyes pin me, because the kid is my fault—"has got the govies like Ashrafi looking hard and fast at the Centries and their playmates."

"So," I tell him, "really the only way to get inside the Hub is to get ourselves on their side. And right now, for all Falcone's military and senatorial buddies, we're more outside than before. With him dead."

"I'm waiting for this proposal."

I go in for the kill. "You have a hold on the pirates, on this network. So far. I can give you the Hub."

Now he laughs. It even sounds genuine. "Kirov, you really are an arrogant son of a bitch."

"Who has the power there to change politics in our favor? Not Damiani and her wheezing breed. Not with Azarcon and his admiral papa focused on where she beds her ass. There's still an organization on that side that not even Azarcon can penetrate. Because they hate the strits as much as we do. They don't trust those damn aliens. They haven't been fighting them for decades only to have one rogue captain with high ideals and a bleeding heart come roaring in to upset the status quo. And threaten the borders of humanity."

Caligtiera stares at me.

"Taja didn't spring me," I tell him.

"Clearly," he says. "I ought to shoot you where you sit."

"It's a different galaxy now, Cal. You know it. Everything changed when Falcone died on that dock. A lot of his old rules don't apply anymore."

"What did they tell you? What lies?"

I shrug. "Maybe a lot. But we won't know that until we run the prog. Personally, I think they're sincere." About which part, my deal or Taja's, that's a guess. But to Cal: "I met the bloke. And he's a bastard."

"That's no qualification for alliance, even among our kind. For all I know you're here on his orders because he wants to bring us down. Get you inside, steal our codes, our sinkholes, our allies? Expose it all?"

He's got a gun in his hand, under the table, and he won't have to raise it to my face to kill me. He's got accurate aim, even blind.

"Cal." I lean my elbows on the table. "You may have most of the pirates in your corner now, but you know as well as I do that it's tenuous. With the deep-space carriers hopped up on Azarcon zeal, and pirates being what they are—we're hunted constantly, and in the midst of it everyone wants your job, everyone thinks they can do what Falcone did. So they'll kill you to get it, or everything will fragment and we'll be nothing but a pack of hyenas fighting over Earth-Hub's carrion. And how long do you think we'll last in that environment? Wolves like Taja are just lining up to remove our asses. A solid alliance with a force like Black Ops will make the pack think twice. Because Ops won't deal with anyone but you or me. They know damn well who the smartest ones are in this operation, who Falcone trusted the most. And they can get to our govie allies a lot quicker than we can, with a louder voice."

Laid out like that, even I'm convinced.

"And what's in it for them?" he asks, to the point.

"A fleet of ships on the front line that won't put up with Azarcon's shit. Someone to do the dirty work for them when the Council or Hub Command squint too close at their corners. My contact would be able to explain it better to you, if you were to meet him."

"So they got you out of prison because you're Falcone's geisha with all the pretty words. Is that it?" His stare is hard.

"They got me out of prison because next to you I'm the one with the most influence in the network. And you know it; that's why you don't like me. Aside from the fact I'm less than half your age and better-looking to boot."

"You're a bitch of the first degree, Kirov."

"But I'm picky about who I bed. Geisha don't spread for nothing, and you know it. Now are we going to dance or just get to the good part?"

It pulls a smile out of him, but one with definite angles. He leans forward and removes his crumpled, half-empty cigret pack from his shirt pocket, tapping out a brown stick, then tossing the pack on the table. He snaps his fingerband lighter on the end, and a stinky volcanic smell wafts into the air. "I forgot what it's like to spar with you, Yuri," he says. Which I bet isn't true. He takes a deep drag and blows smoke in my direction. "So get your captaincy back without dying, and maybe we'll talk again."

⋆

Taja tries to grill me on the ride back to the *Khan*, but I don't tell her anything. Not until she threatens to space me, then it's almost funny. I look at her as the shuttle docks back in the bay, grappled and secured.

"Go ahead and space me, and Cal will come for you next.

You want to know what he said? You let me go free on my own ship."

"That's not going to happen, Kirov. Since it's my ship."

I stand, ignoring her guards hovering like angels, and face her when she rises to meet my gaze. "He's not going to talk to you, Taja. I may be geisha, but you were nothing but Falcone's whore. Don't think just because you sit in that captain's chair that it earns you respect."

She tries to deck me, but I grab her wrist, then the guards grab me back by both arms and she hits me then, across the face with her fist. I tongue the bleeding inside of my mouth and just smile.

"You were the biggest whore on that ship," she snarls. "And worse still, you actually loved it. Geisha?" Her teeth show. "Not even Estienne bought that line as big as you. You thought it all pretty, and he knew it was just a façade. Wake up, Yuri."

"Oh I'm awake. Keep saying his name, Taja."

"Words. Geisha words."

"Cal listened to them well enough." To bring it back to the point. When I want to kill her. "When are you going to realize that they played you? They told you what you wanted to hear so you'd get me back here, then get me to talk to Cal. There's no deal for you, only *me*. And if you want to stay alive, you better listen to me. Cal will take this ship unless you let me go."

Her head tilts, like her frown. "I can't do that. But I can let your bedbug go."

"Under guard, I bet."

"Just to make sure he doesn't sabotage my engineering deck. And you can still have shagging privileges." She grins like a death's-head. "Although I might take a sample or two myself."

I don't need to address that. "And I want Piotr to scan my quarters for optics. Thoroughly."

Her smirk disappears.

"Or," I tell her, with my face smarting, my gaze pinned to her face, "you can turn this shuttle around and go offer your services to Cal. On your knees."

That would earn me a shot in the head at any other time. But she knows I'm right. She knows she lost as soon as her ass got ordered to stay behind with the shuttle, but she still won't let go that easily. So we drag it out. And I rub it in.

"Piotr," she says. "Fine." Then she says to her men, "Take him back to his q."

And they do, rough. But I don't feel it. Only my smile.

* * *

Five minutes inside, then Finch comes in, allowed by the guard. I'm sitting on the floor poking my finger at Dexter in the cage, who tries to bite it off. The hatch slams in, Dexter screeches, and Finch rubs his ear, looking surprised that I'm still alive. I open the cage so my pet can fly out. Finch moves away and says, "What happened?"

"We talked." And now I have to plan.

Soon enough Piotr comes in, holding a thin black case, singing like he often does. "Yuri!" he says, breaking off to engulf me in a large hug. He's shorter than me but built twice as wide, solid muscle, and he picks me up off my feet.

"Ah, put me down!"

"I will. But you're back! The nasty rumors are true." He sets me abruptly on the deck. "Pity. Now you will come to my Engineering and order me around again, no?"

"My ship. My Engineering." It's a familiar debate, and he shoves me in the chest until I fall back on the bunk.

"You bother me still, runt. Now what is it you want me to do?" He looks at Finch but knows better than to ask. "Hopefully not him."

"Scan, didn't she tell you? I want some privacy."

"Eh, no doubt." He grins at Finch. Hawk-nosed and strong-jawed, Piotr isn't pretty, but his smile makes up for it. He smiles a lot, and sings while he works as if all the ship were an opera stage. He knows he lives on a pirate, but it doesn't seem to bother him. Maybe because he serves the captain before the work, and he's always liked me.

Finch folds his arms like he's trying not to punch somebody for that innuendo. Probably me. Dexter knows Piotr and caws at him.

Piotr says, "Still with that bird, eh." And for a second he looks at me seriously.

"He gave me this ship," I answer. And I intend to get it back.

"You earned it," Piotr says, then sets his case on the cage and flips it open. Inside are his toys, and he takes out the detector and pokes at it before slowly walking around the quarters, aiming it at every available surface and into the air vents. Finch and I avoid him until he's finished. "Nothing," he says. Then eyes Finch.

Two-legged optics. You don't need a scan for those.

"He's clean." On my side. If only out of necessity, like it's been since day one. "Thanks, Piotr. Now I'm going to need your help."

He nods. "She rotated half the crew and dumped them on other ships. Meyers, Law, Christensen, Dacascos . . ."

My department heads for medical, armory, environmental, and conn.

"But not you."

Piotr grins. "Nobody can keep this ship running but me. But she did ditch half my staff."

"Rika's still here. And Ville."

"Taja'd get nowhere without a Hanamachi, and she knows it."

They hold sway over most of my contacts. The way I intended it, if I wasn't around.

"Then get a message to Rika. I want Taja dead by next shift."

Finch's arms drop to his sides. But his silence persists, smartly.

Piotr says, "Done. But the crew she hired after you were gone will fight."

"Then we're going to need guns. I'll send Finch to the library, have—Angela, is she still around?—have her meet him. He was a lifesystems mechanic, so he can help with the environmental controls. I want a battle strategy done up in two hours, where we can cordon all her goons and get the bridge with a minimum amount of damage to the ship."

"She's going to expect it."

I nod. "Yeah, she will. But she's got no choice. Cal won't deal with her, and she's greedy for some action. She won't try to kill me because she needs me, but she'll clean house in lieu of that."

Piotr shrugs. "We know this. We are not a cruise line. Just tell us where to be."

I can't buy loyalty like that. But when they're willing to die for me, and maybe I wouldn't for them, it's a bittersweet taste.

*　*　*

For long minutes Finch doesn't say a word, sitting on the edge of the bunk with his arms folded against his chest as if he's cold. I sit on the deck playing with Dexter, letting him grab my sleeve and wrangle it with his sharp, tiny beak.

"You're going to kill her," Finch says finally.

I keep my eyes on Dexter's bright green feathers. "I have no choice." And even though he doesn't open his mouth yet, I preempt him. "No different from the man you killed."

"That was self-defense."

"So's this. I leave her alive and she'll always be after me."

He pulls up his feet then, cross-legged, and just stares at me.

"You disapprove?" I glance at him. *You're naïve if you disapprove.*

He doesn't argue with me. "What do they want you to do?" *Black Ops.* "Specifically, what are you doing?"

A reasonable question, delivered in a reasonable tone. He's not going to spin on me.

I concentrate on the little bird. "It might be best if you didn't know."

"It might be best if I'm not in the dark." *Calm voice.*

But *you know too much already,* I could say. About me. The way I feel him watching me. The way he must have watched me when I was asleep and talking.

But this. I don't need to tell him. This is business he doesn't need to know. "Just follow my orders."

"I'm not your crew."

"You're on my ship, you're my crew."

"I'm not your crew, Yuri."

I look up. *I'm not a pirate,* his face says. His face says he's an exception to the rules in my life, sparse as they are, and maybe he's right. I've given him every indication that I'll separate myself for him.

But not in this. I can't be thinking of him when I have to kill Taja. I feel dirty enough.

Somehow he reads that. "You tried to leave before."

This. Piracy. Maybe him. Maybe he means all of it. I don't answer.

"Yuri, why did you never leave before? Before all of this happened."

That ignites me, his curiosity where he has no business being curious. Because we shared a cell? Because I might feel bad for screwing him, and he thinks that makes me saintly? "Finch, don't mistake what this is."

"What what is?"

I make sure to look him in the eyes. "The fact you're here and I haven't killed you yet."

"Yet?"

I cup my hands around Dexter, lean, and slip him back into his cage. Shut the door and watch him flutter. He's safe in there. People think birds always want to fly. But Dexter goes into his cage when he's stressed, when he wants to feel secure. Too much space is freedom for anything to grab you.

"Yet?" Finch says again, a little sharper.

"You wouldn't be so calm if you knew how many people I've killed."

A beat. Then, "I know."

I stand and look down at him. Cramped quarters. "You know what exactly?"

His hands tighten on each other, slow whiteness. He doesn't blink, but it's out of caution, not defiance. "I know you weren't born into this. I know this ship—or the ship you grew up on—I know it hurt you."

The air seems too still, despite the whine of the vents.

"I know," he says, almost stumbling on himself as he stares at my face, "I know why you started to cut." A beat.

"Bo-Sheng." And now his eyes drop to my arms. But not in judgment, and that feels worse.

"You don't know shit." How can one look make me this angry. "You don't know shit!"

He gets to his feet.

"Leave," I tell him.

But he doesn't move.

"Get out!"

Dexter screeches. Finch raises a hand to his head as if to block it out, but his feet stay locked to the deck.

Then, insanely, he says, "I'm sorry."

Aggravation. I go to the hatch. Of course I can't leave. "What the hell for?"

Now he sounds desperate as if he wants me to understand something. "For asking you. In the prison. I never should've asked you because the things you said after—"

"I never said anything after."

"—in your *sleep*. When you walked. The things you said that had happened to you—"

I move away from the hatch, keep my back to the wall. "Get out, Finch. Go meet Angela in the library, make yourself useful."

"I didn't know. I didn't know about Estienne, or Bo-Sheng, or what they trained you to do as a geisha—"

These names and words he says, as if he knows them. My blood feels white with rage. Or retreat.

"And now you're back in this life," he says, "and what it'll do to you—"

I shout into his face, "I never left it!"

Except the fact he's standing here says different in some unexpected way.

He takes a step as if he wants to come closer.

"Finch, I'm getting rid of people in a shift. You don't want to fuck with me."

And why does that sound more like a defense instead of a threat. I mean it as a threat.

He doesn't hear it that way. He never seems to hear the way I say things, only what's in my head. Because of that prison where we had nowhere to run, no corners or shelters, no barriers except our own words. And mine ran ahead of me like unsupervised children. These children that aren't children at all; my sleeping words are old and clotted. That was what he heard, and now he's here because I let him make me weak. But that won't work on this ship. I have my plans, and now he's screwing them up in my head because he keeps walking closer and these quarters are small.

"You only think you know me." The words stop him, or maybe it's my tone.

"I think I know . . ." His voice trails, but not out of uncertainty. His eyes search for the right words. They search me and only need to go so far. "You run a lot into yourself."

This is how I'm bruised. My voice sounds level, but it feels torn in my throat. "I got you out, but I'll kill you anyway, Finch. At some point I'll kill you."

"Like you're going to kill Taja."

"No." He's only a meter away, and now my arms start to fold before I stop myself and force them to stay loose at my sides. "No, I'll kill you slower, and you'll believe it's because I care."

The curiosity again. "Don't you?"

"Not as much as you seem to think."

"Don't you."

There isn't another answer to give. Any questions he might ask now are only because he wants me to ask them too.

Except I don't want the answers in my mind, much less said aloud.

I won't stand with my back to the wall as if I'm cornered. I move to get by him, to the hatch, to bang on it and get outside in the corridor even if it means getting in an argument with the guard.

But as soon as our arms brush he turns, and his arms are around me. Not a straight-on embrace, he just catches me at what angle I'm at in passing and it's both his arms around my body, pulling me in.

I will push him away, but then he says, "Don't go back to it."

I'm leaden, standing there. I'm leaden and lost.

I struggle from his hold, but in a snap he encircles me again, and for a second I think, No use. No use. And it's strange to be held when you don't want it. You don't want it just because it feels so good. His body is warm and surrounding but not for geisha trade, not for prison protection, it's just his arms, and they seem to crumble me in their grip.

"Stop." I push at him.

Not hard enough. I think he's scared, and maybe he's not holding me so I can feel it, but for himself. He should be scared, he should remember why he avoided me before, when I taunted him. I can't have his fear on me, polluting me against what I need to do. This ship will pollute him, but he's muddying my thoughts.

I shove harder and cuff him across the head. "Stop it!"

He backs up, fast. I'm out of breath as if he had me running.

He leaves without a look, and the hatch slams in.

And I flinch.

He makes me pace. Before a major action, when I need to retake my ship, and he makes me pace. I try to sit on the bunk, but he was sitting on it, so I'm up again, and there's nothing in my quarters to cut with. There's nothing sharp here except my memory. My own fingers are too blunt, and what the hell is going on now?

I pace and claw at my arms.

What the hell is going on now.

*　*　*

Dexter is quiet, and I'm on the bunk, on my back, arm over my face. Listening for activity, some indication that I've won. That this thing could get going again—my ship, this plan, my life. Help Lukacs, whatever his agenda, but stay ahead of the game. It isn't an old notion, it's inbred at this point.

The hatch rattles briefly, then yawns open. I lean up on my hand—Taja? Come in to threaten me?

But it's Finch again, holding bird food in a clear plastic bag. He glances behind him as the hatch shuts and holds out the bag to me.

"Rika sent this. Taja won't let her in."

"Did she say anything to you?" I slide up and take the bag, open it. Dexter hops and screams at me, recognizing a meal.

"Rika or Taja?" He sounds surprisingly normal considering the shit he pulled.

"Both." I stick my hand in the bag, feeling the colorful pellets roll between my fingers.

"Rika just gave me the food." Not mentioning Taja.

I look up. His face, forced impassivity. But his collar's a bit torn, and my hand shoots out, grabs it and pulls it aside so I can see the red marks on the side of his neck. Fingers and teeth.

He shoves my hand away.

"The hell, Finch?" I forget the bag, look at the hatch.

"Forget it, Yuri." He steps into my sight line. "Look, she can have her thrills, and I'm not *telling* her anything."

But my thought wasn't on information. Faced with it in bruises I thought only of what's mine. What Taja has no right to touch. This instinctual leap that's got me into trouble since prison.

"I can handle it," he says, and I look at him. He has a geisha face, the kind of features that would show stark under paint. I can almost see my color on his skin. I don't know what he sees, but he stares kind of concerned. "What?"

This heaviness in my chest. It's not even what I touch; everything I look at is somehow tainted by my eyes. But I still look at him and how he's handling it. Giving in because there's no way out. This is how it starts.

"Rika didn't give me anything but this food." He gestures to it to draw my attention.

So I look down. It frees him to break expression if he wants. "Not just the food." I feel around some more and pull out a tightly wrapped scroll of paper, bound by an elastic, and a small card of cigrets. My spacer brand. Rika, you beautiful bitch. "Here, drop some of this in his feed cone." I hand the bag to Finch.

He takes it but stares at the paper in my hand.

Rare paper. But Rika's a geisha and likes fine things. I slip the elastic around my wrist and read her calligraphic handwriting.

*Talked to Chris. He passed private messages to the ones
I know are on our side. Piotr'll block off Engineering with
his people down below. Angela'll take your boy and a team
to the biosystems for the sabotage. Ville's got the Hanamachi on command crew deck, flight, and the armory—
our bedbugs will help—and Buckell, Chance, and Rickert
are going to move on the bridge. Chris is there too. Will
pump smoke through the environmental controls, seal off
forward deck sections C to F, knock them all on their asses,
sort them later. Bridge needs to be barricaded and Taja
taken down. Then the rest won't put up a fight. Fence-
sitters will capitulate.* Then she added, *Brig's going to be
crowded.*

But only by the fence-sitters. The ones around Taja as her
personal squad will be vented. Anyone who puts up too
much of a fight will be killed. But Rika knows that. And my
saliva tastes sour at the thought.

These quarters seem too small. Worse when I read the
smaller print beneath the brief. *Where do you want your boy
after?*

I look across at him. He's on the deck poking his finger
at Dexter, trying to get him to bite it. Not afraid anymore,
but then it's just a bird, and they're both inside something
larger. Maybe he feels my silence. He looks over his shoulder at me.

"After you help Angela I want you to go to your quarters," I tell him. "And stay there."

He doesn't say anything, but it's plain in his eyes. No. He
doesn't want to hide, he wants to help, like he thinks he's
helping by bedding Taja or whatever it is she's got him

doing, and the thought of it scrapes me again. I should be yelling at her, but I yell at him.

"I said you'll go to your quarters and not move your ass!" Now, until you're needed. After, or you'll regret it.

He doesn't attempt to convince me otherwise. But when he leaves I have nothing but the echo of my anger.

* _* *

I let Dexter out of his cage so he can hop or flit around, then I lie on the bunk again with a lit cigret and look at the ceiling. Waiting. Smoking to calm myself, to distract myself, but it doesn't really work because I listen too closely to the environment. Finch doesn't come back even though he's stubborn and he can. And that's for the best. It'd be best if he wasn't on the ship at all. But everything's gone too far for that.

Taja knew from the moment I set foot again on this deck that it was going to come to this, but maybe, despite the Ops deal, she knew already that she had to show her hand in a big way. To the *Khan*, to the rest of the pirates. She needs to have it out with me—instead of winning the ship by default—or she's never going to get anywhere in the organization or with our clients. And certainly not with Caligtiera.

No captain retires on a pirate ship. There's only one way you lose your seat. And if you want to be a pirate captain, and you serve aboard a ship already, there's only one way you can get it. Unless you're a protégé.

Caligtiera is a patient man, and he had genuine respect for Falcone. But like any snake in the grass, he waited to strike. His ship has no Hanamachi. That's one part of Falcone's vision that he never did agree with and will never perpetuate. For whatever reason.

Protégés perpetuate protégés, that's the theory, but I was the first to get my own ship. No other ship turned out a geisha protégé. That was Falcone's gift, and his failure.

Except now.

I'm still alive, and there will be more deaths. I smoke to settle nerves and cloud my sight. I smoke and blow the tendrils to the lights. The lines perform ballet in the air with an accompaniment of distant violence. When the shots grow closer outside my hatch Dexter launches himself across the quarters in a flurry of bright green, a dart of color in the gray.

* * *

Eventually the hatch opens again, bringing in a strong acidic wave. When I smelled that from the air vents I knew things were well under way. Now Rika stands here with a rifle slung on her shoulder and blood smudges on her cheek. The guard's dead at her feet. She tosses me an LP-150.

"Bridge?" I check the ammo read on the side of the weapon's pulse pack. Still well over 70 percent.

"Waiting for you, Captain." She grins.

"Taja?"

"Also waiting. With your boy."

"What? I told him to go back to quarters!"

Rika frowns. "He didn't tell me."

This isn't prison. He better learn it.

I lock Dexter back in his cage. He screams at the commotion, the smell, and the sound of the hatch shutting behind me.

* * *

Bodies guide my path all the way to the command deck and the bridge. Some of them I recognize, most of them I don't. Cleanup's going to be tedious, and there's nothing to do but shut down a good part of your brain and your senses. Push them to the shadows so your world is just white.

"How much did we lose?" I ask Rika, as she walks along beside me, her wrist casually resting along the muzzle of her weapon.

"From reports?" She wears a pickup in her ear, hands me one so I can link to the comm chatter. "Forty percent of the crew, maybe. Maybe more. Ville and his team's got the brig covered."

"We're running almost skeletal."

"We have bridge and Engineering."

And that's what counts. The hatch stands open. I step in, see three of the six bridge personnel facedown on the deck. One of them with her hands behind her head: Taja. The three replacements for my bridge, plus Chris, stand off to the side with guns trained, and amid them is Finch. Someone gave him a gun at least.

No time for questions. He disobeyed me. He looks at me, and he feels it. He's going to feel it.

I push my slung rifle to my back and walk up to him. His eyes narrow. Maybe he thinks I'm going to hit him, but I take the gun from his hand, check it. He put it on safety, and I thumb it back to kill.

"Kirov," Taja says. "Listen to me." Her voice muffled in the deck.

"Shut up," I tell her. "Dead woman."

Faced with it in an enclosed space, I see him pull in a rough breath. But he just gets a mouthful of dissipating smoke. The vents are shut, but it still creeps in. His eyes say, Don't. But not for her sake or mine, for yours.

Maybe if my crew weren't standing around. Maybe if I didn't have this deal with Lukacs and Caligtiera waiting off my starboard side. Maybe if I wasn't bred for it. Blooded for it.

Maybe if she'd kept her hands off him. Maybe if he'd just stayed in q like he was supposed to he'd never have to see me quite like this.

"You don't have to," he says. Wrongly.

I feel my crew shift. I feel Rika tilt her rifle, just a bit.

"You have your ship," Taja says. Keeps saying. She knows the routine, but like any of us, maybe, her convictions don't stick this close to death. "Yuri, you have the *Khan*!"

"I know," I tell her, and look away from Finch. I aim the gun and shoot.

"No!" Finch says, a beat too late.

Rika says, "Finally."

*　*　*

Rika takes Finch back to my quarters. The captain's. I go to the comm station and tell it Caligtiera's private link, but not for an open call. I want to leave him to think and contact *me*. With my rifle scope I freeze a shot of Taja on the deck and transload it straight into the message to him. With two words:

Your move.

*　*　*

I'm alone on the bridge with the rifle in my lap, in the captain's seat, watching the console waver in standby, helio images morphing and twisting in the air just above the hard-plate. I can lean over and finger a coil or a command nebula and the ship will power up or fire its cannons and I can go anywhere with it. I can take it to Lukacs and blow him to the strits. Or I can deal him to Cal, and together we figure out this operation once and for all. It sounds so plausible in my mind, but I know better. Reality is never that rosy.

We're motionless in space, anchored to the stars, and Taja sprawls dead behind me on the deck.

The bridge hatch beeps and opens, and I swivel the chair to look. Rika. She steps in and around the body, then drops down in the conn seat in front of me. She's ditched her rifle, and now all she's got is a sidearm, which she places on the console beside her elbow.

"Yuri," she says, "what are you doing with that boy?"

"What are you talking about?"

"That Finch."

"I'm doing nothing with him. In any sense, in case you wanted to know that too." Warning. I look at her.

She leans forward on her knees. Her cheek still has blood on it, like geisha paint. But flakier. Darker. She says as if I don't know it already, "You can't let him question you like that in front of the crew. For your sake and for his." She plows ahead. "He's weak. Any idiot can see she had to be shot."

Because this ship is a pirate.

"He won't do it again. I made my point. He saw it."

I saw it. I'm still seeing it.

"You made your point because he's in love with you, and you want to hurt him," she says.

I stare. "What have you been drinking?"

She answers like she didn't hear me. "Because you're in love with him but he's your protégé. That's not how it works, Yuri."

"I'm not in love with him and he sure as hell isn't my protégé."

"It'd be good if he was, so people know you're on board for it. You never showed interest in getting one."

I have no answer for that. Because it's true and I'm tired and there's a body that's my fault lying bleeding on my bridge.

No I don't want a protégé.

Her eyes say I better want one. The right one. "You're going to severely mess things up if you take him on and you can't separate. I don't know what went on with you on Earth—or Austro for that matter—but it'd be best if you dump him on Hades right now."

I still don't say anything. I just look at her.

She says, "You know I'm right."

"I know that just because you're the Elder Sister of my Hanamachi, you can't assume you can talk to me this way. Especially with wild ridiculous theories. You think I don't know what I'm doing with him? You want this fucking seat?"

"No," she says. "I don't want the seat. But I just helped you get it."

We stare at each other. This captaincy comes with conditions. Of course it does.

How did I forget?

She picks up her gun again. "I'll stay on bridge and get someone to remove the body. You better go . . . do what you have to do."

"Is the ship secure?" I ask dully.

She says, "It's secure." Without the "sir."

So I get up from the chair and leave it behind.

* * *

Rika put a guard outside the captain's quarters where I told her to hold Finch. I'm almost at the hatch when the intercom sounds overhead.

"Captain Kirov, comm one." Rika's voice.

Caligtiera. So I bypass the guard without a glance and go to the library, which is just down a deck, where I'll have comm access.

The room is dark and empty of life. Knowledge here is clogged inside comps and probably not accessed much since I left. I doubt Taja encouraged my crew—or hers—to read, explore, or experiment. I used to. The information might be screened, but a crew ignorant of basic slate-learning can't serve you well. Difference in my captaincy and Taja's. Stop thinking of Taja. When I sit at one of the center consoles I can feel the cold coming off the black equipment, the table, the chair. There's a fine layer of dust on the smooth surfaces.

It's habit to let my expression fall to blankness as I comm Rika to link us. Cal's face appears on the display, bland and lined. He says, "Are you up and running?"

"Yeah. To get from A to B and even fire a few shots."

"Comm your contact and get him out here. Not to Hades. We'll meet at Ghenseti. I'll let you know where specifically on station—later. But first I want you to come aboard."

I tell him, "No. Whatever you want to say to me, you say it now."

"What I want to say won't go over comm. Come aboard, or the deal's off."

He shuts down.

So now he's testing me. Maybe his interest in Lukacs is a lie, and all he wants is to get me back on the *Cross* so he can kill me and take my ship, too easy in its half-staffed stage.

But you don't figure a man like Caligtiera by keeping a distance. And this time I'll go to him armed.

* * *

Rika accompanies me, and two men I vaguely recognize that she assures me are good. The same woman in the gray suit escorts all four of us to the conference room, with three of her own guards. I tell Rika to wait outside with the guards, which she isn't happy about. But she doesn't argue in front of them. Me and the woman go into the room where Caligtiera waits, sitting with a slate in front of him. The woman sits on his right side and I mirror them on the opposite end of the table.

"Did you comm your Ops contact?" he says.

"I want to know what you have to say to me first that can't be said over a secure comm."

"Well for some things I need to see the face up close." He slides the slate across the table, and I stop it with a slap of my hand before it goes off the edge.

Clearly he wants me to read it, so I do.

They're schematics of the EarthHub carrier *Archangel*. With patrol schedules. Deep-space carriers have six to eight thousand crew.

I look at him. And he's actually sort of smiling as he smokes his toxic brown cigret. He says, "This will send a message to the Hub. And Ops. If they even think to fuck with us."

It'll send a message to the other pirates too.

Macedon's sister ship.

And sitting here my gut tightens and begins to twist. I force myself not to swallow, show anything except that dead gaze Falcone used to say made me look like I was one step from committing an atrocity.

And look, here I am.

I set the slate back on the table. "When?"

"Haven't figured that out yet." He might be lying. I almost bet he is. "But since you went to all that trouble to retake your ship, I expect you to be my bloodmate in this, and if this flies, then I think we'll do all right with Ops."

I nod. "Why're you risking it to tell me?"

"I honestly didn't think you had the balls anymore to do Taja," he says. If he could see my hand beneath this table. My nails dig into my palm. "Since you managed not to do Azarcon's kid. But this has restored my faith in you. And from now until this deal goes down with Ops, you're not leaving my portside space. Understood?"

"Yeah." Of course.

I may have my own ship, but I still don't have my freedom.

$$* \; * \; *$$

On the flight back to the *Khan*, Rika asks what happened so I tell her the bare minimum. Kill *Archangel*. She grins. "Cal has balls, man. You think he can do it?"

"Yeah." I pretend to check my sidearm. But I'm not seeing the gun.

"Take down a carrier." She is impressed. "Especially that one." There's no talking to her about the black dosage in my veins from this, she's still a junkie wanting a fix, and I'm still feeling withdrawal pains. "Only Falcone did that," she says.

"Falcone knew carriers." State the obvious.

"Cal must have someone inside." She admires him. "To get those schems."

But of course he would. Everyone's dirty.

✦ ✦ ✦

Finch is still in my quarters. He sits in front of the cage watching Dexter but gets to his feet when I step inside. I dismiss the guard and shut the hatch. Maybe I should dismiss him too. The cold I felt from the docking bay to these quarters doesn't seem to dissipate. It just settles in my chest and in the room like a broad net, pulling us down.

He doesn't say anything. And it's all right because now I have to speak. Now I feel sick. Nobody else will listen, and if I keep it in my head, it's going to mangle me in some way, or infect me until I have no choice but to give in.

We stand apart, and I tell him, "They plan on blowing up *Archangel*."

A flicker in his gaze. "Is that a ship?"

My quarters. Its forest green walls in some vague semblance of nature, the polar opposite of this ship's angled gray interior. The bed's unmade. Taja's sheets. But I sit on it anyway to alleviate the growing nausea.

"A carrier," I tell him. "*Macedon*'s sister ship. You know *Macedon*?"

He nods. Who doesn't know *Macedon*.

"They're going to blow it up. *Archangel*. Six thousand souls."

Not so long ago they would've been six thousand enemy. But somewhere along the line I lost the flavor of the word.

"Can't you tell them? Comm them?"

I rub a hand through my hair and pull at the roots a little. "No . . . no, I don't know their link code, they change them every week, and even if I did, if they're warned, he'll know who did it and kill us instead."

Finch moves over to me, leaning back on his heels on the floor beside where I sit. Just watches me, thinking of Taja. I can see him thinking it because it's there on the surface of his eyes.

"I had to do it." Like I have to explain myself to him for some reason. As if I hadn't yelled and hit him just a few hours ago. But one death against thousands can bring argument to a halt.

"What about this carrier?" he says.

This is different. The other wasn't completely right, and this would be completely wrong. I try not to make it form too solid in my head though.

"I tried to leave before," I tell him. "It didn't work. You don't just walk away." Maybe I'll have to go through with this. And it's making me sick.

"So," he says, still mild, still watching. "You just keep going? 'Til someone kills you or you kill yourself?"

But that's the pattern of this life.

Hands on opposite arms. I dig.

"Yuri."

"I've done worse." What do you call pulling children into this? Recruiting from a station and sinking them to a planet to rot until some dark ship takes them up and drowns them in its blood.

"So you'll do it again?" Not so much judgment in his tone as a complete confusion. Maybe my mind really is this alien to him.

My words feel like another language. "Which is worse, killing a child or killing a ship? What is it, just numbers?"

"They're equally wrong."

"But say that's your only choice."

He's silent for a long minute, and I don't interrupt it. "Then whatever makes it your only choice is wrong. And the choice itself is a child of that wrong." He answers it, but he's questioning me. Why are you asking these things?

"Then what does that do, absolve you when you actually do choose one or the other? When you're forced to?" Was I forced? Maybe not. Like I'm not in this. Maybe if it means your life or taking lives, you're expected to self-sacrifice.

He rests his hand on the mattress. "People do shit for complicated reasons. Absolution isn't something we get for ourselves. It's given."

I look him in the eyes. "But maybe it's all a lie. Who gives it, anyway. Who is so fucking pure that they can give absolution? The law? The government? Religion?" Distant concepts, like the stars, and when you're just a kid you look to more immediate influences. Estienne, telling me it was all right that he did things with me because my mouth said I wanted it but my mind was in the palm of his hand. So people like me take the children because nobody's truly innocent, everybody's the same. Everybody has to be the same or how can people pick and choose what they care about. Maybe kids are only important when they're yours; otherwise, people don't make the effort. At least not the right people. I can taste my own bitterness, years removed from that bloody Camp. I'm not even so involved that I can't see exactly the track of my own thoughts. They leave deep imprints in the black snow of my memory. Cold thoughts with geisha detachment.

Maybe this is what I tell myself to justify the thing I will be doing and all the things I've done. My gaze drifts to the deck.

"Yuri," Finch says now. With a certain firmness. "What

does all of this have to do with that carrier? It's obviously wrong."

It's obvious but not easy. Like leaving a life. Or a necessary killing. "I don't know what else to do." That's a lie. I know what should be done. I just keep weighing my options, hoping the scales will tip better in my favor.

Finch doesn't speak. He doesn't need to, and he knows it.

"You should go." I say it without any heat. Not like before. "None of this is your decision." Or your life. "I'll drop you off at the nearest port once it's all over." If we're still alive.

He asks as if he didn't hear anything that I said, "What exactly do those Ops want you to do? Don't you think you should tell me now?"

Yeah, there's that. If it's not Caligtiera's agenda, it's Andreas Lukacs's. And maybe it makes perfect sense that the only person I can possibly trust is the one I brought out of prison. But there's Taja . . . I look at Finch and remember Taja isn't an issue now.

"Yuri, *tell me*."

Has he ever said that to my sleeping self? Is that how he knows?

This alliance of one can't hold. So I pull my hands through my hair, just hold them there with my elbows on my knees. "Ops wants me to set them up with Caligtiera— that's the captain of the other ship—" These words to him bleed out of me like a transfusion, he's pulling them out, and I feel less steady with each syllable. "I don't know if those agents really want to infiltrate the operation or if they just told that to me to protect their own ass. They might actually be looking for a real alliance. Either way, Cal wants that carrier dead to give everyone a signal. And now I know and now I have to go through with it or he'll kill this ship, Finch.

He won't hesitate, and we're running on low crew as it is. There's not enough here to fight with. Taja was just the beginning." For me. This ship. My blood tied to this ship, and I don't know where else to be and what else would keep me contained. "This is my ship." I shot Taja because this ship can only be my refuge when I'm in control of it.

But I'm not really in control of it. It's all illusion.

"You can get out of it, Yuri." His hand makes a fist in the sheets.

"I told you I tried. You don't get out."

He twitches as if he wants to touch me, but stops. "Didn't they say—didn't they say on the Send long ago that Azarcon had? Isn't that why all the politicos hate him?"

"I'm not Azarcon. I don't have an admiral in my corner."

"Then approach *him*."

I shake my head. "I tried already. I almost killed his son. He sent me to Earth to be put in prison. He would never listen to me."

"You have information he would want. He'd be more inclined to listen than any other captain."

There are red lines on my arms from my fingernails. Finch grabs my wrist, stops my clawing.

"Yuri."

"He'll kill me, Finch. He'll kill me and likely all of you." *"Tell him what you know."*

What I know.

That I'm a protégé too? I'm Falcone's protégé in blood. I'm what he left behind.

WRECKED

I was ten years old when Marcus took me into my first command crew meeting, which was once a week. None of the ten department commanders, plus Caligtiera, found it odd that I was there, which made it easier. So easy that I was bored. Even though Bo-Sheng had said this ship was a pirate, and Estienne confirmed it, it seemed to run just like any other ship. Not that I knew firsthand. But Marcus went over procedures and costs, cargo and schedules and flagged crew files with meticulous discussion. They also talked about their allies, like *Shiva*, who was their bloodmate, and others in the network spanning all the way to Hubcentral. He made me take notes in my slate, which I had to send to his comp so he could review.

It only got interesting when they talked about punishing people for breaking ship rules—like people who stole from

each other or the ship, or witheld profit that they'd made on
one mission or another. Sometimes the punishment was brig
time, other times it was a thrashing.

Once or twice Marcus just put people in the airlock and
vented them. At the end of my first month of meetings they
talked about this one girl who used to steal drugs from medical. She was a junkie and lied twice about getting on recovery. Marcus said he didn't abide drug use on his ship
because it made people stupid and desperate and dependent
on something other than their Blood (which is what he
called the ship). So out she went. And I took notes.

You couldn't just let people go on stations if you wanted
them off your ship, Marcus said. Because they knew the operations of the ship and the network, and he wouldn't risk
them getting caught and blabbing to Hub authorities. But he
always gave a couple of warnings before venting you. So it
was fair, he said.

She shrieked like a strit. It hurt my ears.

He had me watch because I had to learn to stomach it.
The girl was a shivering, sweating mess—from fear as well
as her addiction. She might've been sixteen or twelve, it was
hard to tell from her drug-abused body. They stripped her
naked and set her in the airlock at gunpoint. Her nipples
were like little withered grapes. She screamed a lot. He'd
taken the ship to a drop point only he knew. There were
dozens, he said, mapped by this ship or the others in the network. Like how Hub ships mapped the Dragons. But the
Dragons were big. And she was just going to be one more
piece of refuse floating toward some star.

Nothing like that was happening in the fifth meeting
though. I knew the routine by then. Before the meeting
wrapped Marcus would tell me to go outside and wait for
him. I figured it was because they wanted to discuss things

that I was still too young to understand, and that was all right, usually by then I'd be so bored I needed a nap. So I stood outside the conference room on maindeck and smoked. And if I had to wait extra long, I always ended up crouched on the deck with my back to the wall, watching the crew pass.

This time Caligtiera joined me for a smoke. He'd done it twice before, just came out while they took a break inside or something, but he never talked to me. He had his own cigrets, small brown sticks that stank up the corridor like a volcanic fart. He hunched there beside me, and muttered something about "Vin getting comms every time they had to discuss payroll," but then he laughed and I guessed it wasn't so serious. Half the time I didn't understand what Caligtiera was mumbling about. He might've been Marcus's second-in-command, but he was a ghost. I barely saw him. And when I did he always looked at me funny and never said much. Like he knew exactly what I was thinking and was amused by it.

"Who's Vin?" I finally asked him.

"Vincenzo. Falcone. Your captain."

"I thought his name was Marcus." I wouldn't put it past Cal to lie to me just for kicks.

"That's his middle name."

"Oh." Cal probably just liked to make me feel stupid. I shrugged and smoked. At least my cigs smelled better than his. And probably cost twice as much. Marcus bought them for me even though I had an account now. He was generous like that.

"So," Caligtiera said.

"So?"

"How's Estienne?"

I glanced up at him. He looked older than Marcus, stout

and well lined, like a chair you had kept around for years. It seemed comfortable until you used it and found the hard edges actually bruised. But the clarity in his eyes seemed younger. Or maybe he just kept the things he'd seen well hidden so they didn't show.

"Well?" he said, flicking ashes so they trailed down near my shoulder.

I scowled and moved away. "Ask him yourself." I didn't have to be polite to Caligtiera. Much. And Marcus wasn't there anyway.

"I'm surprised he isn't jealous," he murmured, blowing smoke to the ceiling.

"Jealous?"

"Of you. You know." He peered at the burning end of his cig as if his fortune was in the glow.

"No I don't know. And he isn't jealous. That's just stupid. He likes me. And he's *older*."

"Mmhm. Likes you even though you'll surpass him?"

"What does that mean?"

"Surpass. Go by him. Or above him." His lips quirked. "To the top."

Because Marcus treated me special? "Maybe I'll *surpass* you first. Or instead."

He held the smoke in his mouth, staring at me. I didn't look away. Then he exhaled, and it streamed from his nostrils like a landed shuttle venting drive coolant. And the smell made my gut twist.

"I guess we'll see, little man," he said.

The hatch to the conference room opened. Marcus stood there. "Don, we're resuming." His gaze flicked to me as I stood. "Yuri. You keep smoking that much and it will break the recyclers. Tone it down."

"Yes, sir. Should I still wait?"

"Yes," he said, then jerked his chin at Caligtiera, who stubbed out the cig against the bulkhead, let it fall to the corner, and stepped by the captain back into the room. Marcus held out his hand. "I ran out. Give me your pack, hm?"

I pouted but handed it over.

He took it, then shoved my head lightly. "Ten minutes. And clean up Cal's cig."

I scowled. "Yes, sir."

"Review the notes. I'll be asking you about them."

"Aww!"

"Yuri." He stared at me, not easy.

"Yes, sir."

He disappeared back inside, and the hatch shut with a clang. I picked up my slate from the deck. And the dropped cigret. It still stank.

The worst thing about a pirate ship, after the people, was the work.

Since Bo-Sheng was on another schedule, I didn't see him at all, but they kept me plenty occupied. My first real job among the crew was in the cargo bays doing inventory on the supply bins stacked in the cold storage area. I wore a skinsuit against the chill and had a slate with a list of serial numbers and itemized contents, names that I couldn't pronounce. They looked scientific or medical, or just numbers and letters. Weapons, I thought for some of them, but wasn't sure, and nobody I worked with confirmed when I asked after a week of working. They just said, Ask the captain. So after that week I asked him, and he said, Where do you think we get the guns that I'm showing you how to shoot?

The contents didn't matter to me just as long as I verified everything every two weeks. It was busiest when we got new inventory, usually off-loaded from *Shiva* since Marcus said he was running *The Abyssinian* in the shadows for a while.

By July I had my solid routine and the regularity of it made the dark corners and tall crewmembers seem more familiar. Or less intimidating. I had goldshift meals with Marcus, then bridge observation and weapons training, then library lessons or research on any kind of topic Marcus or Estienne assigned—which usually had to do with military strategy, mathematics, station and star systems, the most-used languages in the Hub aside from majority, and politics. For fun I got to look up stuff about Earth or entertainment, pick vids to watch in my quarters at blueshift alone or with Estienne. That was all before lunch. Then Marcus or Estienne would have lunch with me, and after lunch I worked on the ship. Until August it was all cargo bay inventory, and after August it was Engineering observation in the afternoons. Before dinner was gym and sparring time. And after dinner was my time. As the months went on, Marcus said, I would learn a new area of the ship. In a rotation.

It was better than school. Nobody treated me like a kid because I was the captain's protégé, and when I did my work well Marcus rewarded me with cigrets or clothes or just extra cred, which I could use to order stuff from Austro. Some of the crew would pick up orders on their outrider forays to the Rim. Sometimes Estienne went because he had business there too. He'd dress up in his black like one of the first times I'd seen him and say he was going to a party on station. Austro was the biggest station outside of Hub-central, and I'd read about how the rich people there had vid premieres and socialite gatherings to raise money for "the destitute" and some of it even went to places like Colonial Grace.

Papa never wrote. And Marcus said the transit station

where Mama and Jascha had passed through had been blown by some symp marauder, and now many of the relocation records were lost. So it was taking a long time to try and track where they might've gone. There were a lot of relocation colonies in the Spokes. Mama and Jascha hadn't shown up at Colonial Grace yet.

I tried not to think of Papa and Isobel. I still wrote to them in a separate part of my journals, which Estienne encouraged me to do, and when I'd gathered a week's worth I gave the file to Estienne to send to Papa. But Papa never wrote back. By September I stopped bugging Estienne to send them, and he stopped asking me. We just stopped talking about my family altogether, and I thought he preferred that anyway. Marcus too. They were sad for me, maybe, and it made them uncomfortable when they had to tell me that nobody on Colonial Grace cared where I was. And neither did Bo-Sheng. He didn't ask for me either, Estienne said. Let Bo-Sheng work, Marcus said. And you do your work. And you'll both be all right.

If it weren't for Marcus and Estienne and all the things I was learning, I would've been a lot sadder.

There were ten other kids on board that *were* on my shift schedule, and sometimes during gym time we'd get a game going with a ball. We weren't supposed to take the gym equipment out of the gym, but I snuck a fist-sized ball in my pocket to my next Engineering observation block. Sometimes the men and women there started to talk among themselves about things I didn't understand, and that was when I went to the bathroom for a half hour, or so I told them. I started to go to a rarely used back corridor somewhere near the supply rooms and bounce the ball on the deck and bulkhead. Bounce-bounce and back to my hand, over and over again, traveling down the corridor as I went if I wanted a challenge.

The fifth time doing this I heard singing coming from the main corridor, then a man appeared, heading for Supply, voice echoing in a language I didn't understand. He spied me midcast and threw up his hands, one of them holding a slate, in mock surrender.

"Please, don't shoot!"

I grinned. He didn't seem like the type to yell at me. "This isn't a gun, it's a ball. My gun's in my quarters."

He approached, hair sticking up in all directions as if he'd just awakened or run his hands through it too many times.

"Still, a ball can kill a man in the right hands."

"It's rubber!" I bounced it once to show him.

"Ah, indeed it is." He caught it before I could and looked at it all over. It was a red marble design. "But, you know, the captain doesn't like these toys just all around the ship."

"It's not all around the ship, it's just here. When I'm bored." I wondered if he was going to report me. "I keep it in my pocket most of the time."

"I see. So you should be working, but you come here to play, hmm?" He held out the ball to me, though, with a smile.

I smiled back as I took it. "What's your name?"

"Piotr Tyborsky. And you?"

"Yuri Mikhailovich Terisov."

"That's quite a name." He rubbed his chin in thought. "But it's much too long. Just too long for me."

"You can call me Yuri."

"Yoo-ree." He emphasized.

I laughed. "Yuri."

"Yoo-ree." He started to sing the name as he punched in

a code to the supply room. "What work do you do for this great ship, Yoo-ree?"

I shrugged. "Stuff for the captain. I'm his protégé."

"Oh, yes?" He glanced down at me, crooked grin, as he disappeared into the supply room. I leaned against the hatch and peered in at him among the high shelves stacked with small bins. A light tracked him overhead as he moved down the aisle, consulting his slate as he went and running his fingers over lit labels. "Protégé, hmm? You are a special boy!"

"Eh." I shrugged again.

"The captain has many special boys . . . ," he murmured, pulling down a bin and setting it on the floor so he could open it.

"What? Does he? Who else?"

"Oh, never fear, Yoo-ree. Nobody else at the moment. I just meant—from before."

"Before what? Before me?" Who else? And where were they now, on other ships?

"I've said a wrong thing," he muttered, taking out an opaque plastic packet from the bin and tucking it under his arm.

"Why?"

"It's up to the captain to tell you, not me. I am sorry." He stood, sliding the bin back into its space.

"No, tell me. I promise I won't say anything."

He shook his head and ushered me away from the hatch so he could shut it again. "Nah. I've said too much." The hatch made a hollow thud as it closed. Then he looked down at me. "Please do not mention it to the captain, Yoo-ree. For both of us. Captain Falcone doesn't really like talking about the others."

I tucked the ball in my pocket. "Um, okay." But I was curious.

He put his hand on my head, still for a moment, before ruffling my hair. "Good boy. Now. Go do some work." He whacked my bottom.

"Ow!" I tried to kick him, but he moved away, too fast, and started singing some ridiculous song using my name as the chorus. "Shut up!" But he made me laugh.

He waved at me and strolled off. That blueshift at dinner in the mess hall I asked Estienne what Piotr Tyborsky did, and Estienne smiled. "He's one of our drive technicians. And he drives the senior staff down there crazy with his singing. Or he would if he wasn't so damn good—with his voice and his fists."

* **

I waited a week into October before asking Marcus, casually over breakfast in the captain's mess, if he'd had any other protégés before me.

"Yes," he said slowly, sipping his caff. "Why do you ask?"

"I just wanted to know . . . if I was the first." I wasn't going to get Piotr in trouble. And I rocked a bit on my chair to distract Marcus, to be cute.

"Sit properly, Yuri."

I clunked back and picked up my toast, bit into it. Sometimes he wasn't in the mood for me when I wanted to act like a kid, but other times he seemed fond of it. He'd tousle my hair and hug me a lot. He seemed this shift to be in a huggy mood because he smiled at me.

"No, you weren't the first, but you're certainly the one to do best so far."

"Yeah?" Grin. "Sir?"

"Yes. All of the others failed me in one way or another. I don't think you'll fail."

"Really?"

"Really." He looked serious for a minute. "But it'll be hard. I won't lie. It's very hard sometimes to work on this ship. But the reward is great. I reward my crew."

"I know." I smiled so he wouldn't be so serious. "How many were there? Before me?"

"Three." He leaned back with his caff and didn't smile back.

I wanted to ask what had happened to them all, but something about the way he didn't look at me anymore made me hesitant, and I left it at that. I never wanted to push too far on his patience or kindness. I remembered the girl in the airlock. There were limits to what he tolerated, like any father, I guessed, and if this crew were his children, then I wanted to be the son he favored most.

For a long time.

* * *

We had a horror vid that late blueshift, Estienne and I, which I liked to watch in his red-and-black quarters with the lights off. He propped his comp on a chair, and we sat against the bulkhead on his bunk with the red material hanging down all around so in the particularly bloody vids it gave a fun atmosphere. He curled his arm around me, and even though I tried not to, sometimes I shut my eyes and made "ew" noises.

"You're going to give yourself nightmares at some point." He laughed.

"You're not supposed to laugh, it's supposed to be scary."

"Okay then. I'll be scared." He hugged me tighter and said in an exaggerated child voice, "Help, help."

I shoved him and he laughed again and the mood was ruined. But it didn't matter because I was tired anyhow and curled up with my head in his lap, watching the vid sideways. His fingers ran through my hair in light caresses, and it made me sleepier. But I remembered my questions and if I couldn't ask Marcus, I always asked Estienne.

"Did you know the other protégés?"

His hand stopped moving for a second, but then continued. "No."

"How come?"

"Well . . ." He started to rub my back, and I liked that the most. "I wasn't here when the first two were around, so I never met them."

"What happened to them?"

"Oh . . . the first one left. Betrayed the captain, I hear. It was really ugly, and Marcus hates it mentioned. The second one killed himself. Apparently he was just unstable. He wasn't suited for this at all. I guess he was weak. Don't talk to Marcus about what I say, okay?"

"I won't, I promise." I fingered the fabric over his knees, the soft worn pants of his sleepwear. "What about the third one?" The one before me.

"He wasn't cut out, so the captain let him go on station. Chaos, I think."

"Yeah?" So I was doing well, or else he would've kicked me off too.

"Mmhmm." His hand slid up the back of my T-shirt and started to rub. This always got me sleepy real fast because the pads of his fingers had slightly rough calluses that just seemed to tug my eyelids shut with every stroke. I forgot my questions in the lull, then he said, "Want to sleep here this shift?"

"Okay."

So he ordered off the vid and lay down with me, and caressed my back just like that until I fell asleep.

4.10.2189 EHSD — The *Khan*

I didn't see Bo-Sheng for three years. For my thirteenth birthday Estienne threw a party, which I figured had Marcus's approval since Estienne made a huge deal of it. He hadn't done it for any of my prevous birthdays. Before it had just been dinners between me and him, or me and him and Marcus. Small gifts like extra time on stations or like last year Marcus had given me my own LP-150 rifle, just like soljets had, but it was never a *party*. Turning thirteen was an occasion though, despite the fact I did what plenty of adults did anyway, but for the sake of dates and numbers, it was a deal. Or maybe three years later I'd finally earned the right to be fussed over outside of work.

Estienne went all out. Full-surround decorations, invitations dropped in comps and alerts, and lots of presents. He tried not to imply that he was giving me anything beyond the party, but I saw the way he watched me when I was in his quarters. If I poked behind too many cases or into his lockers or behind this or that curtain, he was ready to take my arm and distract me with talk, food, or games. I played along. If I truly ruined it for him, he'd make me pay in training. And it would get back to Marcus, because I knew Estienne reported on my progress to Marcus, and when it was Marcus's turn to test me or make me work he'd be sure I paid too, in some way—doubling me with the smelliest crewmember to oversee cataloging of supplies we'd hauled in from one ship or another, or making me itemize the weapons with the meanest son of a bitch assigned to the ship's armory. It was his way of punishing me and training me at the same time. Sometimes I went to sleep bruised, but it was never serious. I was special in the crew, like Estienne was special. The crew never touched him either so whatever roughing up he got it must've been from his clients.

He had clients that we met at ports in the Dragons or that he flew to see on other ships or stations. They left him some shifts unwilling to leave his quarters, so he'd comm me in a croaky voice and say I should just catch up this shift. Never knew exactly what he did at that point, and he never explained, but it was important to Marcus, and Estienne didn't seem to mind (always back the next working shift without any change of behavior). It seemed to require expensive clothes and a knowledge of weapons. And sex, I suspected. Which I knew about from watching vids and talking to the other crew—and Estienne, even though most of the time I got the feeling he wasn't telling me everything. Later, he kept saying. Now I had to learn languages. Or guns. Or fighting. Or planetary trends, weather systems and terraforming and satellite communications across leap space. I read a lot of old literature, and new, and they even let me learn music. I also had to know military procedure, even though *The Abyssinian* wasn't a military ship. But Marcus had been a carrier captain and I learned about EarthHub carriers.

But sex was what I thought about. I wanted to ask him so many times—how did it feel when you did those things specifically beyond just kissing. Kissing was easy. He kissed me a lot, on the cheek and the hair and the mouth sometimes, but it wasn't anything like some of the crew did in the mess hall or the lower-deck berths. That kind of kissing took skill and I didn't have it yet; nobody would take me on, which I figured was Marcus's or Estienne's doing.

Sometimes I was tempted to go through Estienne's belongings while he was still asleep or if I was waiting in his q while he was in the bathroom. But I never did. He'd kill me, really. But I thought about it. A lot. About what he knew from experience and I only knew from observation. Especially when I cuddled with him. That was nice, and I slept better with it, but I thought about it, who he'd been with and why and what he did, and how did that help our ship?

He shouldn't have been with other people. He liked being with me the most. He said so.

But whatever *it* all was, he kept it to himself. He loved a little mystery, and my birthday was a great excuse. He made me wear a blindfold for the party, even when I said I'd keep my eyes shut.

"I don't trust that you won't peek. You're such a rascal." He laughed and slipped down the black mask over my eyes, then took me by the shoulders. We were in his quarters but that wasn't where the party was going to be. "Okay, walk."

"I'm gonna trip!"

"You won't. I won't let you. Now just walk."

I spread my hands in front of me so I wouldn't bump into anything, not entirely trusting he wouldn't let me run into a bulkhead just for fun. His quiet laughter didn't let up as he steered me through the corridors. I heard low voices and little giggles as I went. Estienne's hand was firm on my shoulder, his other one gripping my waist. I mapped the turns and steps we took and soon knew exactly where we were going. The captain's mess.

Private party.

I heard a hatch open, and Estienne said, "Step over."

The threshold, which I knew, so I did, and immediately the smell of warm, spicy food—my favorite, rice and dal and peppered roti—hit my nose, then my stomach, making it rumble. I grinned, and Estienne squeezed my side. "Don't take it off yet!"

Something chirped.

I smiled wider. "What's that?"

He growled at me and made me walk to the left, positioning me in front of something. My toe hit what might've been the leg of a clamped chair. I felt other people crammed in the room, the heat of bodies and the silence of stifled voices. Estienne held me now on both sides of my waist, and said, "All right, take off the mask."

I yanked it off and blinked, pushing hair from my eyes. In front of me on the long table sat a tall cage, and inside it was a hand-sized green bird with a dusky peach face and a curved beak. It hopped along its perch, opened its mouth, and screamed. Its round black eyes blinked at me as if it had no idea or didn't care that everyone in the room (and possibly the entire ship) cringed.

"Ahh!" I leaned over to peer into the cage. "You're loud!" I put my fingertip through the thin black bars.

"Be careful, he might bite," Marcus said, standing right beside it. I hadn't even noticed him. I looked up, and he was smiling. "I'm hoping you'll train him to be quieter. Do you like him?"

"Yeah! He's so colorful. He's mine?"

"Of course he's yours. Happy birthday."

"Thank you!" I threw myself into the captain and hugged him. He wasn't nearly as demonstrative as Estienne, but he never spurned my affection. He didn't even care that there were others in the room—like Caligtiera, who still tended to lurk around the captain. I felt his eyes. I always felt his eyes.

Marcus hugged me then, patting my hair. I had grown, longer-limbed, and the top of my head reached the bottom of his chin. I pressed my cheek against his shoulder, then pulled away and put my face back near the cage. "What is he? I mean, what kind of bird?"

"A lovebird," Marcus said.

I looked up, and the whole room was silent. Nothing but the sound of the food sizzling on their heated plates. Marcus held my gaze, and I tried not to blush. He never did anything just for the hell of it, but I hardly thought he'd be so blatant. Behind me Estienne said nothing.

So I said simply, "I love him."

Marcus smiled. "I'm pleased."

Estienne hugged me around the waist from behind, lifting me off my feet. "Now cut the cake!"

I laughed and pounded on his arms to set me down. The lovebird called, fast kind of shrieks, and I wriggled out of Estienne's grasp toward it, placing my hand flat on the cage. The bird arched its beak and pecked at my palm.

"Dexter," I said.

"Hm, what's that?" Marcus said as he motioned the steward to bring over the plates of food.

"His name! I've decided."

"Dexter?" Marcus said.

Everyone in the room chuckled or outright laughed until Estienne said, "It's a great name for a bird. All of you shut up."

I'd had a dog called Seamus, and I couldn't remember where I'd gotten the name. Dexter must've been lodged in the same place in my memory, because it was an outrageous name for a thing that size, with that color. The little bird screeched at me, and it pierced all of our ears until I let him nibble at my finger again. His wings fluffed, and his head twitched, as if everybody outside of his world frightened or fascinated him.

* * *

I sat scraping chocolate icing off my plate and licking the back of my spoon. Everyone had left, even Estienne, who'd promised to give me his gifts in private instead of in front of everybody. I liked the sound of that. My other gifts included gameware, clothes, and a lot of certificate numbers so I could order things for myself and pick them up when I got to station next. It was a good haul.

Marcus sat with me in the quiet room, and even Dexter had calmed now that we were alone. I watched my new pet as he hopped from one perch to another in the large cage, occasionally flitting to the colorful, ropy toys that hung from the bars like streamers. He liked to pick at those with his crescent beak. I leaned on my elbows and put my nose to the cage, watching with the spoon in my mouth.

"I'm glad you like him," Marcus said, on the other side of the long table. All the dishes and plates had been swept away already by the stewards. Nothing but the scent of food lingered in the air. "They say they die of heartbreak if you separate the pair, but it's just an old romantic myth. These birds will take to human owners just as well."

Dexter stopped his nibbling of the rope and looked at me, opened his beak, and yawned. He even had a tiny tongue. I grinned and set the spoon on the table. "You think he'll take to me?"

"Why wouldn't he?" Marcus smiled.

I got up and went around the table and hugged his shoulders as he sat. "I had the best birthday. But I guess tomorrow is work?"

"Yes, next shift is work. Which is what I wanted to talk to you about." He put his hand on my arm and lifted it from his neck, guiding me around so I could lean at the edge of the table and he could look up at me from his seat. He didn't let go, just slid his hand down to hold me lightly by the wrist, his thumb caressing the pulse there. "Your learning and work over the past three years have been exemplary. Both Estienne and I are really proud."

I quirked a smile at him. "Good."

"I think it's time you get the ship's tattoo."

I straightened. "Yeah?"

His hand slid up and he leaned forward so he could touch my chest above my heart. "Right there. But for that you'll have to know the true name of my ship."

"Isn't it *The Abyssinian*?"

"No . . . we're a pirate ship, aren't we?"

"Yeah. So?"

"So it wouldn't be smart to advertise the true name of my ship when I go to port, now would it?"

Of course not. I made a face for being so stupid. "I guess I just didn't think about it."

"Now you will. Because to everybody not in my network, we're *The Abyssinian*. But to others in the Family, we're *Genghis Khan*."

"Family." I chewed on my lip.

"That's what we are."

"Like that antialien group? The Family of Humanity?" The Hub called them terrorists, but I thought they were only protective of humanity. I'd done my reading.

"No, not them." He looked up at me, serious. "Yuri, I want you to listen."

When he said that it meant I better Remember. That it was *for always* if I wanted to stay here. More than just training; between him and me—his protégé. I'd looked that up too, and he hadn't just taken me under his wing. He gave me another life. And even though he never said it directly, I knew he loved me.

"I'm listening, sir."

His thumb still stroked my pulse. It almost made me sleepy, with my belly full of spiked punch and food and cake. Behind me I heard Dexter flitting about in his cage like a beating heart.

Marcus said, "Once you're marked by my ship, you're going to begin training as a geisha. You're going to learn everything that Estienne knows and everything I can teach you as my protégé. Do you understand? You won't be one or the other."

I started to nod, but then shook my head. "One or the other?"

"Halfway between adult and child. Given certain things but sheltered from others. Restricted. You're thirteen now. You won't be restricted. You'll no longer be a child, hidden away. You'll be both geisha and protégé, you'll know the most of anyone on my ship besides me. I've had others before, but none of them pleased me as much as you. None of them succeeded so well at this point. You're my perfection, Yuri. You're the future of my Family."

It seemed to echo in the room, but that was just my own disbelief talking back at me. He was holding my hand. I would be Family, with the mark of his ship on my heart. The true name. And when he said it like that it meant forever.

I'd have everything, even Estienne's name. Estienne's other name. The name he wore when he wore the black. I'd know his mysteries.

Geisha, Marcus said. I said it too. I loved the way it felt on my tongue.

* * *

With my arms around the birdcage and Dexter screeching at me from the movement, I headed to Estienne's quarters. It was up a deck, in that barricaded corridor, but my tags worked to open the doors. Once at his q I had to kick the hatch because I didn't feel like setting down the cage. By then Dexter had quieted and just fluttered around from one corner to the other. Little bits of his bright green feathers drifted to the bottom.

"Excited? Once I get you in my quarters I'll let you out of this thing." Maybe Estienne would let me release Dexter in *his* quarters. I had my mind set on sleeping here this shift, after Estienne gave me my presents, and I could grill him about the geisha duties. I made faces at the bird, and he tilted his head at me, then flapped and squawked when the hatch grated open.

It wasn't Estienne at the entrance, but a girl. With an open shirt and low-slung pants, messy hair and a slender way of standing that gave attitude as much as it gave skin. She had dark eyes and thick lips, young in every way, but older than me. Estienne's age. Her body and the hatch hid the inside of the quarters.

Her eyes flickered, and she said, "Est, it's your boy," and turned away to look behind her.

I felt my insides tighten. I wanted to hit her, just like that. Hard. For the way she looked at me and the way she called him *Est*. I thought about kicking, but at that point Dexter let out a long squawk, and the girl turned around, a hand to her ear.

"What is that *thing*?"

"He's my bird!" I stuck my fingers through the bars on the cage door. "Should I let him out so he can shit on your head?"

Her lip curled, then Estienne appeared behind her, obviously in a hurry for something. He raked half his shirt onto his shoulder and blinked as if he'd just woken up. But not from sleep, I'd bet. The belt on his pants was undone.

"Yuri . . . did the captain send you?"

As if the only reason I wanted to see him was on Marcus's orders?

"No, but it's still my birthday, and you haven't given me my presents yet."

He and the girl exchanged glances—the kind adults gave when they had things to say that they thought should be kept from children.

Except I wasn't a child anymore, even the captain had said.

"You can go," I told the girl. Because I was Marcus's protégé and even Caligtiera didn't order me around.

Estienne lifted his chin at her, which made me mad. My words weren't good enough? She moved then, zipped up her shirt, and edged by me (because I didn't move and I was glad when Dexter screeched at her), off down the corridor with a small glance behind. I glared after her to make sure she went in the lev and disappeared, then I looked back at Estienne and shoved the cage at him.

Which wasn't fair to do to Dexter, who flapped inside and protested sharply. Estienne stepped back, nearly tripping since I'd surprised him, and hurriedly set the cage on the floor. I walked in and shoved the hatch shut.

"So who was she?"

He pushed his hair from his eyes and straightened, patting the cage to reassure Dexter. He looked at me for a silent moment, then went to his desk where his bronze-and-black cigret case lay. He flipped it open and tapped out a stick, then struck the end with his fingerband.

"You sound jealous for a reason?" he said.

"I'm not jealous! I just asked a question!"

Dexter added to my voice.

"Dammit, Yuri, shut it down." He pointed with the cigret. "And shut down that bird."

"He's not a comp."

"These are my quarters!" Estienne yelled suddenly, his hand twitching as if he meant to open a blade. I froze, mouth clenched, until he came over just as swiftly and hugged me to his chest. "Sshh, all right," he murmured, like I was upset. But I wasn't. I stood there, still angry and just a little unnerved. He rubbed my back and kissed the side of my hair, stroking his cheek against it until I finally hugged him back. "I'm sorry, I'm just tired," he said.

"I guess I interrupted."

"Nah." He let go and went to his bed. The sheets were kicked to the foot, the pillows shoved against the bulkhead. He sat and patted the mattress. "C'mon so I can give you your presents." Now he smiled.

I wandered over, not too keen to sit where that girl might've been. But he grabbed my arm and pulled me down beside him, and it was so familiar here in his quarters that I forgave him the girl. Sort of.

"Is she your—girlfriend?"

His eyebrows rose and he laughed. "No. That's just Taja. She's a bedbug."

I made a face. "Is she part of your geisha duties?"

His chin tilted. "No . . . and he told you, huh. About being geisha?"

Now I smiled. "Yeah. And you're gonna teach me."

I thought he'd smile back, but he didn't. Instead he said, "First let me give you the presents." He stubbed out his cig in the ashtray at his feet and went to one of his lockers behind a long strip of gauzy curtain, edging it aside. It obscured his hands in a crimson film. He came back with a thin gold-wrapped box, less than thirty centimeters and too narrow to house a knife. A fork maybe, but not an actual fighting blade. I forced myself not to frown in disappointment.

"Happy birthday," he said, placing the gift in my hand and closing my fingers around it. Then he kissed me on the forehead.

"Thanks." I smiled at him for that kiss. And forgave him a little more for Taja.

"Well open it," Estienne said, shoving my shoulder.

I pushed a finger beneath the envelope of paper and ripped it off. The box was the same color. I lifted the lid, flicked away the top layer of silver tissue paper, and lying embedded there was a smooth black thing. Looked like two chopsticks stuck together. "What is it?"

"Take it out, I'll show you."

I lifted it out, set the empty box aside. The two chopstick things slipped apart a bit, yet they were connected by what looked like folded paper. So I spread it open and a painted image appeared on the delicate golden surface. A white face with black crescent eyes, wearing a long dress covered in colorful flowers.

"It's a fan," Estienne said.

"Oh," I said. "Um. Thanks."

He laughed, when I thought he'd be insulted. "For the geisha. Look." He took it carefully from my hands, closed it, and stood in the center of his quarters. With a flick of the wrist he snapped open the fan and turned it face out, its curve covering the lower half of his face.

Now I smiled, because his eyes were bright.

Then he began to dance. In his party black with the paleness of his hair like the reflection of a sun. His eyes never quite connected with mine, a flirtation. He moved so fluidly it was as if the room danced with him, the walls and the curtains and the air that I breathed. All of them took turns to slide around his body as he gave me his back and his shoulders and the side of his face. The fan closed and opened like a gilded eye, in whispers. He held it sometimes like a shield, other times like an invitation, and when he was finally done, paused in front of me and bent at the knees with his eyes cast down, I wanted to lay my hand on the top of his head and pull him toward me. Because nothing that beautiful should go untouched.

I reached toward him, but he straightened, and my fingers grazed the air. He was smiling at me, but secretive, and held out the folded fan.

"You'll learn," he said. "And you'll break people with a look."

Break him, maybe? I took the fan. I stared into his eyes. "What's my other gift?"

"Rascal," he murmured, holding my gaze. Then he took my head in his hands, his fingers threading into my hair, and leaned down. My eyes shut, I didn't know why, but I just breathed in, and it was Estienne everywhere. The imprint of his quarters behind my lids, the movements of that dance, and his fresh scent. He whispered into the top of my hair, "Go next door. To the right."

I looked up. Our noses touched. "It's in that q?"

"Just go," he said, and released me.

I wanted to stay here. A heat had started at the base of my stomach, and it spread down. But when Estienne walked to his desk, the cool air in his quarters washed it all away.

"Aren't you coming with me?"

"No," he said.

Sometimes I didn't understand his games at all. So I got up and set the fan on top of the cage before I left.

* **

My tags worked on the lock, not surprising at all considering Estienne's rein on this ship. I shoved the hatch open and stepped in, looking around. It was the same size as Estienne's quarters, but unpainted.

Bo-Sheng sat on the bunk.

I squinted. It must've been him, even though his hair was finger-length short, and his face seemed harder. His cheekbones stood out more, sharp planes that angled sweetly against the tilt of his black eyes.

He stared at me and rose from the bed.

"Bo-Sheng?"

Stupid to ask. But I couldn't believe it.

The heat that had melted in Estienne's quarters started to spread again from the base of my belly. His shoulders had broadened, he was taller but not quite as tall as me even still, and beneath the gray mesh sweater, as he crossed his arms, long muscles drew a taut outline.

I grinned and engulfed him in a hug. I hoped he wasn't still mad about our last conversation, which I barely remembered.

He didn't return the embrace. Instead, he wriggled and pushed me back. "Stop it."

I stared at him, clenching my jaw. First Estienne and now him? Playing these games?

He looked down as if I intimidated him. And for some reason that made me feel a little ashamed.

"Why're you here?" I moved away and dug into my

pocket, taking out the Red Star brand of cigrets that Marcus had introduced me to way back in the Camp. The rich scent filled the quarters in no time. Bo-Sheng still smelled like his cheap smokes.

"They told me it was your birthday," he hedged.

"Oh." I tried a smile. "It's good to see you." Even though you won't even hug me. "They put you on that different shift, and we never crossed paths."

He nodded a little, still didn't look at me.

I blew out the smoke and tilted my head, resting my elbow on one folded arm. "What've you been doing?"

"Working," he said. "Technician stuff. I'm sorry I never tried to, you know, send a comm or something."

I chewed the inside of my cheek. "Well . . ." I hadn't either.

He looked at the walls.

"I'm sorry too." For the fact we're not friends anymore. But maybe this was what happened when you grew up. One incident and you became awkward around each other and it was never the same.

But he came toward me then, looking somewhere at my feet. He put his arms around me and pressed his nose into my shoulder.

I should've set him back, because it didn't feel like he meant it. This robot wasn't the same Bo-Sheng who used to chase me down the shore in the Camp. But maybe it was that memory that made me return the hug.

I felt his chest pushing against mine as he breathed. I tightened my arms.

"I'm sorry," he said, muffled in my shirt.

"You already said that. Don't worry about it."

"For bringing you here."

He was warm and small in my arms. Felt narrow and

slippery, so I squeezed. He was older, but I was the captain's protégé. Ships had rank, and I'd stepped over Bo-Sheng. "I'm not sorry about that."

He didn't answer.

I pressed my fingers into his back. He didn't squirm this time, but his body was tense. I tried rubbing his back like Estienne did with me, eventually moving one hand up to his neck, feeling for the pulse.

"How have you been?" he asked, in that close silence.

"Good," I answered, even though I wasn't thinking of answers at all. "You?"

He didn't speak. His heart ran, I felt it. He was feeling it. It was like candy, but better. I moved my cheek from his hair and rubbed it against his temple.

He stepped back with a little shove, breathing in as if he'd been burned.

"I'm—going," he said, making for the door.

"What's your *problem*?" I could've hit him for that. My skin tingled with it. Heat. And now irritation.

"I can't do this, Yuri."

"Then when?"

He paused at the hatch, a hand pressed against it, and looked back at me. I started to smoke the forgotten cigret again. It was almost burned down anyway so I dropped it on the floor and toed it out. Scowled.

"When?" he said. Stupidly, I thought.

"Yeah, when. When can we spend time together? You weren't this way when we got on board. And suddenly you don't want anything to do with me?"

"I do," he said, glancing at the walls. Afraid to look me in the eyes, maybe. "I was worried."

"I told you there was nothing to worry about. We haven't seen each other in ages, and I want to—" My teeth clenched.

"I like you. I've always liked you. Why don't you like me back?"

"I like you," he said. But he refused to look at me. His fingers picked at the scars on the hatch.

The heat had traveled to my head. The room felt tight, the floor too sunken. The color of humiliation was a bruising red, and it filled my sight.

"Just go," I said.

I wanted him to stay and knock me over like he used to do when I got an attitude.

But he just left, quietly.

*   *   *

I waited enough time until I was sure Bo-Sheng would've got in the lev, then I went back next door, to Estienne. I kicked and pounded the hatch until he opened it, swearing at me.

"Some other people on this deck are in their sleepshift, you—"

I shoved by him and went to Dexter and picked up the cage.

"What's wrong?" Estienne said from behind. "Didn't you like your—?"

"Some gift! Thanks a lot! Bo-Sheng's all weird with me, and I don't even know why you bothered!"

"Bo-Sheng wasn't the gift," Estienne said. "Well, not only. I thought you'd want to see him. Why, what'd he do?"

Dexter set up a squall. He flew from one corner of the cage to the other and punctured the air with his cries.

"Dammit, Yuri, you better teach that bird to be quiet. I don't know why the captain would give you such a noisy pet." He rubbed the side of his head. "It echoes in this ship."

"I like him, so shut up!"

"What'd Bo-Sheng do, Yuri? He wasn't the gift, I just thought you'd like to see him. The quarters were your gift. New quarters. And I'll help you outfit them, however you want. Won't come out of your pay."

I was at the hatch. I paused and turned. Dexter stopped squawking and rustled beneath the paper at the bottom of his cage. The tiny shape of him moved around under the cover, like he was hiding from something.

Quarters next to Estienne. It dampened my temper. My embarrassment at Bo-Sheng's reaction to me. But I didn't say thank you.

Estienne said, "What happened?"

I shrugged. "Nothing. He's just all different and weird. I don't wanna see him again. It was obvious he didn't wanna see me."

"Aw, Yuri." He came toward me and extricated the big cage from my grip. He set it on the floor carefully then hugged me to his chest.

I pulled away.

"Now what," he said. "I swear you have more moods than a girl."

"Shut up."

"See?"

I looked at him from behind my hair, murderous. But he never took that seriously. He knew it would pass. He knew I couldn't stay mad at him, especially when he grinned at me. He said, "Next shift is geisha training. And you're tired. We'll move you over to your new digs too. But for now, if you don't want to go back down to your old q . . ."

I looked at him full in the face.

He smiled. "Go get ready for bed."

My heart was trotting. I went into his bathroom and

brushed my teeth, because he always kept toiletries for me in there since I stayed over a lot, and Marcus was big on me keeping good teeth. By the time I emerged again Estienne was already tucked in his bunk with the sheet and blanket pulled up. But his shoulders were bare. Which was different.

I tried not to breathe as loud as it sounded in my head.

I remembered vids and talks with Piotr and joking with some of the other younger crew. Images and words all mingled in my mind. But they were distant things.

I didn't feel so distant, looking at him. I was still wearing my party clothes, my good sweater and pants, but I sat on the bed and took off my sweater at least and threw it at the desk chair where it sloppily hung. I started to tuck under the blankets but Estienne said, "You'll ruin your pants."

Ruin? With wrinkles, maybe, which laundry could press out anyway. But he gave my back a little push so I slid off the pants and tossed them after the sweater, then hurried up and tucked under because it was cold when all you wore was underwear that cut above the knees.

He wasn't wearing anything but underwear either. Our legs grazed as I stretched out, and I swallowed. His had short, almost wiry hairs. Maybe they were even as pale as the hair that fell into his eyes. I lay on my back and didn't move because this was different from hugging with all your clothes on. Different from even wanting to be kissed. And I liked it when he kissed me, but this wasn't it.

It was one thing to know the mechanics and to laugh at the vids from embarrassment, and then be in the situation. It didn't matter how many things I'd seen. Just then I didn't know what to do. My curiosity got trumped by nervousness.

I knew he was watching me, but I stared at the ceiling. The lights were still on and I wished they weren't.

"What're you thinking about?" he said, quiet.

"Nothing." My voice seemed too loud. But I couldn't seem to make it soft. "I mean . . . um. How come you're not one of the captain's protégés?" I just wanted to talk.

Estienne propped his head on his hand and fingered my shoulder. "I don't have . . . well, I don't *want* the command responsibilities that you'll eventually have."

"Why not?"

"Yuri . . . let's not talk about this now."

I kept staring at the ceiling. "I wanna talk about it. He said I'm going to be this thing, and I wanna know what it all means."

"You'll find out what it all means."

"Why protégés? Why's he got this—system." Not that I minded, but it wasn't anything nonpirates did as far as I knew. I pulled the blankets tighter against my body. It made him move his hand, and he sighed.

"You know how in the military people go to academies and get training, and if they want to do like specialized things or get on the command track, they take extra training that's harder and more focused? Well that's the idea. Marcus used to be in the EarthHub Armed Forces. He grew up in that system, I think his whole family served. But instead of applying all that training stuff broad like that he wanted to do something more personal. Because he believes it'll create better captains. Ones that would be loyal to each other because they had this special thing in common. Ones that would be most loyal to him because he set the bar and trained the first."

I listened. It was his vision, then. Like the govies talked about their vision for a safe Hub against the strits. Marcus had a vision for his crew and the ships we ran with. "Do all of them have protégés? All of our allies?"

"No. Just certain captains that Marcus handpicked, who he thinks could actually train one properly. Like Captain Townsend on *Shiva*. I mean, it's a long-term thing, right? To train someone from when they're a kid. Marcus is kind of thinking about it in generational terms. He wants his business to last. And it starts with you." Estienne smiled a little. I heard it in his voice. "Or the others. But I guess it took a while for the captain to get it right, it's not like math or something. But you're doing well. You have what it takes to do what the captain does, eventually. You'll see." He slid down and tucked against my arm, his head near mine on the same pillow. "Now can we stop talking about it?"

I couldn't think because his breath was warm against the side of my face. I'd run out of questions anyway.

"Don't you like this, Yuri?" he said.

I wanted Dexter to make a noise, but I thought he was asleep. He didn't peep. And I thought about crawling out except Estienne put his arm over me then, like he usually did when we were both in sleepclothes and just went to sleep. That was all it had been before. But now my eyes weren't shut, and I knew his weren't either.

"Do you like this?" he asked again.

"Like what?"

"This. On your birthday. When you're going to get your tat tomorrow of the *Khan*, and be a real part of the Family. And everything else."

I dug my fingers into my forearms. His arm lay across my neck, warm and defined. I was getting muscle from all the training, but I was still girl-thin and unmarked. He had nine years on me. He was adult.

But so was I, wasn't I? What did time and standard dates mean to deep spacers on ships? I'd killed a strit when I was ten. I knew how to shoot a gun and I had a knife.

His hand slid down and caressed my arm. "I'm not going to hurt you," he said. "You've been wanting me to do this for a while, haven't you? When you left earlier you wanted this. It's going to be okay." Then, "Lights, fifty."

They softened to shadows and glow. The red fabric canopy looked like a sunset. And I was almost sleepy from the way he touched me, all slow and light, and the feel of his breath on my cheek.

Almost.

"Are you okay?" he asked.

No. Yeah. I couldn't decide. It was hard to think. But he was familiar. And he stopped the caresses and just hugged me, like we always did, except as I rolled into his arms, I felt how warm his skin was, and smooth, and how some parts of him were soft and others were not, because of his muscle. He wasn't bulky, but it was there. Just—more. Than me.

It didn't take much. He must have felt how rigid I got, all over, but he didn't say anything. His leg moved, his knee slid a bit between mine, then up, and I made a small sound and tried to pull away, because now all the heat in my body was moving fast to just two places—my brain and below my waist—and, even though I'd seen vids, this wasn't a vid, it was me, and he was going to laugh or something.

"It's all right," he murmured, a hand on my back. "Yuri, it's all right. This is supposed to happen, I don't mind."

Maybe I minded. Except—it felt nice. And scary. And nice. I ached. And I wanted to roll over and hug the pillow and stop feeling down there. Or something. But I didn't.

His knee moved again. Not an accident. And he was soothing me with his voice and his hand on my back, so I started to move against his leg, I didn't know, it was an awkward little dance, and it didn't last long, I couldn't help it when all the suns in the galaxy seemed to die behind my eyes, flood my limbs, and burn me to the core.

And afterward, the cold of space.

Except he hugged me, even though I wriggled, and I was damp and weak and embarrassed.

I couldn't think past that. He held on despite my struggling, until I hugged him back, just fit against him like a familiar sweater. I didn't want to move.

"You're fine," he said. "It was fine." Rubbing my back.

And it felt so good, just like that. It felt so good that I was guilty.

*　*　*

When I woke up he was gone. As soon as I climbed out of the bunk Dexter squawked a greeting. So I went over and poked my finger through the black bars, and he fluttered up to it and nibbled. There was a feed cone hanging in the cage, so I gestured to it. "Breakfast, go on." Eventually he got it, or he got bored of me, and went to it. I checked my tag for messages, and Estienne had left a short one: *Go to medical.*

I was sticky in my underwear from last shift, and it made me glad he wasn't around. Medical for that? What were they going to say? It had happened because of Estienne instead of just during sleep, but was that such a big difference?

I took my time in his shower, and looked in the mirror afterward with my hair damp and combed back. Of course I didn't seem any different. Maybe I needed a haircut, but I liked how Estienne played with it, and he couldn't do that if it was too short. Maybe he wanted me next door because it made things like this easier? I knew he was going to teach me about geisha duties, but I always thought he liked me best. And not just because I was the captain's protégé. He didn't need to like me for that since Marcus treated him special too. And he'd said that girl Taja was just a bedbug. I wasn't just a bedbug.

My tag beeped. I palmed it, and it was Estienne.

"Medical, Yuri. Now."

"Okay." I smiled. His stern voice.

I landed up there, and both Estienne and Marcus were waiting for me, wearing their work faces. So I straightened my shoulders a bit and swept my eyes around. Doc Wachter wasn't in sight, but there was a small girl sitting beside one of the examination tables near Estienne and the captain, her head bowed as if she was looking at something in her lap. Medical was an oval room, smooth surfaces splattered with arthritic-looking scan equipment that clawed and poked you when they used it. Pitiless doctors and medtechs. Whether a flu or a broken bone, they seemed to think it was all your fault. It was plenty of incentive for me to remain healthy and unmarred, so I didn't have to see them except for annual checkups.

Marcus motioned me over to the table now.

Closer, and the girl looked up, the long black hair parting away from her face as she tossed her head. Her face startled me so much that I stopped. It was covered in tattoos, right down her neck to the collar of her shirt. What exposed skin I saw on her hands was also inked. It was such an enmeshed puzzle of images that I could only make out familiar shapes here and there that created something identifiable—a bird, a gun, a sword, flames . . . words in stylized red or blue or black lettering that made cryptic statements like "truth is beauty" and *"eimi hosti eimi."*

When she smiled her teeth made a white line across a colored landscape, like a scar.

"This is Mnemosyne," Marcus said. "She's going to give you the *Khan*'s tattoo."

"My name means 'memory,' " she said, "and you're not gonna forget where you come from. Take off your shirt."

I did so, rolling it in my hands, and smiled at Estienne to say hello. He smiled back, but with reserve, and patted the examination table. "Lie up here."

I hauled myself onto it and lay back, tilting my head to the girl. Reading her skin. Mnemosyne swung over a tray with little bottles and what looked like a needle gun. I sat up.

"No injet?" Nobody used needles to ink tats. That was old. And it looked like it hurt. A lot.

Marcus pushed me back down, not hard enough to bruise but firm enough to keep me there. He didn't smile like Estienne had. He hovered in view, blocking Estienne behind his shoulder. "This ship is your Blood now," he said, "and you're going to feel it."

* **

Genghis Khan's symbol was a black horse reared on its hind legs, with red flaring hooves and red eyes. Marcus said the ancient Mongols were great horsemen, and Genghis Khan spread his empire from the back of the horse. He told me to read the history, so I did eventually, and even though the tattoo hurt, it was good. The pain kept me alert, and the color on my chest was a mark of my new status. In Captain Falcone's fleet. That was what he meant by network. And empire. He had a fleet, of sorts, of ships that weren't going to let the Hub tell them what to do, and didn't have to hand over aliens in this war. Marcus said the *Khan* was lying low for a while, but it didn't mean we weren't going to work. It was the perfect time, he said, for me to learn.

Even though people couldn't see the tat beneath my shirt,
I thought they saw it on my face. I kept my Serate handgun
tucked in my backwaist and walked those corridors with
Estienne to begin my first shift as a geisha and a protégé. We
weren't going to his quarters. He said there was a room.

I glanced up at him as we walked. He saw me looking,
smiled, and slung his arm around my neck.

"Ow," I said, because even a little movement stung.

"Ah, you can take it. I can't wait 'til it's all healed up."

"Why?"

"So I can touch it." He grinned.

I blushed. I felt it to the roots of my hair. And he laughed,
but not meanly.

"Don't you want me to touch it?" he said in a sly voice.

"Shut up."

He ruffled my hair, hard, so I dodged my head. "How's
Dexter?" he said.

"I let him out in your quarters." I grinned.

"No you didn't!"

I grinned. "No I didn't, but I got you."

He laughed again. "Demon."

We went back up to the sequestered deck where his quarters were, and my new one. He said, "These are the Geisha
Quarters. So you know. We call them the Hanamachi, from
the old name of the geisha districts in Earth Japan. Flower
towns. It's kind of pretty, the name."

"It's just you and me in this whole section?"

"No." He smiled. "There are others. You're going to meet
them now."

"But I've never seen them around here . . ."

"They stay hidden rather well." His smile had secrets, but
he gave my shoulders a squeeze and took me through a
hatch I'd always passed but never entered. Inside was a wide

lounge with painted brushed-gray panels on the walls, lined by thin columns of lights so that the ambience was soft white and close. Streams of the same pale color fluttered from the ceiling to the floor, which was carpeted. Surprisingly. In the shadows it looked blue, like water. Dark couches circled a bottom-lit table. There were tall drinks laid out, and people seated around them. Five in all. A drink per person. They all stopped talking when we entered and looked over.

Three girls and two boys. I thought. They were all very pretty.

Estienne put his hands on my shoulders and guided me closer, walking behind me. "Hey everyone. This is Yuri— finally." And to me, "They've been all curious to meet you."

"Yeah?" I tried a smile and a small wave. "Hey."

"Yuri," Estienne said, gesturing with one hand to the left-most person, a black-haired girl with skin almost the same shade, so deep and smooth that the light made her seem metallic. "This is Hestia, your Elder Sister. The rest are your sibs. That's how we refer to each other here. Hestia and I are your Elder Sister and Elder Brother, and the others you call just by their names. Rika—" He nodded to a brown-haired girl sitting beside Hestia. Then continued around the couch, "Yasmin, Ville, and Jonny." The last two were the boys.

Jonny shifted closer to Ville to make room on the end of the couch crescent. "Have a seat, Yuri."

They were both dark-haired, the boys, almost black, with pale eyes, but where Ville had a vague arrogance in the set of his mouth, Jonny's smile was quick, without edges. I sat beside him, and he smelled a bit like sweet musk. Estienne joined me and spread his arm along the back of the couch.

"Yasmin is our dancer, she'll show you those moves with the fan that you saw earlier. The others . . . well, you'll get to know what they do. Sometimes we'll meet like this but one or the other will be absent. That's because of clients."

"What do you do for the clients?" I had to ask it before Estienne rolled over the issue. Now that I was here, in this circle, he couldn't just avoid it.

"Have sex with them," Hestia replied, leaning forward to pick up her drink, which she sipped briefly. "Or just talk. Or rather, get them to talk. Sometimes when the captain has meetings he wants us there to relax the situation, and we don't do anything but play music and dance for them, or serve them drinks and food."

"Like real geisha, you mean?" I'd long ago read about it, but I hadn't thought there were many similarities except in the name.

"Something like that," Estienne said. "The clients are all people who do business with us. The ship. So it's business, always. You understand?"

"Even the sex, you mean. Like bedbugs."

"Well, not even. Less than bedbugs. These people aren't our friends."

I nodded. I was starting to get scared of the idea.

Ville said, "Don't worry, it's not nearly as exciting as it sounds. Mostly you just put your mind elsewhere."

"But the perks are good," Jonny said. "Some of our clients really give us lots of stuff. And that makes the captain happy too."

They weren't helping to calm me down. I looked at Estienne.

"It's okay." He could read me easily. "By the time you're ready it won't sound so bad. That's why you're here. We're going to train you. Mostly me, but your brothers and sisters too."

When he said it I thought of Isobel suddenly. And Jascha.

And I had to bite my lip, hard, to stop any more images that way. They were all silent, staring at me, maybe seeing through to my thoughts. They had eyes like that, like they knew all your little movements and gestures, things you weren't even aware of.

"You're very sweet-looking," Hestia said. "Like an angel, really, with those eyes and lips. The ones they paint on churches."

"A cherub," Yasmin said suddenly, very quietly.

I didn't know much about all of that, but I said, "Thanks. I guess."

Jonny laughed, and that seemed to break the muted pauses. "He doesn't even know when he's paid a compliment, Elder Brother. We really have our work cut out for us."

* * *

And they did. I thought I knew stuff, but when Estienne told me what the six of them did—and me, seven—it was clear that I didn't know much at all. I knew guns and fighting (which Estienne said was still good to know, because sometimes Marcus sent the geisha to kill betraying clients) and how a ship basically ran, and stuff about the Hub and other kinds of slate-learning, but geisha life was different. Geisha knowledge was . . . gentle and brutal. And they talked about it all, especially Estienne, with a frankness that shocked me.

Dancing, he said, came in all forms. You danced just to dance for someone, to tease them or to begin something. Or you danced with words and songs. You danced with touches too, danced with bodies in a bed. Or you danced with weapons. Like the captain's tattoo, the woman with the knives and the hands hanging from her belt.

Ultimately it came down to one thing—what was best for the ship. That was the captain's bottom line, and if you kept that in mind, he rewarded you, like this whole section of the deck to keep his geisha apart from the rest of the crew, because they *were* apart. We were apart. We were special, privileged, soft-edged with art and perfume and expensive clothes, and sharp with words and eyes and the freedom to kill other captains, politicians, and officials. Those people were all some of the *Khan*'s clients. And Marcus repaid betrayals.

Silk and steel, Estienne said. That was our world. That was my world at last, and once I'd learned it no one would ever hurt me again. Not without consequence. And I'd deal it myself, with skill. I'd end the dance myself, he said, one way or another. Geisha always did.

* _* *

The fan was our symbol.

At the end of the shift, after dinner and after Estienne had helped me clean my new quarters of dust and grit, then moved my few belongings, he promptly took over my shower to wash himself of the sweat and dirt. I sat on the floor and twitched my fingers at Dexter, who didn't seem to care that he was in a new place, I guessed, because he was still in his little cage. Dexter burrowed beneath his paper, and when I stuck my finger in and pushed at it he darted forward and tried to bite me. It reminded me of Seamus for some reason and I laughed.

Then Estienne came out, completely without clothes on, and I saw the fan tattoo just below his navel, spread there like an open eye, except it was red and gold and black, with the chevron end pointed down. And then I wasn't looking at the fan at all.

I was looking at Dexter. Fast.

"Yuri," Estienne said. I heard his voice but didn't see him. I didn't see anything, I was so fixed on not looking anywhere, even with both eyes open. "Yuri, this is training. I want you to look. You have to learn to look."

But the shift was over, we were still training? I asked him that, absently poking through the cage.

"Yes," he said. "Once I say so, we are. No matter the hour. So look at me."

And I had to. So I did. I saw him like that, naked, for the first time, head to toe, but I didn't much look into his eyes. I was too embarrassed. And I couldn't, even then, seem to move my gaze from his privates anyway. Even though that was far more embarrassing a thing to look at. But there it all was, all of him, and he was older, I knew, and bigger.

I wanted to shut my eyes, but this was work.

The hairs on his legs were just like on his arms. Sparse and pale and soft-looking.

It didn't feel like work when he came over and slid his hand into my hair.

"You really are sweet," he murmured, "like Hestia said."

Dexter started to toss up a ruckus for no apparent reason, but he was a loud bird and probably didn't need any. I looked at him and patted the cage. "Dexter, sshh."

But Estienne pulled me to my feet. "Leave your pet, he'll be fine."

"You said you don't like how he screams."

"I don't care now, he'll settle down in a bit I'm sure."

I stood, not knowing where to land my gaze.

"We won't do anything much," Estienne said, in his soft

way, reading my mind again. "I just want you to get used to it. Go take your shower, then come on to bed."

"Here?" It was hardly as nice as his quarters. Not yet anyway.

"Yeah, here. This is your place now. Where do you think?"

His voice had a hint of impatience, so I just went to the bathroom. I ran the water and stood under and looked at myself. Did he expect me to come out naked too? Well now I had to because I'd forgotten to take a change of clothes in with me, all I had was my dirty ones from the shift, and if I put on dirty clothes after taking a shower, he was going to frown.

I stayed in the shower for a long time, poking the cycler three times. Until a banging came on the door and Estienne opened it, and said, loud above the water, "You're wasting it. Hit the dryer and come out here." The door shut.

So I did come out, eventually, blasted dry, smoothing my hair and going straight to my locker where my sleepclothes were. He was already in the bunk with the blankets up to his waist. I was so aware of him I didn't even need to look.

Dexter was silent. I glanced at the cage, and he was hidden again under the paper.

"Am I so awful to be around?" Estienne said. "You're around me all the time during our goldshift. What difference does it make just because we're not in clothes?"

I didn't answer, just tugged on my pants.

"Leave the shirt," he said, "and I want you to answer me, Yuri. I want you to think."

"It's different," I said. Snapped. "Of course it's different."

"Why?"

"Because!"

"Don't give me that," he said, just as sharp. "You aren't

going to get away with little-boy answers anymore. Come here and sit your ass down."

I went over and sat on the edge of the bunk, my arms folded and my back to him.

"Yuri." His voice was soft. He could change it like that, in a second, and for the first time I wondered if that was part of being geisha too. His hand touched my bare back and moved around, light, in circles.

Without thinking about it, I let out my breath.

"Yuri," he said.

"Do you even care about me at all?" I asked, still with my back to him. "Or is this all just part of—training?"

"I think you know the answer to that."

"I don't. That's why I'm asking."

His arm came around my stomach and gently pulled me back against his chest. "I think you know." Somehow his nose found the side of my neck and it made my shoulder curl. "Sometimes," he whispered into my skin, "we have to work. And other times we get to play. That's just the way it is. But I like it better that it's me training you, just because we're like this, and it's not somebody else. I want you to know what you'll always come back to, no matter what clients you have or who else trains you. It's always this, you and me. Do you understand?"

"But I'm thirteen, and you're—"

His fingers dug. "I don't want to hear that. Age means nothing here. Did it matter that you were only four when the strits blew up your home, and you lost your mama? People like to make such a big fucking deal about age and this sep- aration of children from adults, but people like you and me, when were we children? When? If it's so bad for me to love you just because of some number, then why's it okay that my family died when I was five, all of them, the strits just

blew our ship because we were in the way between a battleship and a marauder, and I spent a week in a pod waiting for
someone to pick us up and you know nobody ever came?
Nobody. Nobody until the *Khan*. So fuck it all. If they want
to say some things are bad because of age, then everything
ought to be, everything should be watched and listed and
made better for kids, but they don't do that, do they? They
don't fucking care. So we make up our own rules. And I love
you, Yuri, this isn't a weapon, I'm not killing you. I love
you, and what's so wrong about that?"

Nothing. Nothing was wrong. I turned around and
hugged him because I heard the tears in his voice. And the
rage. And I knew them both like we were family.

* * *

Yasmin taught me the dance with the fan, there in a special room with mirrors on the walls and a warm faux-wood
floor. We had to watch ourselves, like Estienne had wanted
me to see him, because you couldn't be self-conscious about
your body if you were going to use it. You had to be aware
of how you looked and how others saw you, or you could
never control what you said—with your body or your
mouth or your eyes. She taught me how you could use your
body to speak, to capture, and to control. If they were fixed
on your body, they couldn't see your eyes. If they were fixed
on your eyes, they didn't see your hands. When you knew
your body and how it moved, you could move among people and not be noticed, or you could walk into a crowd and
demand attention. I'd thought she was quiet and shy, but
when she danced she seemed to hook me with a finger and
pull me closer without taking a step in my direction. Her
hair was wavy and long, like her body, and my eyes were

fixed on it, her body with its softer curves and smoother skin. I wondered what it would feel like pressed up against mine, fitted into mine like I fitted into Estienne and his harder angles. And she caught me watching and laughed, pointing at my nose and giggling until I laughed with her. Because she had just proved her point.

Ville taught me music, singing, and soft guitar. Clients liked talent, they liked you to be in a room soothing them, making a nice background, and if you did that and listened at the same time, you picked up a lot. People were drawn in by song. People fell in love with someone who could make their voices soar and whisper in a heartbeat. My voice was undeveloped, but he said it was workable. I would never belt out an aria, he said, but enchantment came just as readily in rawness. Ville was so pale and his hair so black that he seemed to be a reversed sort of boy, half-there, with spirit gray eyes that made me think of those feral dogs I saw sometimes in the Camp, the ones even Seamus had avoided. But Ville was soft-spoken, despite the sullen set of his mouth and the way he grinned, teaching me, as if it fed him in some way to know that he knew more than me but was generous enough to let me in on it all.

Jonny taught me language, and the weapon of words, how to pick up on what people truly said despite the shape of what came out of their mouths. We watched vids of interviews, formal and not. We read reports. He explained how to pitch your voice to be pleasing or commanding, and when in pleasant conversation what sorts of things you had to say that would steer the other person to talk about what you wanted. And when not to speak at all. There were so many shades of it, but Jonny said not to worry. Soon I would see and hear it all without even knowing, and I'd respond to it the same way, like walking. Or breathing. Jonny had a gentle sort of accent and a fast smile. At some angles, as I watched him over the horizon of my compscreen, he seemed far too plain to be a geisha, far too thin and long-faced, too ugly to be a girl and too pretty to be exactly masculine. But then he smiled or his eyes focused on me with unblinking attention, and the force of that was powerful, the way beauty was.

The second week of training he sent me a message on my tag that he couldn't make it this shift because he had a meeting, and I caught him in the corridor heading toward the lev, in geisha black, shiny as ink, with his hair long about his shoulders, wet-looking, reflecting lights. And through the outline of black on his eyes, his stare was half-lidded, smoky blue, deep. In this role and in those clothes he even walked differently. It was true what Yasmin said.

Rika taught me the silent and subtle ways to incapacitate someone who touched you the wrong way. I knew some fighting but not the quick-and-dirty things she said you had to do sometimes to keep yourself alive. And where to put small weapons on your body or in your clothes so even if you were naked, you knew exactly where they were and how to get to them. How to be quick, and how to keep your distance. Rika didn't smile much at all, and Estienne asked if she scared me even a little, and I said, "Yeah. A lot." And instead of laughing, he said, "Me too."

Elder Sister Hestia taught me about service, drinks and food, and if I had to sit with someone, how to be pleasant in movement and posture. The worst thing to do was knock over a glass in a client's lap. That would end any deal right there, or just add stress to the situation, and it was all about flow. You should be so smooth they didn't even know you were there unless they wanted to. Unless you let them.

They all knew these things, like I was learning all of it,

but they were particularly good in one or the other, and so they taught. They were all older than me—I thought Hestia was the oldest, even more than Estienne—but none of them were more than twenty-five. Or so I guessed. Not that it mattered. I was the captain's, and they didn't treat me like a kid or haze me like a newcomer, and when we had our meals in our private mess hall in the Geisha Quarters they even let me pick the dessert first. Yasmin liked to poke me at unexpected times and for no reason. Jonny loved to hug me even though he never went further than that ("You belong to Elder Brother," he said). Hestia watched me sometimes as if gauging just from my face if things were going all right. Rika and Ville didn't say much, they seemed too involved with each other, and I asked Estienne one shift if Marcus didn't mind that, and Estienne said, "Of course not. The closer we are, the better we work."

A month into it and Elder Sister Hestia took me into her quarters. She reclined on the small couch there, her thumb and forefinger caressing the smooth pink thumbnail on her opposite hand, and motioned me to sit on the bed. So I did, bouncing a little. It was very soft.

"You like Estienne a lot, don't you."

I nodded. Liked him in lots of ways, which I thought she meant.

"Good. You'll enjoy learning from him. But you know some things he can't teach."

She waited, so I said, "Like what, Elder Sister?"

Her teeth were straight white when she smiled, prettily contrasted to the dark of her skin. "Women, for one." Then she stood with smooth purpose and began to disrobe, sliding the long material off her shoulders. "You do the same, Yuri."

There wasn't the same kind of warmth in her tone, but that was all right. I didn't expect it. For a second I didn't

move, just stared at her as she revealed her body. It was dark
everywhere, and when I reached out my hand it looked pale
and sickly against her skin.

When we were both undressed she joined me on the bed
and took my hand in both of hers. She was warm and I was
cold. And when she placed my hand on her breast I was
shaking. It was hard to breathe just like when I stood too
long outside in the winter on Colonial Grace. The air took
away my breath.

Here in her quarters, the rich sweet scent of her skin
made it difficult.

But her voice and her movements were easy with me.

* * *

It was regular with her for a while, but completely just
training. Women needed to be handled differently from men,
she said. People, she said, liked to homogenize the genders.
Whatever a man could do, so could a woman. And vice
versa. And while that was true in some cases, she said, it was
idiotic to believe that men and women were just the same.
With all of her instruction though, she never encouraged me
to stay longer than it took, so I still bunked with Estienne in
off shifts, either in his quarters or my new one.

He helped me organize and dress up my new cabin so it
was all shades of green and blue, with little sparks of orange.
I thought Dexter liked it. It wasn't too soft or dark like Estienne's space and it wasn't going to stay quite as neat, because I just couldn't seem to keep things that straight, but it
was colorful when all the lights were up, and when they
weren't it felt like a jungle. Mostly we just slept, pressed up
against each other in the black. He'd touch me and cuddle
and once in a while he got me off just by that. But nothing

more. Maybe he didn't want to interrupt what I was learning with Elder Sister Hestia, but as the weeks went I could feel it, every sleepshift, building.

I wanted to, with him.

Too slow, it seemed. With thoughts of dance and words and song, I wanted to know everything he could teach me, everything that complemented what I was learning elsewhere. Everything I learned I showed him in private, except for sex, and he'd test me on the mundane things, and he was testing me with this because all the affectionate touches he had didn't stay my curiosity.

What else? I wanted to shout. Show me.

I didn't go much into the other parts of the ship anymore, everything was in the Hanamachi, our Geisha Quarters, except for when Marcus called me down for meetings or more training in things like drive basics and flight, things geisha didn't know and didn't have to know, but protégés did. After the first month he invited me for a private dinner in the captain's mess, just me and him, and he gave me a hug when he met me at the hatch.

"You're looking well."

"Thanks." I smiled at him and went to the table, waiting for him to sit before I pulled out my chair and followed suit. The steward brought the first course, a spinach leaf salad with what smelled like raspberry vinaigrette. The wine was light. I sipped as he did. Our cutlery flashed under the half-cast lights.

"Your Elder Brother and Sister are really pleased with your progress," he said, leaning back as he chewed. He picked up his crystal water glass. "How are you about the things they're teaching? Comfortable, uncomfortable?"

I swallowed, took a sip of the wine before responding,

putting my hands in my lap. "I was uncomfortable in the beginning but . . . it's better now."

"How is it better?"

"I understand it now. It's like a game, but not . . . I don't
mean like some fight contest. It's conversation. It just uses
everything, not just your speaking voice. And it's fun on that
level. Knowing all the levels when most people don't."

His eyes appraised me. I wasn't telling him anything he
didn't know already—not just the meaning of what I said,
but that I said it at all. Estienne and Hestia were reporting on
me all the time. They never said so, but of course they
would. Before I was theirs, or a geisha, I was a member of
the *Khan*. And all of this was Captain Falcone's idea.

"How is Estienne?" he said, changing the subject. But not
really. He was dropping lines to know what I'd cast back.

"I like him," I said, with a smile.

"He likes you," Marcus said.

"I know, he told me."

"When do you think you'll be ready for your first assignment—as a geisha?"

"Whenever he tells me."

"But you might have to tell *him*. Do you think you're
ready now?"

I hated to admit it. "No, sir."

"Why not?"

I resumed eating. The steward brought the soup, a
creamed broccoli. I waited until he'd left and sat quiet for a
second, not wanting to just blurt out a deflective answer.
That wouldn't work in this room, at this table with the
captain.

"I don't know how I'd like having someone touch me
like that. All the other stuff, even the killing, I think I'm fine
with. But Estienne touches me, and I like that. I even like it

when Elder Sister Hestia does it. I like it when *I* like the person. What if I don't like some client?"

"But it's not about like or dislike," Marcus said. "Not with a client."

"I know, but . . ." I should've kept that quiet. That was the sort of interjection that got you nowhere and didn't make anything happen in the conversation except let the other person know you were more undecided than you let on.

"Estienne's explained to you about work and play," Marcus said.

"Yes, sir."

"Your body's a tool, Yuri. It's something you wield with skill, like a gun or a knife. In and of themselves those things are harmless. It takes someone who knows what they're doing with them to make them dangerous. And my geisha are dangerous. That's what I intend. You don't have to hurt people to be dangerous. Giving other people an appearance of power puts you in control. When you sit with clients, or sleep with clients, whatever it is that you'll have to do, they will all think that they are the ones with power. But you know what you're doing when you let them touch you. It's not love or affection. You're not giving them anything that means a thing to you. They want the motions of it, and you give it to them, and if you didn't, they'd be in want. And who then has the power?"

I listened, hard.

"So when you go to work," he said, "you take your knives and your gun and your body, they're all weapons. Do you understand?"

I thought. He watched me.

"What's your question?" he said.

And he did want to hear it. He wanted me to work it out. So I said, "But my body and mind are connected, and it's my mind that wields those weapons. I choose to take up a gun or a knife, and I can put them back when I'm done. But I walk around with my body, it's a part of me. When I look in the mirror I see it, and when people touch me it does things to me. How can I separate that from a client?"

"Control," he said. "Before you can properly control other people you have to learn to control yourself."

I thought about that. I ran his words through my mind, and he let me. We didn't speak for the rest of the meal. But we didn't need to. He'd said already what he wanted me to hear.

Power and control. Two sides of the same idea. Like a geisha and a protégé.

* * *

I wanted to talk to Estienne about what Marcus had said, so I went to his quarters. It was already at the end of the shift, time to relax, roll into bed, and do nothing for a while. My head felt a little warm from all the wine, a glass only but I thought it was expensive stuff.

I buzzed Estienne's hatch and waited. He was usually in quarters by this time, catching up on comp work or reading or something. Sometimes we sat in his bunk and did individual work, propped up against each other with our backs to the bulkhead, and that was my favorite way to spend the end of shift.

His hatch opened, and Taja stood there, looking just the same as she had the last time I saw her. On my birthday.

I pushed by her into the quarters. Estienne was still putting on his pants. He wasn't wearing a shirt, and his chest was ruddy and damp.

"Hey," Taja said.

I turned around and shoved her out of the quarters.

"Yuri!" Estienne said, reaching for my arm, but I darted away and followed her into the corridor.

"What the hell—?" she said, putting her hands up to deflect my pushes. Trying to shove me back. "Stop it, you little weed!"

"Get the hell out of my *face!*"

"I'm not *in* your face!" She knocked my fist away, and her leg moved to trip me. I jumped to the side, hit her at the back of her neck. She fell forward.

"Yuri!" Hands grabbed me around the upper arms, but I drove my elbows back. They met air, and I cut free. I turned, but Estienne dodged, and his hand shot out, grabbing me around the throat. He shoved me to the bulkhead. In his other hand a knife snapped up and pointed at my right eye. "Stand still," he said.

Hatches opened up in the corridor. My brothers and sisters and Elder Sister Hestia peered out at us. Quiet.

I breathed. Shifted my gaze as Taja got to her feet and gestured at me. "That boy is crazy! You better *train* him, Estienne!"

"Fuck you!" I yelled back.

Estienne's fingers tightened. I started to cough.

"Go," Estienne said.

She stared at me, cheeks sucked in.

"LEAVE!" Estienne said, at a level I'd never heard before from him.

She went. Straight, without looking back. And he held me there, pinned, until the only sound in the corridor was my breathing.

"Are you going to behave?" he said, in a normal tone. Still pointing the knife at my eye.

"Yeah," I said. "Let go of me."

He did, slow. Snapped the blade shut and turned his back to me. Hestia looked at him, and maybe he looked back because she shut her hatch then, two down from his, and once that happened they all shut themselves in, and I was alone, watching him walk off.

I rubbed my neck. I coughed and spat after him, "You defend her over me! Fuck your *lies*!"

He whirled and came back to me at a clip, grabbed my arm, and shoved me into his quarters, right onto his bunk, with its soiled sheets from his sex with her. I tried to get up but he pushed me back down.

"I told you long ago that she was nothing but a bedbug. What's your problem?"

I stared up at him, gripping the mattress. "Why do you need to shag her anyway?"

"We just do it. You don't have to be stupid about it. And before you think of attacking her again, she is the captain's alpha right now, so you better not mark her up in any way. Pulling my knife on you was saving *your* ass."

"His *what*?"

"Marcus screws her on a semiregular basis. He likes her, for what it's worth. So messing around with her in a good way only helps on this ship. Messing with her in a bad way will get you brigged or worse. Even if you are his protégé." Estienne set his knife on his desk. He hadn't looked at me at all. "You don't know everything yet, Yuri. Tread lightly until you do."

I watched his back, the fingernail marks on his shoulder blades. From her. And something coiled in me, black and thick and pitiless.

"Fine. I'm going to quarters."

I left, and he didn't stop me.

* *
*

I didn't go to quarters. I went down the decks to the forward crew, with my Serate and my switchblade. The curves and angles here were all dark, imploded, sharp night on a ship that knew no day in the first place. But the rib-cage arc of the corridor made you feel like you were inside something that might just belch you out if you disagreed with it. The rumble and scream of the drives sounded louder there than in the Hanamachi. The walls were scarred.

I had the ship specs memorized by now and made my way to the lounge. It was noisy and crowded, smelled of caff and smoke and bodies. Blue haze hung above the people, lights or stale air or something of both. I looked around but didn't see her in the shadows or the blue. So I pushed my way in, ignored the looks, and unclamped one of the empty seats in the corner. I climbed onto it.

"Anyone know where Taja is?" I yelled.

Talking stopped. Faces turned up to me. A blunt silence.

"Taja," I said again.

"What d'you want with her, kid?" a man said, and I tried to see who it was, but bodies shifted, and it was impossible to tell. Three men approached my seat. None I recognized offhand from my training.

"That's my business," I said.

I heard someone say, "That's the captain's boy."

Good. Now they'd know not to touch me.

But one of the men suddenly grabbed my legs and jerked me from the chair. I fell to the deck with a yelp but managed to kick myself free. I rolled over and sprang up, hobbled a bit toward the wall with my gun in my hand.

"Touch me again," I said, aiming at the one who'd

grabbed me. Blurs of faces, dark eyes, dark skin, paleness and ink. They kept their distance, but I was sure they all were armed. "Now where is she?"

"Just tell him," some girl said, "before he peashoots us to death."

"Put him to use. Our crew needs culling."

"Berth 20C," another voice said. With laughter. "Go there. The captain will thank you."

"He wouldn't thank you for coming down here with a gun and your little threats."

Untethered voices floating from the mash of faces and the smoke.

But it didn't matter. I had a number. I walked to the door. "Pissant."

No such silence and respect, as I'd got when I was new, but then I never went to the crew decks, and I hadn't been a geisha. Maybe on the captain's orders things had changed for them, maybe not. Pirate crew. They must've known I wouldn't go running to Marcus.

"C'mere and say it." I looked into the crowd, kept my back to the wall just right of the exit. "Come up, unless a kid with a gun's got you all anonymous and brave."

A man stepped out. Old, rangy, his arms just taut flesh over whipcords. He said, "Don't waste our time."

I shot him. Twice. One in each leg so he tumbled to the deck.

I heard guns being gotten all through the room.

But I walked out. And gambled that nobody would fire.

And nobody did.

*　*　*

Berth 20C. I buzzed the hatch and held my wrist behind my back, the free hand holding the Serate. I wasn't going to kill her, of course, but she could back off Estienne, I didn't care even if she was the captain's wife. How did she manage to be alpha anyway? She wasn't even that pretty. And the fact Estienne didn't do anything but defend his actions made my insides burn. Maybe I should've gone back up and shot him instead?

The hatch opened, and Bo-Sheng stood there.

I blinked. We stared at each other before I said, "Taja's shagging you too?"

"What?" He squinted at me. His lips looked parched, his hair tousled as if he'd been sleeping.

"What're you doing in Taja's quarters?" I said, trying to see over his shoulder. I gave up and just shoved him back, going in myself.

"Taja? These are *my* quarters."

And they were. It was obvious a boy lived here, one bunk with clothes strewn on it and a mess of what looked like electronic supplies. His work?

Damn adults played me. *Our crew needs culling.* They wanted to put my gun and temper to use. On Bo-Sheng.

I turned around and looked at him.

"Why do you have a gun?" he asked slowly.

I remembered it, tucked it into my waistband. "Never mind. I'm—"

He looked scared. His arms wrapped around his body and he kept blinking at me, rubbing the side of his face.

I was sober enough to know when someone else wasn't. "Are you high?"

"No." He scowled.

I moved him aside and shut the hatch. "Bo-Sheng, you can't be high. The captain doesn't *like* that shit."

"You come all the way down here from your high mountain just to scold me? Screw you!"

Maybe I should've been angry. But instead I said, "What's happened to you?"

He snorted. "Oh, that's a jewel coming from you."

"What's that mean?"

"Look at you!" His hand jerked in my direction before tucking back against his body. "You're the captain's whore, they all talk about it."

My teeth pressed together. "I'm not his whore, I'm his protégé. He's never touched me. For your *information*."

"Well it isn't like he hasn't before."

"Before what?"

"With his previous 'protégés' . . . or whatever you call it. He likes to fuck kids."

I reached to him and shoved him against the bulkhead, my fists in his shirt. He didn't struggle, just stared at me with wet, black eyes.

"Who's saying those things?" I pushed my face into his. "What're their names?"

"Like I'm gonna tell? They'll kill me."

"*I'll* kill you!"

He didn't answer. And my words rang.

Then he said, "Yuri . . ."

I heard it. And all the anger just vented from my system. My fingers unclenched, and instead of bruising him, I hugged him. And he didn't fight this time, his arms locked around me. And then he said, "Where's your family, Yuri?"

For a second I didn't understand why he'd ask that. It was obvious—my family was here. The geisha and the captain . . . and Estienne. But he tilted back his head and blinked at me. "Where's your mama and Jascha, has he found them yet?"

"No," I said, releasing him and walking to his bunk. I

fumbled out my cigrets and lit one, shoving the case back in my cargo pocket.

"Why not? He said he would. Maybe your mama's in a good place, and we can leave here and go see her. Or go back home to the Camp."

The pleading tone grated on my nerves. "Fuck the Camp. I'm never going back there. What would we do if we went? Sit on those old boxes and piss at the lake 'til we got sick and died?"

He sniffed, rubbed at his nose, then his arm. "Then we should find your mama ourselves and go to her."

"Bo-Sheng, don't you get it?" I stared at him and sucked hard on the cig in frustration. "Nobody wants us! Papa never *once* tried to comm me, so what makes you think my mama would care where the hell I am?"

"Of course she'd care! And how do you know he never tried? The captain told you? Why do you even believe him?"

"You believed him! You brought me here!"

He recoiled as if I'd struck him. "So you blame me."

"No I don't *blame* you. I like it here! Look at what he's given us. Why the hell do you wanna leave?"

Estienne was here. I was never going to leave.

"Yuri," he said, "they do bad things. They kidnap kids and force them into this life. Just because we came here in total ignorance doesn't make what they do all right."

"Force them?" I laughed, sheer surprise. "Nobody here is forced."

"Maybe not up where you are. But down here's a different story."

I shook my head. "Estienne would've told me . . ."

"Him? He fucking *recruits* for Falcone!"

I still shook my head, but my mind started to spiral. "You're wrong."

"They lie, Yuri." He came close and took my shoulders, fingers digging. "I bet he's been lying to us all along, in everything since we got aboard. Since before. They had your papa sign papers like this ship was a legit merchant, but it's a pirate, and those papers don't mean shit. None of what they told your papa or the Camp officials means shit. *They took us.*" He blinked rapidly. "They—"

I broke away. "I like it here, Bo-Sheng. I don't wanna leave. So what if we do some bad things? What would you rather do, go off and live in a foster home on some station? Or be held in some detention center until the govies figure out we didn't mean to get on this ship? Oh, except we did. And I get a better education here than anything those tired old grown-ups in the Camp coulda given. I got my own weapons, my own berth, my own pay. So what if we steal cargo here and there. So what if it's hard. You earn what you get here, and that's more than the Hub would ever allow anyone our age." I took a drag from the cig. "And Marcus has never touched me, that's just fucking rumor."

"Maybe he knew you could be got in other ways. What about Estienne?"

I hit him. Ashes flew from the cigret, and he knelt in a heap on the floor, holding his face. Crying. And I bent down and hugged him because I didn't want to fight with him, I just wanted him to be happy here. I held on tight. "Maybe I can get you moved up to the Hanamachi with me, and you'll see. It's not bad at all."

"No." He wrenched away and staggered to his feet, putting his back to the wall. "I'm not gonna be your whore!"

I could've shot him for that. But he was pathetic, his face muddy with tears. I could've made him regret those words.

"Then stay," I said instead. "Do your drugs and live down

here and don't ever talk to me again. Then maybe you'll learn."

I left him. Without killing him. Even though I wanted to, right then.

* * *

I was in my quarters, on the floor, with the cage door open and Dexter on the lower bars, ducking his head at me so I could scratch it. So much like a dog it was funny. He made me smile, and for a while I forgot about Taja and Estienne and Bo-Sheng.

But then he let out a screech, and a second later the hatch beeped and swung in. I'd locked it, but Marcus had a command override, and he stepped in. I got to my feet and Dexter flew from the cage with another screech and perched himself on my desk, flapping his wings before settling. The captain gave him a glance, then looked at me, not smiling.

"You went to crew deck?"

He was going to brig me or worse. "Yes, sir."

His tone was calm. "Tell me, Yuri, what fucking business is it of yours to go hunting another member of my crew when she did nothing to you? Then shooting a man in the process?"

"He bitched at me in front of all of them. I wasn't going to take it. How'd they respect me then?" I wasn't going to answer about Taja if I could help it.

He walked right up to me, two strides that changed the expression on his face. "Before you go shooting my crew you find out who the hell they are!"

Dexter launched from the desk and flew about the room, squawking, biting at my nerves, but Marcus ignored him completely. His shout was louder than the bird. "That man is one of my drive engineers, and I can't fucking afford to have him lying abed in Medical!"

I couldn't move.

"I expected better," he said, in a sudden normal voice. "You did something rash because you're pissed that Taja is screwing Estienne. What the hell did we talk about at dinner? Are you being led around this ship by your dick and your silly notions of romance? I want it out of your head, Yuri, do you hear me? I don't give a shit that you and Estienne snuggle on off-hours, but your entire stay on my ship isn't all off-hours. You're going to work for what you get here, and if that requires you to bare ass when I say, you will do it and not complain. Do you read me?"

I couldn't answer. My chest was too tight. I couldn't breathe.

He hit me at the side of the head, so fast I felt it some seconds after the fact. And then the pain, sharp.

"Do you read me?" he shouted.

"Yes, sir!"

"What you're feeling now for Estienne," he said, "is false. What have you been learning here if not that fundamental fact? You can control your emotions. You can use other people's emotions to control them. This will save you a lot of grief in the future, in your work. You may have affection for people and make attachments, but you learn to balance it. And not let it consume you." His voice was kinder then, as if he regretted having to yell. "Do you understand?"

I nodded. I did. Even when I'd offered kindness to Bo-Sheng he'd done nothing but spit in my face.

"Estienne will always be here for you." Marcus said. "Like the *Khan* will be. But sometimes we have to go off ship for missions. That doesn't mean you're forgotten. Just because he sleeps with other people or you're both geisha doesn't mean that central part of your relationship is void."

I nodded again. Tried not to let my eyes leak. I kept them open, and the cool air dried me out.

He said, "You saw Bo-Sheng again, didn't you."

I said, "Yeah. And he doesn't want anything to do with me." It hurt.

"He's been difficult since he came here. Jealous of you because I saw more in you than in him."

I didn't say anything. I didn't want to believe it. But Bo-Sheng seemed determined to drag me back to the Camp with him. That fucking Camp.

Instead I said, "Marcus, you haven't found Mama yet?"

Marcus said, "No."

And why should I doubt him? Even a pirate, maybe even especially a pirate, wouldn't have had ready access to Hub information.

I said, "Is it true you kidnap children? Is it true you raped your other protégés?"

He stared down into my face. "What do you believe? What do I have to do, let you interview every crewmember until you decide you can trust me? It's time to make up your own mind. It's long overdue. Have I ever been truly awful to you?"

The truth was I wanted to be here.

So I shook my head, and said, "I'm sorry, sir."

He nodded. "Fine then. No more shooting my crew. Now that you're older they have little restriction in how to deal with you. So I'd advise you not to troll belowdecks for a little while." His mouth tugged at the corners just a bit. "You definitely made an impression though."

But of course I had. I was his.

* *
  *

I didn't see Estienne until he commed me early next shift, before breakfast. Some part of me thought about apologizing for the whole deal, but then he didn't even open the hatch for me, I just saw the light go green, and I opened it myself.

Estienne said, "Sit."

It wasn't a tone that invited argument. Maybe Marcus had come down on him for my behavior?

I went farther into the q and perched on the end of the desk chair. He was dressed in geisha black, but it all had a slightly transparent quality to it that gave his skin underneath a wet sheen. He was sitting on his bunk, but when I sat, he stood, and took the two strides to get in front of me. I had my hands on my knees and didn't know what to look at. Up into his eyes was suddenly too intimidating. I remembered the knife in my face. So I settled on his navel, which showed through the unseamed bottom half of his shirt.

My palms were damp. I didn't know why. For weeks I'd stirred with wanting just exactly this. So what was different now?

Maybe it was just a little too abrupt. A little too conscious. And if he was angry at me still, was it going to hurt?

"Look at me," he said. Gently. No anger.

It struck me that we'd never really kissed. Not like the way a geisha should.

So I looked at him.

His eyes were dark. His hair was long. And when he leaned down to my upturned face, the ends of his hair grazed my cheek, and things were blurry for a second, then not there at all because his lips pressed to mine. I felt his hand snake around to the back of my neck.

He was kissing me.

And I sat there, sweaty palms.

He said with warm breath against my mouth, "You have to kiss back, Yuri."

So, really, what was I waiting for?

I didn't have to wait anymore.

I reached up to touch his face, but he pushed my hand down.

"Kiss," he said, still so close I couldn't really see him at all.

I leaned forward and up, put my hand somewhere on his shirt to steady myself even though I was the one sitting down, and I kissed him, soft lips, open mouth, tasted the caff and the cigs on him, inside him, and it was all wet and smoky and did things to me that maybe or maybe not were supposed to happen. So much different from Elder Sister Hestia, just because I cared about him in a different way.

His tongue pushed my mouth wider, so I guessed that was what he wanted, or what he wanted to show me, and I let him, but just as it was threading a warmth down through my body he leaned back, licking his lips, and said, "Do something. Don't just wait for me. You have to initiate."

And damn it all, he was frustrating me. So I stood, forcing him back, and twisted his shirt in my fist. His hand clamped around my wrist, and I knew he was going to protest, but I said, "You want me to. So shut up and let me."

"*Kiss,*" he said. "Nothing more."

"Tease," I said. "So forget it." With my knuckles grazing his bare belly. The fan tattoo.

I thought he'd smile, push my head in that playful way he liked to do, but there was nothing playful in his face. He grabbed my wrists, painfully, and disengaged my hands from his body.

"This is work," he said. "Not play."

"Can't it be both?"

His eyes narrowed. "Yuri."

"But I know that I know you. That we—we do things already. I know it'll be different with a real client, but do we have to pretend that's now?"

He said, "Yuri, don't confuse the situation. Just because I touch you and we fool around doesn't mean you know what you're doing when you have to do it for a reason other than getting off. You have to learn. Despite the fact it's me—keep your heart out of the equation. Copy that?"

He sounded like Marcus. And his voice was studied. I wasn't in his equation now.

I clenched my hands at my sides. "Copy *that*."

"Good," he said. "So kiss me." He didn't smile. "Properly."

He didn't mean to be proper. He wanted me to manipulate.

So I watched his face, etched my gaze along the curves of his lips and the lines of his jaw, down the stretch of his throat to his collarbone. And I took a step until we were chest to chest, and I could feel him breathe. I slipped a hand to his waist, curled a finger in his belt loop, and pulled his hips closer. He was watching me with his hands at his sides. I leaned and kissed him, barely a tilt of the chin, so our noses brushed. I bit his lower lip, gently, and tugged on it, then tongued his mouth wider, delved in like into a burndive. Forget the edges of the real world, the dirty color and mundane solidity. His world was a soft pressure, wet warmth, and all the colors were behind my eyes in flavors. Caff. Cigs. Heat and smoke.

I trailed that kiss along his cheek, his jaw, down his throat when he tilted back his head. And I felt his hand in my hair, and maybe it was just training the way he said, "Good, good," in a low voice, but if it was, I was determined to train him. He was going to learn. This was going to be more than work. In the end it was going to be worship.

And even as I touched him I wondered if he felt this way with Taja. If he felt anything at all now that wasn't so conscious and so deliberate. And maybe my seeing Taja twice like that hadn't been an accident. Maybe he was making a point to me.

I bit the side of his neck, and he pushed me back.

I smiled.

He said, "This isn't going to work. Turn around."

"What do you want me to do? You said kiss. Didn't that work?" My gaze slid down to fix pointedly on his crotch.

He took my arm and faced me to the bed. "Lie down. On your stomach."

All the joking left my brain. I glanced over my shoulder and smiled at him, but he didn't smile back. "Lie down." Softer voice. So I did that, and he climbed onto the bed and straddled my hips. I raised myself on my elbows because now—

Couldn't breathe.

"This isn't fun," he said from behind me, as I stared at the side of the lockers pushed against the top of his bed. "If someone wants this, **you** build them up if they want it, there's no emotion involved. Sometimes they don't want all the buildup though, so you just go to this." Echoing parts of what Hestia had said. As he spoke his hands slid underneath the back of my shirt and pushed it up. Not quite the same way he did when we were just casual in his quarters. His fingers pressed my ribs on their way back down. He raised himself off me. "Lift your hips."

I tried to roll over, free now, because this wasn't how I

pictured it would be. I thought he'd hold me a little first, or talk to me in his real voice, not with this sort of voice as if he were standing at the side of the room, watching.

But he didn't let me roll over. One hand pressed between my shoulders. "Lift your hips," he said. "Please."

So I did. I thought he was going to reach under just to touch me, but he unseamed my pants and tugged them down, and didn't touch me at all.

"Estienne," I said.

He moved off me without a word, and I wanted to look back at him, but I didn't for some reason, I just kept staring at the side of the lockers, their dented metal covered in a fall of red fabric, and maybe I heard him rummage around for something beneath the bed, maybe I heard him remove his own pants, but it was just me and the lockers and my grip on one of his pillows, my chin pushed into it. I was flat on my chest. Then he said he had to prepare things so he put this stuff inside me and it was cold and I squirmed but he pressed a hand to the small of my back to keep me mostly still, and I wanted to say Stop, but of course I didn't because he wasn't going to and I had to learn. Then it happened. He put himself inside me in slow increments, all of him and all of me, until all of me was just wet and red, like the pillow beneath my face. He didn't talk to me, not really, except for telling me what to do and how to move. He wasn't brutal, but he wasn't kind. He wasn't even really touching me.

It wasn't him. And it wasn't me.

It was just the geisha in this room.

* * *

He sent me back to my quarters, just like Hestia had. I wanted to go because I hurt. And as soon as I got there I threw up in the bathroom. Grasping the cold steel seat I tried to remember that Estienne loved me, that as long as he loved me it made anything right, because how could anything bad come from those feelings. I tried to keep those thoughts in my head, but as I coughed and spat they wanted to come out of me like the sick. They wanted to revolt.

* * *

Early next shift Rika buzzed my hatch. I was still in bed, and she came in, maybe I'd forgotten to lock it, I couldn't remember. She saw me curled up beneath the blankets, and said, "No fight training today I guess."

I shook my head.

"No anything today?" she said.

"No." I watched her as she came closer to the bunk. "Can you tell Estienne? Or Elder Sister? I don't want to leave here."

"Sure, but they might not go for it." For all her general ruthlessness, she could still be caring. She cared a lot about Ville, the way they sometimes held hands at meals. Now she reached down and touched my hair. "You did it finally with him, didn't you."

"Yeah."

"You need to go see Doc Wachter."

"Later."

"This shift, Yuri. It's important you go." She sat on the side of the bunk. Now I wondered if Estienne had sent her.

I wondered why he didn't come here himself. "You want anything? Food, drink . . . a gun for target practice?"

It made me smile. It was a good thing to think about and not the fact Estienne hadn't visited before her.

"I'll come back in an hour to take you to Medical," she said, standing again. "And don't worry, it does get better."

In general or with him?

But I didn't ask that. She wasn't the one to ask.

* * *

Doc Wachter said I was dehydrated (because I'd been throwing up most of the shift), so he told me to drink lots of liquids and gave me an injet of something, then he examined me and did something with a bot-knitter spray and told Rika to bring me back at the end of the shift. I didn't see Estienne for the entire shift. And I had to go stand on the bridge for two hours right after medical for my regular training watch, with my envelope of water. I had to pay attention to what was going on so I could see all the things Marcus had made me study about bridge command.

Except I didn't pay attention to any of it, not even Caligtiera and his looks. All I thought about was Estienne.

After another checkup I skipped dinner in the Hanamachi mess hall and just went straight to quarters.

And Estienne was in there. He held out his arms as soon as he saw me, and I hesitated.

"It hurts," I said.

"I just want to hold you," he said. And, "I'm sorry, but you need to know, Yuri. That was work. And now I just want to hold you."

And he looked so sorry. So I dropped my slate on the

desk and went to him, and he hugged me just like that for the
rest of the shift.

* * *

We worked in his quarters. We played in mine. He was
normal Estienne in my quarters.

He told me I was going to get my geisha tattoo after my
first client. He asked me one sleepshift if I was ready, with
months of work and play making my body grow in ways that
I couldn't see when I looked in the mirror, but it was there,
I felt it inside. And I told him, "I'm scared."

"I know," he said. "But after the first it's easier. Trust me."

This made it better, he said. When we came home to this,
just him and me and the ship. After shopping runs to station
or even when I went as a protégé with Falcone to other ships
like *Shiva*, checking up on their operations. My brothers and
sisters all told me the same—you came home to the *Khan*.
And I couldn't keep putting it off, so one shift I just told
him, "Yes, I'm ready." Because I'd learned where to put my
hands, my mouth, what words to say and how to say them,
how to move and how to defend myself, and this was my
work now.

This was work.

6.19.2190 EHSD—Debut

The party for my debut as a full-fledged geisha took place
on Chaos Station. Geisha from *Shiva* as well as our own
Hanamachi were all going to be there, with our captains and
a bunch of clients. Marcus said the clients were arms deal-

ers and sympathizers—humans who sided with the strits.
He was helping them get together because the sympathizers
wanted better weapons for the war, and the arms dealers
needed to unload their stash somewhere, to someone. Marcus knew a lot of arms dealers, and he'd lately been in contact with some symp leaders from the other side of the
Demilitarized Zone.

"Why are we helping the strits?" I asked, there in the captain's office as he explained the situation. As his protégé I
was going to be by his side. For this meeting he didn't want
me to circulate that much. He was going to assign me the
client himself.

He said, "Nothing in this war is black-and-white." He
scrolled his comp for a minute, sitting behind his granite
gray desk, then paused and looked up at me. "Are we going
to have a problem?"

"No, sir," I said.

"I've sent a file of dossiers to your comp. Memorize
them, they're the information on the dealers and the symps.
And you'll be wearing this." He took a commstud from one
of his drawers and flipped it over to me. "You might not be
directly beside me in the room, and I'll want to talk to you.
Gather at the main airlock in twelve hours, we dock in ten."

* * *

Estienne watched me dress. He was already in his geisha
black, a stiffer shiny material this time that made his silhouette as sharp and dark as a blade. My black had tiny crystals
embedded in the fabric, so I glittered like a jewel. *Tama*,
Estienne said. The euphemism for payment. Geisha wages,
in the old days. That was how they were counted, when you
were sold. Jewels.

Except I wasn't going to be sold. The transaction wouldn't be that cut-and-dried.

"He'll save you for an important client," Estienne said. "I have an idea who, but . . . he wouldn't want me to say until he does. But this one likes them new."

I tried to ignore that. I was getting good at it, all the talk and thoughts of working with someone other than Estienne or Elder Sister Hestia. So I turned around from the mirror and smiled. "My eyes don't look right."

"I'll do it." Estienne unfolded from my bed and came over to take the red inkpen from my fingers. He held my chin to keep me steady, and murmured, "Look up." So I did, and he carefully ran the pencil around my eyes, making a smooth catlike upsweep past the corners of my lids. Still gripping my chin he leaned to the desk and took the red shadow, rubbed the pad of his forefinger in it before filling in the lines so my lids were the same nebula crimson. He dusted the indents at the corners with some star black. Then he took the gloss stick and rubbed the sponge over my lips. "Clear," he said, "because your lips are just naturally all bitten up and pink."

"Shut up." I gave his chest a shove.

He laughed and tossed the makeup on the desk. "And your skin is so pale, you don't need powder at all." He patted my cheek.

I snapped my teeth at his fingers.

"Vicious," he said, pulling his hand away, still smiling. Trying to put me at ease. I went along with it, because I wanted to be, even though the gnawing in my gut told me otherwise. "Look." He turned me to the long mirror on the wall.

I reached up to move the hair from my face, but he swatted my hand down.

"Let it fall."

In my eyes and down in soft spikes on my cheeks. My hair was a darker blond than his, and while his eyes were fogged black on the lids, I had the maiko red. Apprentice until after this party.

The last thing I did was slide my switchblade up my right sleeve into the little pocket I'd sewn there, then held it in place with a pullable tab.

"Ready," I said. A lie.

"Beautiful," he said, which wasn't.

＊ ＊ ＊

All seven of us waited at the airlock. All in black, all carved with makeup around the eyes and powdered to a perfect sheen. Hair was glossed, tied back except for mine, as polished as our nails. Jonny smiled at me. "You're like a murdered angel," he said, which made me frown, and Estienne squeezed the back of my neck. "Don't make a face," he said. "The way you look now can break a body."

So it began. And while we stood waiting, I saw their expressions form. Become silent and still and unreadable.

I tried not to fidget, pull at my forearm sleeves, or shift on my feet. Estienne kept his arm loosely around my neck and smoked a cigret. I bummed one off him because I'd left mine back in quarters. Of all the times to forget my cigs.

Soon Marcus walked up with Taja and a male crewmember I didn't recognize. Taja. She looked at me but didn't say anything, and I just blew smoke at her. I hadn't seen her around Estienne since we fought, but that didn't mean she hadn't been with him. They just didn't let me see now. Marcus moved in front of my line of sight, putting her behind his shoulder, and his eyes grazed me. I looked back. He wore a tailored dark suit, the first time I'd ever seen him in anything so expensive. The lines made him seem taller and accentuated a feral leanness that I'd never really noticed before even when he was shirtless. His hair was combed back from his eyes and his eyes—chemical blue.

"Good," he said, as he watched me. "Good."

It wasn't approval; it was assessment.

The seven of us and his two guards followed him out the airlocks and down the ramp, merchant crew off to a party. The IDs he presented to Chaos Station Customs said we were legal, and what else were merchants going to do when they docked and emerged in party finery?

They waved us through and by the time we got to the high doors of the inner station, my cigret was smoked down to its filter.

* * *

The gathering was in the VIP lounge of a club and den called Tartarus. It was a dark décor with embedded floor lights of gold and orange, tattooing the room with flames. Aside from our group of ten from the *Khan*, *Shiva* came with their captain, their captain's protégé, a couple of guards, and three geisha, dressed similarly to us except their predominant color was red (with the black). Our clients were already circulating when we got there, served by the *Shiva* geisha. A quick count came up at twenty. I recognized faces from the files. Ten dealers and ten symp buyers.

Estienne squeezed my hand then headed off with everyone else in our Hanamachi to work the room, leaving me with Marcus, who strode over to the *Shiva* captain. So I followed. I recognized her protégé from my first visit to their ship. He looked older, naturally. His hair was longer. But his face was still sullen, and he looked right through me.

"How do they seem?" Marcus asked the other captain.

"Cordial," she answered. She wore a form-fitting white suit and held a tall glass of a pale green drink. "But nobody's going to break out in a firefight with Marines on station. At least the symps have that much common sense."

"Don't say that word too loudly," Marcus said. "They're touchy about it."

I listened with one ear and scanned the room. Already half the eyes were straying toward the captains, and consequently toward me and the other protégé—Evan, I remembered. He wasn't in geisha attire, and I didn't think he recognized me, years removed and with my different look. I turned away from him when I caught movement on my left—one of the arms dealers approached us, drink in hand. A short man with eyebrows too dark for the rest of his hair, which was a sienna brown. Gregory Arnell, or so his file had said. Ex–Army colonel with a penchant for young things. I didn't say anything as he scanned me with a stare.

"Captains," he said, holding out his hand. Earth-raised.

"Good to see you," Marcus said, taking it. They exchanged boring pleasantries even though they all had guns inside their clothing. Then Arnell turned to me, an afterthought since he was already paying attention to me with everything but his eyes.

"He's new," he said to Marcus, but facing me.

"Yes, this shift is his debut," Marcus replied.

"Oh?" Arnell smiled at me. "That's why he's so serious."

I supposed that was what superiors did—talked about me when I was standing right there. As a reminder that I was owned, maybe.

"I don't have to be serious," I said, unasked, because the
file had noted that he liked to spar.

"Oh no?" he said, with a bit of a sneer.

I smiled at him as if I hadn't noticed, locking eyes. "Oh,
not at all."

And it was true then, everything the other geisha had
been telling me. I practically saw his heart rate increase.

I had him then. That quickly. Even when Marcus diverted
his attention back to business, I had him.

* * *

They danced around each other, the symps and these
dealers, like proper lovers waiting for a chance to consum-
mate their commitment. Marcus acted as the go-between,
Shiva's Captain Townsend as a second ameliorating factor
and a ship willing to escort the weapons to the DMZ and beyond, and we geisha circulated with food and drinks, open
ears and soft words. Ville played music and halfway through
the meeting Yasmin danced with her fan. It was all very
pleasant and cooperative. We were trying to establish a long-
term deal, and Marcus had it in mind to treat it like any other
business transaction. Just because we were pirates didn't
mean we couldn't be civilized. Even symps.

The symps were Hub-born but for some reason sided
with the strits, and I restrained myself to blank looks when
any of them cast an eye my way. If I hadn't done that, I
would've been too tempted to hit one or two of them with
my serving platter. Strit-lovers. Every once in a while Marcus called me back to his side and whispered in my ear to
linger a little longer at one person or the next, and so I
danced too, in sly subtle ways, powdered and painted and as

unobtrusive as the walls, woven among the conversation like a needle stitching all of our allies together.

When the party finally started to break up, over three hours later, Marcus motioned me to his side. I strolled over, and he rested his hand on my shoulder. "I want you to go with Arnell." He nodded toward the ex-colonel.

"Yes, sir." Now my gut started to twist again, as if I were back in Estienne's quarters being touched for the first time.

"When you're finished, come back to the ship. He won't care for you to linger." He patted my back. "You did well, very smooth. The deals are made, and Arnell is a happy man. Don't mess it up now. Reward him." He didn't ask if I was up to it, of course, he just squeezed my arm and walked off to Captain Townsend.

I looked around for Estienne, saw him talking to another of the dealers, a rather tall blond woman. Why couldn't I have got stuck with her? Instead, Arnell and his contrasting eyebrows stared at me from the corner with a spiced rum drink in his hand. He'd been drinking it and refilling the entire time.

Ville said to take your mind elsewhere. So I made sure my face was in a proper neutral expression, glancing once into the column of mirror on the wall, and headed over to Arnell at an easy pace. The symps were already leaving, bowing or shaking hands with Marcus; but Arnell hadn't touched the symps the entire time, could barely even hide his disdain for them. But whatever hate he had, it wasn't as loud as the mewling voice from his bank account.

"The serious young man," he said, when I got close enough to hear his low voice.

"Not always," I replied. "As I mentioned."

"What will make you smile again?" he said.

Jonny's training didn't go to waste. Or maybe this man

was just too easy to please. "I could tell you," I said, "but I'd rather show you."

It was up to him to direct things from here. I was sure this wasn't his first time with one of the geisha. His mouth quirked, and he rolled his shoulder against the wall, turning toward an exit at the back of the room. This one led to the club's main rooms, which would lead us eventually to the den.

I followed him, mapping the route, noting the exits, staying just behind his shoulder. But he turned, taking my arm lightly and pulling me up to his side. Less out of courtesy and more out of a sense of paranoia that I might simply shoot him in the back regardless of the deals he'd just made.

"So what's your name?" he asked, still holding my arm like we were two friends out for a stroll.

"Yuri," I said. Never give your last name.

"And how old are you?"

Never give them your real age either. "Sixteen."

"Really? I'd thought you younger. But I suppose deep spacers . . . it gets pretty tangled, doesn't it?"

"Yes, sir." He knew I was fourteen or thereabouts. He just wanted to be lied to so he wouldn't have to think about the fact I was underage.

Our stroll took us through the main bar area, which was lit and lively with people, music, and much alcohol. Despite the shadows and activity, he seemed to know exactly where he was going. And of course he did. He'd probably done this before.

Eventually he directed me to the den entrance, deep through the hallways there. It was a high-end warren of rooms, no junkies or dross hanging out the doors, no thin walls where embarrassing noises might filter. Arnell stopped at a door marked twenty-nine and lifted out a key from his breast pocket. He smiled at me and pressed it to the lock, the door clicked open, and he motioned me in first.

I thought I should be back on ship in a half hour, an hour at the most. This man didn't seem too terribly exciting, and with any luck I could just admire the room design, get him off, and leave before he could smudge my makeup.

I walked in and stood at the foot of the bed. The walls were velvet red, with spacescape hotel art shimmering and morphing all around us. Everywhere smelled of hospital. I doubted this was even the room that he was truly staying in, but at least it was clean.

"Have a seat," he said, tossing the key on the dresser.

I perched on the bed, and he came over and sat beside me, immediately placing his hand on my leg, above the knee. His fingers clenched.

I could feel it all happening, even though a part of me wanted to separate, stand, and walk across the room to face the corner.

Instead I faced him, and he was smiling.

"Your first time," he said. "Ever?"

"No. Just here." Maybe he didn't know how the geisha trained. Probably not. I didn't see Marcus making that common knowledge even with his clients. Or especially with men like this.

"Scared?" he continued.

Disgusted. But I said, "No, sir." Ex-Army, he'd like the false respect.

He released me and shoved me back on the bed. I tried to sit up, reflex, but he pressed a hand to my chest, and I stopped myself. No, this was the way it had to happen. Right? This bastard was all into the power thing. He held himself aloof from the symps, sneered at me like I was stupid, walked around like the Hub owed him something. So confident, so smiling. My heart galloped, and he could feel it with his hand there and maybe he took it to mean I was liking this because he leaned down, kneeling there on the bed, and slid his hand up to my hair, gripping.

"You know what to do, don't you?"

Someone like him wouldn't want it any other way, so I nodded once. When he let me go I rolled over.

"You don't talk much," he said.

The blanket on the bed smelled like detergent and flowers. I said, "Would you like me to?"

"It might make things more interesting," he said, grabbing the waist of my pants.

"I can give you a critique as we go along," I said, because I knew it'd make him laugh.

He did. He worked my pants down. I barely felt the air on my skin before his hand gripped my ass.

"Well, would—?" I started.

But he hit me on the back of the head.

It stunned me quiet.

"Shut up," he said. "I know you think you know me and what I like. But you don't."

I thought about getting up, tossing him back, leaving the room.

Except Marcus said not to mess things up.

So I lay there, quiet, and heard him unzipping, didn't need to look to know he was getting himself ready. Just heard the silly sounds he made, and I rested my cheek against the smooth pattern of the blanket and stared to my right where a chair sat in the corner, empty and a little worn about the handles, with a table beside it and an interface menu bobbing unused just above the surface. Waiting for a command. The lamp was up halfway, so the shadows cut the wall into shards.

He didn't prepare me at all. He didn't warn me or say a word, he just shoved himself into me, and I couldn't help it—any training went out of my mind. I yelled and struggled. I swore at him, but he shoved my face into the bed, and this wasn't what his file had said, it never mentioned anything about cruelty or humiliation or an inclination for extreme roughness, yet he didn't stop, and I couldn't breathe. Couldn't see. I lost my voice in the pain until I was deaf from it. Blind from it.

It rolled over me like a machine.

The more I moved the worse it felt, so I just stopped.

I stopped.

The menu above the table nodded, expectant, waiting for someone's hand to intervene and make it come alive.

* * *

"Well, pull your pants up," he said.

I couldn't move.

"You're not passing out here, pull your pants up and get out."

I bled. I felt it even past the numb. I tried to push myself up to my knees, and I guessed I wasn't moving fast enough because he grabbed my arm to drag me from the bed.

And it was reflex. Or revenge. My switchblade landed in my hand somehow, popped from its sheath in my sleeve. It snapped open, and I stabbed.

Into his arm. He recoiled with a curse, and I stumbled to the floor. Saw his boots. I drove the blade into his foot.

He fell back with a cry, heavy on the carpet, and he hadn't even pulled up his pants all the way so I saw his thing, all wet and red and still half-aroused, that thing he'd used to rip me apart, and he hadn't warned me, he knew the rules, he must've known, and still he had something to prove, or he was just that cruel. I had tears on my face, but I crawled onto his chest and stabbed him in the heart, just like I'd done with that strit long ago.

Stabbed him to make him bleed, like I was bleeding.

And he bled. A lot.

* * *

I commed Estienne. I told him the room number. Then I curled in the corner and watched the stain grow on the carpet.

* * *

"What've you done?" Estienne said, standing over me. "Yuri, what've you done?"

"He hurt me!"

But Estienne wasn't looking at me, he stared at the body. Its pants were still down. "Come on." He grabbed my arm and dragged me to my feet. "You have to get the blood off your hands before we walk out of here. Put that blade away. At least you're wearing black, so it doesn't show up."

"Stop it!" I could barely walk, but he made me hobble to the bathroom anyway and waved on the tap himself. Water gushed out and he pried the blade from my hand, folded it, and shoved it into my pants pocket. Then he took my wrists and put my hands under the water. I had no tears. "Why're you doing this?" I meant, Why don't you care?

He said, with a little shake in his voice, "The captain is going to be mad."

* * *

Before he took me to see Doc Wachter, he took me to
Marcus, who was in the primary cargo bay looking over
some of the arms shipments. Crates of it lined up like soldiers on the deck, falsely labeled and electronically sealed.
Marcus paused in his conversation with one of the crew and
stared at us. At me. Seeing my state.

"What the hell happened?"

"Arnell's dead," Estienne said.

Marcus didn't ask him. He said to me, "What the fuck did
you do?" His voice was slow and a cut below an outburst.
But his eyes raged. Flame blue.

Everyone was staring. Crew in the bay, Marcus, Estienne.
I wasn't going to act like that bastard hadn't deserved it, so
I looked the captain in the face, even though I was feeling so
sick I thought I was going to puke on his shoes.

"He raped me," I said into his face.

Marcus moved a step until we were toe-to-toe. I
would've backpedaled, but Estienne was behind me. "That's
what you're trained for!" he shouted down at me. "It's not
fucking rape when you're assigned to fucking take it! Do
you know what you did?" His hand shot out and grabbed me
by the side of my hair. Wrenched my neck to the side. He
yelled right into my ear. "Do you know what you just did?"
Then before I could answer, move, or make a sound, he said
over my shoulder, "Get his friend. Now!"

I heard Estienne go away.

Marcus shoved me to the deck, just pushed my head so
hard I lost balance.

"You're going to learn," he said. "I know you have it in
you, Yuri. You were doing so well. Now what's gotten into
you that you can't follow simple orders?"

I lay there, half on my side because it hurt too much to
actually sit. Supported my weight on my right hand and

didn't want to stand in case the captain decided to toss me down again.

The logic of everything just seemed to stand in columns in my mind.

Don't look up.

Don't move.

Don't make a sound.

I just breathed. It was all I felt.

Then footsteps came up behind me, and Marcus said, "Get up."

So I hauled myself to my feet and Estienne had Bo-Sheng, holding his arm. Bo-Sheng's eyes captured mine, and he was scared. He tried to wrench his arm from Estienne's grip, but he couldn't, and Bo-Sheng said, "Yuri," in a choked voice, red eyes, red like his tears were made of blood.

Marcus held out his gun to me. "Shoot him."

Now I couldn't breathe. I looked at the captain. I didn't move.

"Take my gun," Marcus said, slowly, "and shoot your friend in the head."

Bo-Sheng was crying. I felt my chest start to heave, to force myself not to join him.

"Take the fucking gun!" Marcus shouted.

It made me jump. I took the gun. It almost slid right out of my grip, but Marcus grabbed my wrist, swung me to face Bo-Sheng, and lifted my arm to aim.

Estienne stepped out of the way.

Bo-Sheng turned and looked at the exit, but two of the crew from the deck were standing there with their own guns out.

"No," Bo-Sheng said. "Please."

"You kill him," Marcus said, "and I'll call it even for what you did to Arnell."

"No," Bo-Sheng said. "Please, Yuri. Please, Captain."

But Marcus wasn't listening and my ears rushed with blood.

"He's injetting drugs," Marcus said, "and he's had warning. He's weak. I don't want him on my ship. It's either this or the airlock."

The airlock, I thought. Like a coward.

"Shoot him," Marcus said. "And make it count or you'll be making it worse."

"Don't," Bo-Sheng said. Started to back up, but Estienne gave him a shove to set him back in front of me.

Estienne. He didn't even look at me. His eyes were on Bo-Sheng.

My hand shook. I couldn't aim. I didn't want to aim but it didn't matter. It was point-blank range. And the captain was right beside me.

"Are you weak? Are you going to screw me again?" he yelled into my ear. "Pull that trigger!"

"Please please please," Bo-Sheng was saying.

"Do it or you're next," Marcus said.

So I him Bo-Sheng. In the head.

* * *

I didn't cry. I handed Marcus his gun. He grabbed me around the neck, and I thought he was going to break it because now they had to clean up the deck, but he just held me and stared into my eyes. I stared back, but I didn't really look.

"You're going to do just fine," he said. "You kill for me. You kill for this ship. You don't take it on yourself when you have specific orders. Copy that?"

My voice was hoarse. "Copy that."

"I want you to think about this, Yuri. Control. For the sake of our Blood." He meant the *Khan*. There wasn't any other blood between us. Not the kind that bonded, anyway.

"Yes, sir." I remembered that much. The words fell out like some more awake part of me pushed them with a blunt finger.

Marcus let go of me. "Estienne, take him to see Doc."

I still felt the pressure of his hand. But he wasn't going to kill me.

But I couldn't properly breathe.

And now Estienne put his arm around me, held me close. As we walked out he murmured, "It had to be done, Yuri. It had to be done. Arnell made a deal, and now it's threatened, but if the captain tells them he punished you properly, it might appease them. The deal will go forward. It'll be all right."

Fuck the deal, I thought.

Fuck you, I thought.

But I didn't say anything all through the checkup in Medical, didn't speak as Estienne took me to my quarters and inside, and held me there in his arms. He said, "Do you want me to stay?"

I said, "Do what you want," and went into the bathroom. I locked the door. I took out my switchblade and flipped it open and there was blood still crusted on the steel and all over the handle. From that man's body.

My legs lost their strength. I crouched on the floor, rocking, the blade in my hand.

Why couldn't I cry?

I wanted to tear at my hair. Claw at my eyes. When I rubbed them my fingertips came away red from the makeup.

My nails were too blunt as they pulled and stretched my sleeves, pushing into my arms.

Why couldn't I cry.

I was sweating. I was cold. The air sank to the floor and swirled around my ankles and all of my body hurt in the distant way of a half-forgotten dream. Not even the pain would come when I most deserved it now.

So what if the blade was dirty?

So was I.

I pressed the edge to my forearm. Nothing but a pressure, and it wasn't enough. Not to make me feel.

So I drew it back along my flesh, and the red came out in a line, my scarlet fever. It painted my skin like a tattoo.

THE DEEP

4.14.2198 EHSD — Caged

Taja's blood is on my hands, and if I don't do something, so will *Archangel*'s be. This is what it comes down to, what Finch doesn't have to say because I hear it already in my head, in the captain's quarters. My quarters again. But different. Different sheets, different scent, different occupation because of this person I had no intention to save or protect beyond the walls of a prison.

But he's here, and he wants to protect me. Not in any way physical. But quieter. Intangibly. He sits on the deck in this cabin while I pull at my hair. While I try to claw my arms with my fingernails. He's never seen me cut, I was always careful about that; but he's seen the scars on my skin, and he says he knows why I started. He's heard things from me when I didn't consciously tell him. But isn't that what I was trained to do too? Geisha can read people like people read the Send. So many stories.

I want to know yours, he says. Because he doesn't believe I'm a pirate. Not truly. If he did, he would never touch me.

And if I am completely a pirate, I guess I wouldn't let myself be touched. I'd never consider doing what we're going to do. I'd never be feeling this need, like my scarlet fever, to tuck myself away from my memories. To go back, somehow, to another birth. Search in some other womb for answers, because this one suffocates. The mother fluids try to drown, or she's a drug addict pumping filth into my system. This is what it feels like, even here on my own ship. My lungs are black from breathing someone else's shit.

No, Finch says. Just by the way he sits here with me. Just in how I can read in his eyes that killing *Archangel* would be another layer of taint. There is an umbilical cord to Caligtiera and I need a sharp blade.

It's so tempting to cut. It's what I want, it's my release. But now Finch looks at me and stills the clawing on my arms.

*   *
  *

Caligtiera wants me to set up the initial meeting with Lukacs at Ghenseti, but Finch and I work out a plan. I tell Cal that Lukacs wants a pickup from Austro Station, no arguments, because he's doing business there, then I comm Lukacs from the memorized codes in my head and tell him Caligtiera wants me to pick him up at Austro Station. It's an old trick, usually reserved for setting up blind dates, but it works exceptionally well when the parties in question aren't communicating. We'll all rendezvous at Ghenseti. Finch is coming with me to Austro and while I meet with Lukacs and his partner, Finch will find Otter to tell him about Cal's plans for *Archangel*.

Otter. Tunnel kid on Austro Station, sympathizer contact working for the Warboy, but also someone who knows Captain Azarcon. If I can't get to the captain directly, this will have to do. I'm risking Finch, but I can't trust anyone else, and Finch says simply, I'm not staying on this ship if you aren't here.

It makes sense I'd take him with me anyway. Everyone already thinks he's my protégé.

With Taja dead, my loyal crew wouldn't be keen on Ops. They didn't know about Taja's deal anyway, so in a command meeting in my office I just tell Rika and Piotr that I'm running an errand for Caligtiera to pick up a couple of clients. Captains don't have to overly explain themselves, and it isn't any surprise that Caligtiera might want to test me in some way. Rika will be left in command, and she's pleased about that, not because she wants the seat on a permanent basis, but unlike Estienne she rather likes it on occasion.

And Finch is here, in my quarters, two hours before we plan to leave. I sit looking through the comp to try and crack Taja's security protocols. To get into her files. To not look at Finch as he sits on the bunk with Dexter next to him on the locker talking in bird voice.

"Yuri," Finch says.

I keep my back to him, staring at the comp. I've stopped seeing the words a long time ago.

"You should go sleep," I tell him, not turning. "You mightn't be able to for a while."

I hear him shift, the flap of a blanket that he went ahead and found somewhere and changed with the sheets while I was talking to Rika and Piotr. Just like he removed everything that was Taja's from the quarters while I was gone.

Now he's in my bed, not saying a word. I keep staring at the comp until I start to hear him breathe, then I turn and look. He's a cocooned shape beneath the heavy brown blanket, curled toward the bulkhead. Steady rise and fall of breaths. Maybe this is the first real sleep he's had since we left Earth. Even Dexter's asleep on the locker, beak beneath his wing.

I stand and walk over, look down at Finch. He trusts me. But of course he does, we slept in enclosed quarters for two months.

But there's more here. He put himself near enough to the bulkhead to give room for me to lie down. Why this change? Because he saw me break a little? Because Taja treated him worse?

I could sleep on the deck. I tell the lights, quietly, to dim to 20 percent, then I fold down beside the bed to sit, leaning my arms on the mattress, watching his back.

I don't realize my head drops to the hollow in my arms and I sleep until I start to feel a hand in my hair, stroking. And there's dark until I take a deep breath and lift my eyes. Finch has rolled over and watches me now. Still half-lidded with sleep.

"Come up here," he says.

Maybe it's my fatigue or the fact it's an invitation without any expectation in his eyes, but I crawl up beside him and lie on my stomach on top of the blanket, head turned away and arms beneath the pillow. So he doesn't have to look at my face. He can roll away if he wants.

But instead he folds his half of the blanket over me and I feel his arm make a tight line across my back. To hold the blanket there maybe. Or maybe just to hold me. I've taken the pillow, but he doesn't ask for it, he doesn't need it, he just rests his cheek on the back of my shoulder, a shell against my side. I feel his breath against the ends of my hair, his breathing against my body. Both of us clothed, but I don't think I've been this close to anyone.

I shut my eyes, and so does he. I don't have to look at him to know.

* * *

Somehow Finch is in my bed, a long warmth against my body. Making me nervous in some weird way, just by breathing. I look at the white glow of the time stamp on the wall. Slept an hour, but it feels like I sank for a week. His head's still on the back of my shoulder, and I think of Estienne.

And even now it builds up pressure behind my eyes, so I sniff, and it's pathetic and old, this feeling, this reaction to roll over, dislodging him only enough so I can put my arm over him and tighten my hold as if this is something that can't be broken. When in fact everything breaks. Especially people.

He wakes up, I don't feel it, but maybe I'm holding him too tight because he says, "What's wrong?"

Of course everything is wrong, we've talked about it, I opened my arm and bled it out for him, this world that he's in. But he asks it anyway because it's not the world he's asking about.

It's dark, and I'm glad of it, but not even darkness can hide a voice. "Nothing."

He shifts onto his back, and I let him, pulling my arm away, but he grabs it and lays it over his chest again, then he rests his hand along it, just easy like that.

"You haven't kicked me out yet," he says, "so it's not so bad."

"I have a knife under my pillow."

"You want me to get it?" He's amused in some way.

"Finch." I really don't understand him. "I've killed in my sleep."

"Is that a threat or a résumé?"

"Why are you joking about this? It's not funny."

"Yuri." His fingers caress the scars on my arm, and I want to pull away, but then what? He'll only grab me again. "If I don't joke," he says, "I'll be scared."

"You're scared anyway."

He doesn't answer. There's truth even in silence.

"Scared of me?" Because he was. He must be.

"Maybe." A pause. "More scared of the absence."

The absence of me. Because he's on a pirate ship, and I'm the only barrier he has. Like in prison. I move to pull away my arm.

"What?" he says.

"You don't have to do this because you think you need protection." I sit up but his hand snags the back of my shirt.

"I know we're not on Earth anymore."

I shrug, partly to make him let go, partly to dismiss it. He can feel the motion but can't see it. "You're not obligated."

"I'm not asking for sex."

I need to see his face. I can't judge otherwise. I call up the lights 30 percent and turn to look down at him. "Then what do you want?"

"I don't know." And maybe he doesn't. "But it's not that. I mean, it's not the prison. How could I be asking you for that? I see what it does."

I reach back and remove his grip from my shirt and turn to put my feet on the deck.

"Why do you cut yourself?"

A lean to the locker where Dexter still sleeps, and I slide my cigrets into my palm, light one. Familiar motion, familiar scent, and taste that calms me just a little. Has he asked me this before? Maybe. Whatever answer I might've given him, if I gave him any at all, probably wasn't a real answer.

"Are you . . . are you trying to kill yourself?"

I shake my head, and my throat closes up, so I just hold the cigret and watch the end burn. I can't be brave enough to kill myself instead of doing these things. Hurting people. Selfishness is a flame that makes good intentions into ash.

He touches my back again, and I hear him sit up so his hand slides under my hair.

I can find my voice if the talk is just business. "You'll need to stay on Austro."

"I can't."

I turn enough to stare at him, to be threatening, exasperated at his stubborn streak, and it's a mistake because now he stares back too.

"Maybe I should be more scared of you." He picks up what I thought I left behind in conversation. He's been thinking of it for these minutes in between. "But what part did I play in that?" He breathes out and leans back on his hands, looking away now. "Maybe what I did to you was just as bad as what my CO did to me."

"You didn't do anything to me. I'm the one that screwed you, remember?" So he's here in my bed out of guilt. I turn back with my elbows on my knees and take a drag.

"I asked. Because—you know what I thought? They say he's a pirate, so he must want to do this. So then I'll be fine in here as long as he wants to do it."

"I don't hold it against you. I did it to you. I could've said no. It's survival."

"I'm tired of surviving."

"There's nothing else, Finch." The cigret's down to a stub, and I should put it out properly, but instead I drop it on the deck and watch it disintegrate.

"There's feeling. You feel in your sleep what you don't allow when you're awake. And maybe . . . that's why I can't be so scared of you. Because I know you're tired of surviving too."

Now that my cigret's gone I look at him again. Clear-voiced. "I could've said no. I didn't. So stop feeling guilty and . . ." I look at the hatch. Direction.

"You didn't touch me again."

"That doesn't mean anything except it served me no purpose. I'm not a whore, I screwed people for a reason, and when there was no reason, I didn't do it."

"I didn't say you were a whore." And in my silence he repeats it. "I didn't say you were a whore, Yuri."

I am.

"That's why you cut?"

Full circle. These words. Just spinning in my mind. And how can he turn me around like this so my emotions are all a blur?

"We have to go," I tell him, standing. You have to go. This is where all the talking ends. This is where I would absolve him from guilt and let him go, except I'm not pure enough to give anything but orders. "None of this might work." The plan to save *Archangel*. I might not be good enough even for that. Despite soft touches and emptying words.

He doesn't answer the doubt. It's too strong, and we are weak.

✦ ✦ ✦

I take one flight team to shuttle us from our sinkhole at Hades, and we leap once to get to Austro Station. *Orlando*-registered, the shuttle's skin ID says to the station. I'm not thinking of Lukacs though; I can't focus on anything except the fact that Finch can quit as soon as he's on station and never look back. He doesn't even have to meet up with Otter. Sixty thousand people here? I don't have the man-power to find him if he runs. He should run. His records from the prison would say he committed suicide, if Lukacs did his job, and all he'd have to do is find new ID. Not im-possible, especially on Austro, with their healthy underdeck criminal activity.

I almost ask him again to do it—order him—as we wait for the shuttle to dock. Just go. And don't look back.

But I'm selfish, maybe, or a coward, and stay silent.

Once we're on deck, passed through Customs with the IDs Lukacs supplied, there isn't any time to dawdle. For all I know Lukacs has eyes on us even now, so I just look at Finch. We're surrounded by a crowd on the busy concourse heading to shops or eateries, businesses or the dockring. We're just two people in the shadow of a tall support column with the comfortable screening noise of activity all around.

He knows to find a maintenance access and just slip in. He won't have to look far for the sympathizer kid. Otter knows the underdeck like it's all his domain. And in a way it is. Those few who know he's a sympathizer refuse to mess with him. He is the Warboy's. Everyone else thinks he's just the head of a gang (which he is), and they stay wide of him for that. Finch can find him. I gave him a gun just in case, along with my commcode. I can change it after a time, when

I decide that I truly want to let go. Maybe he won't use it anyway except to tell me if he got through to Otter.

"You'll come back and get me?" he says, the question he held to himself all the way over from *Kublai Khan*.

"Yeah," I tell him. "Of course."

Of course it's a lie. I won't say it aloud, that he should not be around me. I won't say it now. But I can say it in my absence from him and not have to look at his face. Because in this odd warmth he's made me selfishly kind. And I don't have the inclination to ruin it with words. Even ones like, Be careful. They're useless now. And they aren't anything that's not understood already.

He understands. His eyes are a bit too wide as he looks at me, maybe he wants to memorize my face like I'm trying to do with him in an unblinking stare that feels all too intimate in this busy open. We don't touch. We have the memory of my quarters.

But now he goes, when not even the memory can hold together against the inevitable, swallowed by the crowd. And I watch his back until it's one of many. Until I can't tell which one is his anymore.

＊ ＊ ＊

I arranged to meet Lukacs at the Hart & Hunter pub in the den district. Pubs are dark, private, and generally ubiquitous on stations. People go off shift, there's always just enough noise to mask level conversation, and it's not out of place to see two or three men simply sitting by themselves with drinks in their hands talking. We could be off-duty pollies, businessmen, furloughed crew off some military ship in dock.

Both Lukacs and his blond partner are waiting for me. I

slide in the booth across from the blond man, with Lukacs on my left.

"Order first," Lukacs says, without any other greeting. Must keep up the appearance that this is friendly.

So I punch in for my White Russian and after the barista brings it by, Lukacs says, "Congratulations on getting your ship back," without a hint of remorse at Taja's death. He has to assume Taja's dead if he knows anything of how pirates operate. But he's still confident, still assuming I need him in some way. And I guess I do, if only to discover exactly what his game is.

"You knew exactly what to tell her, didn't you." I sip the drink, roll the milk on my tongue before swallowing, sweet velvet with that burning underbite.

"She was rather desperate at that point," he says. "How's Finch?"

"Alive."

This makes him smile as if it's a bit unexpected but still something pleasant. "Tell me what went down with Caligtiera."

"First you should probably know the man plans on destroying *Archangel*."

"What?" the blond agent says. A low voice, but fixed attention, leaning forward over his beer. I watch his fingers whiten around the glass. "When?" Harsher.

"I don't know." I watch Lukacs's face. It's blank compared to the other one. I look back at the blond.

He says, "You better be telling the truth about that, pirate."

"The fact I'm even telling you at all should convince you."

Lukacs sips his drink. Not beer, but some sort of deep red concoction. "How does he plan on doing this?"

"He has schematics of the carrier. I'd assume some sort of sabotage. Bombs would be easiest. Bombs by the drive towers." It's how I would do it. "It must be an inside job. Someone he bribed, someone who's disillusioned with Azarcon." They're sister ships. It isn't incredible to believe that crew so close to *Macedon*'s might take exception to Captain Azracon's actions lately. And be more incensed because their own captain supports him. You don't spend years fighting strits and suddenly renew your thinking just because someone calls a cease-fire. "Maybe someone at their last resupply or maintenance stopover, even. And Cal has cred." Falcone's cred. "He can bribe them." That's always a possibility. Very few people don't come with a price.

The blond agent says, "Is that everything you know?"

"Yeah."

He moves to slide out of the booth.

"Wait." Lukacs holds the man's arm. "O'Neil."

So that's his name.

Lukacs gazes at me, and O'Neil tugs his arm free. Lukacs says, "If this plan is stopped, will Caligtiera assume the leak was through you? Who else has he got in on it?"

"I don't know. But he's not a man to brag. He's interested in the deal if it'll give him a solid foothold, and he knows it'll only come through me. So this might be a test." It is probably a test. "To see if I'll tell you, then to see if you're in earnest about wanting a deal."

O'Neil gets up.

"Wait," Lukacs says. Sharper.

"To hell with you." He walks off. I stare after him, and Lukacs slides out of the booth and follows at a steady clip. Not fast enough to attract attention but fast enough to catch up to the other man's long strides.

This isn't the reaction I expect. But I sit there and watch

as Lukacs talks the other man toward a shadowed corner. I can't read their lips, but their body language says plenty. Lukacs is trying to speak reason and O'Neil wants to deck him. In a few seconds O'Neil simply walks out of the pub, and Lukacs comes back to me with a dark frown.

"There are six-thousand-plus people on those carriers," I remind him. And this is why Finch has gone to Otter. Because I'm not sure we can depend on Lukacs to do the decent thing.

"Yes," Lukacs says simply. "Now when will we depart?"

I stare at him.

"My colleague is none of your concern. We're still going to meet Caligtiera. I want it to be soon."

I wonder what he'll do if he finds out I let Finch go.

Probably get some other Ops agent to track him down.

So I keep my mouth shut and play along, finishing my drink before rising. "Meet me at the *Orlando* shuttle in an hour."

* * *

I have idle thoughts about going to find Finch, but that would be—useless. To show my face in the underdeck where Otter's gang would probably recognize me. Useless to go back to Finch as if I have anything to offer other than probable death. Protection in the prison, but a death warrant in space.

But I wonder if he's found Otter. I wonder if he's worrying. Like I'm worrying. And wondering. And thinking, What if I try to disappear too.

My feet take me on a meandering path in the general direction of the dockring. They don't lie even if my mind does. I'm going back.

I can go back to the shuttle and just wait for Lukacs to arrive, but I don't want to sit, I've been sitting in holding patterns long enough, switched on and off in intervals by other hands. The station is full of my immediate life before Earth and that prison, and so I pull the hood of my sweater over my hair and walk. Ordinary people on an ordinary schedule, some life that's as foreign as strits and their eyes. What does it mean to be oblivious? Instead of shaping something out of someone else's clay. This is one last tour before Lukacs and Caligtiera and my hand in their alliance.

My ship. Just think of *Kublai Khan* and the fact it's mine for me to go back to. Even if it isn't for long. If Finch succeeds, and Azarcon succeeds in warning *Archangel*, my ship and my life likely won't be for long.

There are no convictions in my thoughts.

I don't get far in the shopping district before a hand closes about my arm. I jerk and turn and see O'Neil, blue eyes just centimeters from mine.

"Over here," he says, directing me to a side corridor toward the public washrooms. He pushes me in, not roughly but not with any opportunity for refusal, and quickly checks the stalls. One is occupied, so he turns on the tap and washes his hands while I light a cigret. When the guy leaves O'Neil goes to the door and leans against it. "My son is on *Archangel*," he says.

I stare at him, blowing smoke. You mean your kind can spawn?

"He's a jet," O'Neil says. "We're going to stop that sabotage."

"Did you comm him?" So that's what they were arguing about.

"They're silent running. I sent a comm to his last link

code, but I haven't got any confirmation. He might be on maneuvers; he might be anywhere."

"Don't you know the carrier's link?" Mr. Black Ops.

He scowls. "Since this shite with Damiani and Azarcon they've been changing their codes every day. Don't know who to trust among govies these days."

Govies who technically are the ones giving orders, even to deep-space carriers. Not that it's true in Azarcon's case or his allies among the deep spacers, but carrier security protocols are the same whether they're insystem or in the Dragons.

"Is Lukacs going to let it blow?" Even I didn't think the man would be so coldhearted—if he's genuine about working in the Hub's best interests. Wanting to dismantle the pirate network. "Are you positive he's playing this right?"

O'Neil doesn't answer.

"You know his cover for me."

"Yeah," he says.

"What are *you* doing in this?" The question that I wondered since in the prison. "What angles are you playing?"

He might not answer me completely. He might not answer me at all. But maybe he went into this thinking I was one way, and this little meeting has proven different.

"I'm in it to dismantle the network," he says finally. "Lukacs . . . I'm not so sure."

"Yet you work with him."

His smile is nothing but muscles moving, an emotionless expression. "We have similar goals . . . elsewhere. But maybe now two completely different ways of achieving them."

I'm not going to get more enlightenment than that. "I have a man on his way to sending Azarcon a heads-up. So if you can't contact your son or *Archangel*, then that should

pan out." If it isn't too late. If Finch can convince Otter he's
genuine. I'm counting on the fact that even if Otter doesn't
trust him, he will still tell Azarcon as a matter of course.
Threats like that can't be taken lightly.

"You've got contact with Azarcon?" More suspicion than
disbelief. Skeptical about the veracity of it.

I have no intention of giving Black Ops a position on
Otter. They might not know about the kid's usefulness to
Macedon. "Pirate intel isn't half-bad, you know." Especially
for a geisha.

He straightens from the door. "I'll be keeping tabs on you
on your ship while Andreas brokers this deal with Caligtiera.
You work the pirate, and I'll work my partner. At some point
we'll get verification of this threat."

He says it like it's a foregone conclusion.

"Lukacs would really let a pirate destroy a carrier to further his own agenda." And that's not a question either. But I
still want confirmation from the person who knows Lukacs
best between the two of us.

"Yeah," O'Neil says. "In this case, yeah, if he's in it for
an alliance, not an infiltration. Which is why if it comes to
that, he's my kill."

* **

On the ride out of Austro's system I sit in the cockpit with
my flight crew, away from Lukacs and O'Neil, staring out
the viewport as the station hangs distant and lit, flat curved
modules birthing ships at different dockrings. It's oblivious
to my thoughts or the hard clench in my chest, and too soon
it gets smaller. I stare until it disappears.

* *

Rika and Ville meet us as we disembark in the hangar bay. They're visibly armed with handguns, and her eyes assess Lukacs and O'Neil. Questions there that she won't ask now. She frisks them and takes their sidearms. O'Neil isn't pleased about that, but he doesn't comment.

"The clients," I tell her, leading the way out. "I'm setting them up in quarters on maindeck. I want a guard rotation there."

Lukacs doesn't protest because now he's on my ground.

"Separate quarters," I add. In case I want to say things to O'Neil that Lukacs doesn't need to hear.

"Yes, sir," Rika says.

With my command codes reclaimed I override the locked quarters and put Lukacs in first. "I'll tell you when Caligtiera's ready to meet."

He nods. Suited and carrying a single case, he can be in any kind of regular business that we trade in. Arms, drugs, information. O'Neil looks like a guard in his more casual black. I know that's the appearance they cultivate. Rika and Ville don't question it, but I give them a glance to stay put as I follow O'Neil into his quarters and shut the hatch.

"My gun," he says.

"Standard protocol. If I let you have it, my crew will be suspicious."

Typical Ops, he goes on as if what I said didn't matter. "I'll need it."

"Listen to me, O'Neil." I walk up close enough to infringe on his personal space. He doesn't move away, but then I don't expect him to. Men like him operate just as well from short distances. "You're here, I'm calling it, and I won't have any Ops running around my deck with a weapon." I move to the hatch. "None of this means I trust you."

"You'll have to," he says, with arrogant calm. He sits on the bunk and lights a smoke. "If you want to survive Caligtiera. Or Lukacs."

"Then so will you." And I'm still not giving you a gun as long as you're on my ship. I open the hatch and walk out.

They're both locked in, so Rika allows her rifle to lower, and says, "What was that about?" The private powwow with one and not the other.

I can depend on some aspects of the captaincy. Like terse dismissal. "Business."

It makes her frown, but it also sets her in her place. "Do you need me or the Hanamachi?"

To work either Lukacs or O'Neil. Most clients would take that bit of hospitality, and I would take any information my geisha could provide.

But. "No," I tell her. "These men aren't the type to appreciate that. Just let them be."

She nods. Ville lingers until the guards show up. And I leave them both to go back to my empty quarters and comm Caligtiera.

*　*　*

Ghenseti's an abandoned military outpost, a wart among the stars with its half-exploded sections and dead darkness. It's become a meeting place for pirate deals, two leaps from Chaos Station in the Dragons, gutted and forgotten by the Hub after the last strit attack decades ago that destroyed it one time too many for redevelopment.

It's the place where Falcone lost his captaincy. Or the be-

ginning of his loss. Chasing after a strit attack group out of
rage or pride, he left the base undefended, and a second ambush on the station caused the death of half its people. Worthy of a court-martial.

Falcone never liked to revisit it, but Caligtiera has no
such compunction.

So here we are in the one section of the old base that the
pirates made breathable and walkable, that wasn't entirely
crippled by that attack long ago. The grav nodes might be a
little off, making our steps and our breaths a shade heavier
than normal, but we're not here to set down roots, just shake
a deal.

The room used to be a barracks cafeteria. A few long tables are set up, scarred by time and use, the galley black and
dusted in the corner. Rack lighting above makes all the surfaces too shiny, revealing cracks in the floor. Caligtiera
brings his gray-suited woman and two men with guns. It's
just me, the two agents, Ville, and one of his junior geisha.
Ville and the girl stay standing out of earshot by the doors,
as do Cal's men, but the rest of us sit across from each other.
I take position on Caligtiera's right, so there's no mistaking
who's a pirate and who's a govie. And whose pocket I'd
rather dip into, as far as Cal is concerned.

Lukacs places his razor comp in front of him, O'Neil just
sits with his hands under opposite armpits, near his shoulder
holster.

We're all armed here, I gave back their weapons once we
hit dock, they weren't going to come on deck without them.
A mutual mistrust.

"Kirov explained," Caligtiera says to Lukacs and O'Neil,
to the point as usual. "But let's hear it from you."

Introductions were taken care of at disembark, brisk and

cold. But names are still too personal for this meeting right now.

Lukacs passes over his slate with his proposal in it and launches into his spiel. I watch Caligtiera's face. He's too good to show whether he's buying it or not, but he isn't ordering us shot at least. I can feel O'Neil across from me thinking, My son is on that ship, you bastard. And I don't entirely trust Black Ops, but neither, apparently, do they. Admitting to me that he might not be on board with his own comrade—maybe it shouldn't have been so surprising considering the self-serving nature of their lifestyles (and mine), but I think of little else but the possibility Lukacs might be playing both of us, me and O'Neil, so consequently O'Neil is on my side.

And maybe he does know a way I can get out of this before bedding down with Cal.

Take my ship and just go? Except some of my crew might protest. Not all of them, but given the opportunity to escape a pirate I think some of them might go. They weren't trained as hard as me, and a fear of being caught and thrown in prison at this point is probably what keeps some of them still on board. Like maybe Piotr. Stay with what you know if what you know at least keeps you free.

After a manner, free.

Even with Finch somewhat safely away, I can't yet ditch Lukacs. I can't yet remove this nanotag from beneath my skin and walk away from what they're discussing here.

O'Neil is the reminder why. If I can get the exact plan from Caligtiera, I can stop this. There's no gun to my head. But if there has to be one in order to make me kill sometimes (Bo-Sheng, I don't think it, not hard enough to show), then maybe there should't be one to make me do the opposite. Maybe all of my failures before to leave were dress rehearsals, training, and this is my debut. I'm sitting across from Black Ops, sitting beside a pirate, and despite what they think, there are things they don't know about me. Things they can't touch. My face is blank, and Finch is away from Lukacs and Caligtiera doesn't know about Otter and Azarcon, and with my private knowledge comes a lack of obligation to anyone at this table.

This isn't what freedom feels like. I'm not sure I'd know that flavor. But it's got a scent of power. It's got a taste a little like control.

"It's been leaked among the pirates," Caligtiera says, pulling my attention more vividly to his words now that Lukacs has been interrupted, "that Kirov's back in the *Khan*'s chair and that Roshan is dead."

"Leaked purposely," Lukacs says.

"Of course. Already some of the captains are murmuring about whether he and I will start an internal war, but that isn't so, is it, Yuri."

"Not at the moment," I answer.

"But whether or not we care to trust you is another matter. Tell me, what did you have on Kirov that you got him on board for your little proposition in the first place? Just springing him from prison can't have been it. The govies gave him that opportunity when they asked him to roll on us." Cal doesn't take his eyes from Lukacs except to regard O'Neil, while he lights one of his brown cigrets and leans back to set one hand on the edge of the table. "Or is it that he willingly went to you?"

Asking Lukacs while I'm sitting right here, Cal gets to see our dynamic under the heat of the question. I either have some vulnerability that he's not aware of, or I'm more on the side of Ops than on the network's best interests.

"There's a young man," Lukacs answers smoothly, and I

force myself not to react. "Met in the prison. Pretty enough, I suppose, to be of worth. His name's Stefano Finch. He came along for the ride and is, if I'm not mistaken, aboard *Kublai Khan* now."

And now Caligtiera knows. One more thing for him to possibly hold against me.

"Brought down by a boy," Cal says. "Why am I not surprised?"

"That doesn't change anything about this deal," I tell them both. Let them taunt. "The fact is I'm here, and we either do this or get gone. We gonna get our products moving again among our—how do I say it—hypocritical govie clients?"

"It all looks good written down," Cal says, tapping the slate. Which doesn't mean he buys any of it yet. "How about first we get a show of good faith, from both sides. I have a shipment of arms that's been gathering dust in my hold for a month. The Family of Humanity's always looking for extras, but at the moment they're too nervous to take any deals. Arrange something, and I will, in turn, provide one less— concern—about this off-books alliance between the strits and Azarcon. Azarcon and his mice."

"That concern would be?" Lukacs says.

"I'll surprise you."

"Don't like surprises." O'Neil speaks for the first time.

Cal looks at him slowly. "It's a good surprise."

"By whose standards?"

I tell the Ops, "Take it. Or we end this here." You got your meeting, Lukacs. Now I'm not looking out for your best interests. Whatever they are.

Lukacs doesn't look at O'Neil as he takes his slate back from Cal. He just says, "Very well. Give me a shift to arrange the meet with my Family contact."

"That'll work," Cal says.

I motion Ville to come closer so he can hear. "Take them back to the shuttle." And take their weapons too. He knows that. Hopefully O'Neil can grill Lukacs in some way while I have equal time alone with Caligtiera. Soon the agents and my guards are gone, and I light a cigret and look at Cal side-long. "Works for you?"

"They're completely untrustworthy," Cal says.

"Yeah, but so are we."

He shrugs. "We'll see how far this will go."

I stare at the side of his face. "When's it going down?" His end of the deal.

Caligtiera smiles and doesn't even bother to look at me. He just taps his ashes on the table. "Go home with your agents, Kirov. We're not so friendly yet."

* * *

A silent trip back and my hangar bay seems to yawn its disapproval as we disembark into the cold cavern of its mouth. There is my flight deck crew, severely decimated now, and the depressing sight of shadowed outriders hunched near the bulkheads like tranquilized beasts. Once fierce, now just kind of sad in their inactivity. At the height of it my ship would never be asleep. There was always cargo to ship, prepare for, or off-load. There was always a deal on-going in some way that kept the whole crew busy.

Now there is Black Ops, and the two of them on my deck, even if nobody else knows who they are, feels like some sort of capitulation. Of course it is. But I tell myself they are the stones I need to skip in order to guage the ripples of what I want. Of my actions.

Rika meets us on dock and trails us again with Ville, back

to the assigned quarters. The other geisha melts away. This time I get Rika and Ville to pack O'Neil away while I follow Lukacs into his q.

Once the hatch shuts: "Happy?"

He sets his comp on the small desk and lightly dusts the front of his suit as if being on that station with us created some sort of residue. "It's an acceptable start. Now if you leave me alone, I'll make that contact in the Family. I'll need a coded link to insystem, by the way."

"You're on my ship now," I remind him. "Just in case you think you can still control me when my crew outnumbers you. What's O'Neil's problem?"

"Not aware he has one."

"I see, so that little tango in the pub was my delusion?"

Now he stares at me. "O'Neil is my concern."

So he's a concern. Because he has a son he cares about? Naturally I don't say that.

"And you call us piranhas." They'll turn on each other just as readily.

"Kirov." His eyes are impatient though the rest of his face is studied and bland. "I need that link."

I hit him, a fist to the temple that rocks him on his feet until he sits heavily on the bed. And wisely doesn't come at me, since I'm the one with the gun. But his expression isn't bland anymore.

"Don't fuck with me," I tell him. "I know you're thinking about it. I know you must be running something else. You can tell me what it is and save yourself the trouble." It's cast out there, I don't expect a bite. Not from someone like him. But punching him felt bloody good.

He stands again, blinking a bit from the reverb of that hit. "My deal stands. Give me my link."

I could beat him senseless, but it wouldn't get me any

closer to stopping Cal or figuring Lukacs's real agenda. For his training that would take weeks. I can't do anything but depend on O'Neil where that's concerned, and it burns. Operating in darkness.

"My comm officer will contact you for your code." And you better know we will try our best to piggyback any outcomms you make. I leave him to it and meet Rika outside. She's waited with the guards, but Ville's gone.

"This deal," she says.

I look at her. And wait.

"This deal. These men seem twitchy. Like they haven't dealt with us before. With Cal, even. They new?"

Geisha eyes that can read bodies and faces where other people see only masks.

"We're pirates. They're not. Of course they're twitchy." I start to walk toward the bridge.

"We got Cal's back, then?"

"As long as it's good for the ship."

She says, "You got Cal's back?"

I stop and look at her. "What is this, Rika?"

She doesn't blink. "Where's Finch?"

"Where he needs to be."

"I said to put him off on Hades, not Austro Station." Where he can go straight to authorities.

"I said he's where he needs to be. Why are you ragging me? Do you know Caligtiera? Did you work with him?" Were you Falcone's protégé? I step toward her, and she moves back toward the bulkhead. "I know what the hell I'm doing, and you don't need to know all the details. If that bothers you in some way, then you're welcome to get off my ship."

I remember how she took me to see Doc Wachter after that first time with Estienne. I remember when I stopped being scared of her because I knew just as much as she did about how to kill somebody.

"Austro changed you," she says. That year I was away from the *Khan*. Maybe it was Austro. Maybe it was before, but I can't tell her that. I can't tell her anything, and it's not just because I'm captain, and she's not.

I walk off without looking behind. "You were never in *Macedon*'s brig."

* * *

Once I ditch Rika I circle back to O'Neil's hatch and override the lock code. He isn't surprised to see me, standing in the middle of the space with his arms folded.

"Well?" I ask him.

"He doesn't give up his angles that easily."

Clearly. "What *is* it. Specifically. The part you're not telling me. When you two came to me on Earth you both had something else beneath your offer. Maybe he's working an extra angle, but I want to know what you know. I need to know everything if you want me to work this properly with Caligtiera." Ignorance helps nothing in this case.

He purses his lips and makes the decision in the flicker of his eyes. "We were told by the director of the Agency to forge an alliance with the pirates. Exactly what your cover says. Andreas and I—at least, what I believed of him— didn't exactly agree with that. We haven't agreed with the Agency for some time. So we built and ran our own op: you. To infiltrate the pirate organization under the guise of doing what the Agency told us. In the end we hope to dethrone the current director and basically dismantle our own organization. And then build it back up with us at the head of it."

Layers upon layers.

"Andreas," he says, "is the type to sacrifice one Hub ship for a greater good, which he considers bringing down all the pirates one ship at a time, one contact at a time. To him, that's worth more in the long run than one deep-space carrier or so he says."

"Even if your son's on it."

"You learn," O'Neil says, "as I'm sure you know, to put personal concerns aside."

Except we can't. We don't. We get to a point, and the only thing keeping us breathing is the personal.

"Not everyone thinks that way." Falcone didn't. Caligtiera doesn't.

"No," O'Neil says. "But whether he's been playing me all along in order to expose *me* to the Agency, I don't know now."

"Why you specifically?"

He says without any kind of arrogance, just as fact, "I'm a star-ranked field operative." And that's all he says.

He's in some sort of long-term operation then, something more pressing even than this. Star-ranked? Years of training and experience. If he's going rogue with *personal* feelings, and the Agency knows it, they might go to all this trouble, yeah. To find out what he knows, who else is involved, and what they can use on him.

Like his son. Which Lukacs now knows is not acceptable collateral damage to O'Neil.

"Your predicament sounds familiar," I tell him.

"You reach a point," he says shortly. No need for elaboration. And adds, "We need to leave your ship before this shit comes down."

"Cal didn't tell me anything. He won't. This is his show."

"Then we need to find a way to let *Archangel* know conclusively, or Azarcon."

"It's Finch," I tell him. "I left Finch at Austro to contact Azarcon through a sympathizer I know of. If he gets through he'll comm me to let me know."

He considers this briefly. "Either way, I'm not staying aboard if that carrier doesn't blow and Caligtiera turns his torpedoes on the *Khan*."

"And Lukacs?" If he's on the up.

O'Neil says without a blink, "Even if he's still working our original op, he's going about it the wrong way."

And can fend for himself.

"We have to meet Cal again . . . maybe I can get more from him." Although I'm not counting on it.

O'Neil isn't either. "Every time we meet with that man it adds opportunity for suspicion and for something to go wrong. This is a bad deal."

It doesn't take a long time to figure these things. If something smells rotten, all you have to do is take a breath to know.

* * *

I take Lukacs and O'Neil back to Ghenseti a shift later when Lukacs has the information—and presumably the agreement—for his contact in the Family of Humanity. It's the same group of us in the same abandoned room, and that table with its dents and scratches, witness to numerous past deals just like this one. Except maybe this is the first time two agents from Black Ops occupy a side. Problem is, you don't know which side. I watch Lukacs but am acutely aware of Caligtiera beside me as he reads the proposal from the Family. He doesn't show it to me, just takes out his chip-sheet and pastes it to Lukacs's comp. Transloading coordinates maybe, some message.

"I'll contact them to set up a rendezvous." He peels the sheet back and puts it in his front cargo pocket, then slides the slate back to Lukacs. "Good job." Like he's praising a dog.

Lukacs's lip curls just slightly. "And your end of the deal?"

O'Neil stares at Cal with his arms folded and a disaffected expression.

"Imminent," Cal tells them. "Be patient, and trust me it'll be worth it. You don't approve of Azarcon and his sway? This will say something."

"Like what." O'Neil's voice is a flat skepticsm.

"Like fuck you." Cal stares at him.

No he won't budge. But "imminent" is bad enough.

He looks back at Lukacs. "Once I off-load my weapons, then we'll talk again about the details of your expectations of me and my ships. And ours of you."

His *ships*. Mine, others'. Assuming he's got me at heel, at least for now.

This is no different from Falcone. It might even be worse. He's got no time or training invested in me.

Back on the *Khan* I try one last time to sound out Lukacs as I button him back in quarters. "If we're going to do something about *Archangel*, now's the time. Cal won't cop to the event."

"Stop it now and then what?" He sets his comp on the bed, shoulder to me. Dismissal. "He grows suspicious and murders us all. And then where will that leave things? One live carrier and one still-active pirate network. Status quo."

He can shove his dismissal up his ass. "I might almost think you *want* this alliance. For other reasons." Pause. "It occur to you that I can kill you right now, claim you looked to betray us, and there isn't a thing you can do about it? You have no access to Finch, so you can't hold him over my head."

This doesn't faze him. He taps at his comp idly and doesn't even address my first stab. "Of course you can kill me. And O'Neil. You can even remove that nanotag, but you haven't. Why? Because you're already on my Agency's radar, you know you have been for a few months now. There's no getting rid of us." Now he looks up. "After O'Neil and me there will just be another. This way at least you know who you're dealing with. Kill us, and it will spring up on you, and trust that my successor won't be as magnanimous."

Practicality tends to get in the way of justified killings. "You people fucking spawn, don't you."

He grins. "Like pirates."

* **

O'Neil next door says nothing but, "Your boy better have gotten through to Azarcon. Get me off this ship."

* **

The question is how, with Cal right beside me. Moving O'Neil to space is an issue; moving myself seems impossible. I can opt to go down with my ship if it comes to that, but I'm not suicidal. Or gallant.

I go straight to engineering deck and Piotr, who's running a skeletal division, just him and two other techs at the drive tower monitoring station, the rest of the deck on autoeyes until there's an emergency. The city-block-sized room where the towers are housed is framed on one end by a separate enclosed space, plex-fronted and filled by comps whose jobs I have a fundamental familiarity with, but nothing that I could use to keep a ship running at optimum. That's Piotr's job, and he seems confident in our downsized crew nevertheless. He's humming to himself as I step in. The other two crewmembers look up from their stations, gazes lingering. Knowing I'd shot their previous captain. I don't recognize these two, they must've been Taja's recruits. But not loyal ones. Serve under any captain just as long as they're left alone to work; every ship has those.

Not Piotr. He likes me. "Yuri! Have you brought me homemade cookies?"

I smile. "No, but I'll get Rika on that."

If Rika made a cookie, she'd probably slip poison into it.

"I need to talk to you." I give the other two techs a look in dismissal, and they promptly leave.

Piotr leans back in his chair, rocking, one hand on his section of the comp console. I sit across from him at the neighboring station.

He says, "What's up, Captain?"

I'm conscious of the sidearm under my shirt. There's no point softening him up, he'll either understand what I want or turn on me, no matter how sweet the words. "If you had a chance to leave this, would you?"

One eyebrow arches. "Captain, I would never leave this ship or you. And go where? Straight to jail?" He laughs. "No thank you."

"No, not to jail. I mean . . . on the run, maybe, but not with pirates anymore. Not alongside Caligtiera or any of them who're vying for Falcone's operation."

His amused expression turns concerned. "Including you?"

He still thinks I want control of the pirates. And now I have to be clear. "Say I ran too."

To his credit he doesn't react overmuch. He just looks at me, unblinking, chair still rocking at the same slow rhythm. "If you want to run in this ship, you will need help."

I feel some of the tension bleed out from me. "Not everyone would be on board for the idea."

He shakes his head. "I can think of one offhand."

Rika. And all of the crew who follow her as a geisha and my right hand. She was always my second, despite Taja's ambition.

I rest my elbow on the comp console, interrupting harmless static helio images, and rub my hair back. "It'd require another internal attack, and I don't want to do that to her. But you understand . . . I can't stay here. There's—something going down with Caligtiera, and if I stop it, he'll turn on us. I don't want to be around when he does."

Piotr pinches the bridge of his nose a little, sniffs, and looks at me. "You want off the *Khan*, but you can't leave."

For complicated reasons, yeah. But for this purpose . . . "Either Cal will shoot me or Rika will."

"Eh . . . not if there is nothing to shoot."

"Meaning?"

He shrugs and looks out the plex window to the drive towers. "Sabotage."

Any lingering doubts about him get vented at that one word. For him to even suggest it, on this ship that he prides himself in, is enough to tell me that he counts himself loyal to me first, then the Blood. I don't know when that happened for him, and I won't ask; it's enough just to have it.

And we are actually discussing this. He doesn't need to hear my reaction. He says, "When?"

"The life pods are intact?"

"Yes, sir."

"Cal would take us on. We're not even at half crew anyway. And the rest who were loyal to Taja . . ."

"They get on the pods that we don't fill. I can set the brig to open after most of us have left the ship." He knows I don't want to murder the lot of them. He accepts it, and I have to wonder why he's in piracy in the first place. He reads the question in my eyes and shrugs. "My mother was Blood to *Genghis Khan*. I had no choice. And it was livable. You don't see much when you're down here, in this place." A look around his domain with a little smile.

I think of Finch, suddenly. And the one geisha tactic our elder siblings kept secret from us because it doesn't require a mask. Geisha mind-set never would've allowed that last shift in my quarters before I let him go on station.

"You don't see much in the Hanamachi either."

* * *

I check on the bridge and monitor *Iron Cross*'s activity for a while, but they aren't moving from Ghenseti, and neither are we. Not until Cal gives the order to rendezvous with the Family, so I can do nothing but wait for Finch's comm and Piotr's word. I dread the comm that might tell me it's too late, and *Archangel* is dead, and in the same twitch of thought I wonder what's taking Finch so long to tell me he's contacted Otter, and it's all been stopped. If that would be his comm. He could also comm to tell me Otter wouldn't listen to him or . . .

It's not knowing that makes you spin.

I meet with O'Neil again to tell him Piotr's plan. And even as the words leave my mouth I start to shake. Hands clamp behind my back. But he sees something anyway, and says, "I think you need to sleep."

But sleep won't help the inevitable. My decision. This lived in fear.

I comm Rika to tell her to wake me as soon as Caligtiera or Lukacs or O'Neil even blink, and I return to quarters. Avoiding it does no good. I let Dexter out of his cage and sit on the bed holding him on the palm of my hand, letting him peck kisses on my lips. Lie down, Yuri, and shut your eyes. And don't think about how the blanket and the pillow and the sheets still hold his scent, and this is something you actually miss—even though, or maybe because, it was so fleeting. Don't think about destroying all of this.

Dexter stands on my chest and I stare at the ceiling and this is not something I ever wanted to feel again.

The absence of someone. And something.

And I think it cuts more because it's purer, if that word can even be used for me.

Eventually Dexter flits off, and I roll over, face in the pillow. I imagine there is less room around me, and more of the warmth of his body and the sound of his breathing.

* * *

Rika wakes me. And I'm standing in the corridor with a blade in my hand. She's three meters away with her gun out, pointed down, and I blink at her, my shoulder pressed to a hatch and slowly, slowly I begin to recognize maindeck, a corridor run away from the primary airlock. She says, "Captain, put the knife away."

She doesn't know if I'm awake or not. So I take a deep breath and straighten. And fold the blade before tucking it into the pocket on my jacket.

"That weapon better be set on paralysis," I tell her.

Only then she lowers it and slips it into her backwaist. "For you, yeah." Not otherwise. "Where were you going?"

"Hopefully not out there." I glance behind me in the direction of the lock. I might have to start securing myself now. Tell my quarters not to recognize my voice and have Piotr change the code on the hatch so I don't know it. But then I will have to depend on someone else to let me out, and that thought makes me cold.

I shouldn't be on this ship much longer anyway. And that thought doesn't warm me either.

"You weren't answering your comms," she says. "I was coming to get you. Something came in from your boy Finch." She frowns, still not liking that he was left on Austro. Or not liking that I didn't tell her why.

"Thanks." I walk past her. And once I'm in the lev to go up to the command deck, I lean against the wall and shut my eyes.

Every time I sleepwalk, instead of sleeping, it always feels like I was running instead. There is no rest.

⋆

"I'm on *Macedon*," he says. And even though I'm sitting, I feel unsteady. His voice sounds distant over the comm, though I'm staring right at his image and there is no lag. He stares back, dark eyes, a nervousness in his tone. Gray bulkhead behind his shoulders.

"Are you all right?" If Azarcon put him in the brig.

"I'm fine. Just. They insisted. And Otter—well . . ." He had no choice if the symp made him go. "I told him everything. The captain, that is. About *Archangel*—he contacted them, and they're rendezvousing. We're rendezvousing with them."

"You're on that ship, and they're going to meet *Archangel*?" And if *Archangel* blows—but, obviously,

Azarcon wouldn't put his carrier in the way of harm. "Are you all right?" I need to know.

"Yuri. I'm fine. They've got me in some quarters, and there's a jet here just, you know, staying with me while I send this. I told the captain about you."

"What?" My mind keeps putting Finch in *Macedon*'s brig, and my memories of that place are not pleasant. "What did you tell him?" Sharper than I should probably be.

"How we were in prison. A little. Why I was with you on your ship. Things he needed to know."

"What else?" Because you're holding back something.

"Nothing much." He glances away as if someone is gesturing to him off-screen.

"Who's that? Do they have a gun on you or something? Are they threatening you in some way?" I wait for the comm to cut at those questions.

"No, Yuri, I'm fine. I swear."

"What else did you tell them?" About me. "Are they going to send you back to prison?" Already I start to think what it will take to convince Caligtiera to attack *Macedon* if that happens. Crazy thoughts. Attacking *Macedon* in order to free Finch.

Or not so crazy.

"No, I don't think so. I hope not."

A voice off-screen says, "Not unless you screw us. But then we won't bother with jail, sweetness, there's always one of our airlocks."

A jet. I recognize the voice. "Dorr! You little shit, you lay a hand on him and I'll hunt your bloody carrier—"

"Yuri!" Now Finch looks frightened.

A blond head pokes into view. The hair might be cut from what I remember, molded messily now into a short crest lining the curve of his head from crown to back, but the grin I recognize. The flat challenge in his eyes I recognize. One of *Macedon*'s soljets, and I have murderous thoughts when I see his smile. He places a hand behind Finch on the chair back, leaning close at his shoulder. "'Lo, pirate. Who knew you had such good taste, yah?"

"Yuri," Finch says, before I can respond. "I'm all right."

"Yah, he fiiine." Dorr's grin widens, teeth and tongue showing.

Finch looks at him. Go away, his eyes say, though he's smart and keeps it to himself.

I stew. Sitting there. Unable to do anything else.

"I want to speak to your captain," I tell Dorr. "Now."

"That can be arranged," he says in a highfalutin voice, "if he ain't, yano, gettin' his teeth cleaned or sommat." Grin. And before Finch or I can say anything else, he reaches and blanks the comm.

Sons of bitches on that carrier.

Sons of bitches.

* *
*

In twenty-one minutes I get a direct comm. I'm still sitting at my desk in quarters so I can answer it immediately. And it's Captain Cairo Azarcon, of course. Looking unchanged since the last time we faced each other, when I was on his ship and he wanted to kill me. His son can be kidnapped or his wife just murdered, but you can never tell by the look in his eyes. They give nothing. I wonder if he sleeps. If he has that much control actually to sleep.

Falcone's first protégé. First geisha. First one to leave. First one to single-handedly throw the pirate network into chaos.

At least one aspect of our relationship has changed. I'm no longer in his brig.

"Kirov," he says.

"Azarcon." Mutual recognition like two wolves scenting each other before a spar. I don't wait for him to ask the questions or offer the threats. "Finch is innocent in all of this." In relation to me.

A pause. "Indeed?"

Maybe he's surprised that I address that first. Maybe it will tell him that I'm not quite the same person that refused to talk on his ship. I confirm it with more words. "*Archangel*'s still intact?"

"Yes, they're looking for the saboteur and checking their entire ship. It's going to take a while. Where are you?"

"Ghenseti." The irony of that doesn't escape him either, I bet. The location of Falcone's fall from grace. "Where are you?"

"En route to meet *Archangel*." Which isn't any sort of co-ordinates, but I don't expect anything less from him. "I also hear you've been talking with a couple of Black Ops agents."

If he needs a reason to mistrust me more, this is it.

"Azarcon, I hope you didn't torture this information out of my—" What is he exactly? "Crew."

"No, I didn't. I simply asked him. I would only torture if he wasn't cooperative. He also says he's not part of your crew. And you haven't answered about the agents."

"One of them has a son aboard *Archangel*. I'm assuming Finch told you what operation they were running and why they got me out of prison. There's more to it. This agent—O'Neil—will be coming with me when I—" And it's difficult to say, sitting in these quarters. "When I abandon my ship."

"O'Neil." He recognizes the name, and for a split second there's a flicker of surprise. He would know *Archangel*'s jets too, the two ships used to patrol together and train together sometimes. Sisters. And he is the type to know crews to that level. Falcone was the same. Then, "You're abandoning your ship. How?"

Training provides distance when I need it. "I plan to blow it up." It occurs to me that O'Neil will now want to meet with *Macedon* if they're meeting *Archangel*, and even though it would be better sense if I dumped him at Chaos and disappeared myself, the fact Finch is on *Macedon* now has made my decision for me. "I'd like to bring O'Neil to see his son." Couch it in charity.

He doesn't buy it. "You want to make sure I don't vent this kid you sent to Otter. You realize if I let you aboard, you're going straight to the brig."

"And you're going to send us both back to Earth?" Back to prison.

"Well it seems you've got a habit of breaking out, so probably no." That deadpan tone. And he's got no reason to follow the Hub's laws. Even less so than before. Pirate in a uniform. It's not the first time someone's thought of him that way. The Send can be virulent. "When are you doing this?" he says.

What are you going to do with me? But I don't ask. If I hear the answer, it will just make it worse, this inevitable action. "Now that I've heard from Finch, this shift if everything's set up. But I need coordinates to meet you."

"If this comm number will translate to your transport, then I'll contact you. I look forward to meeting Agent O'Neil."

And me. Again. His eyes say it. He's a hunter. Second best to getting Falcone is capturing me. And since the bird is dead already, I promptly move up on the list.

* * *

It takes so little time to comm Piotr as I release Dexter, catch him and tuck him into my jacket pocket even though he squirms. I feel him fluttering in there like a frantic heart.

Piotr says, "Captain?"

I move to the hatch. "Do it now."

* * *

It's a gamble. You sabotage your own ship to blow up, without going through the authorized self-destruct protocol, and anything can go wrong before you have a chance to get free. But I trust Piotr to know his own limits, to know this ship from plate to plate and bolt to bolt, and if anyone can "safely" bring down a heavily modified merchant from the inside out, it's him.

When I get the comm from the bridge I know he's done it. So I go. Rika is stern but beneath it she's afraid—Piotr's told her there is some sort of leak in the drive coolants and if it gets into the grav nodes on that deck, it will destabilize the nodes and things will go boom. Piotr's colorful language. We have a half hour to fix it, or we'll have to abandon.

So I comm Caligtiera. He says he will take us on if we lose the ship, but I should understand that we'll be under gun for now. That doesn't sit well with my bridge crew at all. I blame Taja. She should've had the *Khan* checked over more recently. It's easy to act indignant.

I order the exodus to the escape pods, just in case, I tell them. "Leave the bridge on remote; if Piotr can't fix this by now, there is no way in hell."

I'm the picture of commanding calm. Inside I wonder if this is the only way to get off my own ship safely. Inside I wonder what makes me think I can just walk away.

Rika insists on shadowing me when I go to get Caligtiera's "clients." "I can do it, sir, you should get to a pod."

The girl is too loyal. Or too suspicious. "No, they're my responsibility, and this deal we have going with Cal is too important. I want to bring them across myself. You get going."

"No, sir. Your sister won't leave you behind."

I could order her, but she won't listen. Two of them and one of me, is her math, and even though I'll have guards, none of them are geisha. None of them assassins.

So she follows me to their quarters, and I point her to Lukacs's. When I open the hatch to O'Neil's, he's already standing by it. I slip him a sidearm that he tucks under his shirt, then we're back out in the corridor and Rika's got Lukacs in hand. O'Neil gives me a subtle look as we start off in a brisk walk.

"What is this?" Lukacs says. "What's going on?"

"The ship," I tell him. "It's gonna blow."

"What happened?" Demanding. As if he's the captain.

"Taja was a lousy khan. Don't worry, we're going over to the *Iron Cross*." My dead voice can translate as rage and grief, maybe. Mostly it's an absence of thought. It doesn't feel real walking these intestinal corridors, hearing that alert as if the nerves of the ship itself are going into stroke. The entire crew flows around us to their own designated escapes.

I remember coming aboard for the first time, thinking it was my freedom.

How am I going to get Rika to another pod? Because if she intervenes, I might have to kill her, and I can't think of that. It would devastate Ville. It would be one more deep cut on the flesh of my intentions.

In the last turn before we reach the command pod, Piotr runs up.

"Captain." Quick glance to Rika. Caution.

I don't know if that tips off Lukacs in some way, but in midstep he turns and spins Rika to the bulkhead, arms going around her in a full nelson. Her rifle dangles from its strap but she drives her heel down toward his foot. It glances off as he moves his leg and all of our guns come out—O'Neil's, Piotr's, mine. Pointing at him.

Lukacs notes O'Neil's aim. "So," he says. And in one move he flings Rika toward me and Piotr, yanking the weapon off her shoulder as her arm flies out.

They fire on each other, O'Neil and Lukacs. Point-blank. And both go down.

Dexter, in my pocket, sets up a squall.

"Son of a bitch!" I lean down to O'Neil. Rika's weapon was set on red kill.

Mine, given to O'Neil, was on paralysis.

Piotr says, "*Captain*. We have to go!"

Rika: "The hell is this, Yuri?" She retrieves her rifle from Lukacs's writhing form. The pulse hit him in the chest, but his limbs still twitch. It's spreading.

But he manages to say, "Traitor."

Me or O'Neil, I don't know who he means. But O'Neil has a large rifle-shot wound in his chest, and his eyes are wide-open. That clear blue.

"Captain!" Piotr reaches down and grabs my arm.

I shake him off. "Get to Cal," I tell Rika. "Go!"

"Where are you going?" A blazing look. Confusion and shock and not a little anger.

Azarcon would brig her or worse, because she'd go on his ship firing.

"Pick him up." I motion to Lukacs. Looking at Piotr.

"Yuri," Rika snaps. And suddenly steps over the body,

blocking Piotr. "What the hell are you doing?" Her rifle comes up.

The ship says we have five minutes.

"We go now," Piotr says. "Or we die. This is not a time for debate."

She isn't going to move. She sees it's a client of Caligtiera's, and I have no intention of joining her on his ship.

"Yuri," she says. But the gun doesn't lower.

There isn't anything to do but turn my back. I won't kill her. "I'm sorry, Rika," I tell her. Inadequate, maybe dishonest words. Sorry for some things, not for others. I still go. Piotr covers me as I open the hatch to the pod. I wait to hear the pulse, but she doesn't shoot before it closes again.

* * *

I pilot the pod as we streak away from the collapsing ship. Dozens of similar pods arc out like blood spatter from all points of the *Khan*'s skin, dots along the wall of black. So many, and the *Iron Cross* will take them all and not even notice one pod veering away from the group on its own separate trajectory. He won't know until Rika tells him.

I take my bird from my pocket and let him perch on the flight console. He screeches at Piotr, but the man ignores it, too busy checking our lifesystems.

"We're good for a week," he says.

"We won't need that much. *Macedon* will come get us."

This shocks him. "Yuri," he says, "that wasn't what I had in mind exactly."

None of this is what I had in mind exactly. Since I was four. I stare at my ship. Already little thunder and lightning flashes can be seen through the partially imploded hull.

Chain-reaction explosions from within. It would be almost pretty if it weren't so devastating. It won't be destroyed in one complete boom. Death like this takes time. It took me a lifetime.

It gets smaller the faster we go, as we build up to a full flight velocity.

Fleeing to *Macedon*. None of this was what I had in mind when I blooded the captain's son. I might have shot him to kill, like I am killing my ship, but it was I who bled. I am the one who's bleeding.

A BREATH

1.13.2196 EHSD — Boysdeck

I got my second and third ship tattoos after killing Bo-Sheng. A brand or a collar, in a way, or maybe just a reminder like you'd wear a wedding ring. Tattoos were that. My second was a smaller version of the one over my heart, the rampant black horse, and Mnemosyne inked it just below the inside of my right elbow. The ship's nanocode went into the ink and beneath my skin. A mark of ownership. Falcone dealt violently with the people who touched his possessions, and that was what we were. My geisha fan tattoo, inked at the same time as the one on my arm, said I belonged to the Hanamachi. We all belonged to the ship.

I was chrono twenty, but it didn't mean a thing. I'd worn the first tattoo for six years, and been on *Genghis Khan* for eleven. And that was my real age. Eleven years in service to the Blood.

Estienne told me not to show them my tattoos when I went to Austro Station, down into Boysdeck, so we covered them up with that semipermanent industrial skin that actors and physical trauma victims sometimes used. The people on station might not recognize the geisha fan, but chances were someone might know the two from *Genghis Khan*. There were some ex-pirates underdeck (not from the *Khan*, since Falcone didn't just let people go), or people who dealt with pirates, and the less they knew about me the better.

I got a new name. Yuri Kirov. Not Terisov. Nobody would recognize me, not even Papa. He said I wasn't allowed to try to contact Papa or find Mama, and the threat was implicit. It didn't matter. I had new Family now. I didn't want to talk to my family because what would I say? They wouldn't understand what geisha meant. They couldn't know what I did.

It was dangerous for pirates—especially now. *Shiva* was dead, captured by Captain Azarcon, the thorn in every illegal deep spacer's side. Word seemed to pass from one carrier to the next that the strits weren't all that important anymore; instead, they must track down pirates and their caches. Falcone raged.

He wasn't Marcus anymore.

This is what I did. I recruited for him.

And everything Bo-Sheng had told me seemed to plant under my skin and wither there for lack of light. So black and twisted and small not even Estienne felt it. Or if he did, he learned to ignore it like geisha could.

There were a lot of things different now that I was allowed to go on station and recruit for the ship, now that I was physically not a child anymore and I'd cut as many people for getting in my way as I had scars on my arms. I never went anywhere without my switchblade, and once I even stabbed someone in my sleep. I didn't know when it began, but I started to take walks in my sleepshift. In my sleep. Someone tried to wake me up or touch me or something— I couldn't remember—and I'd reacted like I was awake. I woke up next shift back in my quarters, and Falcone called me into his office and told me a man was dead, and I had done it, someone had seen me from in the shadows. And they said I was a ghost.

So then Falcone began to lock me in and put a guard on my hatch, so even in sleep he had me caged, and Estienne was the one who opened it for me in the goldshift—if he didn't sleep over. I told Estienne maybe he shouldn't stay over in my sleepshift because of my walking. But I couldn't put a real threat behind it. I liked him there too much, and I wanted him to lie to me in that way he'd been doing since I got on board. They were good lies, tangled in truth. They were the kind you could feel calm about in the dark.

The crew basically left me alone. Word got around that I could kill even in my sleep, and it became a bit of a grim joke.

They left me alone because after Bo-Sheng there were others, names that I chose to forget in waking hours, on *Genghis Khan* alone. Then one time a geisha kid on *Shiva,* when that ship was alive, didn't like the way I criticized her work when Falcone sent me over to review their Hanamachi and their protégé. This geisha kid was so new and not yet so unafraid because *Shiva* was no *Genghis Khan,* and she called me a bitch and a high-handed mother, and I slashed her on the face so badly they didn't want to use her anymore, even with a bot-knitter fix. After that *Shiva* didn't give me problems, and her captain picked better geisha.

They all got in my way or up into my face for one thing or another, and Falcone had always said that if you didn't take care of things right at the flash point, you just got burned later on. Even Caligtiera stopped mocking me quite so much, and Taja sure as hell stayed clear—of me. Not of Estienne I was sure.

With all my tattoos and the freedom to walk off the ship anytime I wanted as long as Falcone okayed it, Estienne deferred to me. He asked me if he could sleep in my quarters or if we wanted to stay in a den together on station when we got leave or if there was anything I wanted, and sometimes it hurt because he was my Elder Brother, but I was the protégé, and now if he ever drew a knife on me, I could kill him and not be punished.

Sometimes I had to go away on stations for assignments like recruitment or finalizing of shipments; that took me even as far as Hubcentral, where many of the arms dealers originated. Shipments of guns from Earth, the planet that battled on its surface in a hundred different conflicts, and what weapons you used in ground combat could easily be used on a station. Cutters and howitzers and high-tech bombs for terrorist protests. After a while it became almost as routine as sitting in senior staff meetings, taking notes, or checking up on ship division commanders to report back to Falcone.

But those weeks away from the ship took me from Estienne and always before I left he told me he'd be there when I came back. As long as I came back to the ship, he'd be there.

Boysdeck was going to be my longest assignment away from the mother, off ship and not counting leap time, at least two weeks of recruiting in Austro Station's underdeck. Estienne said the shift before I left, "Just be careful," and "I'm going to miss you."

"Of course I'm going to be careful," I said, curled beneath his arm in my quarters, in bed. "It's not like I'm meeting clients." There was always a danger in clients, if not for us, then for them. I hadn't killed any more for fucking with me, but one or two I'd had to cut or shoot for screwing Falcone on a deal. I said, "I'll miss you too."

In the dark I just felt him push his nose against the side of my hair. "Guess what," he said.

"Hm, what."

"I heard the captain talking. He thinks you're almost ready to get your own ship. So this assignment? It might be one of the final things."

"What kind of ship?"

"Komodo. Like this one."

"Are you serious?" I turned my face to him, just to feel his breath, and somehow I knew he was smiling. Then I heard it in his voice.

"Yeah. Full crew . . . so recruit those kids wisely, they might be under your command."

It set my heart racing. My own end of the operation. "Am I the first?"

"First what?"

"He's never had a protégé that went this far, has he?" It was a risk for him then, with me.

Estienne said, "No. The first one, remember I said? He betrayed the captain long before he got to this stage." Silence. Then he said, "You know who the first protégé was, don't you?"

"No . . . you never said."

"Azarcon."

I stared into the dark. "Liar."

"No. But don't talk to Marcus about it."

I had to let that sit. I could barely encompass it. And yet there was a certain symmetry to the claim. Azarcon had a reputation for disobeying Hub Command orders, recruiting avidly from the least desirous sections of the population like orphans and petty criminals, and his jets were notoriously ruthless. "Why doesn't Falcone tell the Hub? It would ruin Azarcon's career, and he wouldn't bug us."

"I don't know. Maybe because nobody would believe it? Or maybe because he was the first . . . Marcus has this old-fashioned notion sometimes of dealing with people directly. Like for revenge. I think he'd like to just shoot *Macedon* himself."

That made sense—for Falcone.

But the irony of it made me laugh, that Falcone would be screwed over now by a former protégé in the shape of a Hub carrier captain. Estienne had to shush me, as if he were afraid somebody might hear. I said, "So when I get my own ship, it means he trusts me."

"Yeah," Estienne said.

"What about the Hanamachi?"

"Well, you'd make your own."

"But I can't be a captain and train geisha at the same time."

"No, I mean, you'd *have* your own." His arm tightened.

"You? You'd help me?"

Silence.

"Estienne?"

"No . . . I'd have to stay on the *Khan*. Here."

"Why? You could be the Elder Brother of my Hana-machi, and I'd be the captain, and it'd be perfect. We'd run ops for Falcone but we wouldn't have to . . ." Do everything he said. But I stopped because that sounded disloyal.

"I can't, Yuri. This is my Hanamachi, Marcus recruited me, and I can't leave it. But you would take one of your brothers or sisters, or one of each, and they'd become Elders on your ship. That's how it'll work."

"But I want you." I felt for his shoulder in the dark then slid my hand up into his hair, gripped it. "Maybe I can talk to the captain."

"No," he said. And I didn't know why he was so against it. "This is the way it is. The protégé will have his own ship, and his own Hanamachi, and Rika or Ville or Jonny or Yasmin have to advance. That's how they advance. And then I'll have to recruit more here."

"Why can't Rika or Ville or both of them advance, and you and Elder Sister Hestia come to my ship?"

"Because," he said, "I belong to Falcone. We belong to Falcone, Hestia and I."

And it was that simple, and that cruel.

He kissed me, but in the dark he missed my mouth and caught my cheek. And I said, "Don't you want to come with me?"

"Of course," he said, trailing kisses down my neck.

To distract me.

So I let him do what he wanted, but I couldn't let myself get caught in it like I usually did. His distraction only made me think that now it wasn't going to last.

* * *

Boysdeck was a section of the underdeck where mostly orphans roamed. There were a lot of orphans in this war, and maybe not even specifically because of the war. Pirates made orphans too. I knew that now.

If we had crew to fill we kept the kids young enough to mold or old enough to seduce with promises of empowerment through violence. On the system that had wronged them. Community, I told them. That was what we had. And I wasn't even lying.

The ones who still grew up hating, plotting, or otherwise rebelling, if Falcone was in a good mood he simply sold them to other ships or illegal establishments on stations (brothels, gunrunners, drug cartels), or dumped them at sinkholes. In a bad mood, he vented them into space. Either way, though, we were never at a loss for kids.

I appeared in Boysdeck wearing ragged clothes, with no weapons but my switchblade, and prowled the shadows of the station's transsteel guts like a wraith. What maintenance workers came this way usually came armed, the pollies made sweeps every few months; but the denizens of the black, the graffiti, and the many narrow tunnels leading to dead ends and violence always reoccupied like an ancient town after an army had marched through. The people had nowhere else to go, whether they were criminals, homeless, veterans, or forgotten. And especially the kids.

It was easy to spot the prostitutes, low work imitation geisha without the history or the training. Of course they didn't know we had something in common, because theirs was a common trade, and mine was not. They had no idea that there could be a higher purpose to their skills. It was just survival for them, and some older kid or destitute adult gathered these kids together, advertised abovedeck in the subtle code these kinds of people knew, and those who were interested braved the dark and the dank, sometimes with bodyguards or escorts. Cocktails, all of them. Rich, sometimes old, sometimes fat, always justifying their behavior.

The kids were easy to talk to, especially the young ones, seven- and eight-year-olds. I told them about the ships, and traveling in space, I took their names and the locations of their hangout spots, and I told them all to keep it our secret because when the time came I would take them away from these dirty tunnels, but if they told, then it might be difficult.

Kids are awfully good at keeping secrets if you give them a good enough reason.

The third goldshift underdeck I got approached by a girl, maybe thirteen years old, who saw me crouched below a sweating pipe that dripped some sort of coolant into a shallow puddle on the cement. I was smoking a cheap cigret, since expensive ones would just make people look twice, and eyeing the lanky boys who patrolled aimlessly past my sight from one nook to another, dealing or searching for something to fill their time. I wasn't interested in drug addicts, so at least half the kids I left alone.

The girl had dusky brown skin and clear dark eyes, not an addict. Surprisingly well-groomed hair even though her clothes were ragged, threadbare at the elbows and at the collar. She held out her hand to me.

"Smoke?"

You never refused someone a cigret, so I took out the wrinkled pack from my pocket and handed it to her. She pulled out a stick and leaned down so I could snap the end, then she straightened and inhaled and blew the gray toward my face.

She said, "My name's Delsie. What's yours?"

Maybe she was looking for a cocktail. "Yuri." I peered up at her. I didn't stand. I thought she liked looking down at me, and if I stood the dynamic would change.

"My brother wants to see you," she said, and jerked her chin. "C'mon." Then she started off down the tunnel, tapping her cig over the deck.

Her brother could've been a pimp or a drug dealer, but I got up and followed. Direct requests I had to investigate. "What does your brother want?"

"Talk," she said. She didn't turn around. I could've stabbed her in the back, but she didn't seem to care. Some of the kids watched us with shadowed eyes as we passed. Silent. Maybe envious, though I didn't know why I'd get that vibe.

"How old are you?" she said, still walking ahead of me, light footfalls. Her shoes had holes in the heels as if she'd played with them until they tore.

"Bio or chrono?"

She shrugged. "Either."

"Chrono sixteen," I said, which was a lie, but twenty was a little too old in these circles. Twenty sometimes implied you had intent for being here beyond *life sucked*, and I didn't need the added suspicion, however slight. And it was easy for me to pass as younger.

"Tall," she said.

"Tallish," I replied, because she was petite, barely up to my chest. Malnutrition or genetics, you couldn't tell.

She didn't answer. She led me past a spidery wall of cracks and painted lines, language you'd have to be born here to know. Behind a long mesh curtain tied to the pipes overhead stood a boy, hard to tell how old he was because he was small-boned like her, with the same skin and hair color. He wore a mobile comp, the red eyes fixed over his own, so he might've been looking at me or looking at something in the interface.

"This is Yuri," she said to the boy.

He said, "You're new."

Maybe he was some sort of kingpin down here. It might've been a good contact. "What's your name?"

Kid said, "Otter." Which was a little ridiculous considering the lack of water or wooded areas on a space station. "You've been talking to a lot of kids," he said.

"Yeah. How'd you get that mobile?" They weren't cheap.

"Gift," Otter said. Then he just stood there silent, and I realized he was reading something on the interface. Then he said, "Okay. You can go now."

"Go." I stared at him, at her.

"You can go, Yuri."

"What did you ask me here for?"

"Just wanted to meet you."

Delsie smiled at me, standing at her brother's shoulder.

So I walked out, and felt at least one pair of eyes on my back.

* * *

Nobody talked about Otter, though they all knew of him, aside from mumblings about the fact he led a large gang underdeck. That might've been an explanation for the reticence, and it certainly was an explanation for how he seemed to know what I was doing. Any kid I passed or talked to could've been part of his gang. I tried to find any common tattoos or other markings that might set them apart but saw nothing consistent. He and his sister were like some kind of dirty little secret that I couldn't penetrate; so for fear of it getting back to him that I was grilling this child and that, I stopped asking.

The children wore me down. I went abovedeck every other full shift and commed in the possibles from an out-of-the-way public console so Falcone could look over the files. Since this was my first major recruitment, and he wasn't going to spend resources getting them off station if half of them turned out to be duds, I had to be thorough. So over the shifts I collected data on the kids, kept an eye out for Otter or his sister or anyone who might've been their spies, and ran into quite a few political aides and professionals. They'd sneak down to pick up people for their bosses or themselves. From police officials to Merchants Protection Commission officers, the cocktails were wide and varied. Men and women. I noted them too. It was helpful to know when powerful people had certain vices.

I didn't so much mind reporting on the adults. But the kids. After a full week I just sat up at a café facing the main concourse in Module 7, had a hot drink, and didn't think about how trusting they were.

Falcone had gone to Colonial Grace, he told me later, to meet with a contact he had there. Even in the refugee camp. Some of the supplies that Hubcentral shipped for the destitute families got diverted to pirates, and his contact helped to make that happen. He'd told me this maybe expecting a reaction, but by then I was numb. I'd killed Bo-Sheng, and the Camp was somewhere distant and blocked off. Best not to think of it. Really best not to let Falcone see me thinking of it, even a little. He liked to test me that way, drop hints of things to do with orphans or rapes or shootings—key words that would tell him if I still had a problem. I guessed I worked through my problems with the cutting and the sleepwalking, because I was able to look him in the eyes, impassive.

All the truth came out in afterthoughts, when it no longer mattered. What would I do with this information now?

I never asked him why he chose me. Estienne had sort of explained a long time ago and when it came down to it, this grand vision of a protégé, of the geisha, was all Falcone. He had in his mind how to restructure the galaxy to suit his own ambition, how to create a fleet of ships that would be cored by specially trained people strongly loyal to captains who were strongly loyal to him—and along with the mind behind that came some sort of instinct. You were supposed to hone it for command.

He'd had an inkling about me, through my dynamic with Bo-Sheng, through talking to my father, through a dozen different signals, all confirmed when I was in training, like these kids I was recruiting were going to be trained. Not in the technical parts of pirating, but the mind-set.

He trained me so well I could recognize it, but that didn't stop me from living it still. Obviously I wanted it to some degree. Or else how had I got so far? It was who I was now, and maybe it had always been a part of me.

Sitting on a station picking out children like you'd pick out a pair of shoes.

It was too easy to walk among children. They flocked around your legs, even the suspicious ones, if you showed the proper face. Promised them better things.

The people around me at other tables stared at my rough clothing and disheveled hair. Of course I had cred to cover this fake lifestyle, but the appearance set everyone on edge. These were the same people who did nothing to help all those children I was recruiting underdeck. How would they feel if I took their children? I put that in my stare when I looked at them. Maybe I should follow you home and take your children.

Eventually I returned to Boysdeck. And Otter caught me. He sent Delsie again, who bummed another cig and told me to come along. I looked at her narrow back as we walked, looked at the shadows on every side. She took me to the same corner of the tunnels, and her brother was there, without the mobile this time. Instead now he had a gun.

"What the hell is this?" I fingered the end of my sleeve where my switchblade was tucked.

"Sit," Otter said, pointing with the muzzle of his gun to an overturned crate in the center of the space.

I sat. Kid with territorial issues? I hadn't seen them all this time, but maybe some of the dross I'd talked to walked their observations to his ears.

"You make an awful lot of comms abovedeck," he said.

So he had me tailed even there. Must've been real good because I hadn't spotted one. "And this is your business?"

"Who're you comming?" The gun didn't waver, and Delsie moved behind my shoulder, out of sight and still out of reach.

So these kids knew their shit. I said, "My ship."

"What ship?"

I stared at the muzzle. "I don't like answering stuff at gunpoint."

"At gunpoint should be the only time you answer stuff," he said. "So answer."

"You know a lot for a tunnel kid." I turned slightly to peer at Delsie over my shoulder. "Who's paying you?"

This could go on. He knew it too. Unless he shot me. But he wouldn't until he got his answers.

He didn't answer my question.

"Who's paying you?" I stared at him. "I want to know who I'm dealing with."

"Maybe we'll keep you until you talk."

"Black Ops?" He was young, but it wasn't unheard of. "Some other govie agency? You give me something and I'll give you something; otherwise, you might as well kill me now and die in ignorance."

If he had any sort of insight he could see I wasn't bluffing.

So he said, "I work for the Warboy. Who do you work for?"

That had been the last thing I'd expected to hear. I stared at him and all of his barely shoulder height. He was an ally of the big human sympathizer? The Warboy was at the top of the govies' hit list, even ahead of Falcone.

"Who do you work for?" Otter repeated. Not just a king-pin. A symp himself. With obvious connections besides the commander of the strit fleet. A part of the sympathizer network on Austro Station. No wonder I hadn't been able to de-tect a tail.

"Merchant," I said. *"The Abyssinian."*

"Try again," he said. "Merchants don't leave their crew on station, solo, for this long."

So I said, "Merchant that doesn't report all of its cargo."

"Pirate," he said.

"Technically. But coming from a symp, that's pretty ironic."

"Symps don't steal children."

I smiled. The way armed people did, though he was the one with the gun. "Just recruit them?"

"This is my home. They don't steal children. They give us work."

I didn't answer.

"Don't come back," he said, with a jerk of his weapon.

Which was my cue to leave. So I did.

* * *

I had to kill them. I went abovedeck and sat in that café and thought about it.

A long time.

I didn't know why it was so difficult. Not only were they suspicious of me, but they were symps. It wasn't hard to fig-ure. Only one answer for a problem like that.

But I sat at that café, unable. Rented a low-end den and slept there, procured a gun from a trafficker we knew, and dawdled in that room popping out the pulse pack and clicking it back in, over and over. Then I tucked it into my waist and went back to the café. I ordered one milked caff and nursed the thing for three hours, just sitting there watching the concourse traffic flow by.

I didn't see him at first, he was so small and lost among the color, but then Otter peeled himself away from a crowd of tunnel kids loitering abovedeck. He strolled over to my table, stood on the other side of the low gate that separated the outdoor seating from the traffic. "You haven't come back to kill me?" he said.

This odd kid. I didn't answer.

"Why not?" he continued. "Don't want to?" Then he hopped over the gate and plopped down across from me. "Let's talk."

"About?"

He stared at me from behind shaggy dark bangs. No sign of the ruby-eyed interface. "You pick."

I wasn't going to talk.

He said, "Okay, I pick. We want someone in the pirates."

I took a sip of my now-cold caff. There was nothing but thick flavor at the bottom. "To serve you cake?"

"To get us information."

"Why would I do that."

"There something you'd want from us?" He leaned on his arms, scratched his hair, at every glance a wiry, twitchy teenager.

"Not particularly."

"Think hard, Yuri. Think of our resources. There's gotta be something you'd want."

"Symps can read minds?" I looked at him.

"No," he said. "Just faces."

Not my face. "Kid, I'm one minute away from shooting you in cold blood."

"In public? Go ahead. Optics." He nodded his chin up at the second tier of the concourse. Of course I knew that, and of course being a symp he knew it too.

I said, "Go back underdeck and maybe I'll forget we met."

"You're here alone? Nobody else from your crew with you?"

I didn't answer.

He said, "I can get you out."

I stared at him. "Out?"

"Of your ship. Of your life." He shrugged. "Out. Don't most criminals want out in some way?"

No. The immediate answer threaded through my silence. Stitched together my fear.

"I can do it," he said. And maybe he was just tossing out options, hooks, to see which one might snag. "You can be off this station in two shifts and be on your way anywhere in the Hub."

My heart thudded.

"I'm not joking," he said. Then scratched his cheek and rubbed his nose with the back of his hand when I didn't speak. "Tell me the real name of your ship."

"Symps are concerned with pirates?" But of course they were. Some of them bought weapons from us.

I didn't think he was one of them. Not the Warboy's recruit. "Information never goes to waste," he said.

That I knew. I wanted a drink. A stiff one. And I thought of Estienne back on the *Khan*, sleeping alone.

"Offer's open," the boy said, then got up from the table. He pushed the chair back in like a polite son. "See you."

He hopped back over the gate and disappeared into the crowd.

I ordered that drink.

* * *

His words pounded in my mind so loudly that I began to feel sick. And that meant I was actually considering it.

The alternatives were to shoot him and his sister, or leave them alone and forget about them.

After sending another report to *Genghis Khan* about what I'd observed in the underdeck (leaving out Otter and Delsie), the following shift I finally went back, wandered the dank gray until Delsie found me. I knew she'd find me. She led me to the same point of contact, which probably wasn't where they actually bedded down on blueshifts. It was just one of his offices here. He didn't seem surprised to see me.

"Genghis Khan," I said, trying not to twitch at how easy it was to offer the name just like that.

His eyes flickered behind the jewel red interface lenses. *"Genghis Khan.* Yuri. We work together?"

I folded my arms. "Give me a solid proposal."

He said, "I'll be in touch."

* * *

Two shifts later he came to my den room with two other boys, older—muscle. Bold and foolish. I rested my hand behind me at my backwaist, where my gun was tucked. And Otter said, "Your info about *Genghis Khan.* Would you like to trade?"

"For what?"

He said, "I have a contact aboard *Macedon*. A symp. A spy. He might be able to get you a deal. Talk to Captain Azarcon, and you might not have to go to prison."

The proposal had changed. No longer interested in just letting me go? Rely on another symp? Walk straight into the arms of the person who had the most reason to hate Falcone? Who knew him maybe like I knew him. Who'd want to own me too in some way, I had no doubt of that. This deal was no good. "The Warboy doesn't want me for himself, so he shunts me to that bastard? I'm not going to prison either way. You can leave."

"We want you. Azarcon would need to meet you too. Your kind are problems to us both. But we won't help you unless you give us something back," he said.

I barely heard the words as they left my lips, but I felt the shape of them on my tongue. They tasted bitter. "I'm not going to Azarcon. Symp." That was no offer. And I would probably never get a better one, not for who I was. So how would I live if I left? I didn't know how to live outside of this. I couldn't just walk away. Especially to Azarcon, who hunted pirates above and beyond.

He watched me with his red-covered eyes. "So you'd rather recruit?"

I pulled my gun and pointed it at him. The two other boys were quick, but Otter stepped forward, once, and it stilled them with their hands at their waists, on their weapons.

"Mutual amnesia," I said. "I suggest you take *my* offer."

He held up his hand. Between his fingers shone a small chipsheet. He flicked it at me like a playing card so it careened over my shoulder and landed on the bed.

"If you change your mind."

He left. And I didn't lower the gun until the door shut behind them. I didn't look at the chipsheet until the door was locked.

But I put it in my pocket like a thieving hand.

* * *

I went back to *Genghis Khan* after two and a half weeks on station with a final list of kids for one of our bloodmates to follow up with, confiscate, then distribute. Estienne asked me "how it went" and I just looked at him, holding that slate full of names and information. "How do you think?" I said, and it was wrong. Because he sat on my bunk looking up at me, and it wasn't just confusion in his eyes, at my tone. Or concern. He was curious.

"What's going on with you?" he said.

"Nothing. Just tired. The shuttle ride back was long." I pulled some clothes down from my locker and started to change. He came up behind me and ran his hand along my stomach.

"Why don't you go take a shower."

I stepped away. "Good idea." I looked at him. "I'll see you later."

He bit the inside of his cheek, watching me. Wanting me because it had been more than three weeks for him, counting my transit time. He said, "Are you still upset about—me not joining you on your ship?"

I had to wrench my mind around. I hadn't thought of it much in the last little while. "No," I said, even though now that he reminded me, it cut. Again. Even though right now I could barely look at him for some reason, when usually I wanted nothing but to bed down.

He moved closer and held my face in his hands. But my

hand came up before he could do anything more, pushing his arm away so he let go.

"Not now." I stared at the deck.

I heard him release breath. Annoyed, maybe. Sad. But he didn't say anything.

Sometimes I wished he would ignore the fact I was the protégé, and adult. I wanted him to do what he'd done when I was younger. Not be hesitant around me. Stand up to me. Sometimes. In the muddied parts of my mind.

Now I thought he was a little scared of me.

And so he left.

* *

After my shower I put on clean clothes, black and white, and presented the list in person to Falcone in his office. He made me stand there while he perused.

"Good," he said, like he was checking for typos. "Good. Have a seat, Yuri."

I unclamped the chair in front of his desk and dropped down into it.

"So," he said, resting on his arms, leaning toward me. "With this assignment accomplished, I think it's time to tell you that I've acquired a ship for you. Komodo-class, a bloodchild for the *Khan*."

This was something good to hear, finally. I felt my mouth pull into a smile. "Yeah?"

His eyes didn't leave my face. "However, I'm bothered by something, Yuri."

I straightened. "What, sir?"

He said, "You know Estienne won't be a part of your Hanamachi."

"I know that."

"But you don't like it."

I looked at him.

"Answer me," he said, still mild. Except for his eyes.

It wasn't a face you could lie to. And besides, I wanted to see if I could bargain. "No, I don't like it. I'd like him with me."

"Because you think you're in love with him."

Estienne told. I wasn't surprised. He'd been telling things to Falcone since he first set me in quarters separate from Bo-Sheng. But in this. Maybe he was pissed because I hadn't slept with him when I returned?

"Are you in love with him?" Falcone asked.

"No, sir."

His mouth twisted. "Oh, I know you say you aren't. I know on the outside you act like there isn't a problem when you both are with clients. And I know I told you that I don't mind the connection between crew—or geisha. But that relationship should never get in the way of the work. If you're going to get your own ship, and be a captain, you can't be dependent on someone like Estienne."

"What about Taja?" I said, sitting very still. But watching his eyes.

He stared at me. It seemed like only the black pupils were looking at me. They were stark against his blue irises. Then he got up and came around his desk and laid a hand on my shoulder. I didn't expect him to do it, and I flinched. He smiled. "Taja amuses me. But I don't sulk about her other bedmates."

He'd touched me plenty of times growing up, but never in a way that made me uncomfortable. In that way.

But now.

I forced myself to look up at him, wanted to get up and push him back, but I didn't move as he ran his hand over my hair, down the back, lifting the ends between his fingers and off the back of my neck. I didn't move.

He said, "You *do* want your own ship, don't you?"

"Yes, sir."

"I think you'll make a fantastic captain for me. If you just learn to separate what's good and bad for your ship. Control and awareness are good. Deluded fancy notions of romance are not."

What was so romantic about just wanting someone with you? I didn't buy him flowers and chocolate. We didn't hold hands in the corridors.

But I didn't say anything. I stared at his desk while he played with my hair.

"What do you think would happen if you took Estienne over there and some rival captain found out about your . . . love for him. You would be giving this enemy a large opportunity to screw you over just by threatening Estienne. Now is that wise? Or fair to Estienne to be your hostage?"

"No, sir, of course not."

He said, "I don't think you mean it." He dropped his hand.

I said, "Does that mean you won't give me a ship?"

"I had no intention of *giving* you a ship." He stepped away and sat back behind his desk, suddenly all distant business. Not that what he'd been doing wasn't also business. "You know if you get a ship, it'll be because you've earned it." He picked up his slate. "Now get out."

* * *

I slept alone that blueshift. Estienne didn't knock on the hatch or comm me, and out of sheer stubbornness or muted anger at his evident conversation with Falcone, I didn't

comm him either or go to him next door. I had half a mind
to go to Jonny or Yasmin, but decided instead to stay in and
play with Dexter before bed. He hopped around on my desk,
sat on my hand when I input orders for the cargo crew under
my command (if I verbally input he tended to think I was
talking to him and made noises at me), and when I finally
crawled into bed I heard Dexter fluttering in his cage, in the
dark, restless. I lay on my back after coming awake for the
second time.

When the hatch beeped he screeched at it.

"Sshh, Dex. Lights fifty. Open." I sat up, expecting Estienne or at least one of the other geisha—and it was Estienne. We'd cuddle and forget about any distance between
us.

"Hey," he said, moving in but keeping the hatch open.

"Hey . . ." I started to push the blankets aside to invite
him to bed but he shook his head.

"Put on your clothes, the captain wants to see us."

I froze. "Why?"

"I don't know," he said. But that was a lie.

So we went—not to the office, but to Falcone's quarters.
Spartan and gray, it wasn't geisha-decorated in any way,
wasn't comfortable. I hadn't been in there since I'd first
been on the ship, and it looked no different from my vague
memories of it.

He was sitting at his small desk and motioned us farther
in.

Without any other greeting, he simply said, "Take off
your clothes."

Estienne started to unseam his shirt.

I stood there.

Falcone said, "Take off your clothes, Yuri."

"Why?"

He put his hand on the desk. It held a gun.

I stared at him. Estienne was naked and went over to the bunk and sat, unasked.

I didn't know why I wanted to test things, but I said to the captain, "You wouldn't shoot me."

He said, "No?"

"You wouldn't kill me." Even though I said it with more rebellion than I was feeling.

He said, "I don't have to kill you to hurt you. Now take off your clothes and join him on the bed."

My skin turned cold.

"Get on the bed!" he shouted.

My hands twitched. I pulled off my clothes, dropped them to the deck near Estienne's, then sat beside him on the bunk, covering myself, even though—why? I'd stripped for clients, I'd done worse or had worse done to me.

But nothing made me feel quite so dirty as when Estienne started to kiss my shoulder while Falcone watched.

He watched the entire time.

* * *

I walked blind back to quarters with Estienne trailing. He didn't speak. I still felt him at my back even though clothes and distance separated us. I still felt Falcone's eyes.

I barged into quarters so abruptly that Dexter started to squawk. I tried to push in the hatch, but Estienne followed and I turned on him.

"Get out."

"Yuri," he said, looking guarded. As well he should.

"I said get out!"

"It was just a test. That's all it was."

"Testing what! How bloody twisted he is?" I saw Estienne flinch but didn't tone it down. I turned it up. "I don't give a damn if there's kink with clients, but this is us! This is home! And he"—my damn eyes. But I took a breath and finished it dry and strangled—"he watched!"

"You have to let it go," he said.

Let *him* go, he meant.

I wanted to hit him. I wanted to grab him close and tear him inside out with what I felt.

"He's screwed kids, hasn't he." Bo-Sheng's words seemed to swim physically in front of my eyes, demanding attention. Demanding truth. "Didn't he?"

Estienne didn't answer.

"Just like you," I said.

His right fist flew. I grabbed his arm, but he pelted with his left, and for a few violent seconds we shoved at each other, but not enough to truly hurt because both of us could, both of us could kill each other if we had real intent. But then he broke away and went to the hatch.

"I love you," he said, "but if that isn't enough to cancel out all this other shit, then that's your problem, not mine."

I let him leave.

I screamed at the hatch, after the fact, "It's *your* problem!"

But I was the one it seemed to hurt the most. He'd said it as clear as he could in the captain's quarters. When it came down to it, he'd screw me first before Falcone.

* * *

For a week I cut every blueshift before bed until my arms were a webwork of scars and blood, wrapped in bandages and covered by long sleeves. But it let me breathe, it let me go about my work with a face that gave nothing. I told Rika

I was too tired to spar, so avoided her keen eyes. I ditched anything social, and I ignored Estienne. By now the crew just thought I was moody or busy when I got like this. Even Caligtiera tended to avoid me in this state.

But not Falcone. We still had our dinners. On the seventh one since the shift in his quarters, he said, "Some clients might like the scars, but I want you to stop until they're all fully healed. Do you read me?"

Yeah, they were all right as long as they didn't infringe on business. As long as they allowed me to do what I did for him. Whatever it took to cope, when drugs weren't an option.

"Yeah." I speared a block of meat.

"You're still angry," he continued, toneless. "Just because I was witness to what you and Estienne do anyway?"

"What we do outside of clients is personal." I held a knife and fork to cut into the steak again but set them aside to take a sip of my wine.

"Too personal for your captain?"

Maybe the mad mood had taken too much hold. I looked him in the eyes. "Yeah. For the same reason you don't like anyone reminding you of Azarcon, maybe I don't like the stuff between me and Estienne to go further than us."

He boxed me across the face, so fast I didn't have time to set the glass down. It flew from my hand and shattered on the floor, spilling red. My eyes watered, but I kept my seat and stared at him through the tangle of my hair. Breath felt like shards in my throat.

"That's the only warning you're going to get." He resumed eating. "Say it again, and I'll take it out on Estienne."

The next time I went on station to meet a client—Chaos Station, a week later—I took Otter's chipsheet with me.

And I commed him.

The captaincy, whenever I got it, *if* I got it, would get me off the ship. I'd still have to follow Falcone's orders, but I'd be off the ship.

And in the meantime I talked to the underdeck kid. Just to hear what he had to say. Just to hear something in my head other than Falcone's words. Otter told me that it might be difficult to get my message to Azarcon, but he was sure it would get there, I just had to be patient.

I could be patient, I told him.

Patient as a predator.

*   *   *

Neither Falcone nor Estienne ever mentioned it outside of when it happened; but we got called into his quarters every two weeks or so, in our sleepshifts, and had sex for him. And after three months he summoned me to his office and gave me my ship. I managed to smile at him. The expression came from the thought that I'd be my own captain. I knew already I wanted Piotr as my engineer commander. I was going to fill my crew with as many people from this ship as I knew I could trust.

Kublai Khan, Falcone said. *Genghis Khan*'s bloodchild. It was waiting for me at Hades, where we were headed. Silently I wanted to know how he could guarantee I wouldn't shoot him just as soon as I got on my own bridge.

Then he said, "Your lieutenant will be Taja Roshan."

And I couldn't protest. Even then. Though I didn't much hide the faint sneer on my face.

But that wasn't the real reason he had such confidence in

my loyalty. He smiled at me with this gift between us, and he knew exactly why I wouldn't shoot him. And I knew — so did Estienne.

* * *

It was a beautiful ship, my *Kublai Khan*. It smelled new. Polished and painted obsidian bones. I could walk the corridors asleep because it was a Komodo-class ship, like its bloodmother, where I'd spent the last eleven years learning. But it had none of the other *Khan*'s scars, yet. There were no bad memories or troubled dreams to mar its surfaces and seep into its bones. My ship was young and waiting, and our steps along the deck sounded like playful music. As Estienne followed me to my new quarters, holding one of my bags as I held Dexter's cage, I almost regretted that comm to Otter.

My new quarters were twice the size of my previous one, but without the years of lived-in comfort. Blank walls, bulkhead gray, and a stripped bunk in need of occupation. In need of seams and sunken patches that said a body was at home here. Maybe two bodies, occupying one mild depression. One small sadness. "This is all going to change," Estienne said. Like I was changed.

It was mild between us. I couldn't stay angry at him, even though it felt that way sometimes. Even though, sometimes, it felt hollow between us. Here now in my large and lonely new place, I looked at him and was ten again.

But only until he dropped his eyes. Then I set down Dexter's cage and put my arms around him, and Estienne let my bag drop and hugged me back. And leaving *Genghis Khan* was one thing, but leaving him altogether or turning him over to Azarcon was something else, especially when his tears dampened my collar.

"I'm sorry," he said. For everything? Maybe.

I didn't answer, and his fingers gripped me tighter until I said, "It's okay." And of course it wasn't, but right then it was near enough to it.

His voice was muffled. "Our ships will still run together. Just like we used to do with *Shiva*. You'll see, it won't be so bad. You're on your own now, and it's good. It's good to be away. Just a little."

He was right in that. But my quarters were empty. So I asked him to stay, if only for a while.

And he did that for me.

*   *   *

Eventually he left, and I sat on the floor of my colorless new world and watched Dexter hop out of his cage and flutter toward me until he landed lightly on my arm. I rubbed his green head with my finger, and his tail feathers shook. He was one bit of color until I could redecorate and make this place my own. I held him up to my lips, and he pecked his bird beak at me, sharp little kisses.

I still tasted Estienne on my tongue.

He'd touched the scars on my arms. "Maybe you won't have to do this anymore." He'd never mentioned them before. Maybe because he knew why they were there, and as long as *I* was there, they couldn't be helped. Now his fingers were soft along the lines like he was reading them, blind. He said, "Rika and Ville are here at least. You're going to be fine. And you'll take on your own protégé eventually."

I hadn't thought of that, for some reason. It made my stomach clench.

"Birds have to leave their nests," he'd said, trying for a smile. Glancing at Dexter in his black cage.

I let Dexter roam and flit freely, then lay in bed and stared up at the ceiling. I could handle things here, alone. I could walk these corridors, I didn't have to be locked in. A slow smile formed.

This was my ship. It was my arsenal. I was going to run things.

Before I went on my bridge I destroyed Otter's chipsheet under my heel.

1.15.2197 EHSD — Slavepoint

Almost a year into my command and the route to Slavepoint was a regular one, even though it sat behind the Demilitarized Zone in strit territory. Not all symps were like Otter. I learned since my geisha debut that Falcone dealt with sympathizers on the stritside of the DMZ, and these symps didn't support the Warboy. In the war where EarthHub outweighed and outgunned the strits when it came to deepspace combat, the strits and their symp allies relied on guerrilla tactics—fast strikes and quicker retreats. With precision weaponry. They hit stations, depots, carriers, and merchant ships that supported the military effort. But they were still basically relegated to their side of space. And the symps that dealt with Falcone wanted to change that.

We needed somewhere to put the confiscated children when recruitment occurred in droves, as it sometimes did depending on how low-staffed the ships were in the network. Austro was a large pool for recruits, but so were hapless merchants on isolated routes between leap points.

Leftovers were bid on, and instead of tramping a dozen pirate captains through *Genghis Khan*'s decks, Falcone preferred to use Slavepoint.

He supplied weapons to these aggressive symps so they could better blow up Hub stations and ships, and the symps gave us a planet on their side of the DMZ. It worked pretty well. Carriers didn't normally run insurgent missions deep past the DMZ, especially with Azarcon's focus on us, and one planet in a vast space that was partially charted but not visited by Hub ships provided a proper sinkhole to store caches—of slaves.

Mid-January Falcone ordered *Kublai Khan* to the planet as an advance tactic before he came later with the weapons shipment for the symps. He had a mission first by Meridia—to ambush *Macedon*. He'd gotten intel from a contact somewhere in Hub Command; *Macedon* was going to Meridia for a resupply. Pirates in general were high on a recent victory, *Genghis Khan* specifically—he'd teamed with a symp marauder and destroyed *Wesakechak*, a deep-space carrier, out by the Gjoa asteroid belt. Now, once he'd finished with Azarcon, he was going to meet us at Slavepoint. He sent Caligtiera with me to assess some potential new crew for his own ship.

Every month I went down to the planet to see how the camp was running. Sometimes if *Genghis Khan* was there, Falcone sent down Estienne to survey the slaves, and Estienne and I would disappear for a few hours in one of the rooms the camp administrators always had prepared for the visiting captains of the various ships. The rooms for the khans were always well stocked with liquor and clean sheets.

The planet itself was unterraformed, its atmosphere poisonous. It seemed drearier than normal because Estienne hadn't come down this time. He commed me when I was still aboard *Kublai Khan*, in orbit, and said they'd got a new geisha that he had to train. "But don't worry," he said, with a sly grin. "He's not nearly as pretty as you."

I stuck out my tongue. It made him laugh.

The children and what adults we kept in the camp were well taken care of—you couldn't exactly sell damaged merchandise. I took a walk with Caligtiera through the well-lit warren of corridors and rooms, where guards stood at every exit and entrance with rifles. The people in the mess hall or recreation room moved about with the quiet resentment or the total capitulation of criminals in a prison.

I never looked too closely at the children. I tried not to look them in the eyes.

We stood in the prisoner mess hall, Cal and I, which was in the center of the prisoner wing. There were only two wings to the settlement—one for the hundred or so prisoners and one for the captors, with heavily guarded gates in between. Nobody could escape to the surface of the planet, so the bottleneck transfer corridor was the only concern. We'd never had problems since 80 percent of the slaves were kids.

Cal smoked and watched them eating in the pervasive gray-painted room. He said, almost idly, "Was your camp anything like this?"

I was just lighting my own cig to try and cancel out his weed stink, and shrugged. "Don't remember."

"Ah, come on," he said, glancing at me. "Don't tell me you don't sit awake at night here and think about the irony of the situation."

"Oddly, no."

"You're a convincing liar," he said. "Or maybe not."

"And you're an annoying hole." I took a deep drag of the cig. "If it bothered me so much, do you think I'd be here?"

Not even in Slavepoint, but at Falcone's beck and call.

"I don't know," he said. "It could just be that you're patient." He paused, blew a smoke ring. "Or cold."

I looked at him sidelong. Kept staring until he had to look.

Then I smiled. "How 'bout both. And since you're so chatty today, how *are* things aboard the *Khan*, in the captain's second chair?"

Of course he didn't answer. Not out loud.

* **

My comm beeped in the middle of my sleep. Three separate times. The first was Taja back on the *Khan*, telling me the symp marauder had arrived and was simply waiting for *Genghis Khan* to show up with the weapons shipment. Symps were never idle talkers, so it was only a heads-up. The second time, Cal commed to tell me that *Genghis Khan* and *Beowulf*, a bloodmate, had leaped insystem and were now off-loading the weapons. They'd survived *Macedon*, pummeled it in fact, and made off with prisoners. If Falcone had wanted to talk, he would've commed, but he didn't, so I went back to sleep. Lightly.

Falcone was going to be in a good mood for the next long while, for getting *Macedon*. Maybe one of his prisoners was Azarcon himself.

The third comm was from my ship again.

Taja said the Warboy's ship and three other symps had leaped in and attacked both *Genghis Khan* and its buyer.

I made it from my base quarters to the main control room in a mad dash, though the walls seemed to have contracted. Five, ten minutes to get through all the automatically locked doors between base sections. Cal was there already.

He said, "*Genghis Khan* is dead. We need to get to the landing bay."

I didn't understand his words.

"Report!" I barked at him, going to the scan. The floating images there showed three different colored blots. Symp red, Hub carrier blue, and Hub battleship green—two of them.

"That one's our buyer." Cal pointed to fleeing red.

Five symps, two outbound. Our buyer and another symp in pursuit of it. After their own.

Cal said, extremely calm, "The symps took down the *Wulf* and started an attack on the *Khan*. *Macedon* leaped in and shot the *Khan*, and soon after these battleships arrived. Our only escape is your ship."

Macedon? So Azarcon wasn't dead. At least not his ship. Not like—

The words fell from my lips almost before he'd finished speaking. They were ashes cast at sea. "Then let's move."

* * *

I always kept *Kublai Khan* on the dark side of Slavepoint's single moon, with the specific intention to hide it from inbound ships to the system. It was safe, and we took my shuttle back, a modified transport that resembled a symp design so we could fly around on this side with a little more disguise. But *Kublai Khan* itself couldn't face off against that many enemy, so we stayed put. I waited on my bridge as *Macedon* and the symps left the system in pursuit of our buyer. As soon as they were far enough we sent out rescue squads to the remains of both *Beowulf* and the *Khan*.

There wasn't much left, and not many survivors. We did as thorough a job as we could, but there was threat of at least one of the Warboy's fleet ships leaping in to take care of Slavepoint, so we fled. Abandoned the camp and its people.

I aimed *Kublai Khan* to the deep and sent it hard. We would hide out at Hades.

It took hours for my people to wade through the bodies laid out in our primary bay and get to those that were still alive enough to treat. Not all of the crew would ever be accounted for, either blown completely into space or disintegrated from internal blasts.

I saw Rika and Ville, my Hanamachi Elders, and they both ran up to me past the medtechs and the body bags and threw themselves around me.

I didn't have to ask.

*　*　*

I didn't leave the bridge and, unless a crisis came up, nobody was going to speak. Not even Taja, who stayed on shift even though I was up. I sat in the chair and listened to the ambient hum of the comps and my crew talking softly into their comms when they needed something. There wasn't much to do. The ship was moving, the word would be spread: *Genghis Khan* was dead.

Caligtiera came up to the bridge, unasked, and leaned down to me, resting his hand on the arm of the chair, avoiding the controls there.

"One of the survivors said that Falcone was on the symp ship when it fled. Our buyer. He was with its captain."

I stared at him. He didn't say anything past that. He

wasn't going to suggest we go after it—with the Warboy on its ass and *Macedon* not far behind, escorting that damn symp through Hub space no less. Or hunting it.

Cal thought of it too.

The *Khan*'s death meant more than just the loss of the crew. And unless we sent a strong message back, the network was going to falter.

I was his protégé. Caligtiera had no ship now, and he wouldn't challenge me here. Not yet anyway. It was my call.

"Get me *Caliban* on comm." It was a Hub ship in Falcone's pocket, a friend of his from when he was a captain. I'd read that they were assigned, either by accident or not, to replace *Wesakechak*, the carrier *Genghis Khan* had destroyed in the deep.

Now we were going to see how strong the alliance held.

I had to think of these things now. I had to put everything else aside, this black feeling that had one name. This open mouth inside me that wanted just to scream.

*   *   *

It wasn't a good time for pirates to be out in droves. *Macedon* had been damaged, and every deep spacer that patrolled the Dragons took it as a personal insult.

But I arranged with *Caliban* to keep me in touch.

So they told me *Macedon* and the Warboy had captured our symp buyer, and the Warboy had taken it. They told me Falcone was on *Macedon,* and they were headed to Chaos Station. So *Macedon* and the Warboy were working together after all. It made a sick clench in my stomach. *Caliban* told me *Macedon* had arranged to hand Falcone over to Hub authorities so he could be tried back on Earth.

Azarcon just didn't kill him? He had more restraint than me.

But this was good news. We could arrange something between now and then. Like *Caliban* crew snatching Falcone in the handover on Chaos Station. They didn't want to do it, but I reminded their captain of Falcone's stature among the pirates and what would happen to *Caliban* should he die and some of us decided we didn't want their alliance. Maybe we could no longer trust them? It would take only one comm to the right authority to get their ship investigated.

So they agreed, and we waited.

I visited the injured crew from *Genghis Khan*, wandered among them in my medbay or the triage tents set up in the hangar, looking for Estienne. But he wasn't there, and finally Rika came and took me back to her quarters and didn't leave me alone unless I went to the bathroom or the bridge. She didn't say a word, and I was grateful. Silence was better than speech. There was nothing to crack it, because if my silence cracked, so would the rest of me.

* **

Word came down but not from *Caliban*. From a contact on Chaos that said *Caliban*'s dockside attack had failed when the Warboy's crew, moored at the station by Azarcon's order, intervened to help *Macedon*'s jets. This alliance would ruin us. It had already begun.

Falcone was dead, killed by a symp.

Falcone was dead.

* * *

I should have stayed on bridge, been there with Taja and Caligtiera so they couldn't, at least, plot to kick me off my own ship.

But I had to be alone. I had to be in quarters, with the lights down, and lie to myself.

I was free.

And Estienne was dead. Dead or lost back in the remains of the *Khan* that we hadn't gone back to for fear of the Warboy's fleet. His body could be among the ruins, waiting. Yet I knew it wasn't. People didn't wait like that. They lay with wide-awake eyes. The wakefulness of death.

And I wasn't really free. I had a ship full of people, some of whom I cared about, others who wanted me dead now that there was opportunity to advance themselves. Who was going to protest? Not Falcone.

Estienne was dead, and that part of it wasn't a lie.

That was the only truth that seemed to matter, and it threaded through me, a needle. Making holes that gaped and bled.

* * *

Caligtiera came a shift later and stood in the middle of my quarters as I sat on the bunk, my sleeves pulled down, stuck to my skin from dried blood. But he didn't see that, my sweater was black.

He said, "You need to take out Azarcon's son."

I nodded. I didn't have to ask why. It was the way of things. Like all of this, as soon as I'd stepped foot on that ship when I was nine.

Blood for blood.

And I was his protégé.

2.3.2197 EHSD — The Son

Ryan Azarcon was beautiful, physically. Of course by paying attention to the Send, I knew this, since he was all over it lately, the newest fad-face despite (or because of) the fact most of his candid transcasts lately showed him giving meedees the finger. I almost liked him for that. His mother was the public affairs bigwig on Austro Station, his father was every pirate's nightmare, and the two of them together, however two people like them even got together, had reliable genetics for a pleasing face. The kid had that, and he knew it. If people didn't always tell him, I'm sure he saw it when he looked in the mirror.

He was nineteen, but not pirate nineteen. He was affluent, catered to, had a personal bodyguard in the form of a young EarthHub Marine, and spent his time mostly in recreation at parties, vid premieres, and cybetoriums. Watching him cavort from one social engagement to another, I thought of Bo-Sheng and me by the lake, tossing rocks and being cold. I let those thoughts fester, watching this rich boy.

He had an addiction to Silver, or at least a healthy habit. Silver was the number one illegal narcotic for rich stitches all across the Hub, and for the most part he kept it a secret, it seemed, from everyone—but I recognized his dealer at a tech shop called Macroplay. She had a reputation for fine line swack. At least he only put the purest shit in his system. Snobbery even in vice. Drugs just for the hell of it, for recreation. Drugs just because it was the cool thing to do. Drugs to cope with the fact he was his father's son, maybe, whether he wanted to be or not.

I'd arrived on station in a fake merchant uniform, hair covered with a cap, eyes down, and bled myself into the routine of the concourse—quickly. The three kids I used from Boysdeck, who I'd trained before for a previous operation—pirate assets on station—were more than willing to be my eyes and ears when I physically couldn't be. They weren't part of Otter's gang. They could go underdeck when I couldn't. They helped me keep track of Ryan Azarcon and his bodyguard. They were thorough and mocking when they made their reports, usually in my rented room in a low-cred den. I took one of them to range shoot, and he loved it. I taught him about disabling laser trips in heavily secured maintenance tunnels, like the one near the flash houses in the den district's Red River, where I'd seen Azarcon's bodyguard.

My tunnel kid was going to help me in the job.

I killed a maintenance worker with no family and took his access ID.

It was a methodical process, like getting dressed in geisha blacks before meeting a client, or inventorying cargo to be shipped in some deal. Planning a hit was just step-by-step.

I sent reports back to my ship when I checked up on Taja and Caligtiera. Rika and Piotr let me know that nobody had overthrown my captaincy yet. Rika said Dexter missed me.

Hurry, they said. Everyone is dying to see it on the Send.

Azarcon's son. Dead.

And who were they going to blame? There were plenty of people they could've blamed, especially once Azarcon announced that the Warboy and the Warboy's strits that he'd helped in apprehending our gunrunning symp were going to sit down with him in peace negotiations.

It made me laugh, really, in my den, watching on my comp.

Treaty. With the Warboy and his strit patrons.

Caligtiera said, Do it soon. The bastard's uniting them.

But I doubted it.

I watched the grumblings of the Family of Humanity. It wasn't my specific mission, but with this news of possible peace, intel was at a premium. I told my tunnel kids to trail the ones I knew of in the underdeck, because we ran guns with them too, and followed the thread to a woman in the Merchants Protection Commission. I needed to know how far she was connected with the fundamentalist factions of the Centralists, and if they were going to get in the way of my op. If anyone else wanted to get back at Azarcon, it would be the Family of Humanity and their Centralist allies.

Don't let them trump us, Caligtiera said. That kill is ours.

She was in her midthirties, maybe more, but cured in suspended aging treatments; she looked about fifteen years older than me, small brown eyes and long blond hair about a year out of fashion in its blunt, unremarkable cut. She wasn't very pretty, a sedentary woman judging from her size—about four or five above ideal. And she liked to decompress from a long work shift at a medium-scale bar called Goldmine.

One late shift I put on casual dark clothes and found her in the bar. I pretended to jar her elbow as she sat on the high stool. It spilled her drink all over the colormorphing bartop. The basest of beginnings.

"I'm so sorry," I said to her irritated scowl, trying for an embarrassed smile and sneaking peeks into her eyes.

"Really, I totally wasn't looking where I was going. Here, let me buy you another one. What were you drinking?"

Her name was Elizabeth, and despite her dowdy looks, which tended to make her seem as if she didn't care about much, she had a strong sense of purpose and a lot of opinions about the state of the government and the Hub as a whole. That first shift in the bar we talked politics, and I let it slip how disgusted I was that Azarcon would even attempt a peace treaty with the strits after all the grief they'd caused humans on this side of the DMZ.

I played her like a drum, a steady beating of smiles and drinks and eventually sex. A week into it, and I was in her apartment in the executive tower, and she was speaking more openly like the Family she was. And she was only too happy for a young thing like me, someone to divert the passion for her Cause into something that would make her sweat. And I was only too happy to raid her comp when she was asleep.

They wanted Azarcon humiliated, discredited, and worn. But not dead. Because dead heroes became martyrs, and the man had enough mystery.

If they only knew his secret. Knew him as I knew him, as one of Falcone's. Never mind that he was an EarthHub captain now; some part of the pirate must've still lingered.

She asked on that late shift, ten days into our relationship, "Where did you come from?" In that way of sodding romantics. She's asked about my fan tattoo and found it sad when I told her it was to remember an old girlfriend. My ship tattoos I had covered with those semipermanent cosmetics.

We were lying in her big bed, typical postcoital laziness, and she was playing with my hair, propped on her elbow.

This was going on long enough. I needed her to be

hooked completely, not nibbling at the bait. She had a sense of injustice about the war, it was what drove her to be a part of a group like the Family of Humanity. They were all indignant about something.

So I told her, "A refugee camp. Well, not originally. I was born on Plymouth Moon."

Of course this impressed her, as it would any Family. The flash point of the war had been on that Moon, strits and humans fighting over resources.

"They moved the colony from there some years ago, didn't they." Soft voice and sympathetic eyes.

I nodded. "So I grew up on Colonial Grace . . . 'til I was, like, nine. Then I joined a merchant crew, it was the only way to leave that rock."

"No family?" She paused. "Or were they . . . ?"

"They weren't killed. My babushka, yeah, but my parents and my brother and sister . . ."

It had been so long since I'd thought about them that just saying the words made my distant mind falter. I sat up away from her touch. She was a target, though she didn't know it yet, and I'd said enough.

I reached to my pants thrown at the foot of the bed, dug in, and took out my cigrets.

But she prodded. Gently. Looking to comfort. "What happened to your family, Yuri?"

I'd given her my name. And my old name. Terisov. Because it meant nothing now.

I smoked hard and shrugged. "Left 'em. We were separated, then I left 'em."

And suddenly I wasn't thinking about Mama or Jascha, Papa or Isobel.

It was Estienne. And I hugged an arm around my stomach, smoking and choking from it because the tears clogged my throat. She sat up beside me and laid her hand on my forearm, stroked the scars there. Hadn't asked about them, maybe she'd seen something like them before, but her touch was too sensitive on the skin, and I had to get up, get out of there. I pulled away.

"I'm going. I'll see you later."

"Yuri." Her hand reached a beat too late, missed my body, and rested instead on the bedsheet as I yanked on my clothes. "I'm sorry," she said.

"Not your fault," I said, and meant it. The only thing I'd truly meant since I started to play her. But I left and didn't talk to her for two shifts, just stayed in my den smoking, trying to collect myself.

But when you were divided into so many pieces, it was impossible to put yourself together.

* _* *

She finally commed me at the den. She thought I was a ship mechanic between contracts, and it had helped that I had nowhere permanent to sleep; she was quicker to invite me over, feed me, look after me, spoil me. So she did again, said she wanted to cook a meal for me.

I told myself I needed to get more information off her comp, so I would sleep over again tonight and dig. I landed up there with some flowers, something expected and sweet, and put on a smile before I kissed her cheek. "I'm sorry for running out like that."

"No, no." She tugged me inside the apartment. "It's understandable. I got something for you."

"Me?" I watched her shuffle off to the adjoining kitchen to put the lilies in a vase, then she came back and took a chipsheet out of her dress pants and held it out to me. I palmed it with a curious smile. "What is this?"

"I found out where your family is," she said.

I stood there, not smiling anymore.

"I have connections . . ." Her eyes hunted mine, unsure, wanting to please. "My people tracked your mother and your brother from a refugee base in the Spokes, about a leap from where you were on Colonial Grace. They've resettled on Mars now with your sister Isobel. After your father . . ." She stepped closer and I couldn't move. "Well . . . it's all in the sheet."

She let me access it on her comp and it told me my father was dead. But the rest of them were alive, and as I stared at the columns of information she wrapped her arms around my shoulders from behind and kissed the side of my hair.

"You can contact them now," she said.

As she said it, I knew I couldn't. What would I say? There wasn't anything to say to them, my language was lost to anything they might understand. There was no going back, no searching in the womb for answers. Dead things didn't hatch in birth.

Besides, my presence in their lives would put them in danger from fellow pirates who wanted me off.

But I pocketed the sheet to keep, I didn't know for how long, and maybe I was going to lose it somewhere along the line, or be killed before I could do anything with the information, but it was information, and I dealt in that. I committed it all to memory in the way I was trained. And when I turned around to hug her for it, she rubbed my back like I was a child.

* * *

It didn't take more than a full shift before Caligtiera commed me with a direct, "Why isn't he dead yet?"

I asked back, "Why aren't you off my ship? Don't plan on putting down roots, do you?"

In fact, he didn't. Rika told me he used some cred he had stashed away from decades of piracy and bought his own vessel. An Orca-class, of all things, that I knew wouldn't stay its basic shape. The first thing you did when you got a pirate ship was outfit it with weaponry. But while that was happening, with some of the survivors of *Genghis Khan*, he was still on my ship, and I had a mission.

I didn't tell anyone about the contact info on my family. And I didn't look at it again. The more I looked at it, the harder it became to think of Azarcon's son as a target.

So I thought of Estienne instead, even though it hurt. Because it hurt. It hurt enough that I thought Ryan Azarcon should feel it too.

* * *

I followed Ryan Azarcon on the shift of Austro Station's elaborate Chinese New Year celebration. February 17, 2197.

I had my list. My tunnel kid. My position on the second-level tier of the flash house. I had optics that cut through the bouncing lights and pinned my sights on the target.

I saw him there in white, on the dance floor. Suggestive, abandoned dancing as if all the stars and planets were contained in this moment just for him, spinning around his orbit, jeweled in his eyes.

And maybe they were in some way. He was so close to death. In those moments maybe even God paid attention.

Kill him, I told my tunnel kid. Go close in the crowd.

And I watched. Beautiful boy in his beautiful world. This

special son. Did he even love his father? Enough to die for him? Enough to kill for him. Did the captain really love him? His bodyguard did, I'd seen it in the animation of their interactions, and it wasn't true that one shot equaled one kill, a sniper's body count. One kill meant revenge, didn't it, that led to other deaths. And if Azarcon didn't really love his son, he might still take the insult to heart, like all pirates did. It wasn't about love. Revenge was the greedy child of hurt, and I felt it for Estiennne like a scabbed-over wound. My steps were thick through the flash house smoke.

I followed my tunnel kid down to the floor, through the bodies and their ecstatic arms. They danced all around me, oblivious and innocent. But I pushed my way through until I saw him. In my scopes his eyes were very blue. His laughter wasn't laced with drugs, not yet.

Cairo Azarcon's son, so unaware of why someone would want him dead. He had scars too, but instead of wearing them on his arms, he injetted them into his veins, marred himself from the inside out.

He was just a little younger than my brother. By two years.

I just had to shoot him.

Child of a pirate.

But I shot my tunnel kid instead. I shot the girl Ryan Azarcon danced with. I shot the lights out, and the crowd rampaged.

And then I lost him in the madness.

* * *

I told Caligtiera over comm, He had too much security. The flash was too crowded. The conditions were too bad.

He said, "Why didn't you pick another time?"

I said, "You try and assassinate someone on Austro, with hundreds of cam globes and patrolling Marines. This is a rich station with a penchant for paranoia ever since that dock bombing years ago."

I doubted he believed me.

I stayed on the station even after Azarcon blew in, collected his son, and took my target away.

I stayed, and ran the op on Elizabeth, who had so many tales to tell (in her comp if not in her bed) about what the government was doing with terrorists, and the longer I was away from my ship, the easier it became. Madness lulls in isolation, and my world was calmer alone.

4.15.2197 EHSD — The Captain

Elizabeth had recent correspondences in her comp to other Family members of the terrorist cell on Austro, all of them regarding a plan to assassinate Azarcon's wife. She also had a few messages exchanged with an ex-jet from the carrier who was willing, for the right amount of cred, to talk about jet security protocol.

She was soft with me, but in her comms to her allies she said, Get Azarcon back to the station. Take out Junior and send a clear signal to back off.

I thought about warning Captain Azarcon.

I thought about it until Caligtiera arrived on station, met me in my den, and occupied me with news of the network, my ship, how they were going to step up their attacks in protest of this treaty and Azarcon's involvement with Falcone's death.

I said, "It was a symp that killed him."

Some symp, it said, aboard *Macedon*. Otter's contact? How many symps would've been aboard a Hub carrier?

Cal said, "It's all over the Send that Azarcon was a pirate."

Yeah, I'd seen. New Centralist President Damiani made it an excuse to rail on deep spacers.

"It's good for us," Cal said. "Falcone would've been happy."

If he wasn't dead. If so many people weren't dead already.

And it wasn't going to stop.

The radical Centralists with their Family of Humanity ties assassinated Azarcon's wife, on the station, and pointed the finger at the pirates. Because now that Damiani was in power she wanted no part of the Family, even in suspicion. Even though the links went deep. Even though, Cal said, the Family talked about an alliance with us to keep this war going for the benefit of all. Exterminate the aliens, capitalize on the occupied fleet, drive Azarcon to some dead moon, and let him rot.

Azarcon came back to station, with his son, and the funeral was long and publicized.

And Elizabeth had written in her comp to take out Ryan next. I read these things while she was asleep in the bedroom, copied what files I could to my own chipsheet, and in the goldshifts she made me breakfast and kissed me under the artifical sunlight that showered from the ceiling. And I started to think that this must be how normal people lived, how it might've been if you weren't lying in every gesture and word. Doing small things for each other in safe places. Dancing in this innocent manner.

But she was a liar too. She was a murderer like me, except she did it for high political ideals, and I did it for blood.

She wanted to get Ryan Azarcon on the way back from the funeral, when he was the most vulnerable, when it would make the biggest statement. When he was right beside his father.

The man would be traumatized, they thought.

Didn't they know what he'd been through with the pirates? Didn't they have a clue what it meant to be Falcone's protégé?

I'd watched him on the Send deflect all the rampant diatribes about his past. I'd heard of his attacks on pirates and his ruthlessness with the strits, when he'd been at war with them. I'd seen Falcone's hatred for him steep to such a strong taste that it could've only been born of a sense of betrayal. Azarcon had left the pirates, left Falcone, and not just left—surpassed him.

Azarcon wouldn't be traumatized. He'd be brutal in his revenge. An estranged wife was bad enough. For his son, he'd kill.

Caligtiera said, "Do it right this time." He brought out a contact of ours on station and told the man to "help" me. What he wanted was insurance that I'd finish it. He didn't know about the govie plans. He was too busy trying to bed them for his own purposes. Rika said, "Come home. Taja's getting delusions of grandeur."

But I stayed, and used the pirate contact Cal set on me to help with Ryan Azarcon's assasination—this time.

And all it took was some distraction, a separation from his main phalanx of security. I let this other pirate smoke the captain and his son and their smaller security into blindness, and the pirate grabbed the son, and I shot the pirate and took the son, because this didn't involve some stooge of Cal's, this was mine. My decision. A desperate sort of move, I knew it, but every time I commed my ship, and they asked me to come back, I thought of being back in that world without Estienne. I thought of being set adrift by Falcone's death and how any pirate who wanted my seat would gun for it because I had no implicit superior to protect me. The head of the family died, and the son became fair game.

* * *

His eyes were almost unnaturally blue, kitten-large, as he sat across from me in the tunnel, as he breathed and I smoked and he tried not to piss his pants in fear. I'd read that his eyes were genetically tampered because he sure didn't get that color from his parents. He didn't like me staring, but I wondered what it was like to be the son of Cairo Azarcon. I wondered what he thought of his father being a pirate.

"Did you kill my mother?" he said.

And it was funny, in its way, considering I'd wanted to warn his papa about it in the first place.

"No," I said. "That was the govies."

He had attitude. I told him I was saving his life because other people had bad plans for him, and he said with a well-honed sarcasm, "You could save it by putting me back with my father."

And that amused me somehow. This kid amused me. In the face of fear he managed to summon his teeth and his claws.

He was Azarcon's son. I shouldn't have been surprised.

* * *

Somewhere along the line I'd made the decision not to go back to my ship. Maybe it was from watching this kid live out his normal existence and wanting to kill him just for that, but it was ridiculous to think that way; he didn't ask to be born where he'd been any more than I had. Maybe if I'd been Cairo Azarcon's son, I would never have done the things I'd done. Maybe it was something inherent that made you capable of committing atrocities.

Ryan Azarcon looked at me as if I was going to do one on him.

It helped that his papa thought so too. I took Big-Eyes to the cubby in the tunnels I'd scoped out for myself, far away from Boysdeck or most of the underdeck traffic. I commed *Macedon* using the code I'd lifted from Elizabeth's comp, and while it took some finagling to access from that point of entry, eventually I got the ship's general comm. Azarcon came on, I kept the visual off, and he demanded, of course, that I return his kitten.

I told him, "I was in contact with a boy in the underdeck named Otter about a year ago, who was in turn in contact with a symp spy aboard your ship. I'd offered to deal Falcone in exchange for exoneration."

He said he remembered. So my message had got through; I just hadn't followed up.

"Obviously that didn't work," I said, then lied: "I had to cut contact when Falcone got suspicious." If I admitted I had just changed my mind, he would've been even less inclined to hear my offer now. I wished suddenly I could see his face. "You know what I want." *How did you get out?*

He said in a flat voice, "You want out. Falcone's protégé. You've kidnapped my son."

And I should've known then. He was never going to believe me. I should never have taken his blood.

* * *

I managed to deal with him, at least. Told him to find out himself about the pirates, the Family, and the Centralists, because it was all there for someone like him to find. Last gasp, maybe. With his kid looking at me like I was crazy.

I'd saved his life. There *were* people out there trying to kill him, they'd proven it with his mother, but this wasn't much of an argument when I was the one who had him in a dank hole. But you never showed your doubts to people like Azarcon—or Azarcon's kid. Laugh, if it helped. Flirt to make the kid uncomfortable. Taunt him even. Better that they were scared of you or wondered about you. Better that if it came down to it, I could make the hard decision and kill my hostage.

I could always go back to *Kublai Khan*.

Junior said, "You would really kill me?" Doubting my threats. Even though he was cuffed to the pipes on the wall. "How far do you think you'd get if you killed me?"

He was so naïve. And rather untouched. I had to touch him. I wondered again if he loved his father, even knowing what he'd been. If he even knew what it meant. I put my hand on his soft long hair and ran it back to the ends. I told him, "I don't have to kill you to hurt you."

He recoiled. As if I would rape him. I considered hitting him just for that. Instead I reminded him, "Don't be so repulsed. Your father did the same in my position."

And he said, "No he didn't."

So I knew the captain hadn't told him all the details.

I could've shown him. But he had to stay undamaged so his father would know I was serious. Not to touch his little kitten.

So I mocked him instead, just to test, just to see if his mettle withstood a constant pressure.

He moved away from me and shut his eyes.

* _*_ *

I left him there in shadows, asleep, to check on my tunnel kids. They told me some pirate had approached them abovedeck to ask about little Azarcon. They said they were told if I couldn't kill him, then they'd have to. I had to hit the boy and scare the girl to make them believe that I was going to do it, that I was having a little fun first, and that it wasn't any of their damn business.

When I got back to Junior he was staring at my comp.

And it wasn't wise but I pulled it away, then realized he'd been burndiving, and as he yelled from the pain, I knew that I'd made him blind.

Damaged him.

Then my tunnel kids showed up, they must've followed me, I'd trained them far too well, and Junior cried out and I had to shoot the kids and I wanted to shoot him next but it was a flurry to get him away from these bodies. Maybe I could get him back to *Kublai Khan* somehow, maybe then Azarcon would listen once our ships were in space. Maybe the trick was to make this boy listen, show him what his father was, show how it could've been for him if he'd just been born someone else's son.

He refused to move, stopped dead in the tunnels with a fixed expression of rebellion on his face, even shining from his blind eyes.

He told me lies. "My father will help you. But not like this." And, "Docs can fix my sight. You might be surprised what my father can forgive. I'll speak for you; I'll make him listen."

He was desperate. He said anything. He was listening for

the sound of other people in these tunnels so he could yell like he had with the kids. And that would be it.

He thought he had sway over his father? If Falcone was swayed by anything, it was because he'd let it. If Cairo Azarcon wanted me dead, it wouldn't matter if I'd helped his son at all. In any way, even belatedly. To him I might always be Falcone's protégé, whether I wanted to be or not. What was I good for except to be killed? Especially now.

Ryan would always be an Azarcon.

And I was a pirate. I'd been too long on this station alone, away from my blood. I'd let my world become diluted in ragged hopes of other people's promises. Like what this kid offered. But it wasn't an offer, it was a pat on the ass to distract me from the truth. I wasn't any captain's son, I was just a protégé.

So I shot Ryan Azarcon in the chest and ran.

* * *

Otter, as a symp, didn't work alone. He sent out droves of his gang to search for me, to help Captain Azarcon, because his symp contact aboard *Macedon* must've asked.

I saw a tunnel exit, framed by the light of the station deck. I was on my way toward it when they shot me in the back.

Paralyzed. Even my thoughts froze as I fell.

* * *

I woke up in *Macedon*'s brig. A jet sat at a security station outside my cage, reading something on his console. It wasn't that much different from my ship's brig except it was bigger, grayer. Colder. They'd dumped me on the bunk at least, and when I sniffed and pulled myself to sit up, the jet looked over, then tapped something in front of him.

I could barely move from that paralysis pulse, and a bite of nausea gnawed at my gut. I swallowed a few times, but it didn't go away. It got worse when the hatch opened and Captain Azarcon stepped in.

Worse when the jet got up and left.

I sat at the edge of the bunk, clutching the mattress as he strode to the gate and looked in at me.

He didn't say a word.

I stared at him. This man who always seemed too dark around the edges, even when slammed with meedee lights. His features—dark eyes canted slightly at the corners, fine eyebrows, a long nose and gracefully lined jaw, and skin so pale he could've been wearing geisha powder. Except he wasn't, it was the smooth pallor of a shipborn soul. It was a face that knew itself, but not for vanity. For control. His hair reflected the overhead lights in white shards. A piece fell over his forehead like a wing, and I could see, if he were younger, what the appeal would've been for Falcone. The face was already younger than it should've been, like Falcone's had been. Deep space was in his veins, and his blood might have run just as cold.

"Captain Azarcon," I said.

He turned his back and went to the security station, pressed something there. My gate beeped. I hauled myself to my feet, but he was fast, pushed aside the bars and came at me. He was tall, deceptively strong beneath the slender frame, and he had me up against the wall before I could take a breath, his arm shoved up under my chin and his free hand pinning my wrist.

"The only reason you're alive," he said, "is because my

son is too. But I'm still deciding how long to *keep* you alive."

He let me go with a shove to the deck. I braced there on my hands and knees before I pulled myself back on my heels and looked up at him.

"Your choice. But you—"

He hit me. I didn't see it coming and barely felt it for the shock. I leaned on one hand, half-slumped, touching my jaw in reflex. As I saw his fingers clench and unclench I felt it.

"Don't even try to manipulate me," he said. "Nor do I have the patience to listen to taunts. I know you're aware that we have a common past—for whatever it's worth. So you know you won't get anywhere with me."

If I hadn't before, I knew it now.

He walked to the gate and out, slamming it behind him. "I suggest you cooperate with my crew."

* * *

Macedon's brig had a reputation, just like its jets. This was the ship that had captured and killed *Shiva*, among other pirates, as well as its fair share of strits. I looked down at the floor, and it had the scuffed sheen of a surface scrubbed for more than casual cleanliness. There'd been blood here.

They didn't feed me. The water from the sink tasted metallic, but it was clean. And it could be hot if you waved it on first, though it was timed and shut off every thirty seconds. I used it to warm my hands, splash my face to wake myself up, then I sat on the bunk and waited. Nothing else to do.

The ship was moving from the sound of its drives. And I had no hope that *Kublai Khan* would ever get me. If they even knew where I was now.

I thought of Dexter. Rika would take care of him. But I

pictured him pining for me and dying of loneliness, like Falcone had said lovebirds did if they didn't bond to another soul—be it bird, human, animal. On the outside it didn't make sense. But on the inside I felt it. Emotions or lack of them could kill you well enough.

Azarcon sent jets. Two of them came in, in their blacks, a tall blond with the name patch Dorr, and a shorter dark-haired one—who didn't wear a jet uniform on closer inspection, just black clothes. He held my comp in his hand. Must have been retrieved from the tunnels. Otter.

The blond said, "Falcone Junior."

And I hated them all, right then, with such purpose and direction that it drew me to my feet to face them.

"I think he's pissed," the blond taunted. "He didn't die well, your big pimp."

I rushed the bars. I screamed at them and I didn't know what I was saying, but they kept saying his name, Falcone, and he was dead. Marcus was dead, had died a long time ago, and my resentment for Falcone had laid itself where there'd once been some kind of safety and a child's sense of love. Protection. There'd once been that, and kindness, shadowed in my memory and brought low from lack of air. From lack of light. You couldn't grow without some form of kind attention.

He was dead, and it felt cruel, as if he hadn't deserved it. And it didn't change a thing, really, what came out of me in rage and tears and violence. Banging the bars, trying to shake them or reach through them, and the jet stepped back, the other one was well out of the way, and they looked at me like I was mad, like I was some wild creature that needed to be put down.

Until I staggered to the corner and sank into it, pulling at my arms, my hair, one after another, with nothing in my

head but Falcone. And Estienne. I couldn't think of one
without thinking of the other.

*   *   *

Ryan Azarcon came to see me. They'd fixed his sight, or
I assumed so since he watched me, even though he blinked
a little more than average, and the soft skin around his eyes
looked sore and bruised. I didn't know how his father allowed it, probably didn't, but the kid came anyway for some
unfathomable reason—testing himself?—and stood on the
other side of the gate and tried to convince me to cooperate
with the jets. With what his father wanted—everything I
knew. Then he asked me about my family.

He asked me about my family. As if he knew.

But I didn't say anything. There was nothing to tell.

*   *   *

He kept coming back, like that blond jet Dorr and his
silent partner who knew a thing or two about comps, because they got past my password gates to even the most embedded files and asked me about what was in there. The
woman I'd been spying on, my contacts on Austro, my little
network on Boysdeck.

Maybe if I cooperated, and it got out, I would just die in
prison. If I went kicking and screaming, at least I had some
honor left among the pirates. Threadbare though it was. And
Azarcon and his jets didn't deserve a thing from me.

Especially when Dorr came into my cell and kicked me
off the bunk while the other one watched without a word.

"You nearly killed our captain's kid," Dorr said, staring
down at me. "You pale-arsed pirate whore."

And what could I do? I couldn't deny it.

I didn't speak, and they bruised me. They kept the lights on, they strung me up, they let me sleep but not enough, they fed me just enough to keep me alive and once in a while they dragged me out to the showers and doused me. Then they put me back, and it all began again. It all frayed my nerves. It made whatever was alive inside of me blow out like a row of overburdened lights. One by one. Shift by shift.

And Ryan Azarcon visited. Twice, three times, and by the fifth I wondered enough to ask, broke my silence and just shouted at him, "Why're you here?"

He didn't say anything for a minute. Kitten eyes in a self-aware face. But not pirate-trained. Meedee-trained. Maybe a little inherent Azarcon guile. The intensity of his stare was much like his father's, despite the blue eyes.

He said, "I don't think anyone's ever believed in you, at least not for the right reasons."

I was tired. Maybe his deceptive benign questions were just another angle to this torture, to bring me out of myself and make me his father's whore. One captain to the next.

So I kicked at the bars. "Get out of my face! You sick little wank! I'm not your pet project!"

He backed up, but didn't flee.

So I banged the bars with my fists and screamed at him. "I should've shot you in the head!"

That made him go. And he didn't come back.

*　*　*

His father returned. I had no idea how much time had passed, but they got no information from me. And it warranted a visit from the captain himself.

He looked in at me again, much like the first time. Much like his son. He said, "You're going to Earth for trial."

I shrugged. "They tried that with Falcone, didn't they."

"Yes, but this time it'll stick."

So sure? Kill me yourself. I wanted to ask him, just to see if he would if he were taunted enough. I kept my eyes to the deck, not out of deference, I was just too weak to lift my head.

"Why don't you kill me," I managed to ask. Why hadn't you killed Falcone when you had the chance. "Isn't that the way it's done?"

"Only if you're a pirate," he said. "It's easy to be a murderer. All you do is lose control."

"It takes plenty of control to put a gun to your head and pull the trigger."

He said, "You don't think everything he ever told you was a lie? Even now?"

Now I looked up and stared through the bars. Bo-Sheng with my gun to his head. His child's face in quarters, begging me to leave with him. Falcone had lied from the beginning to get us off the Camp. But people lied all the time, didn't they, just to get off in one way or another.

I got up from the bunk and shuffled to the gate. Azarcon didn't step back even though I could've reached through, at least my hands, and grabbed the front of his shirt. He stood that close. Like a dare.

"His lies? Compared to what?"

He said, "Compared to the truth. His words are lies. They may be wrapped up in some sort of twisted logic, but at the heart it's only a lie."

I peered into his eyes, but there was just a wall. He was no cocktail, no client. Nothing but a wall. "Then everything is a lie, and there is no truth. Because even you—"

"Even I what?"

I felt my lip curl. "You stand there in judgment when all the Hub knows you did exactly as I did. Exactly. Except I did it better. And maybe it's just a matter of perspective. It's easy for you to brush off the dirt when you're on the other side of this gate."

"And how do you think I got here? By swallowing those lies? That man can control you if you let him, even in his absence. Is that what you want?"

I couldn't answer beyond, "I don't wanna be in this brig, but I'm here anyway." Some things you just couldn't control. Like who you were born into, who you fell in love with, and when your loved ones would die.

Maybe he thought it too, in some way. He said, "All of your actions impact something. It's up to you in what way."

And he left. Given up on me or just disgusted. His voice lacked emotion, he wouldn't allow himself to feel anything around me, he just wore all his words with a cold as bitter as this brig.

* * *

He put me off on *Archangel*, his sister ship, because apparently *Macedon* was on the run after illegally locking down Austro Station when I'd kidnapped his son. Earth-Hub—or President Damiani—wanted him out of the stars. The jets talked as they escorted me to my new home. I pieced it together, even as I felt myself falling apart.

Archangel would take me to Earth, personally, a deep spacer going insystem. Far insystem, it went, to the narrow core. Narrow as a lack of choice or the gaze of an enemy.

MY DREAM

4.20.2198 EHSD — Bird

This might be what it feels like to wait for death, Piotr and I in our pod, some kind of preparatory coffin ready to be shot to the sun. Space makes ambient noise if you know how to listen, with instrumentation, but otherwise it's a muffled darkness so vast you are stifled in its arms. I can't see my dead ship anymore, which is a mercy. We've drifted out of reach and out of sight, and this part of space looks like any other, maybe, like the embodiment of what took me to Earth less than a year ago.

When *Macedon* left me behind. I wonder if it will do the same here, or simply sneak up and shoot us without question.

But the comm from Azarcon comes soon enough, we've barely dug into the pod's stores. He sends a Charger to pick us up, and the carrier turns out to be only a leap away from our position near Ghenseti. Piotr and I sit in the crew benches behind the cockpit with two jets guarding us, silent, with silence from the flight crew. Dexter rustles in the equipment case they'd given me for him, the lid up, but he has sense enough not to fly here. Then the jets must've heard something on their pickups from the pilot because they suddenly look at each other, straightening a bit where they sit. Rifles haven't lowered toward us, but now their attention becomes doubly fixed.

"What is it?" I have to ask.

They hesitate, but the senior of the jets stares at me. A woman.

"Your kind just blew our sister ship." More rage at this point than immediate grief. Rage is so much easier to handle. And for a second I dread that they will kill us right here and orders be damned.

But then I think of that carrier and sink back against the bulkhead. Piotr says nothing, doesn't move, he trusted me enough to follow me, and I might be killing him too. There's no getting around death once it marks you as a child. You succumb, or you serve it. I can't look those jets in the eyes.

"We're meeting up with *Macedon* at the site," the second jet says. "And you better pray the captain's feelin' magnanimous this shift."

Somehow I doubt it.

Because I wouldn't be.

* * *

I look out the small square view window in the Charger as we tilt—after a manner of speaking—on approach to one of *Macedon*'s hangar bays. The angle happens to sweep on half of *Archangel* in the near distance, hunter-killers and

bombers and Charger APCs all buzzing around the bodies of
the two ships like carrion flies. Guarding and gathering.

Six thousand and more people. The carrier's honey-
combed by explosion damage, hollowed out in places, and
the debris floats around like magnified dust specks made of
transsteel and—bodies. Whole bodies, probably, sucked out
from hull breaches, spinning in an inertial danse macabre.

I look away, and thankfully the Charger tilts again, and
the clang of the grapples taking hold jars us for a bit. As
soon as the lights brighten in the compartment the jets stand.
The back ramp hisses and growls as it lowers, and the guns
are on us, motioning us ahead.

I can already hear the noise in the bay, even before we
emerge into brighter light. We disembark under guard, two
more jets there—and I go still because one is Dorr. He
stares at Dexter in the case. "What in bloody hell is that?"

It seems a ridiculous answer, even though it's the obvious
truth. "My bird."

He transfers that stare to me for a second, then motions
one of the jets from the Charger to take the case.

"Please." I'm desperate now, a sudden stab of panic, and
I don't care that they see. "Please don't—"

"Shut up," he snaps, then tells the other jet, "Take it to
that other one."

"What other one?" Finch? "Dorr—"

He doesn't answer, just grabs my arm and gives it a violent yank to shut me up. It works. Dexter screeches as Piotr
and I are pulled away by Dorr and his female counterpart.
They take over from the two on the Charger and escort us
through *Macedon*'s corridors. Slate gray, narrow, not as or-
ganic in design as the *Khan*. The ship is nothing but grim activity, and I hear Piotr's breaths becoming more audible as
we go. Mine are the same, ragged in my ears at the sight.

The sounds. The injured and the dying, medical personnel and their mobile equipment trailing after them like sheep, and the thrum of the drives, a struggling heart—they all surround us, unavoidable to the senses.

Dorr has his hand tight around my arm, but there's no point. Where would I run?

We pass a particular jet, and Dorr stops suddenly and shoves me to the bulkhead. "Stay put." Piotr leans beside me, and the female jet covers us with her rifle. I have nowhere to look but at Dorr as he leans down and snags the arm of an injured jet who's just sitting on the deck among two dozen others, lining it like pieces of black garbage blown against a wall.

"Rick," Dorr says, and the jet looks up. It's shocking when they embrace. The hard grip of grief or comfort.

But these ships know each other. And so does the crew. They're blood, in their way.

I'm standing there with long arms and a medic in red-smudged gray goes by. She says, "Erret, we need your help. The bays are overloaded, and we gotta move the bodies."

"I gotta take these pirate asses—"

She eyes us. "They look healthy. We can use them."

"Fucking pirates!" Dorr says, his hand gripping the other jet's shoulder.

"He's one," she says. "And so's his friend. And we need all hands. If they caused it, then the least they can do is see what they've done."

"I didn't cause it," I tell her, but nobody's listening, and maybe it's a lie anyway. In some way. As the blood makes trails along the deck as far as I can see down the corridor. Lines of red, smudged in places. Tears on a mottled face.

"Are you all right?" Dorr says to the injured jet.

"My leg and my arm, but I can stand, and the bleeding's mostly stopped. I can guard them at least if you need them."

The medic says, "Do it and come on." She heads off, pushing through the press of somnambulant crew.

So Dorr hands his sidearm to the injured jet—Rick?—and he hauls himself to his feet, determined and iron-eyed. Dorr waves his rifle at me.

"Good then," he says. "We'll work."

* * *

It's not work, it's torture. There are people with burns, cuts, and lacerations, and blown body parts. Lost arms or legs or eyes. There are people so covered in blood that you can't tell gender through the sameness of the uniforms. Slight bodies made smaller by shock and despair.

These people used to have a home, and now they don't.

Now I don't.

Dorr puts me through it, me and Piotr, with his friend at our backs, gun pointed. We help one body or the other onto stretchers, into corners, tagging them for triage, or delivering basics like water and sealant. Piotr's eyes are hollow and shadowed, maybe mirrors to my own. We look at each other occasionally, but there's nothing to say. I'm glad he's with me, even though I want to know where Finch is; have they put him to work too among this, or is he still locked in quarters somewhere? I don't see him in this bay, but there are a few bays, and they are all probably filled. Now isn't the time to ask about Finch, there are too many bodies and not enough hands to hold or help them all.

There's a blond in the corner wearing jet black, but for a second when he raises his eyes I think of Estienne in his geisha black, and maybe he sat in his quarters like this while *Genghis Khan* disintegrated, waiting for me to help him.

After a while the jet really doesn't need to guard me. Everywhere I go there are dead bodies in one state of decay or another, all dead or getting there, or just dead in their gazes. I imagine the decks look the same for all of us. Flooded.

And I stop smelling the blood eventually, or seeing the injuries, or hearing the sobs and the moans. None of this can be fixed and this isn't my ship or my deck.

It's just Mishka and Jascha and Mama I see. On my Moon. Mama. And any minute now she's going to let go of my hand.

* * *

Dorr's friend is named O'Neil. Rick O'Neil. He gets called over by the corporal and I stare at his eyes, and they are blue like his father's. I catch the stark similarity in the lines of his frown. Why didn't I notice before? Because his father's was another death I witnessed, and I don't want to see any more.

It's strange the connections we encounter. As if the universe is trying to tell you something but you're too blind to see it without touch.

He's never going to forget this shift, this jet. Rick O'Neil. He's going to live with it for a long time. Because now I have to tell him. Who else is going to tell him? There's nobody else here that knows, and maybe it's better to hit him with it when there's already so much numbness seeping into his system.

I leave Piotr at a body bag and approach O'Neil and Dorr. O'Neil's stripes and badges say he's a sergeant. "Sir," I tell him, it comes naturally this respect. Or maybe it's just a mutual acknowledgment. If he was on a pirate, he'd have to call me "sir."

Dorr says, "What the hell do you want?"

Even when I was across the bay I felt his eyes on me.

"I need to—to talk to Sergeant O'Neil."

O'Neil looks at me, surprised, hobbling on his injury with a faint grimace on his face, but the kind that comes with familiarity. His physical pain is nothing compared to the other kind.

"His father," I start, and I have no idea how to finish it.

"My father what?" He stares at me, and it's so much the same as the dead agent that I can't hold it, suddenly. I didn't know the other O'Neil for long, and we were barely helping each other at the end, but this is his son, this is something I never thought I'd face in this way, with conversation. From someone else. The grief of a child at the loss of a parent. "My father *what*?" he says again, sharper, and Dorr's hand snaps out and cuffs the side of my head.

I stagger a bit, but catch myself. Tangle one hand in my hair and look up. "Your father's dead," I tell him, O'Neil. "I'm sorry." The apology might've been something you always say when you precede it with what I did, but I don't know that I've ever meant it as much as I do now.

He glares in shock. Dorr glares in rage. "Please." Listen. A strange word for this, but I say it anyway. "Please, on my ship, he—"

"You killed him?" Dorr takes a step forward, but the sergeant has more sense or maybe he sees something in my eyes, because he grabs the corporal's arm, holds him back. I can't break my gaze from his face, it's like watching my own confusion and tears, the things I feel at a distance.

"How the hell do you know my father?" he says. "And how could he be dead?"

He has no idea what his father was.

This has become too much to say, as if it weren't enough already. This is a plummet of words too weighted by revelation; but I've started now, and they both wait, a hair trigger away from shooting me for beginning in the first place.

"Your father," I tell him, disembodied voice, shaking hands, "your father was a Black Ops agent, and in the end we were working together against—against Caligtiera . . ." Does he even know that name? But I see recognition in both their eyes. "—and his partner, a man named Andreas Lukacs who . . . he's on Cal's ship right now I think, if he got out . . ." If Rika managed to get him out with the others, and maybe she did, I hope she did, that she got out and she's there and maybe at some point we can meet and she won't want to kill me. ". . . and we weren't sure if they were working together or . . ." This ramble about nothing.

O'Neil snaps me back, his voice thick. "You're a twisted, lying son of a bitch. My father's a security chief for my mother's company!" Yelling it into my face.

I step back and suddenly there are two more jets there, drawn to the distress of their comrade. I spy Piotr in the corner, still and standing, under gun.

"I'm not lying." I look at O'Neil, hoping he'll see that it's not out of pleasure that I open my mouth to speak. "I swear I'm—"

Dorr moves to me like a cat, rifle up, but a voice flares out in sudden command from a short distance away.

"Corporal!"

And there's no mistaking that tone or the owner of it.

I turn, no more relieved than a moment ago when I thought I was going to be shot.

Captain Azarcon approaches.

I'm aware that I'm covered in blood as he gets closer, threading his way through the bodies both healthy—his crew—and not. I'm surprised he even sees that it's me. Maybe he commed Dorr first. Dorr, who stepped back immediately at his captain's command, and now both he and O'Neil just stare at me, pale death.

There's a crack in the captain's façade when he looks at me, surrounded by this. And maybe there's one in mine too. He doesn't say anything but, "Come with me now."

And so I go.

* * *

His office has a black desk, a sheer smoothness that reflects the lights overhead. His comp is up, and there are holocubes at the corners of the desk surface. I catch glimpses of his son's face in some of them, and in others his dead wife.

He motions me to sit even though I might stain. But I take the offer and he takes his seat and there is nothing between us but that desk and my words. I tell him everything I told O'Neil, just letting the last twenty-four hours pour out as if I'm serving him some delicate drink. If I spill any of it over the confines of the glass, it will drown us both. "Cal's still free," I finish, "but I know his coordinates. If he's still there . . ."

"We're in no shape to go after him at the moment." Still loading bodies. Refugees.

"The ship . . ." *Archangel.* "Nothing's . . . I mean, the captain . . . ?" I get images of the woman on her bridge watching sections of her ship exploding on some internal scan, where I might've stood if I'd stood to the last, that old notion of going down with your ship and your crew. Perhaps she had. When I glance into Azarcon's face I can see that she had.

"She's lost," he says, meaning both the captain and the ship, maybe, and he doesn't have to define it further. They are one and the same.

It's one thing to be shot at and lose. It's another to do it to yourself, in suicide.

"Survivors from the *Khan*?" he asks, reading my thoughts. Or more likely just my face.

I shake my head. Then have to shrug. "On Cal's." This false nonchalance that neither of us believes. "Would you have?" All my words come stilted, severed. The limbs of my syllables flail distant from their bodies. But he understands.

When you left, you didn't lose a ship. When you left you just killed yourself in some way? And there he sits with his own ship, in exile. But it's his and he is alive. As I sit here feeling like less.

"If I could have," he says, "I would have killed the *Khan* before I went."

I wonder if he'd had an Elder Brother. But it's not something he will tell me or that I have a right to ask, and it's a wonder maybe that he confessed that much. Maybe because it's obvious. Of course you'd kill the thing you no longer want to be.

I look into his face, and suddenly all of that is secondary to the question pressing at the back of my eyes.

"Finch?" I ask him. And it must be that I'm tired or everything else, but the name pours through me like water when I hear it aloud, and I don't know what I'm doing, but I cover my face, elbows on knees. My head bowed. Dry breaths, don't break down in front of this man, some part of my mind keeps saying. Except I don't care. I don't care anymore what he sees or what he wants or even what he might exploit in me.

My hands start to shake, and they won't stop.

The silence persists from his side of the desk.

"You want to see Finch," he says at length, not really a question.

I nod.

So he stands, and whatever else he wants to say to me will wait. He isn't feeling vengeful, apparently, despite *Archangel*. What I see in his eyes when I finally look up is mercy.

* * *

Walking through *Macedon*'s corridors escorted by her captain, we get a lot of looks, but nobody says a thing or approaches. The way this crew regards Azarcon could be similar to the way it was when Falcone walked his ship, except here there is more open respect that isn't grounded in fear or intimidation. And he walks me himself, the captain, with no other escort. He's armed and I'm weary and even when we get to crew quarters where there are less crew, all of them on maindeck helping survivors, he doesn't balk. He shows no sign of hesitation.

Instead he opens the locked hatch with his command override, and after I step through he shuts it behind me.

Finch sees the blood all over me, but I don't try to explain. As soon as he stands from the bunk I just lock myself in his arms and he can feel that I'm not injured, that the bleeding's not from me. He can feel that I'm whole like he's whole, and solid, and just there.

It's a long time like that, in the kind of silence you get on a deep-space carrier. It isn't absolute, it echoes your insides.

"Are you all right?" Quiet question, an encompassing one.

I can't speak. Because the answer isn't simple, at least

not on my side. But his hand slips into the back of my hair, entangles there, holding my head to his shoulder.

And that's all I need. It's all that I want, and he gives it.

* * *

Dexter's in the quarters with us, asleep and still in his box. So jets have a sense of mercy too. Finch and I sit on the bunk, and I tell him, "They got *Archangel*." In case he hadn't heard.

The worry in his eyes darkens, but he doesn't say anything. There're no words for atrocity. All language is just abstract.

"I was helping." The blood on my shirt, it's dry and stiffened now, encrusted in the folds of the fabric like they line the skin of my palms. Lines of blood that I stare at, flaking at idly with my fingernails. "We should help." I look up because maybe he can't. Maybe it's too brutal, and I don't even think I can handle it, another hour or two or five of shuffling those bodies, dead or alive, from one kind of care to another. I don't know if Azarcon would let me again, but I can't sit in here now.

I can't just sit.

And maybe Finch is scared, he feels scared in the coldness of his hand when it closes over mine. Or maybe it's just because he hasn't been touched so much in a way that makes him warm.

"All right," he says. "We can help."

* * *

I knock on the hatch in the off chance there's a guard out there, and it's not a guard, not a jet anyway. Captain Azarcon. He waited, knowing maybe I'd want to talk or confess or ask for something that I have no right to ask for. I tell him we'd like to go back to the hangar bay, and he sees Finch behind me, looks a long moment before staring back into my face. He doesn't say anything but, "Good."

* * *

When he takes me and Finch there he calls O'Neil over and the two of them leave the bay. I turn and first see Piotr, on his way over from a triage tent, then Dorr, following with his gaze where O'Neil and the captain went. His eyes are red at the corners, his face tight from the effort of holding in his emotions. He turns to me, pale restraint.

"What do you think you're doin' back here, pirate?"

I don't rise to his anger. Instead I walk over to a relief station and gather a few envelopes of water to distribute to the crew. Finch follows behind me and piles some into his arms, staring concertedly at the deck instead of at the bodies. They seem to have multiplied since I left. More refugees.

"What're you doin'?" Dorr says again, behind me now.

"What I need to," I tell him.

And he lets me pass.

* * *

I lose time in the work. Then Dorr approaches, looking as ragged as I feel. He says, "Come with me. All three of you."

We weave our way through the encamped survivors, uniforms of black and gray and blue. They're bruises all over the skin of this deck; touch them, and they wince.

Dorr leads with two other jets behind us, through the corridors again, these unmarked corridors, plain and gray and military compared to the bone architecture that *Kublai Khan* had been. Finch's arm bumps against mine in fatigue, his gaze bleary and fixed ahead of him so he doesn't, probably, walk into a bulkhead.

The jets take us to a full washroom. Showers and sinks and clean unbadged shirts and fatigues. They are all deep blue, laid out in front of each stall.

It takes no explanation or encouragement.

The water feels like forgiveness, but it's cycled and timed, and the cold bites heavy through the steam.

* *
*

A fresh squad of jets escorts us afterward to one of the conference rooms on the same deck, maindeck, and inside is Captain Azarcon and a youth I vaguely recognize. Maybe I'd seen him before when I was on *Macedon* the first time. He sits behind a black razor comp, a pencil-thin interface wand tucked against its edge.

I sit with Finch on my right and Piotr on my left, and even cleaned up and wearing *Macedon* surplus I feel like a criminal across from the captain. Maybe it's the look on his face. Mercy doesn't come without reprimand sometimes, and I don't expect absolute grace from him.

Even with the horrors of what we've been doing the last few hours, he doesn't give us more than the minimum rest. He says, "This conversation's being recorded. Yuri Kirov, please recount the events leading up to your release from the Kalaallit Nunaat Military Prison on Earth and everything that occurred thereafter."

I drag my mind together, hands clenched between my knees beneath the table. I want to shut my eyes and put my head down and just not think.

But my words start fractured, and the more I talk, the more they break.

* ⁎ *

He gets statements from all of us, then we're separated. Finch and Piotr are led away as they take me to medical to remove the tracking device from below my skin. It's a simple procedure, just an injet to disintegrate the nanotag, it doesn't hurt at all. Or maybe I'm still too numb. Afterward the jet, my permanent fixture now, takes me to the captain's office, and by now I can barely keep on my feet. When I sit again across from him at that black desk I just prop my head on my hand, elbow on the arm of the chair.

"Caligtiera and Lukacs are still free," he says, "and according to you, Lukacs's interest in the pirates might not be in the best interests of the Hub. So you've got a decision to make, Kirov."

I've been making them.

He says, "What do you want?"

It makes me look up and into his eyes. No, he's not playing with me; there isn't any trap or hostility in the question. It sounds like a question Falcone would ask except the tone is different and so is the way he looks at me.

I shake my head.

"Yuri," he says. "What do you want most."

"If I can get out of this," I start, unsure where my words are going, where any of this is going, but it doesn't matter. I hadn't known that when I followed Falcone into space, and this man is not Falcone. He was the first, but he must've sat where I am sitting at some point early on, with the admiral who later adopted him. And I don't expect any grand commitments from this captain or his ship, he just asks a simple question, and my answer comes with the simplicity of bone-deep capitulation. If he doesn't listen, then there's nowhere else for me to go. I just hold the words close even though I tell him. I hold them close because they're honest.

"I want . . . Finch. And . . ." I remember. "Some point I want my family. I know where they are, I just haven't . . ."

This stumbling thing, my mind and my words and my intentions.

But he seems to understand. "You know I can't let you leave."

I don't have to nod.

"And my ship isn't entirely legal. But—it doesn't stop me from doing what I can. Your staying here, with Finch and Piotr, will be rough. My crew have no love for pirates."

"Finch isn't."

"He's with you." Stated fact, and I do know it, but then Azarcon adds, "This may not be where you wanted to end up, but it's where you are. I can let you contact your family, monitored, and you will help me track Caligtiera and Lukacs and whatever else I need you to do."

I stare at him. There is resistance to that command. Like there would be with Falcone. Out there in deep space we were equals, but inside of his ship I'm under his benevolence and his whim.

But maybe if I were allowed to just be out there on my own it would be all too easy to find a ship again and start to take what I want, within reason, and then maybe it would build and eventually return to some familiar state, my life. I can see the pattern as if it's stitched to the stars. So for all the pain this is, being brought low before this man, there's also a kindness in humility. Self-kindness that tempers arrogance and greed.

"How did you," I ask, and some part of me still expects

him to take me to the brig and forget about me. But he's calm behind his desk, he's compassionate in his way and I wish I knew how he survived it. Why did he, why have I, and there was one that killed himself. Too many questions in this weird kind of freedom that isn't freedom on the out-side—I'm still serving some other captain. But Finch is here, and there is no Hanamachi, no clients, no gun to my head to tell me to shoot. They won't even give me a gun.

And I see he's thinking about my question and all of the questions behind that one that I don't need to ask. And of course the answer isn't simple, it's not anything I think he will truly share. If it even can be shared.

But he does give this much, and it's a gift. He hands it to me like one, the kind you shake to hear what's inside—but not hard enough to break it.

He says, "Listen to your future, not your past."

*   *
   *

The jet from the conference room that I almost recog-nized escorts me down through the decks, back to the crew quarters. With Finch, I hope. This jet who, looking closer, isn't wearing a jet uniform. It's just black, and his eyes are steady and evaluating as we walk, no hurry, and if he's armed I don't see it, and I wonder that they set just one slight kid to guard me. Maybe because I'm in no condition men-tally or physically to fight anyone or anything, or maybe this kid is deceptive in his stature and his delicate looks.

We are almost to the quarters, I see the guard outside the hatch, when the kid says, "I ran away. Why didn't you?"

His tone is hard to the point of judgment, and I look at him. Surprised.

Ran away.

And he speaks like he knows me in some way.

It's not a far leap. Azarcon's gathered the other protégé here and something in me smiles. The one who Falcone had "let go" on Chaos Station. I don't know his name, but I don't need to. This brother of mine. He stares with jewel blue eyes. A color like Azarcon's son, but different in their thoughts. This one can kill, and maybe he's one step from shoving me to the bulkhead and doing just that.

"I don't think he treated me the same as you at the beginning," I tell him. "Besides, I had nowhere to go."

"Neither did I," he says, "but I still ran."

"I ran. Just eventually." And because I know he doesn't want to hear it, I add, "It wasn't all bad, all of the time."

We stop in front of the hatch, and this kid, who isn't a kid despite how he looks, these looks are just deceiving the same as any geisha paint, he says, "You can acclimate to any environment, but it doesn't mean it's a good one."

I ask him, "Here?"

He watches me silently for a minute. No rush for words and no expectation of them. But— "No," he says. "Here is good."

* *
*

Finch waits inside, with Dexter, dark color and vibrant green. And it feels like I've walked the entire length of this ship to get back to these quarters, and talked enough to fill an encyclopedia of my life. Or maybe this is just the weary feeling I get when I lose the things that weigh on me like some sort of alien gravity. The heaviness leaves, and if I'm patient enough it can be replaced by something I need, something that would fill instead of drown and let me breathe instead of bleed.

About the Author

Karin Lowachee was born in Guyana, South America, grew up in Ontario, Canada, and lived for nearly a year in the Canadian sub-Arctic teaching adult education. She holds a creative writing and English degree from York University in Toronto. Visit her on the Web at www.karinlowachee.com.

VISIT WARNER ASPECT ON-LINE!

THE WARNER ASPECT HOMEPAGE
You'll find us at: www.twbookmark.com, then by clicking on Science Fiction and Fantasy.

NEW AND UPCOMING TITLES
Each month we feature our new titles and reader favorites.

AUTHOR INFO
Author bios, bibliographies, and links to personal Web sites.

CONTESTS AND OTHER FUN STUFF
Advance galley giveaways, autographed copies, and more.

THE ASPECT BUZZ
What's new, hot, and upcoming from Warner Aspect: awards news, bestsellers, movie tie-in information . . .